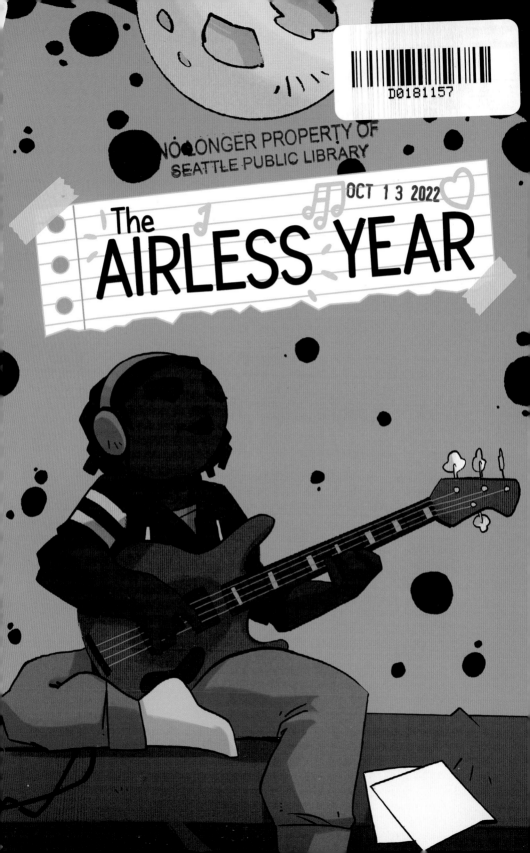

The AIRLESS YEAR

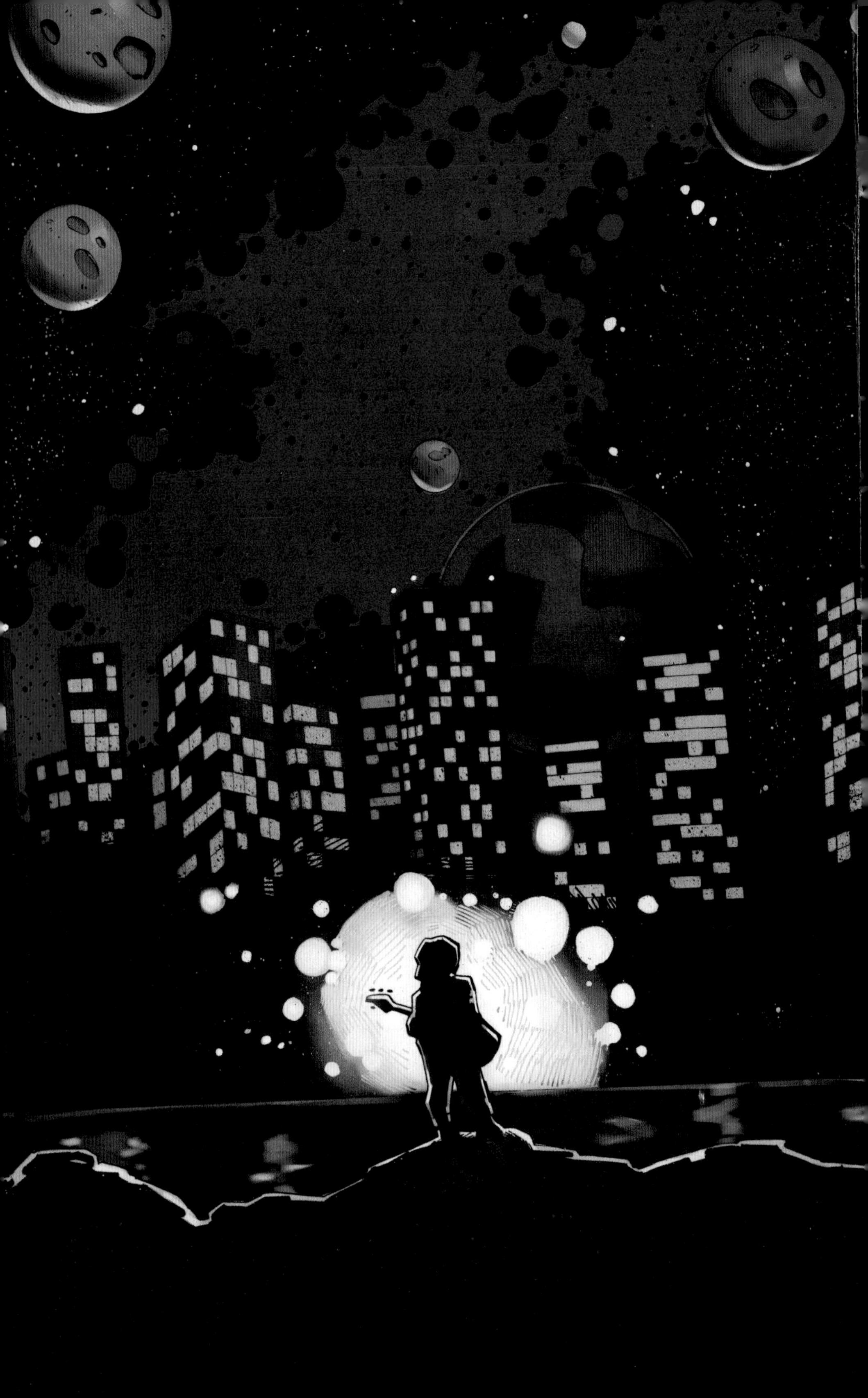

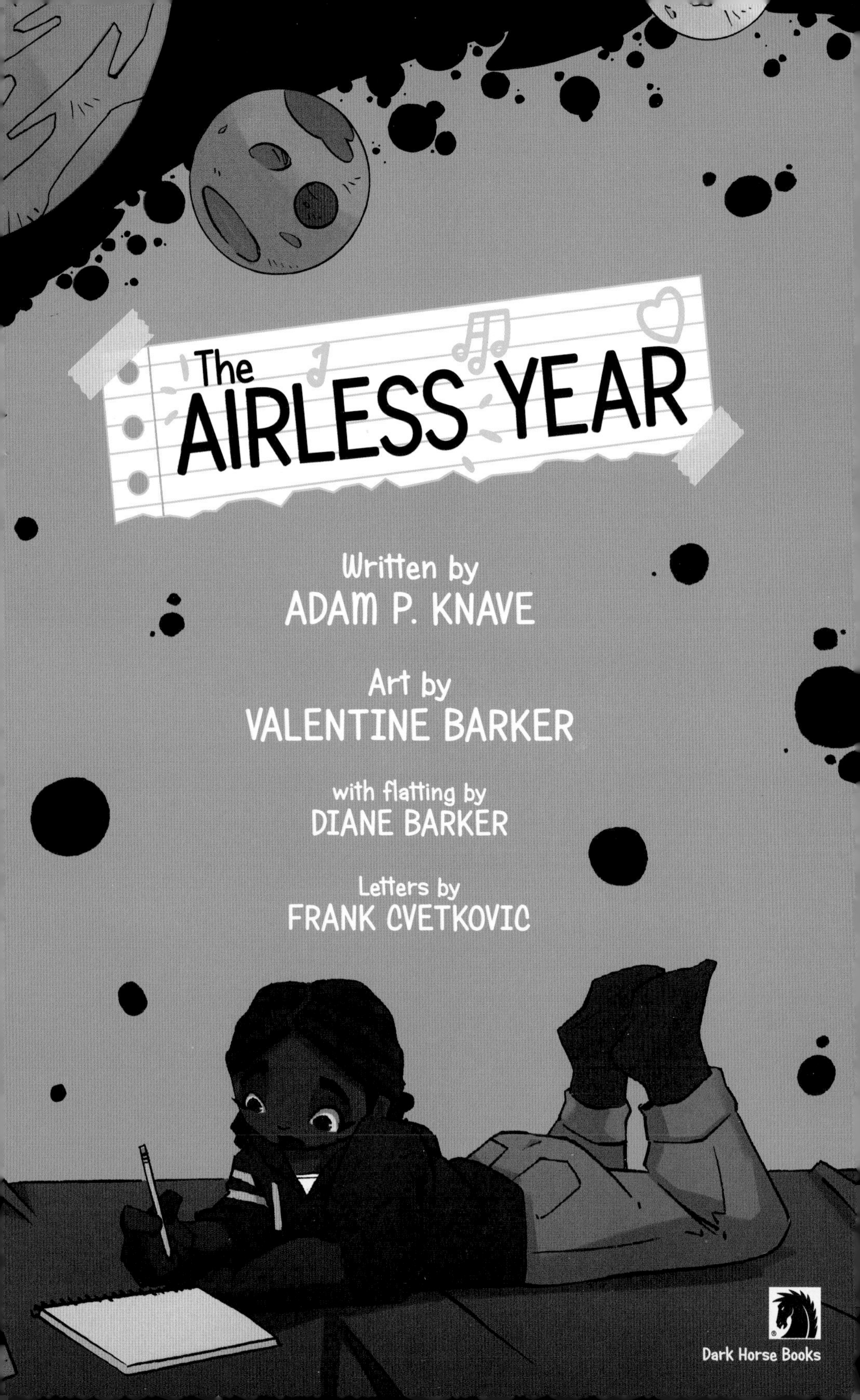

The AIRLESS YEAR

Written by
ADAM P. KNAVE

Art by
VALENTINE BARKER

with flatting by
DIANE BARKER

Letters by
FRANK CVETKOVIC

Dark Horse Books

President and Publisher MIKE RICHARDSON

Editor JENNY BLENK

Assistant Editor ANASTACIA FERRY

Designer MAY HIJIKURO

Digital Art Technicians JOSIE CHRISTENSEN and SAMANTHA HUMMER

NEIL HANKERSON Executive Vice President TOM WEDDLE Chief Financial Officer DALE LaFOUNTAIN Chief
Information Officer TIM WIESCH Vice President of Licensing MATT PARKINSON Vice President of Marketing
VANESSA TODD-HOLMES Vice President of Production and Scheduling MARK BERNARDI Vice President of
Book Trade and Digital Sales RANDY LAHRMAN Vice President of Product Development KEN LIZZI General
Counsel DAVE MARSHALL Editor in Chief DAVEY ESTRADA Editorial Director CHRIS WARNER Senior Books
Editor CARY GRAZZINI Director of Specialty Projects LIA RIBACCHI Art Director MATT DRYER Director of
Digital Art and Prepress MICHAEL GOMBOS Senior Director of Licensed Publications KARI YADRO Director
of Custom Programs KARI TORSON Director of International Licensing

Published by Dark Horse Books a division of Dark Horse Comics LLC
10956 SE Main Street, Milwaukie, OR 97222

DarkHorse.com || Comic Shop Locator Service: Comicshoplocator.com

First edition: June 2022 || Ebook ISBN: 978-1-50672-036-4 || Trade Paperback ISBN: 978-1-50672-035-7

13 5 7 9 10 8 6 4 2
Printed in China

MIX
Paper from
responsible sources
FSC® C109093

Library of Congress Cataloging-in-Publication Data

Names: Knave, Adam P., 1975- writer. | Barker, Valentine, artist. | Barker,
    Diane (Comics artist), artist. | Cvetkovic, Frank, letterer
Title: The airless year / written by Adam P. Knave ; art by Valentine
    Barker with Diane Barker ; letters by Frank Cvetkovic.
Description: First edition. | Milwaukie, OR : Dark Horse Books, 2022. |
    Audience: Ages 10+ | Summary: For Kacee, a queer Black girl in middle
    school, everything feels like a struggle, but when she fails a class as
    a result of her stress and ends up in summer school, she begins to
    discover her own power to improve the things in her life she can
    control.
Identifiers: LCCN 2021055433 (print) | LCCN 2021055434 (ebook) | ISBN
    9781506720357 (trade paperback) | ISBN 9781506720364 (ebook)
Subjects: CYAC: Graphic novels. | Self-esteem--Fiction. |
    Self-realization--Fiction. | Identity--Fiction. | LCGFT: Graphic novels.
Classification: LCC PZ7.7.K84 Ai 2022 (print) | LCC PZ7.7.K84 (ebook) |
    DDC 741.5/973--dc23/eng/20211123
LC record available at https://lccn.loc.gov/2021055433
LC ebook record available at https://lccn.loc.gov/2021055434

DECEMBER 31ST

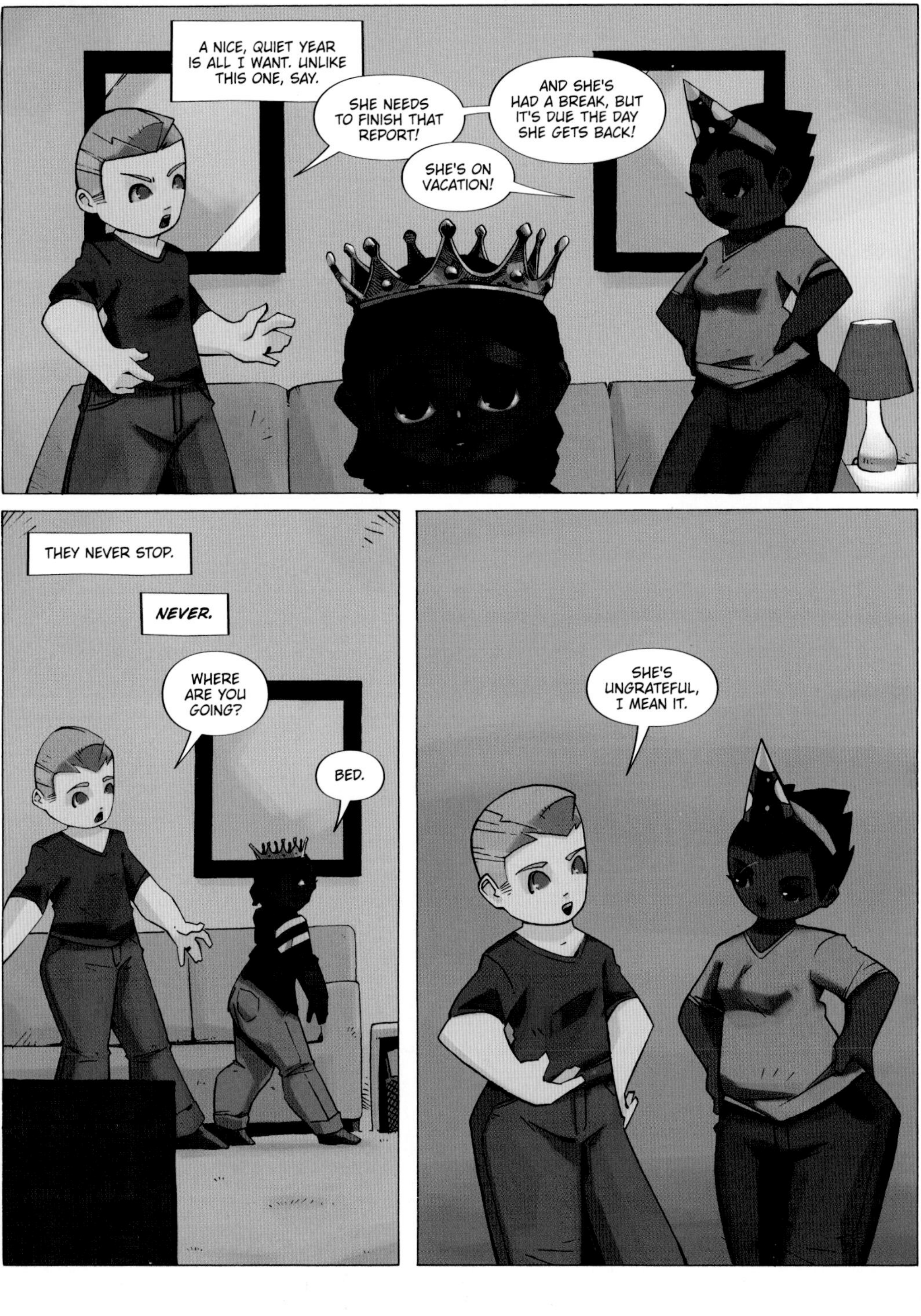
A NICE, QUIET YEAR IS ALL I WANT. UNLIKE THIS ONE, SAY.
SHE NEEDS TO FINISH THAT REPORT!
AND SHE'S HAD A BREAK, BUT IT'S DUE THE DAY SHE GETS BACK!
SHE'S ON VACATION!
THEY NEVER STOP.
NEVER.
WHERE ARE YOU GOING?
BED.
SHE'S UNGRATEFUL, I MEAN IT.

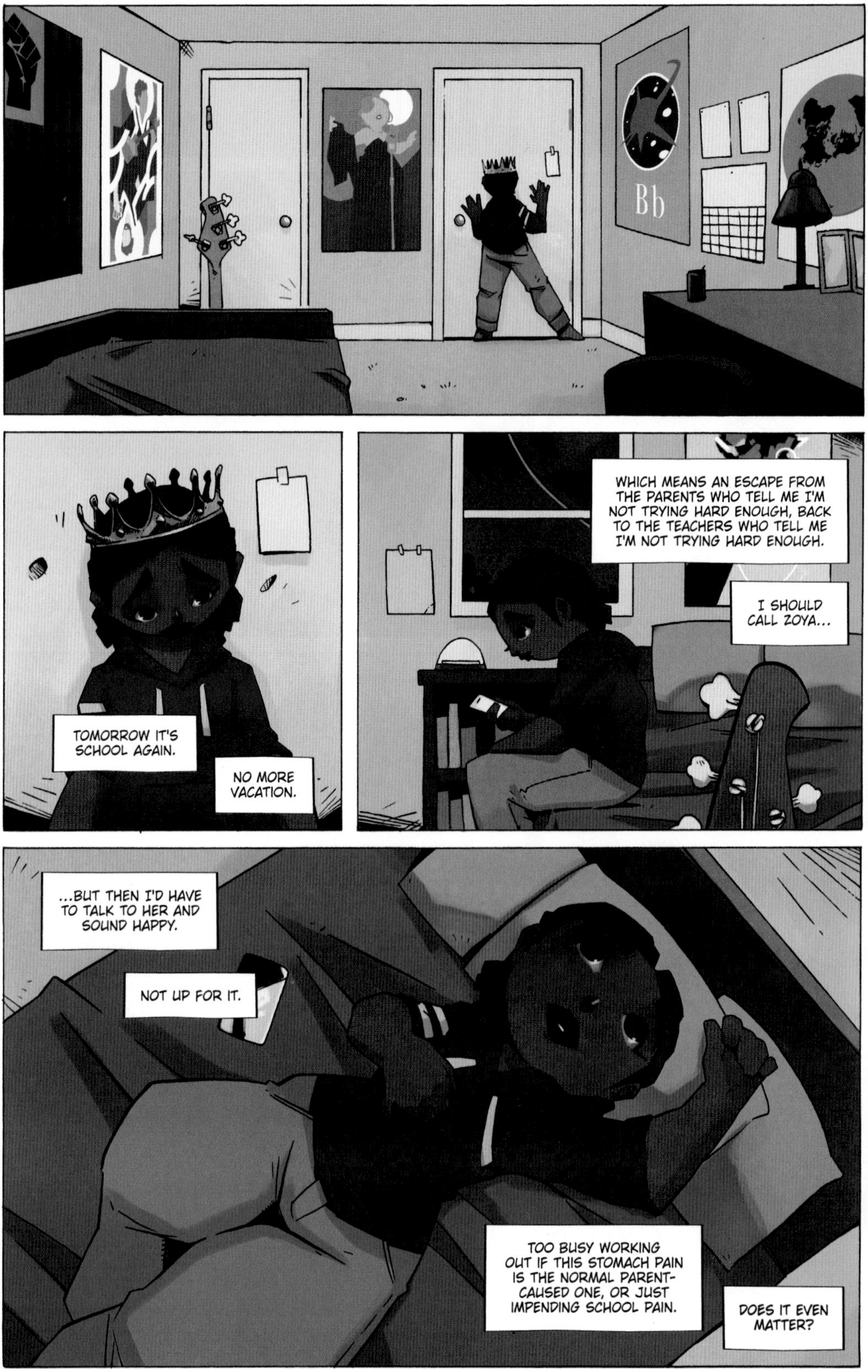
TOMORROW IT'S SCHOOL AGAIN.
NO MORE VACATION.
WHICH MEANS AN ESCAPE FROM THE PARENTS WHO TELL ME I'M NOT TRYING HARD ENOUGH, BACK TO THE TEACHERS WHO TELL ME I'M NOT TRYING HARD ENOUGH.
I SHOULD CALL ZOYA...
...BUT THEN I'D HAVE TO TALK TO HER AND SOUND HAPPY.
NOT UP FOR IT.
TOO BUSY WORKING OUT IF THIS STOMACH PAIN IS THE NORMAL PARENT-CAUSED ONE, OR JUST IMPENDING SCHOOL PAIN.
DOES IT EVEN MATTER?

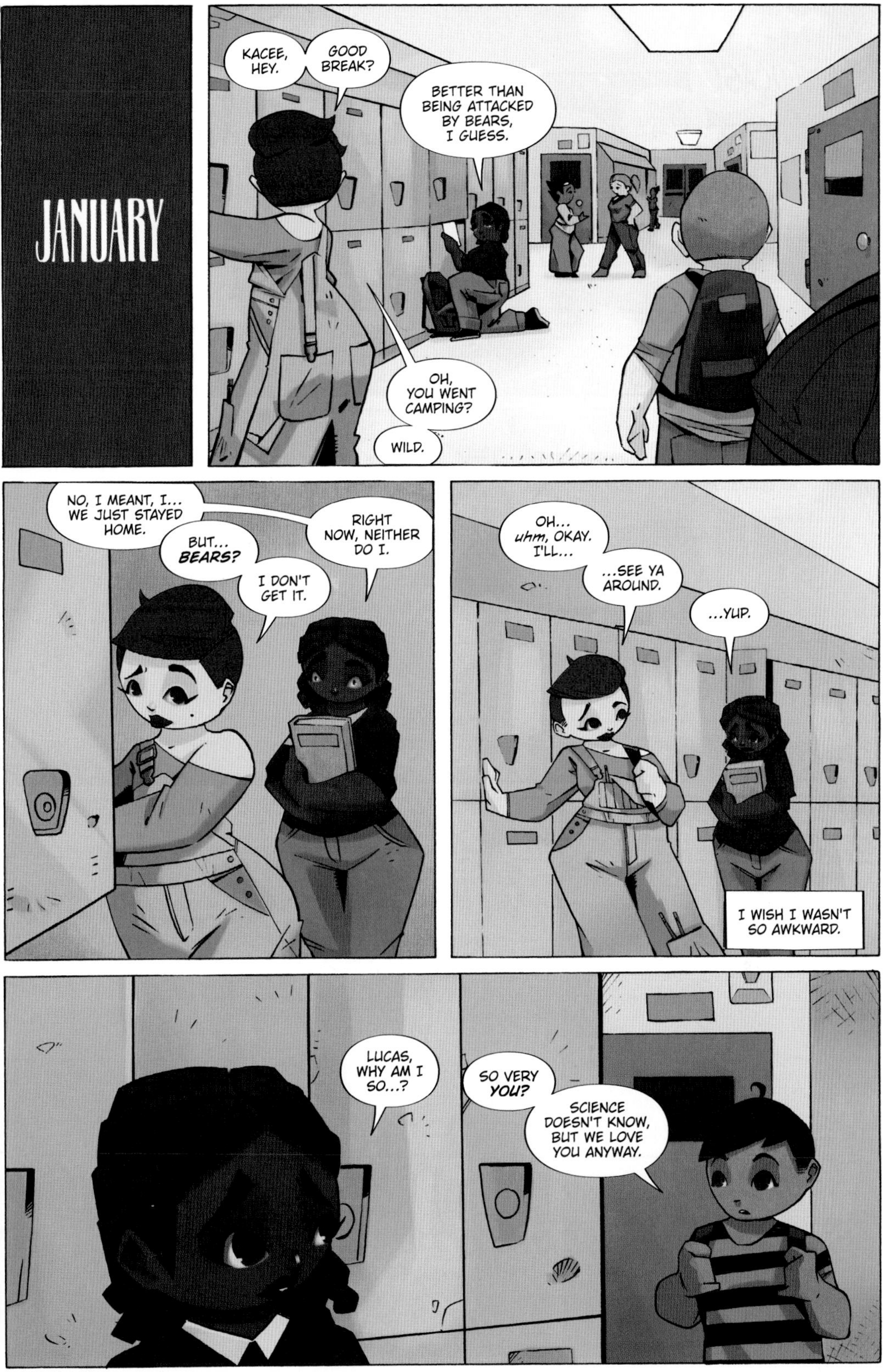
JANUARY
KACEE, HEY.
GOOD BREAK?
BETTER THAN BEING ATTACKED BY BEARS, I GUESS.
OH, YOU WENT CAMPING?
WILD.
NO, I MEANT, I... WE JUST STAYED HOME.
BUT... BEARS?
I DON'T GET IT.
RIGHT NOW, NEITHER DO I.
OH... uhm, OKAY. I'LL...
...SEE YA AROUND.
...YUP.
I WISH I WASN'T SO AWKWARD.
LUCAS, WHY AM I SO...?
SO VERY YOU?
SCIENCE DOESN'T KNOW, BUT WE LOVE YOU ANYWAY.

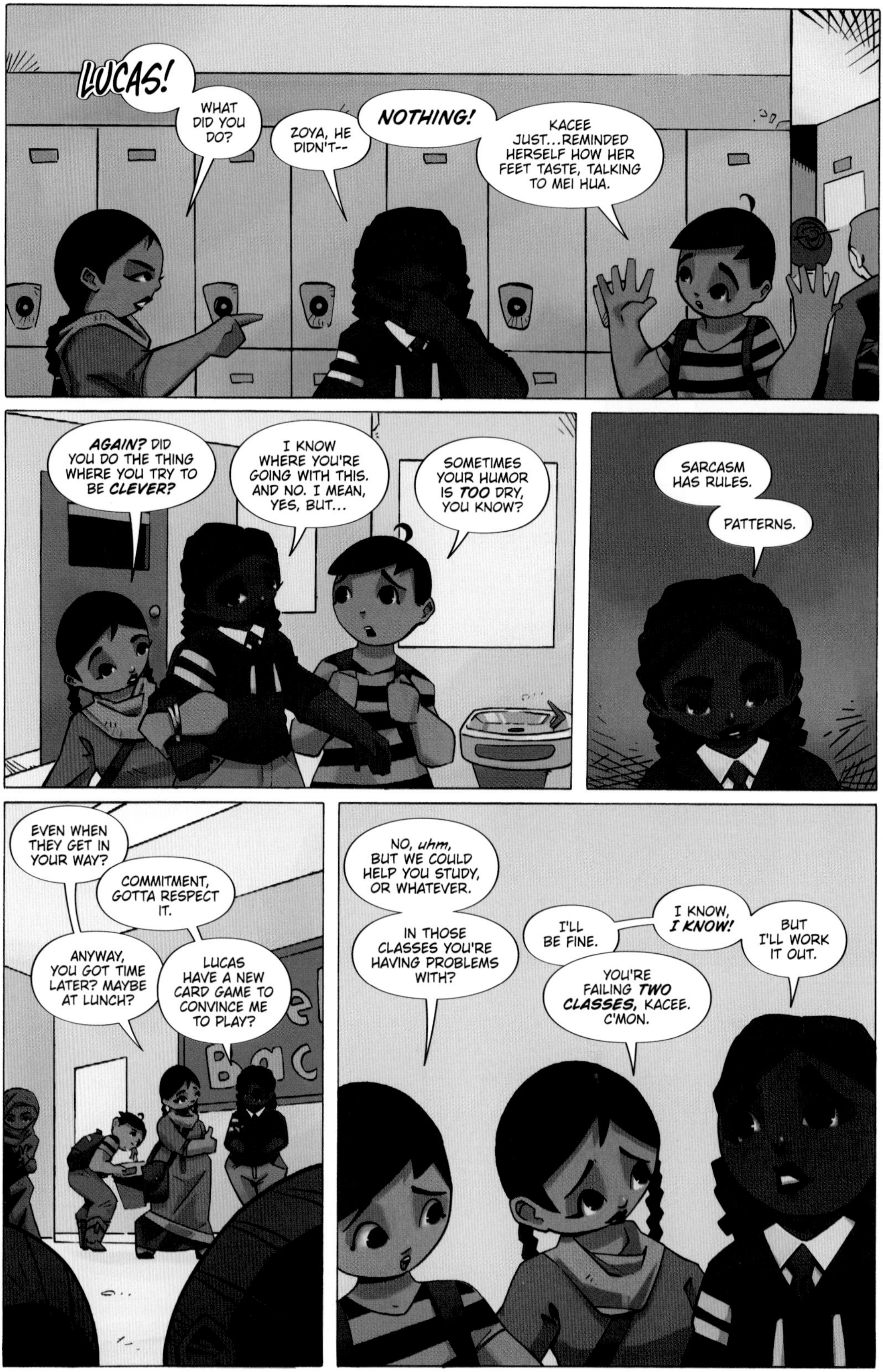
LUCAS!
WHAT DID YOU DO?
ZOYA, HE DIDN'T--
NOTHING!
KACEE JUST...REMINDED HERSELF HOW HER FEET TASTE, TALKING TO MEI HUA.
AGAIN? DID YOU DO THE THING WHERE YOU TRY TO BE CLEVER?
I KNOW WHERE YOU'RE GOING WITH THIS. AND NO. I MEAN, YES, BUT...
SOMETIMES YOUR HUMOR IS TOO DRY, YOU KNOW?
SARCASM HAS RULES.
PATTERNS.
EVEN WHEN THEY GET IN YOUR WAY?
COMMITMENT, GOTTA RESPECT IT.
ANYWAY, YOU GOT TIME LATER? MAYBE AT LUNCH?
LUCAS HAVE A NEW CARD GAME TO CONVINCE ME TO PLAY?
NO, uhm, BUT WE COULD HELP YOU STUDY, OR WHATEVER.
IN THOSE CLASSES YOU'RE HAVING PROBLEMS WITH?
I'LL BE FINE.
I KNOW, I KNOW!
BUT I'LL WORK IT OUT.
YOU'RE FAILING TWO CLASSES, KACEE. C'MON.

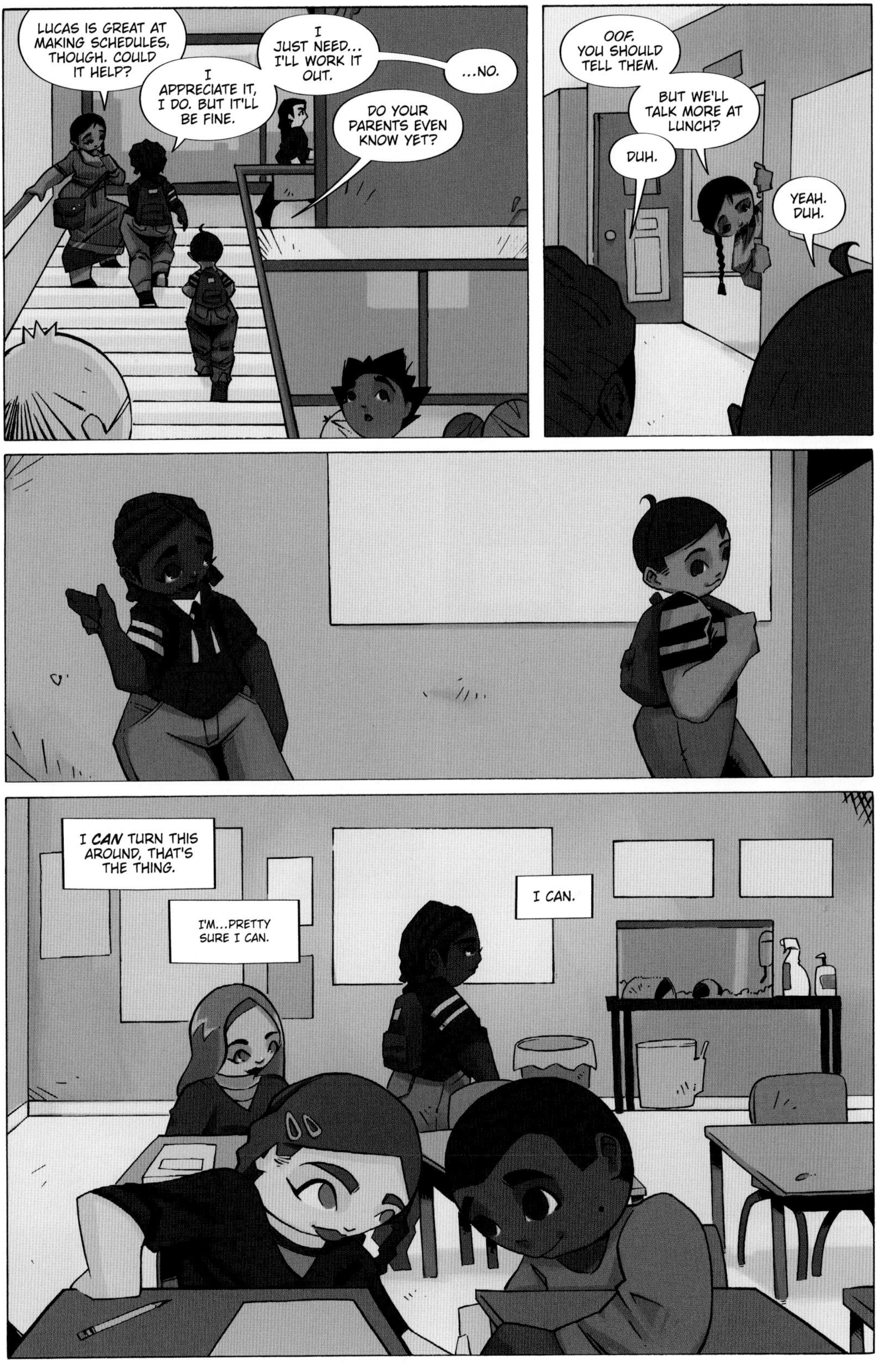
LUCAS IS GREAT AT MAKING SCHEDULES, THOUGH. COULD IT HELP?
I APPRECIATE IT, I DO. BUT IT'LL BE FINE.
I JUST NEED... I'LL WORK IT OUT.
...NO.
DO YOUR PARENTS EVEN KNOW YET?
OOF. YOU SHOULD TELL THEM.
BUT WE'LL TALK MORE AT LUNCH?
DUH.
YEAH. DUH.
I CAN TURN THIS AROUND, THAT'S THE THING.
I'M...PRETTY SURE I CAN.
I CAN.

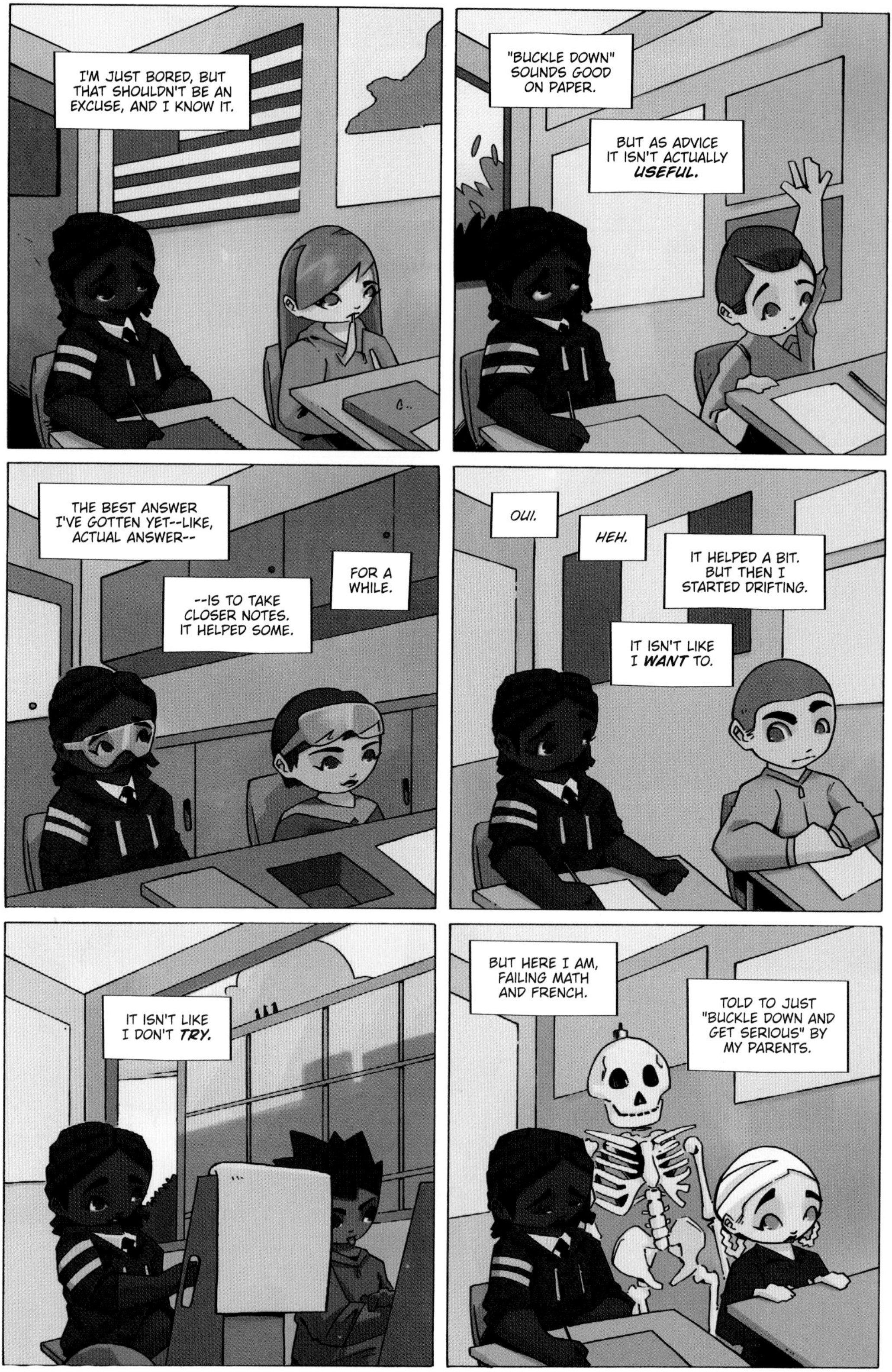
I'M JUST BORED, BUT THAT SHOULDN'T BE AN EXCUSE, AND I KNOW IT.
"BUCKLE DOWN" SOUNDS GOOD ON PAPER.
BUT AS ADVICE IT ISN'T ACTUALLY USEFUL.
THE BEST ANSWER I'VE GOTTEN YET--LIKE, ACTUAL ANSWER--
--IS TO TAKE CLOSER NOTES. IT HELPED SOME.
FOR A WHILE.
OUI.
HEH.
IT HELPED A BIT. BUT THEN I STARTED DRIFTING.
IT ISN'T LIKE I WANT TO.
IT ISN'T LIKE I DON'T TRY.
BUT HERE I AM, FAILING MATH AND FRENCH.
TOLD TO JUST "BUCKLE DOWN AND GET SERIOUS" BY MY PARENTS.

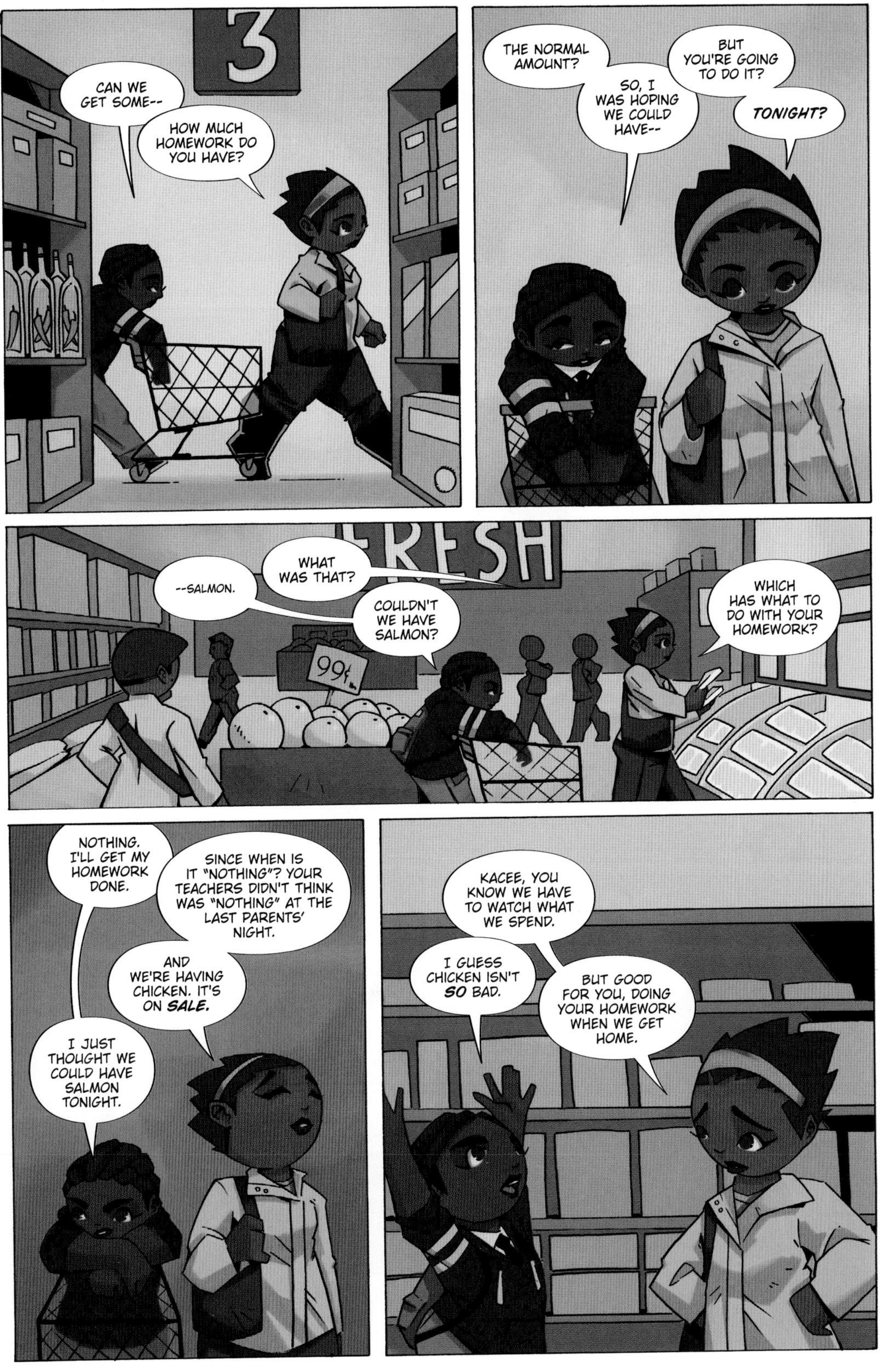
3
CAN WE GET SOME--
HOW MUCH HOMEWORK DO YOU HAVE?
THE NORMAL AMOUNT?
SO, I WAS HOPING WE COULD HAVE--
BUT YOU'RE GOING TO DO IT?
TONIGHT?
FRESH
--SALMON.
WHAT WAS THAT?
COULDN'T WE HAVE SALMON?
99¢
WHICH HAS WHAT TO DO WITH YOUR HOMEWORK?
NOTHING. I'LL GET MY HOMEWORK DONE.
SINCE WHEN IS IT "NOTHING"? YOUR TEACHERS DIDN'T THINK WAS "NOTHING" AT THE LAST PARENTS' NIGHT.
AND WE'RE HAVING CHICKEN. IT'S ON ***SALE.***
I JUST THOUGHT WE COULD HAVE SALMON TONIGHT.
KACEE, YOU KNOW WE HAVE TO WATCH WHAT WE SPEND.
I GUESS CHICKEN ISN'T ***SO*** BAD.
BUT GOOD FOR YOU, DOING YOUR HOMEWORK WHEN WE GET HOME.

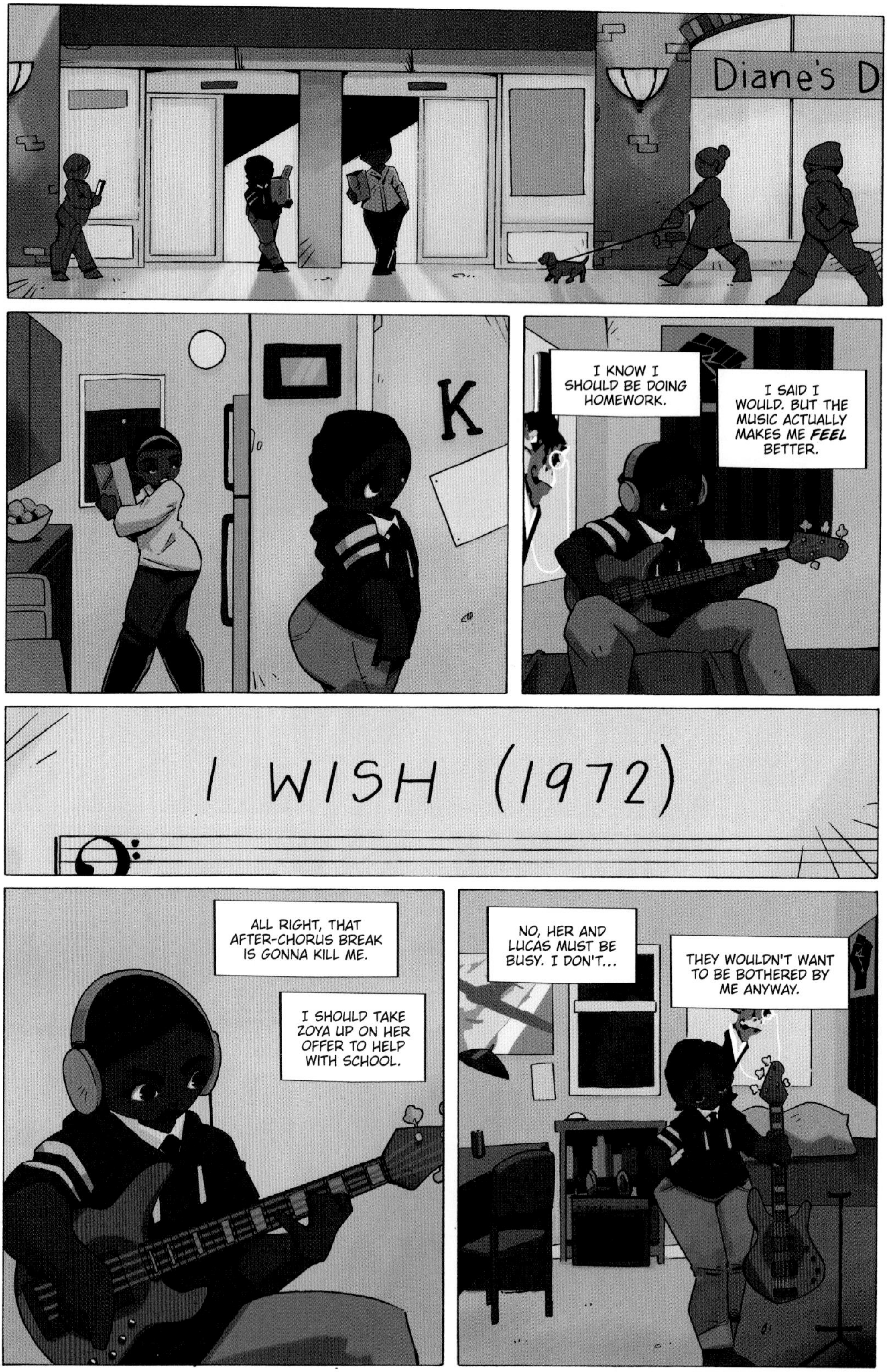
Diane's D
I KNOW I SHOULD BE DOING HOMEWORK.
I SAID I WOULD. BUT THE MUSIC ACTUALLY MAKES ME FEEL BETTER.
I WISH (1972)
ALL RIGHT, THAT AFTER-CHORUS BREAK IS GONNA KILL ME.
I SHOULD TAKE ZOYA UP ON HER OFFER TO HELP WITH SCHOOL.
NO, HER AND LUCAS MUST BE BUSY. I DON'T...
THEY WOULDN'T WANT TO BE BOTHERED BY ME ANYWAY.

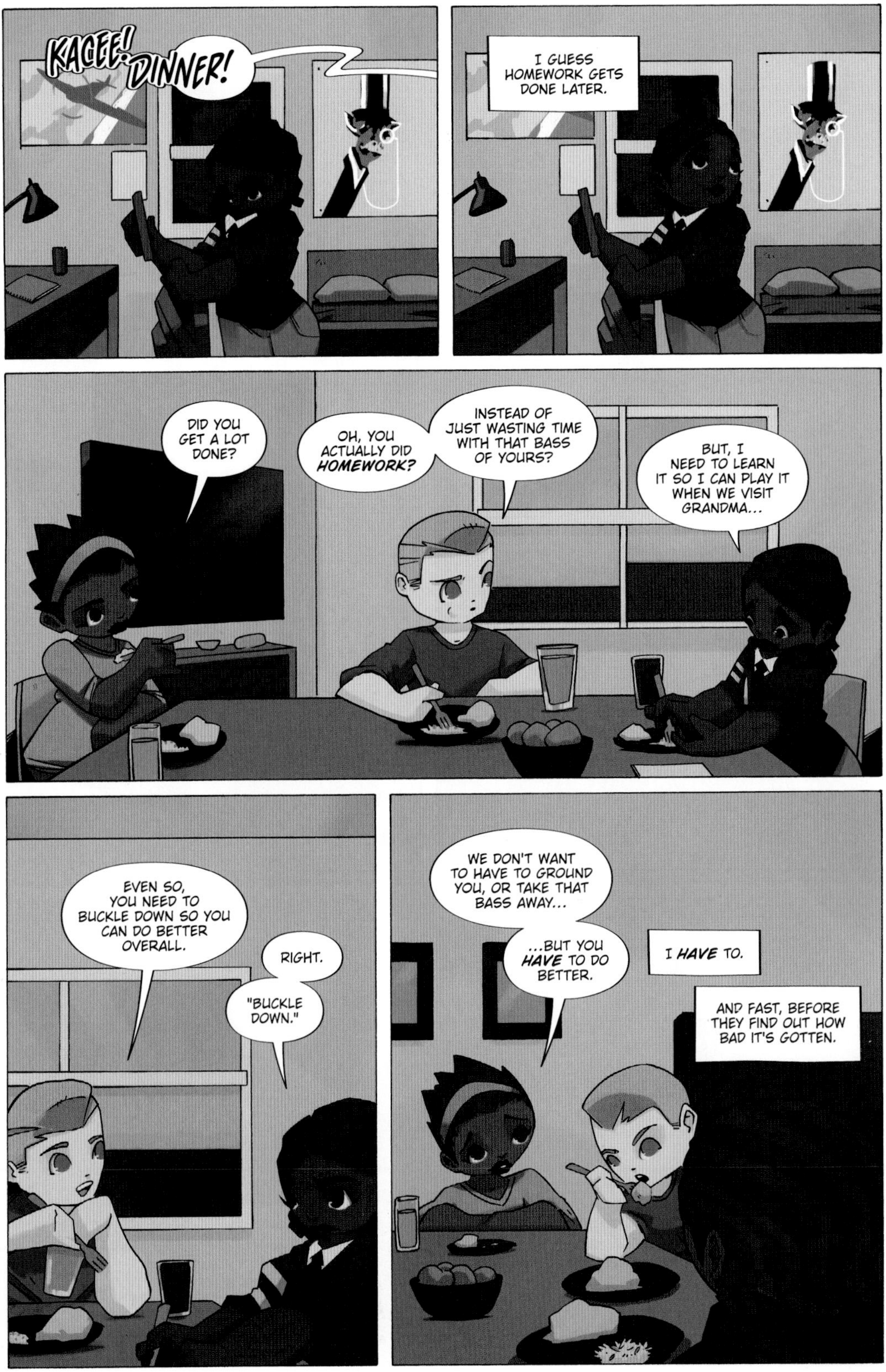
KACEE! DINNER!
I GUESS HOMEWORK GETS DONE LATER.
DID YOU GET A LOT DONE?
OH, YOU ACTUALLY DID *HOMEWORK?*
INSTEAD OF JUST WASTING TIME WITH THAT BASS OF YOURS?
BUT, I NEED TO LEARN IT SO I CAN PLAY IT WHEN WE VISIT GRANDMA...
EVEN SO, YOU NEED TO BUCKLE DOWN SO YOU CAN DO BETTER OVERALL.
RIGHT.
"BUCKLE DOWN."
WE DON'T WANT TO HAVE TO GROUND YOU, OR TAKE THAT BASS AWAY...
...BUT YOU *HAVE* TO DO BETTER.
I *HAVE* TO.
AND FAST, BEFORE THEY FIND OUT HOW BAD IT'S GOTTEN.

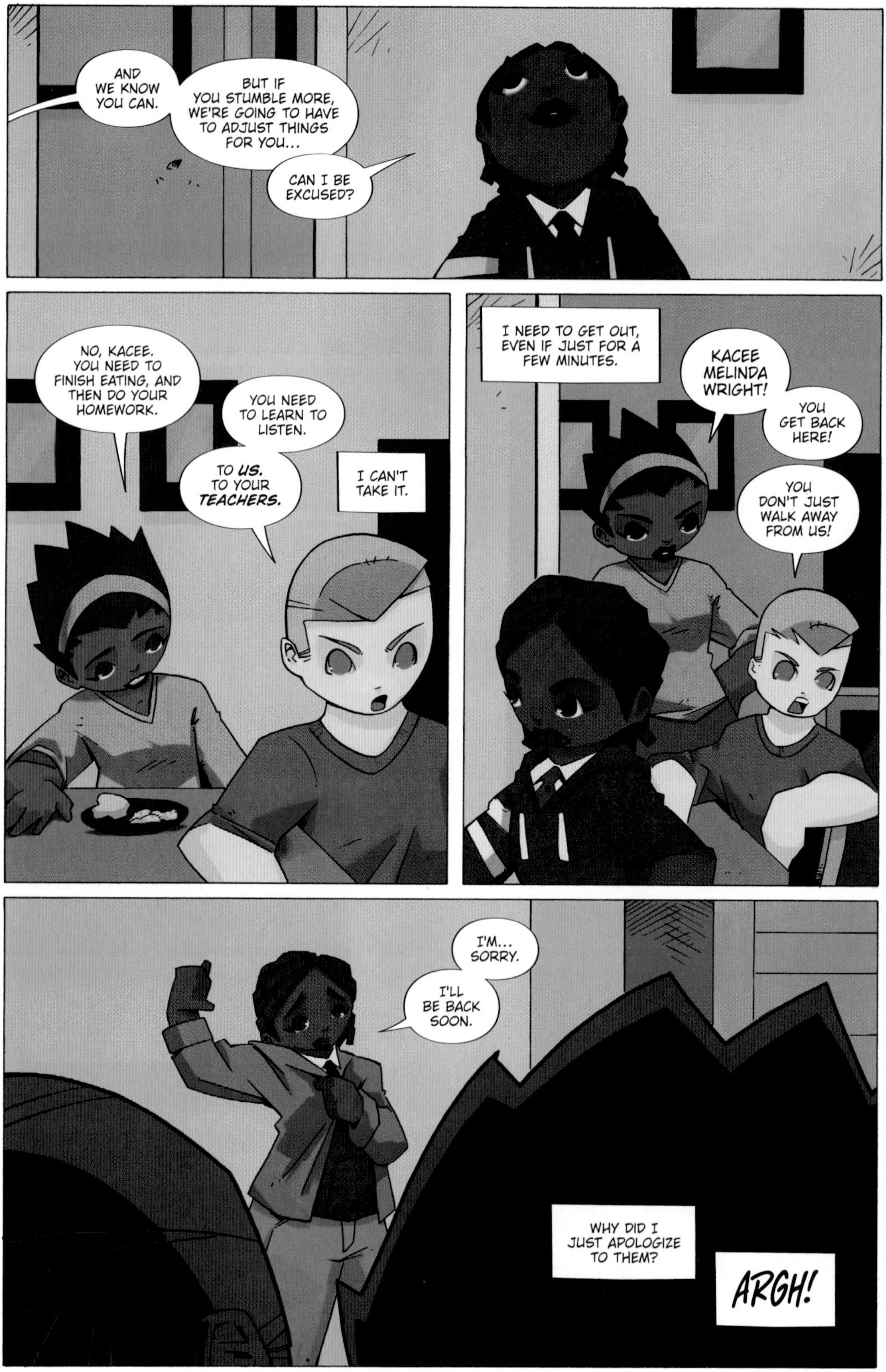
AND WE KNOW YOU CAN.
BUT IF YOU STUMBLE MORE, WE'RE GOING TO HAVE TO ADJUST THINGS FOR YOU...
CAN I BE EXCUSED?
NO, KACEE. YOU NEED TO FINISH EATING, AND THEN DO YOUR HOMEWORK.
YOU NEED TO LEARN TO LISTEN.
TO *US.* TO YOUR ***TEACHERS.***
I CAN'T TAKE IT.
I NEED TO GET OUT, EVEN IF JUST FOR A FEW MINUTES.
KACEE MELINDA WRIGHT!
YOU GET BACK HERE!
YOU DON'T JUST WALK AWAY FROM US!
I'M... SORRY.
I'LL BE BACK SOON.
WHY DID I JUST APOLOGIZE TO THEM?
ARGH!

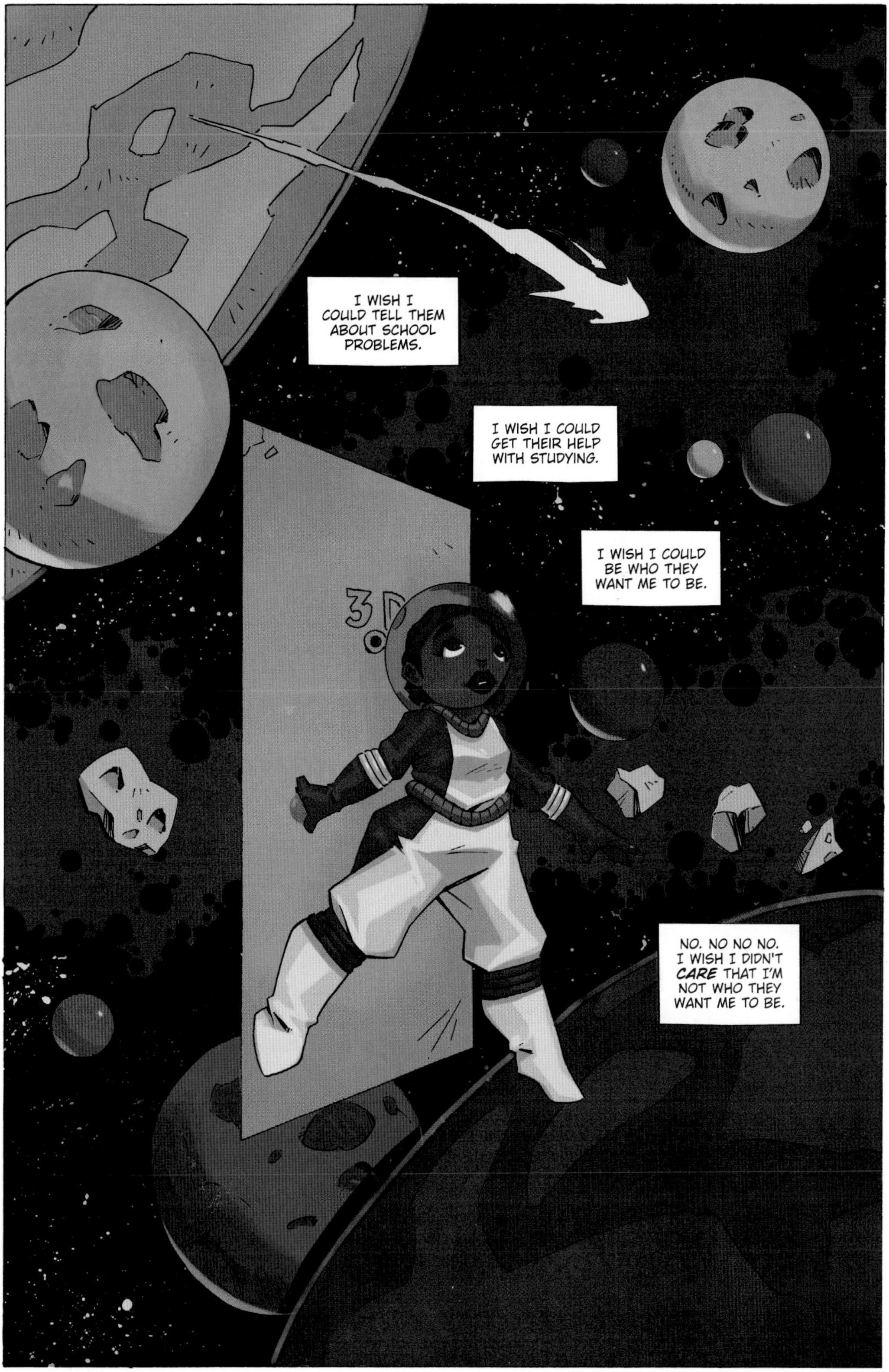
I WISH I COULD TELL THEM ABOUT SCHOOL PROBLEMS.
I WISH I COULD GET THEIR HELP WITH STUDYING.
I WISH I COULD BE WHO THEY WANT ME TO BE.
3D
NO. NO NO NO. I WISH I DIDN'T *CARE* THAT I'M NOT WHO THEY WANT ME TO BE.

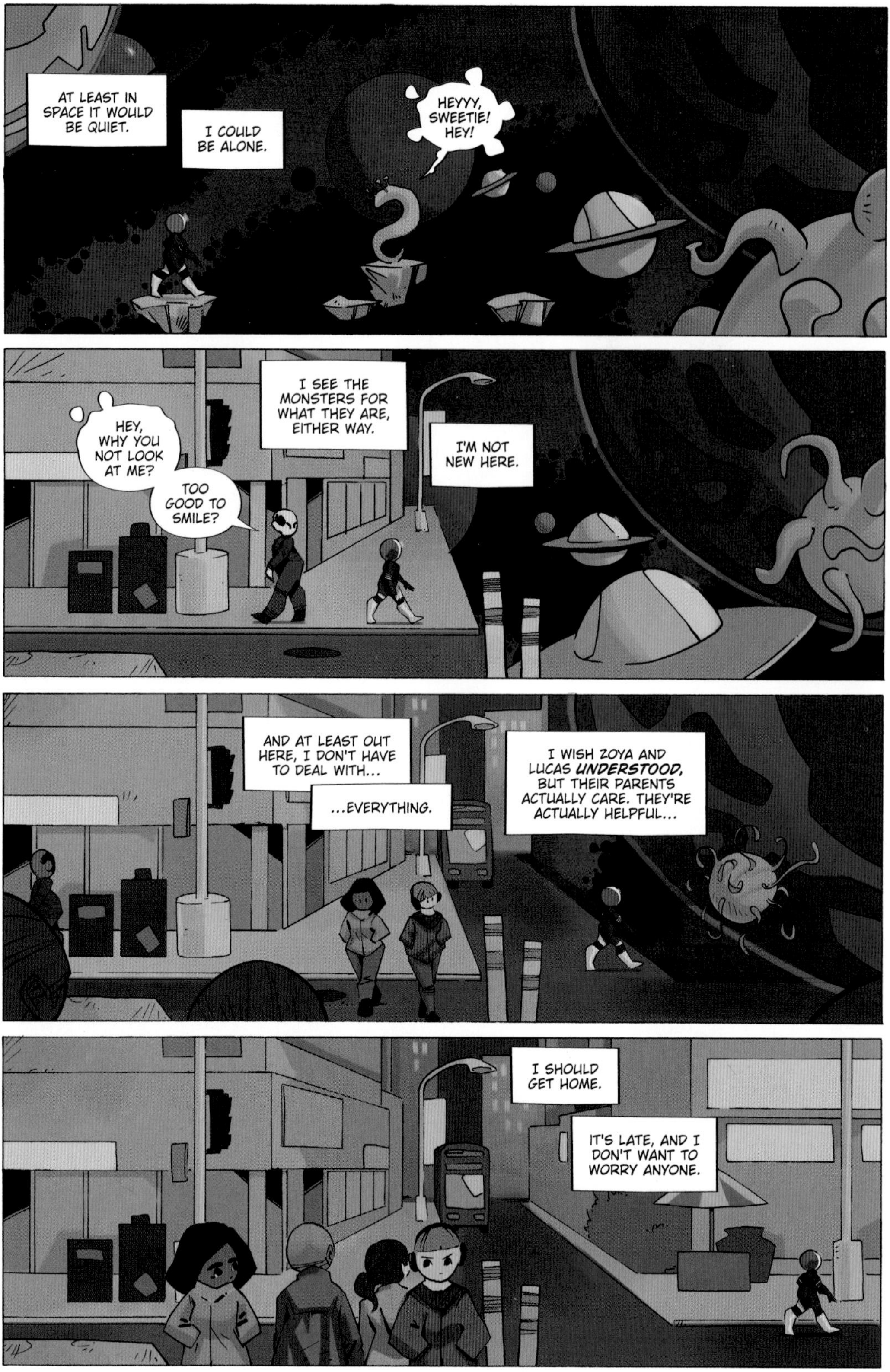
AT LEAST IN SPACE IT WOULD BE QUIET.
I COULD BE ALONE.
HEYYY, SWEETIE! HEY!
I SEE THE MONSTERS FOR WHAT THEY ARE, EITHER WAY.
HEY, WHY YOU NOT LOOK AT ME?
TOO GOOD TO SMILE?
I'M NOT NEW HERE.
AND AT LEAST OUT HERE, I DON'T HAVE TO DEAL WITH...
...EVERYTHING.
I WISH ZOYA AND LUCAS UNDERSTOOD, BUT THEIR PARENTS ACTUALLY CARE. THEY'RE ACTUALLY HELPFUL...
I SHOULD GET HOME.
IT'S LATE, AND I DON'T WANT TO WORRY ANYONE.

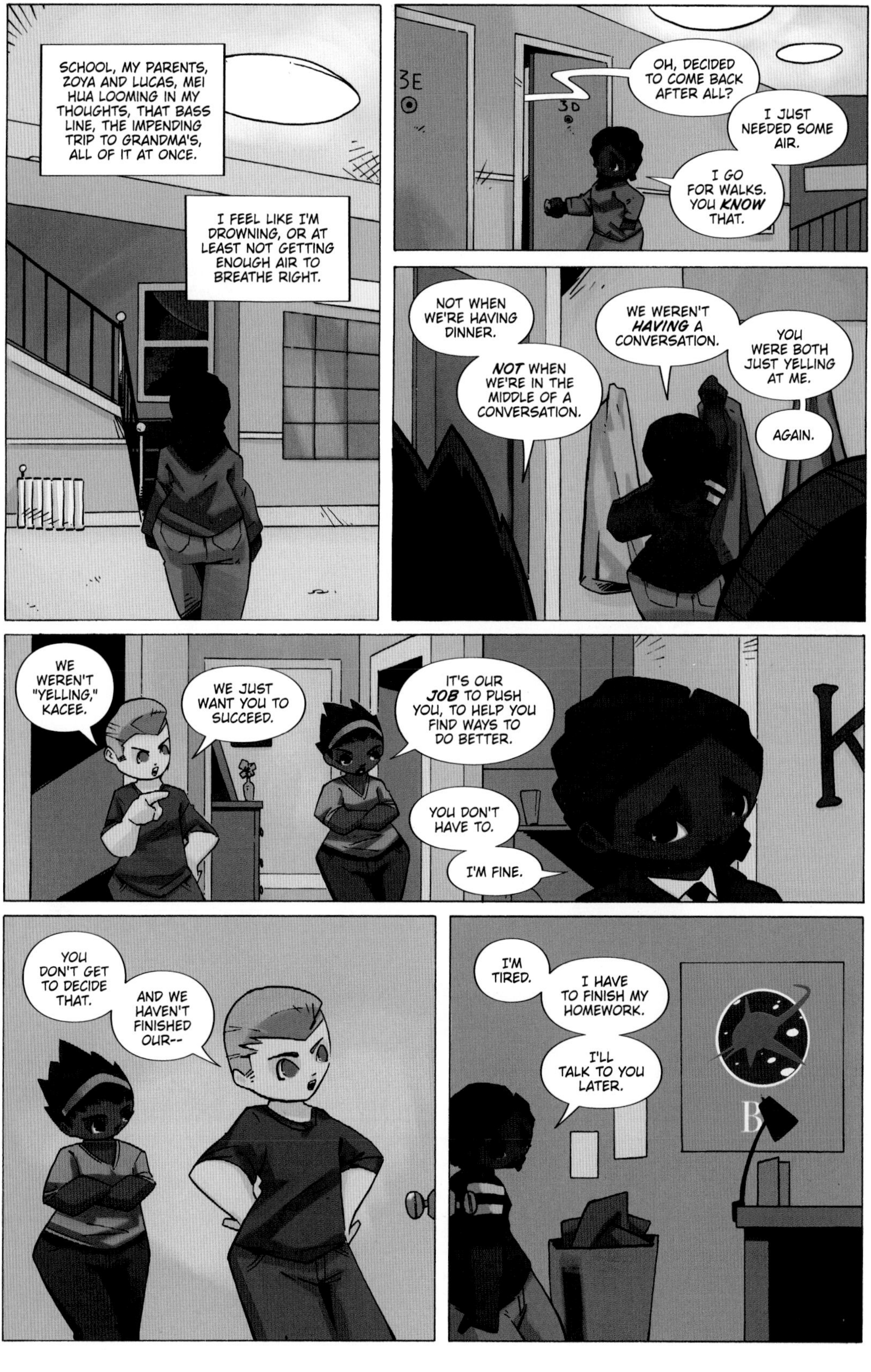
SCHOOL, MY PARENTS, ZOYA AND LUCAS, MEI HUA LOOMING IN MY THOUGHTS, THAT BASS LINE, THE IMPENDING TRIP TO GRANDMA'S, ALL OF IT AT ONCE.
I FEEL LIKE I'M DROWNING, OR AT LEAST NOT GETTING ENOUGH AIR TO BREATHE RIGHT.
3E
3D
OH, DECIDED TO COME BACK AFTER ALL?
I JUST NEEDED SOME AIR.
I GO FOR WALKS. YOU ***KNOW*** THAT.
NOT WHEN WE'RE HAVING DINNER.
NOT WHEN WE'RE IN THE MIDDLE OF A CONVERSATION.
WE WEREN'T ***HAVING*** A CONVERSATION.
YOU WERE BOTH JUST YELLING AT ME.
AGAIN.
WE WEREN'T "YELLING," KACEE.
WE JUST WANT YOU TO SUCCEED.
IT'S OUR ***JOB*** TO PUSH YOU, TO HELP YOU FIND WAYS TO DO BETTER.
YOU DON'T HAVE TO.
I'M FINE.
YOU DON'T GET TO DECIDE THAT.
AND WE HAVEN'T FINISHED OUR--
I'M TIRED.
I HAVE TO FINISH MY HOMEWORK.
I'LL TALK TO YOU LATER.

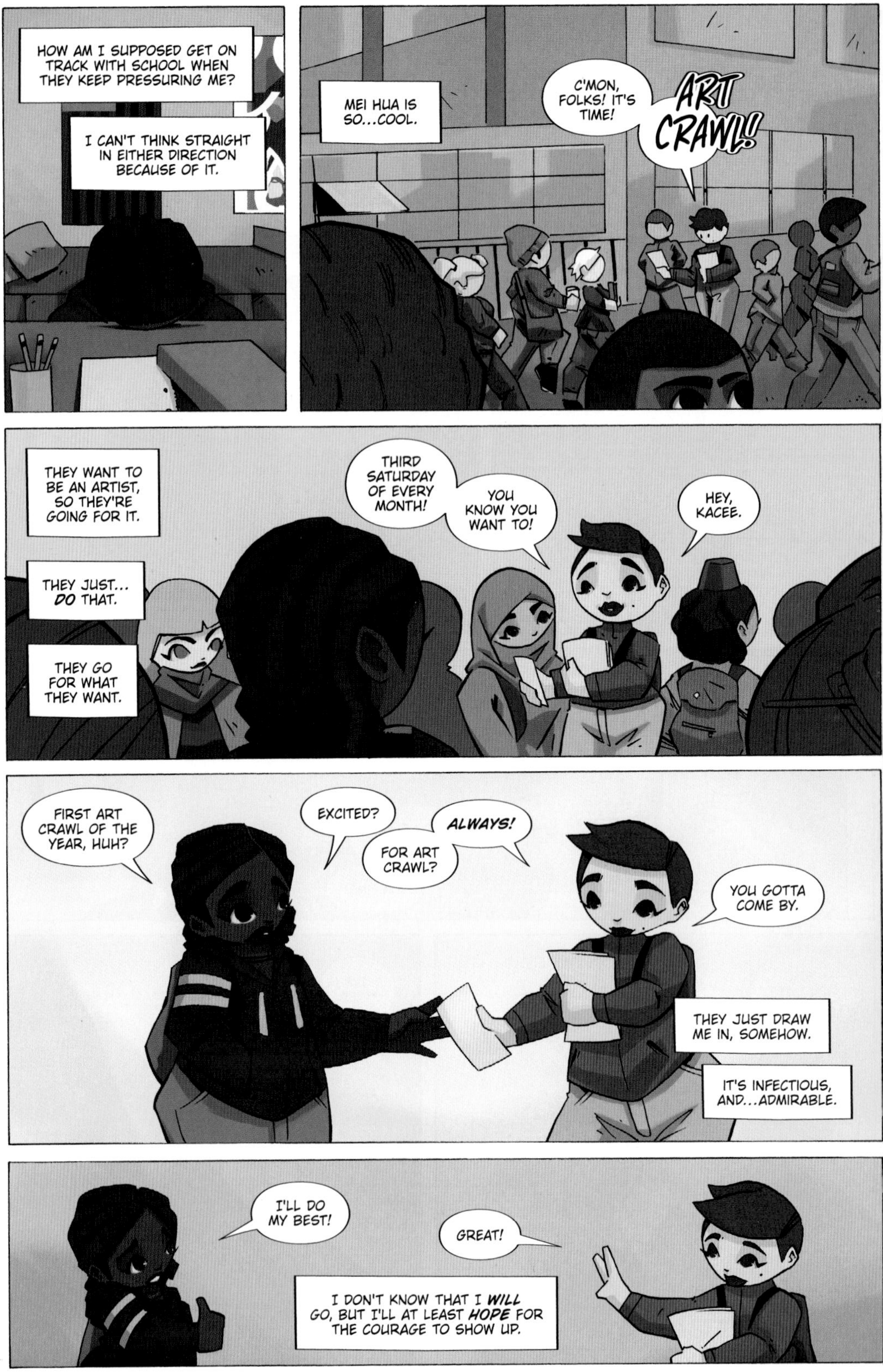
HOW AM I SUPPOSED GET ON TRACK WITH SCHOOL WHEN THEY KEEP PRESSURING ME?
I CAN'T THINK STRAIGHT IN EITHER DIRECTION BECAUSE OF IT.
MEI HUA IS SO...COOL.
C'MON, FOLKS! IT'S TIME!
ART CRAWL!
THEY WANT TO BE AN ARTIST, SO THEY'RE GOING FOR IT.
THEY JUST... DO THAT.
THEY GO FOR WHAT THEY WANT.
THIRD SATURDAY OF EVERY MONTH!
YOU KNOW YOU WANT TO!
HEY, KACEE.
FIRST ART CRAWL OF THE YEAR, HUH?
EXCITED?
FOR ART CRAWL?
ALWAYS!
YOU GOTTA COME BY.
THEY JUST DRAW ME IN, SOMEHOW.
IT'S INFECTIOUS, AND...ADMIRABLE.
I'LL DO MY BEST!
GREAT!
I DON'T KNOW THAT I WILL GO, BUT I'LL AT LEAST HOPE FOR THE COURAGE TO SHOW UP.

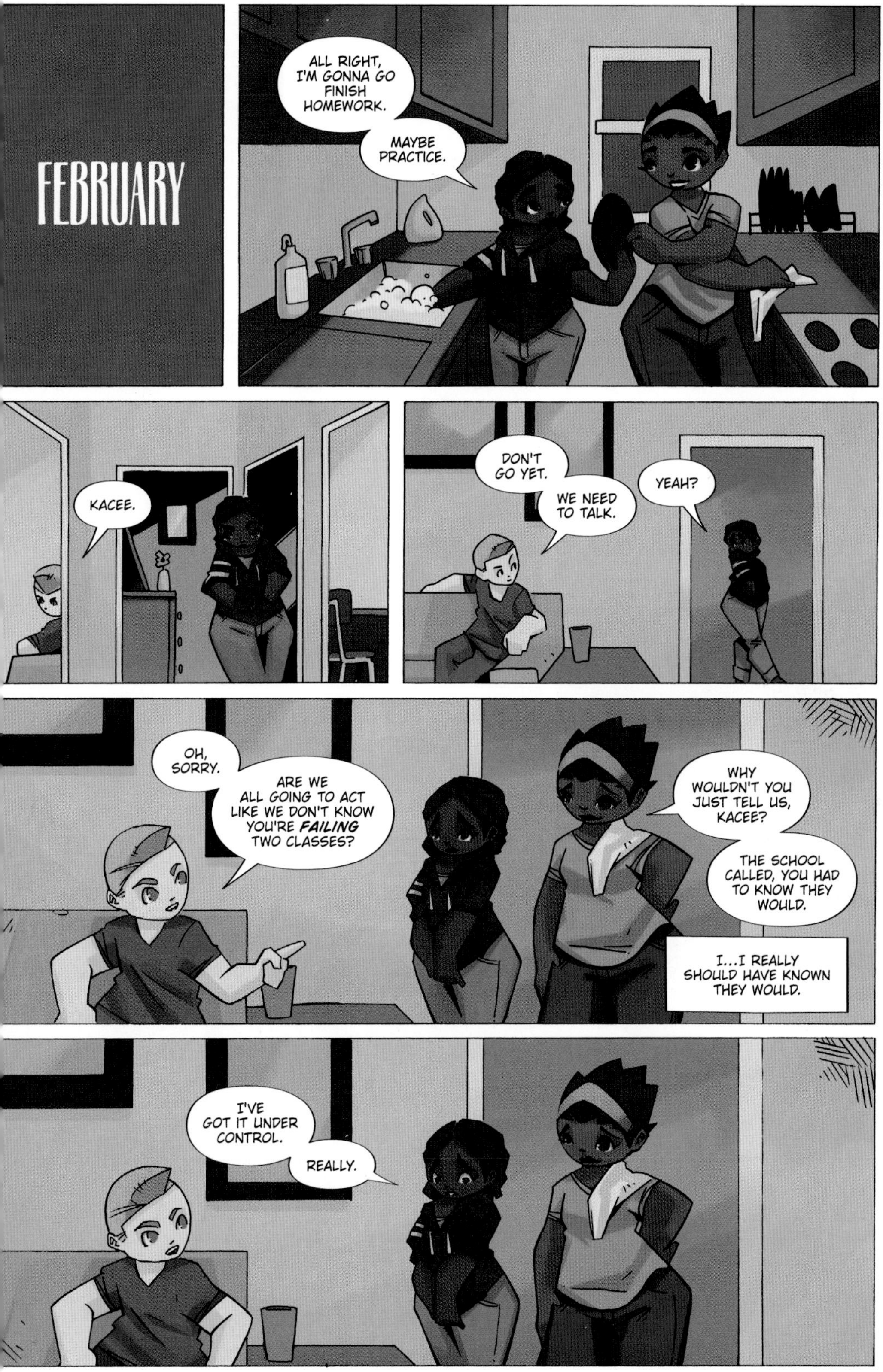
FEBRUARY
ALL RIGHT, I'M GONNA GO FINISH HOMEWORK.
MAYBE PRACTICE.
KACEE.
DON'T GO YET.
WE NEED TO TALK.
YEAH?
OH, SORRY.
ARE WE ALL GOING TO ACT LIKE WE DON'T KNOW YOU'RE ***FAILING*** TWO CLASSES?
WHY WOULDN'T YOU JUST TELL US, KACEE?
THE SCHOOL CALLED, YOU HAD TO KNOW THEY WOULD.
I...I REALLY SHOULD HAVE KNOWN THEY WOULD.
I'VE GOT IT UNDER CONTROL.
REALLY.

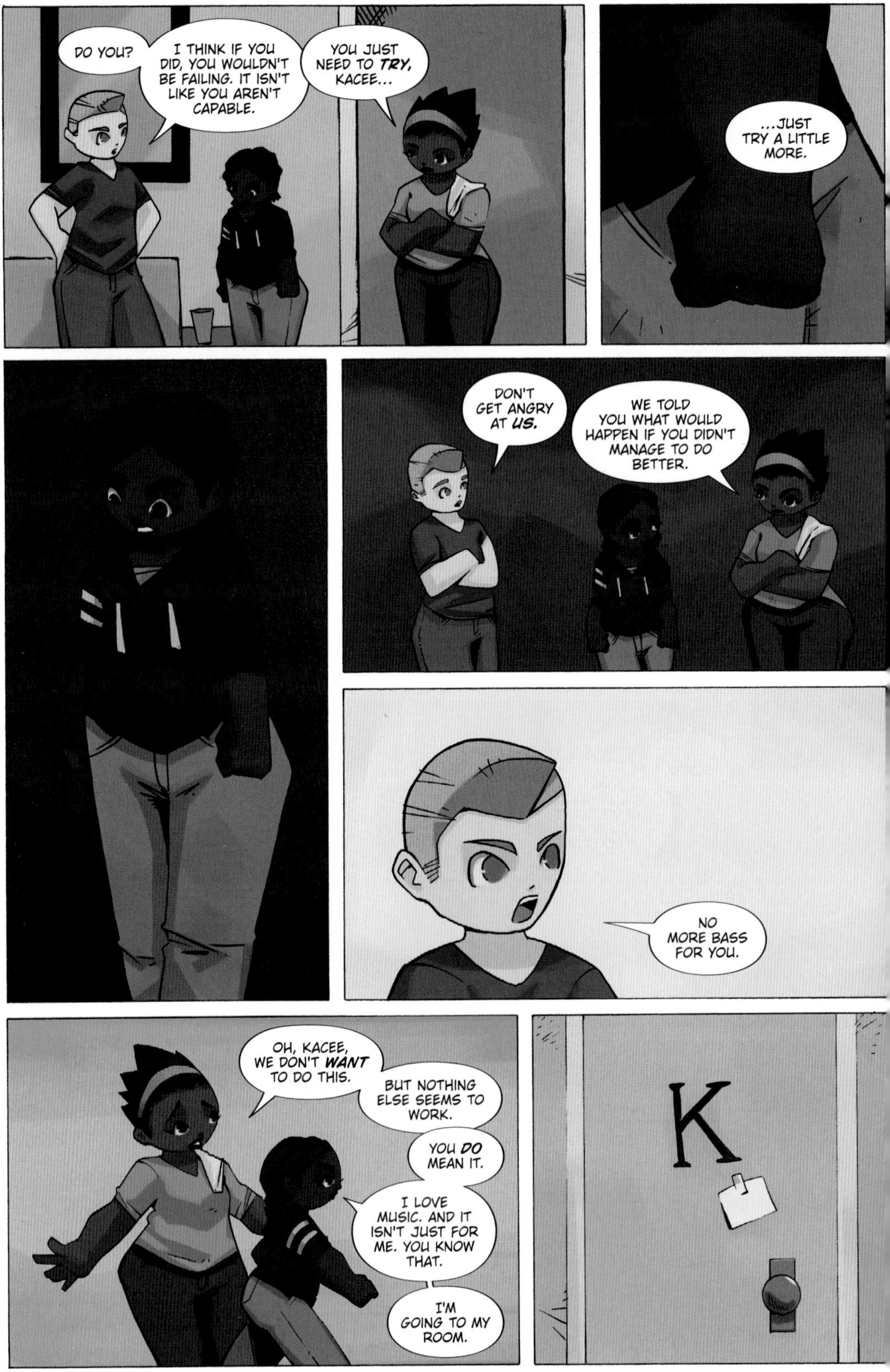
DO YOU?
I THINK IF YOU DID, YOU WOULDN'T BE FAILING. IT ISN'T LIKE YOU AREN'T CAPABLE.
YOU JUST NEED TO *TRY,* KACEE...
...JUST TRY A LITTLE MORE.
DON'T GET ANGRY AT *US.*
WE TOLD YOU WHAT WOULD HAPPEN IF YOU DIDN'T MANAGE TO DO BETTER.
NO MORE BASS FOR YOU.
OH, KACEE, WE DON'T *WANT* TO DO THIS.
BUT NOTHING ELSE SEEMS TO WORK.
YOU *DO* MEAN IT.
I LOVE MUSIC. AND IT ISN'T JUST FOR ME. YOU KNOW THAT.
I'M GOING TO MY ROOM.
K

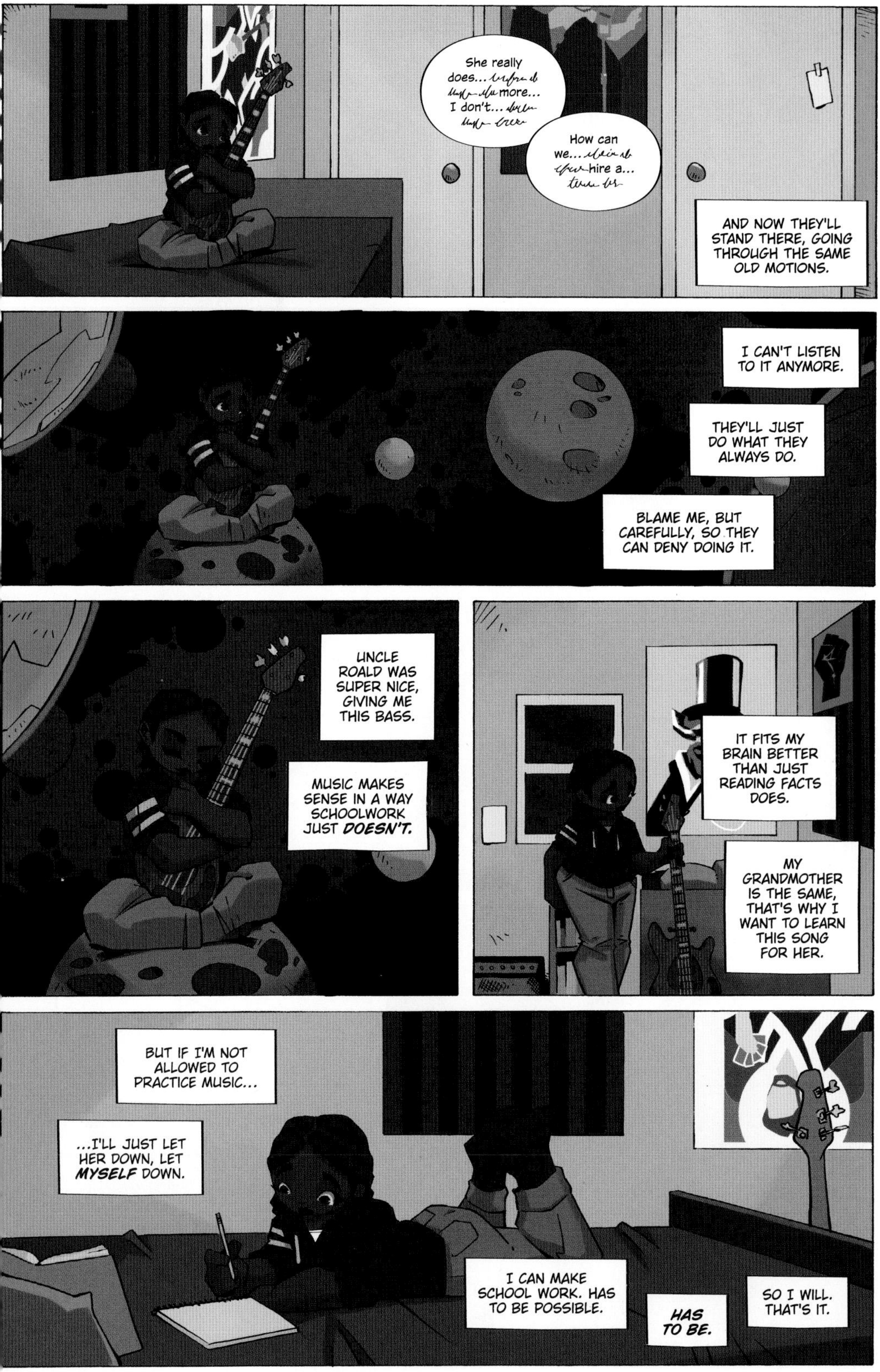

She really does... more... I don't...
How can we... hire a...
AND NOW THEY'LL STAND THERE, GOING THROUGH THE SAME OLD MOTIONS.
I CAN'T LISTEN TO IT ANYMORE.
THEY'LL JUST DO WHAT THEY ALWAYS DO.
BLAME ME, BUT CAREFULLY, SO THEY CAN DENY DOING IT.
UNCLE ROALD WAS SUPER NICE, GIVING ME THIS BASS.
MUSIC MAKES SENSE IN A WAY SCHOOLWORK JUST *DOESN'T.*
IT FITS MY BRAIN BETTER THAN JUST READING FACTS DOES.
MY GRANDMOTHER IS THE SAME, THAT'S WHY I WANT TO LEARN THIS SONG FOR HER.
BUT IF I'M NOT ALLOWED TO PRACTICE MUSIC...
...I'LL JUST LET HER DOWN, LET *MYSELF* DOWN.
I CAN MAKE SCHOOL WORK. HAS TO BE POSSIBLE.
HAS TO BE.
SO I WILL. THAT'S IT.

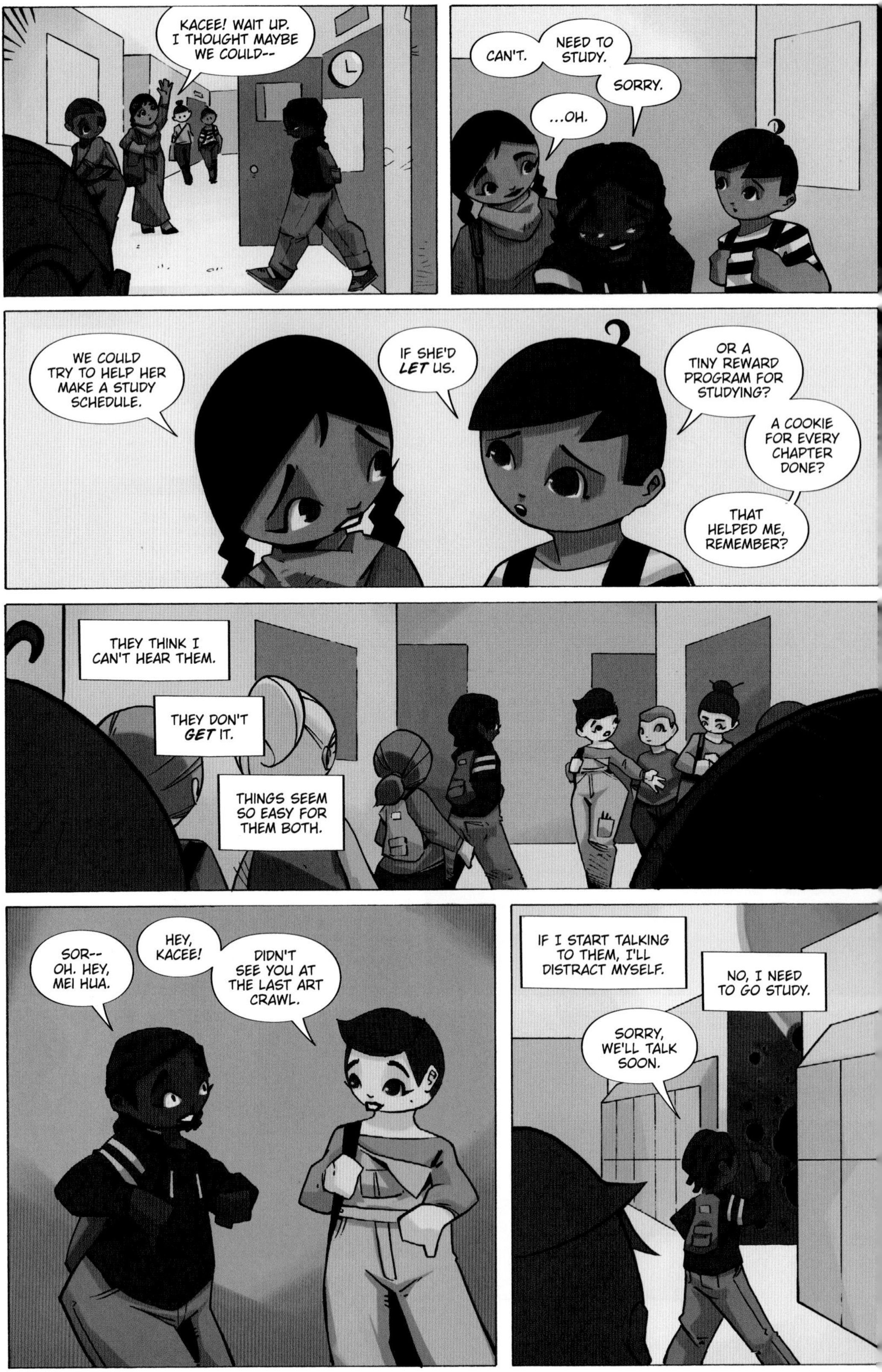
KACEE! WAIT UP. I THOUGHT MAYBE WE COULD--
CAN'T.
NEED TO STUDY.
SORRY.
...OH.
WE COULD TRY TO HELP HER MAKE A STUDY SCHEDULE.
IF SHE'D **LET** US.
OR A TINY REWARD PROGRAM FOR STUDYING?
A COOKIE FOR EVERY CHAPTER DONE?
THAT HELPED ME, REMEMBER?
THEY THINK I CAN'T HEAR THEM.
THEY DON'T **GET** IT.
THINGS SEEM SO EASY FOR THEM BOTH.
SOR-- OH. HEY, MEI HUA.
HEY, KACEE!
DIDN'T SEE YOU AT THE LAST ART CRAWL.
IF I START TALKING TO THEM, I'LL DISTRACT MYSELF.
NO, I NEED TO GO STUDY.
SORRY, WE'LL TALK SOON.

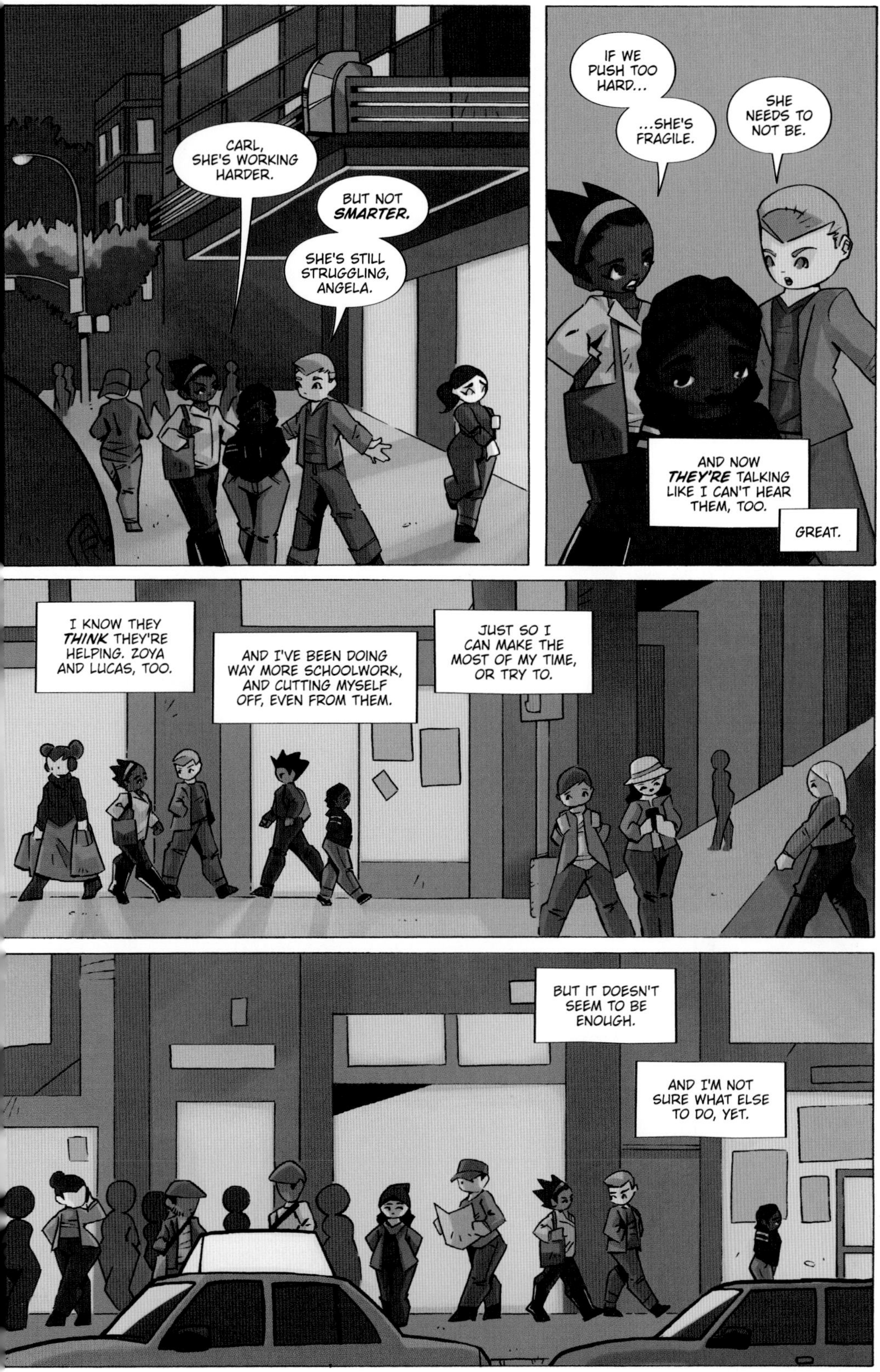
CARL, SHE'S WORKING HARDER.
BUT NOT SMARTER.
SHE'S STILL STRUGGLING, ANGELA.
IF WE PUSH TOO HARD...
...SHE'S FRAGILE.
SHE NEEDS TO NOT BE.
AND NOW THEY'RE TALKING LIKE I CAN'T HEAR THEM, TOO.
GREAT.
I KNOW THEY THINK THEY'RE HELPING. ZOYA AND LUCAS, TOO.
AND I'VE BEEN DOING WAY MORE SCHOOLWORK, AND CUTTING MYSELF OFF, EVEN FROM THEM.
JUST SO I CAN MAKE THE MOST OF MY TIME, OR TRY TO.
BUT IT DOESN'T SEEM TO BE ENOUGH.
AND I'M NOT SURE WHAT ELSE TO DO, YET.

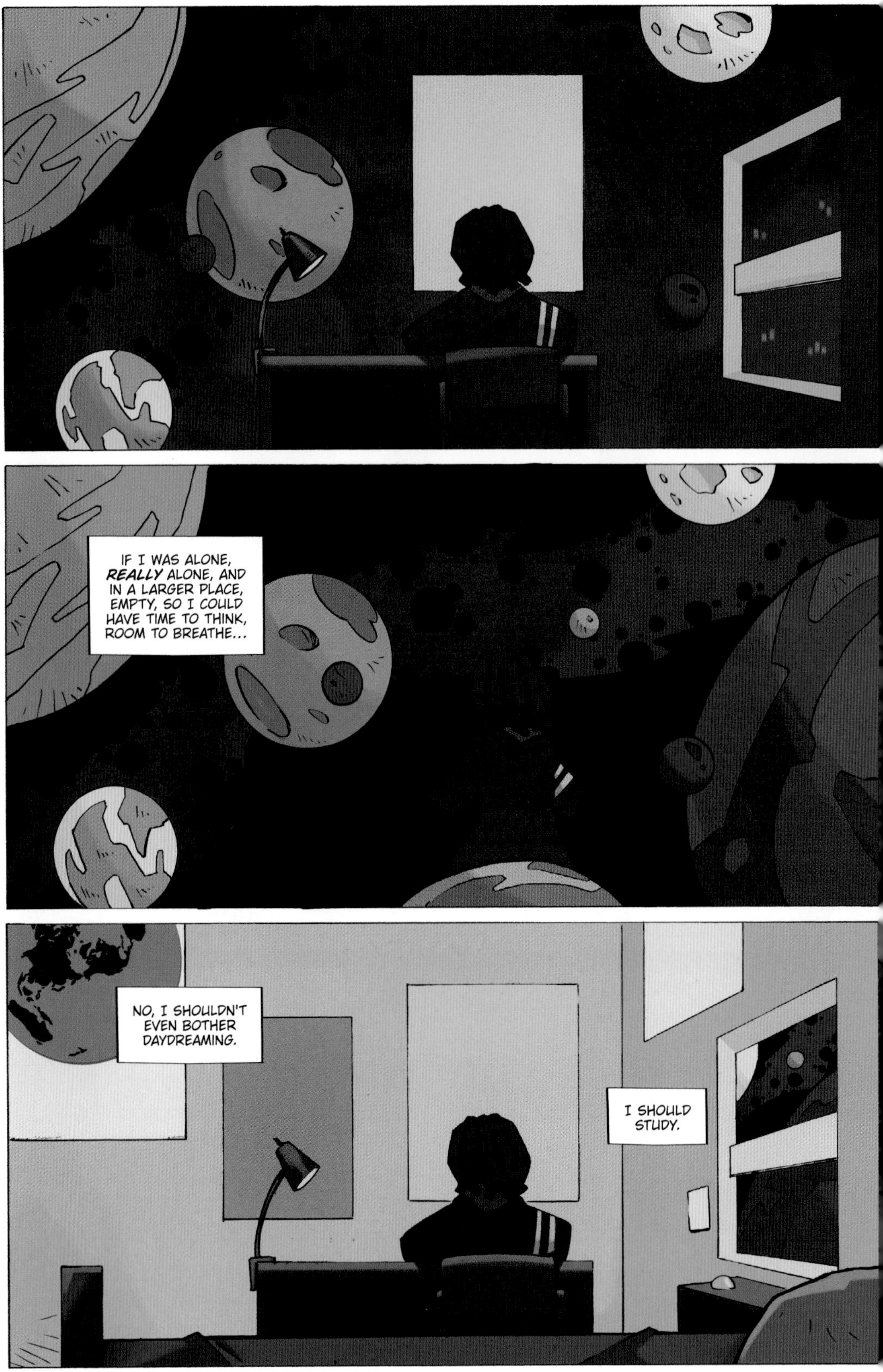
IF I WAS ALONE, ***REALLY*** ALONE, AND IN A LARGER PLACE, EMPTY, SO I COULD HAVE TIME TO THINK, ROOM TO BREATHE...
NO, I SHOULDN'T EVEN BOTHER DAYDREAMING.
I SHOULD STUDY.

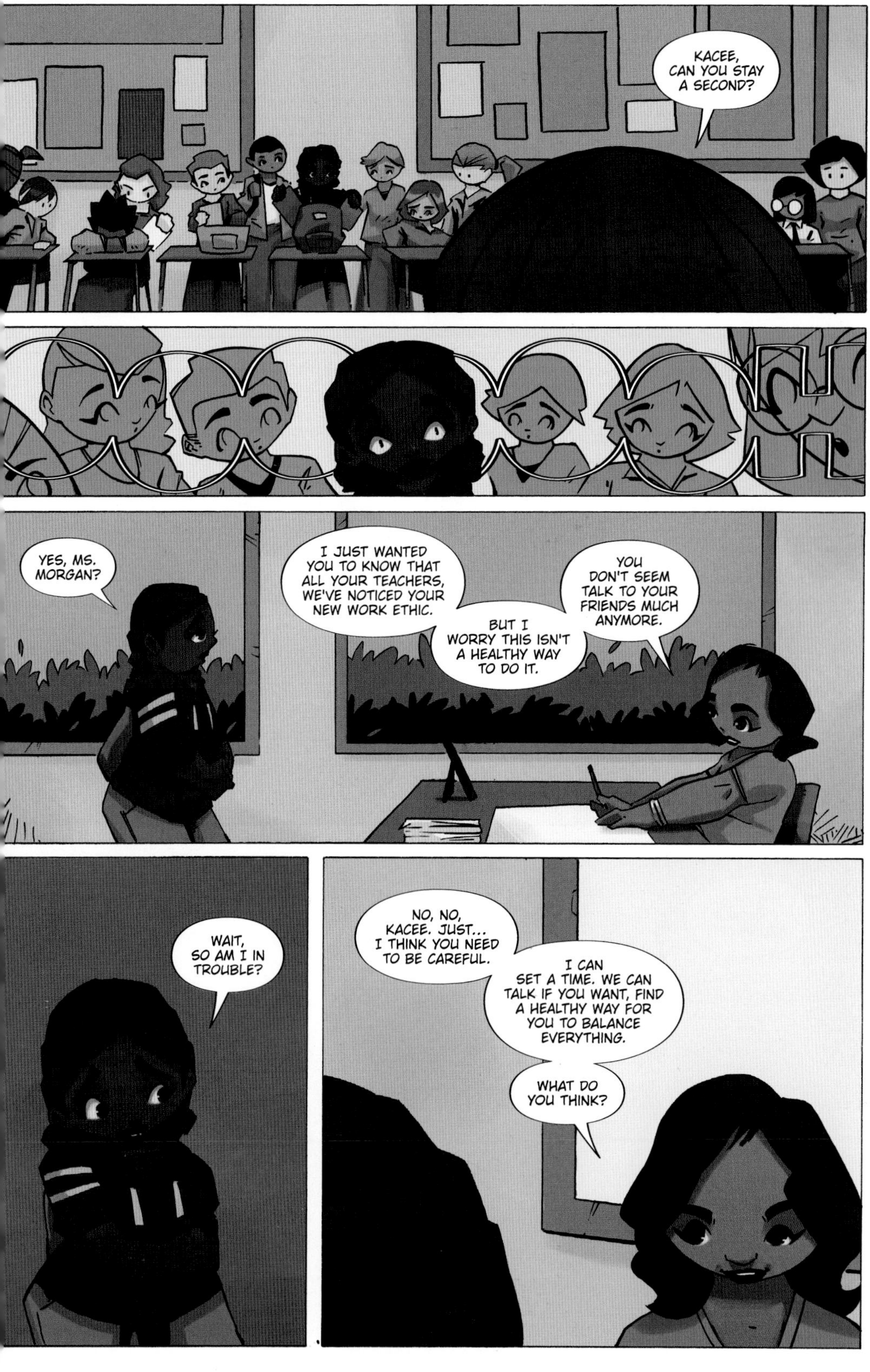
KACEE, CAN YOU STAY A SECOND?
YES, MS. MORGAN?
I JUST WANTED YOU TO KNOW THAT ALL YOUR TEACHERS, WE'VE NOTICED YOUR NEW WORK ETHIC.
BUT I WORRY THIS ISN'T A HEALTHY WAY TO DO IT.
YOU DON'T SEEM TALK TO YOUR FRIENDS MUCH ANYMORE.
WAIT, SO AM I IN TROUBLE?
NO, NO, KACEE. JUST... I THINK YOU NEED TO BE CAREFUL.
I CAN SET A TIME. WE CAN TALK IF YOU WANT, FIND A HEALTHY WAY FOR YOU TO BALANCE EVERYTHING.
WHAT DO YOU THINK?

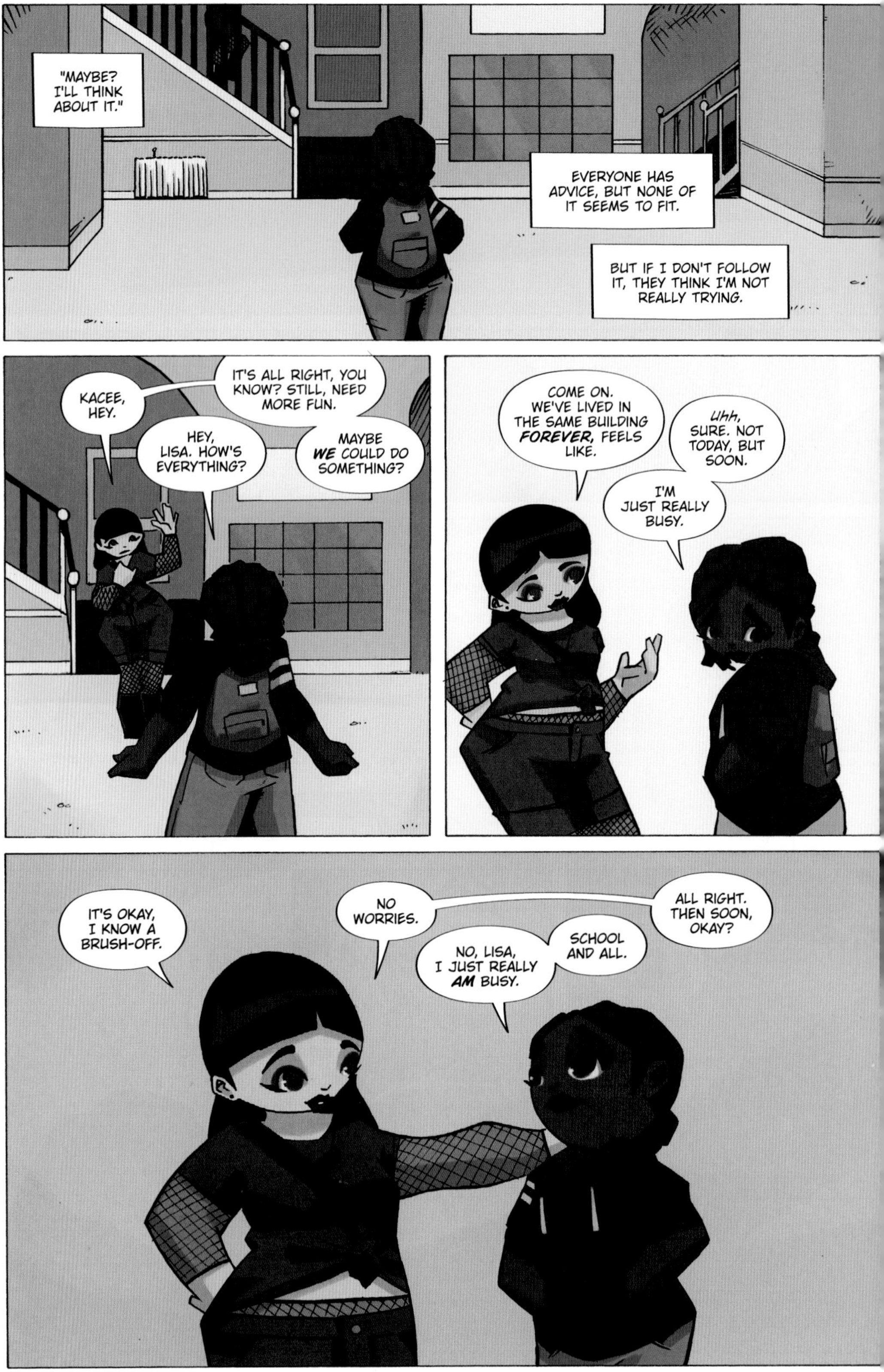
"MAYBE? I'LL THINK ABOUT IT."
EVERYONE HAS ADVICE, BUT NONE OF IT SEEMS TO FIT.
BUT IF I DON'T FOLLOW IT, THEY THINK I'M NOT REALLY TRYING.
KACEE, HEY.
HEY, LISA. HOW'S EVERYTHING?
IT'S ALL RIGHT, YOU KNOW? STILL, NEED MORE FUN.
MAYBE WE COULD DO SOMETHING?
COME ON. WE'VE LIVED IN THE SAME BUILDING FOREVER, FEELS LIKE.
Uhh, SURE. NOT TODAY, BUT SOON.
I'M JUST REALLY BUSY.
IT'S OKAY, I KNOW A BRUSH-OFF.
NO, LISA, I JUST REALLY AM BUSY.
SCHOOL AND ALL.
NO WORRIES.
ALL RIGHT. THEN SOON, OKAY?

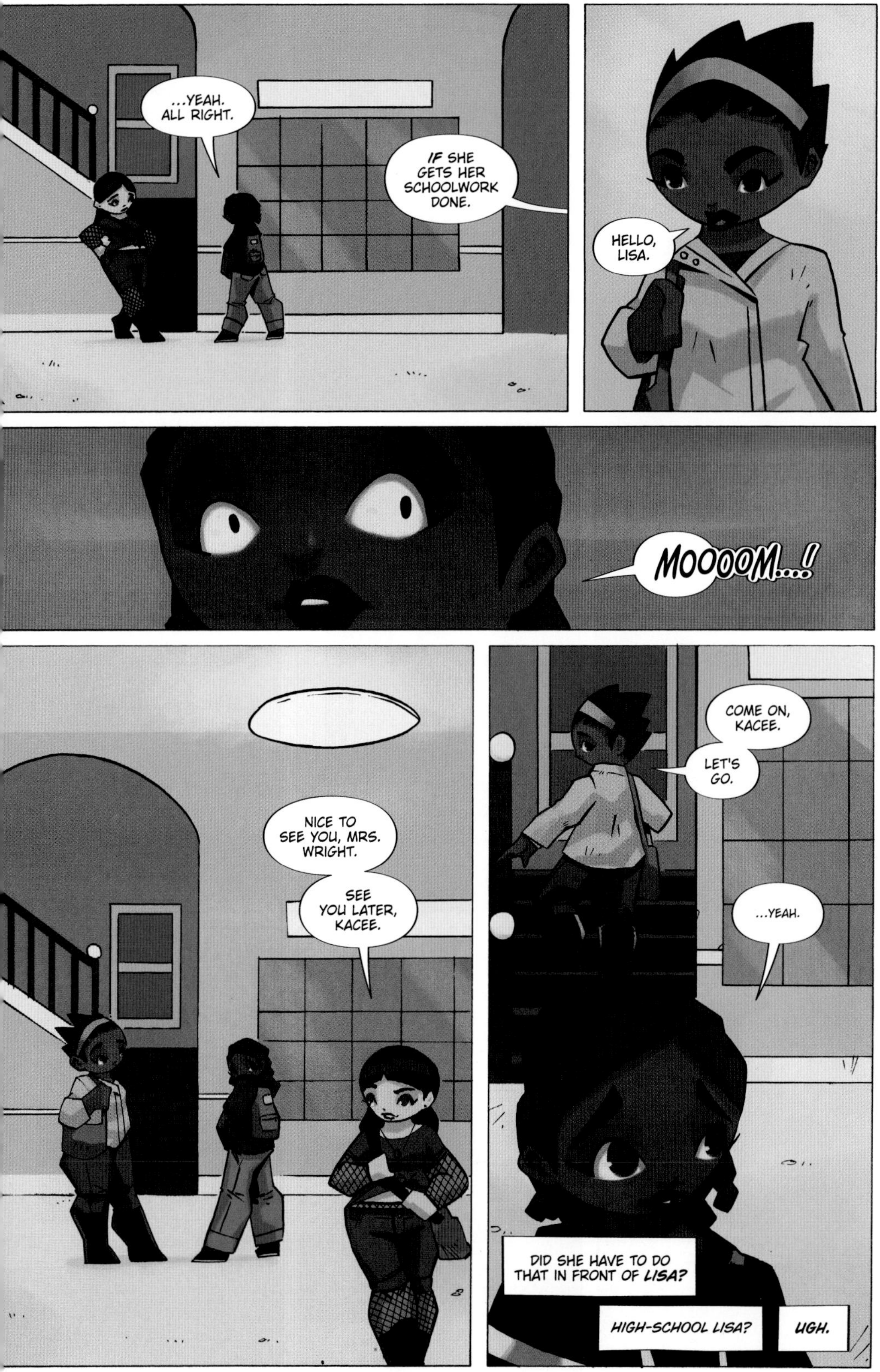
...YEAH. ALL RIGHT.
IF SHE GETS HER SCHOOLWORK DONE.
HELLO, LISA.
MOOOOM...!
NICE TO SEE YOU, MRS. WRIGHT.
SEE YOU LATER, KACEE.
COME ON, KACEE.
LET'S GO.
...YEAH.
DID SHE HAVE TO DO THAT IN FRONT OF LISA?
HIGH-SCHOOL LISA?
UGH.

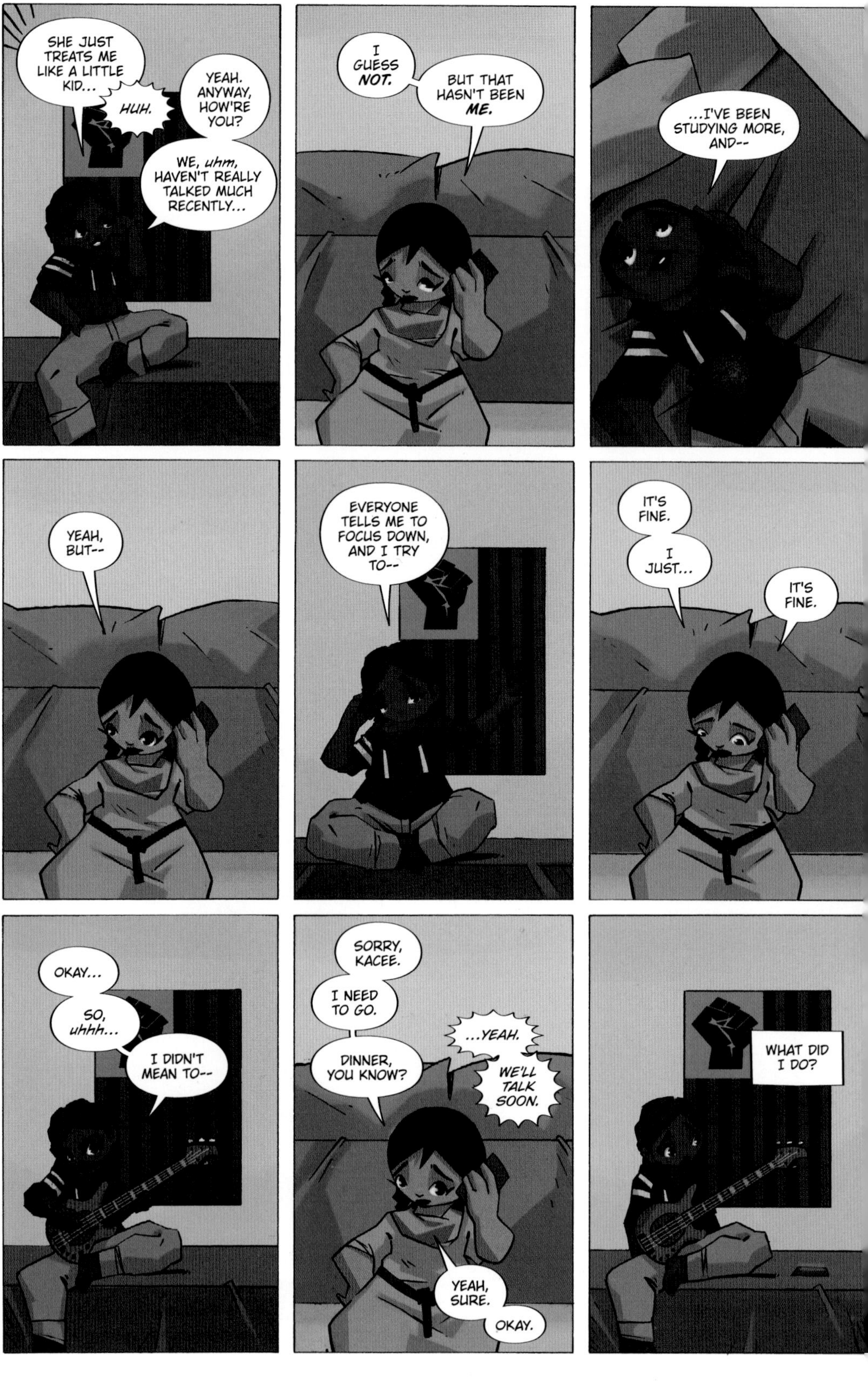
SHE JUST TREATS ME LIKE A LITTLE KID...
HUH.
YEAH. ANYWAY, HOW'RE YOU?
WE, *uhm*, HAVEN'T REALLY TALKED MUCH RECENTLY...
I GUESS *NOT.*
BUT THAT HASN'T BEEN *ME.*
...I'VE BEEN STUDYING MORE, AND--
YEAH, BUT--
EVERYONE TELLS ME TO FOCUS DOWN, AND I TRY TO--
IT'S FINE.
I JUST...
IT'S FINE.
OKAY...
SO, *uhhh...*
I DIDN'T MEAN TO--
SORRY, KACEE.
I NEED TO GO.
DINNER, YOU KNOW?
...YEAH.
WE'LL TALK SOON.
YEAH, SURE.
OKAY.
WHAT DID I DO?

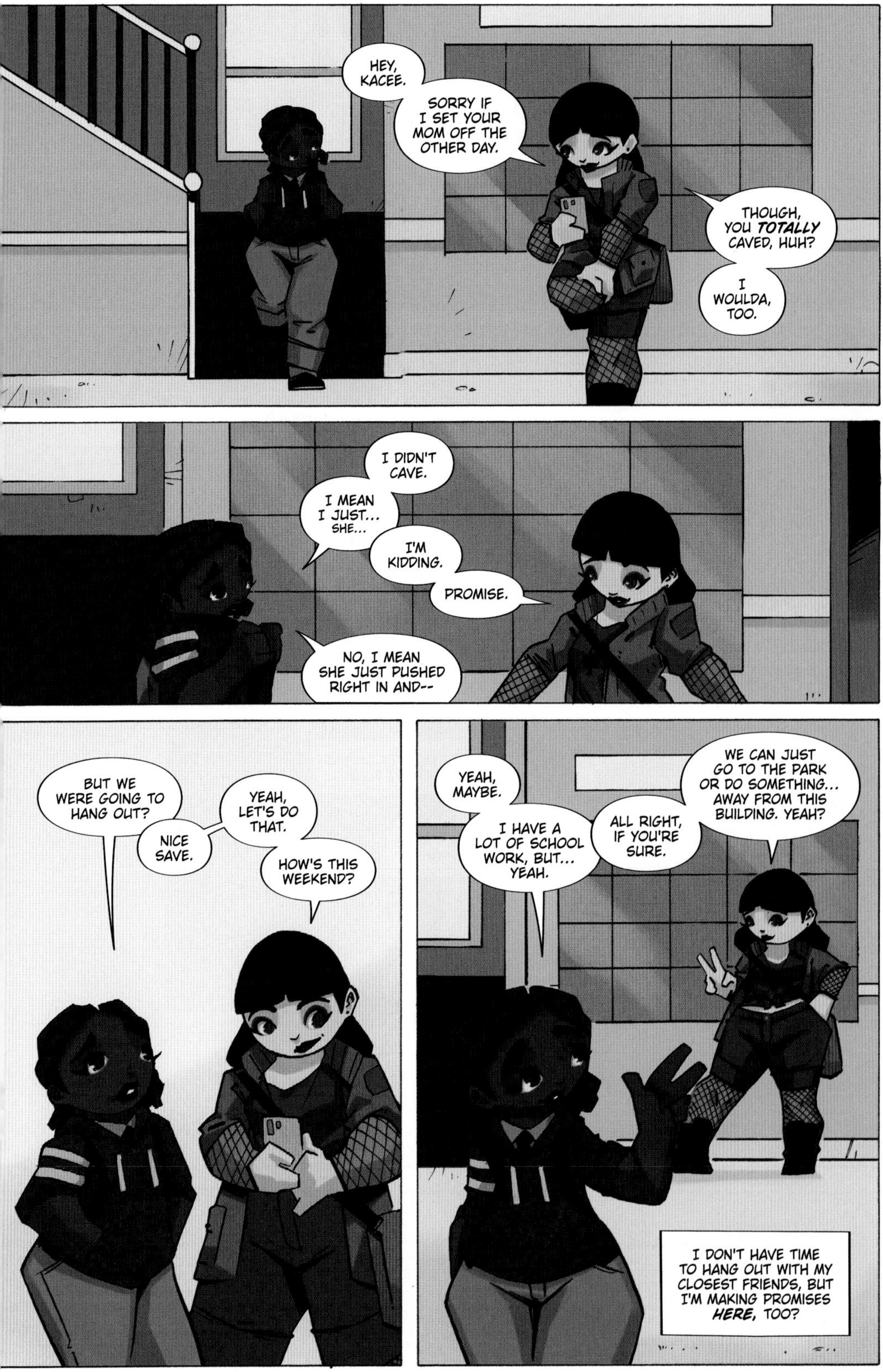
HEY, KACEE.
SORRY IF I SET YOUR MOM OFF THE OTHER DAY.
THOUGH, YOU *TOTALLY* CAVED, HUH?
I WOULDA, TOO.
I DIDN'T CAVE.
I MEAN I JUST... SHE...
I'M KIDDING.
PROMISE.
NO, I MEAN SHE JUST PUSHED RIGHT IN AND--
BUT WE WERE GOING TO HANG OUT?
NICE SAVE.
YEAH, LET'S DO THAT.
HOW'S THIS WEEKEND?
YEAH, MAYBE.
I HAVE A LOT OF SCHOOL WORK, BUT... YEAH.
ALL RIGHT, IF YOU'RE SURE.
WE CAN JUST GO TO THE PARK OR DO SOMETHING... AWAY FROM THIS BUILDING. YEAH?
I DON'T HAVE TIME TO HANG OUT WITH MY CLOSEST FRIENDS, BUT I'M MAKING PROMISES *HERE,* TOO?

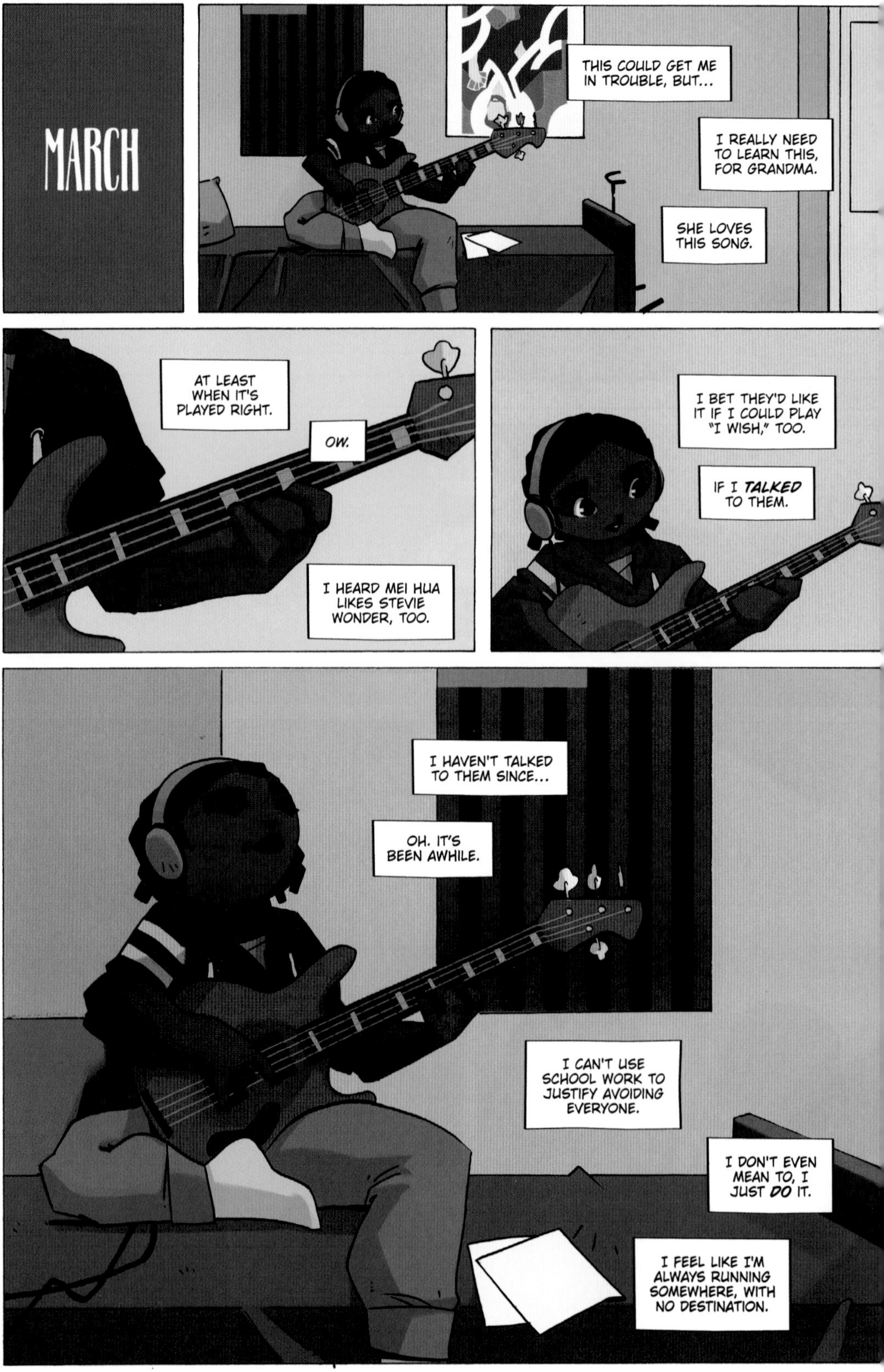
MARCH
THIS COULD GET ME IN TROUBLE, BUT...
I REALLY NEED TO LEARN THIS, FOR GRANDMA.
SHE LOVES THIS SONG.
AT LEAST WHEN IT'S PLAYED RIGHT.
OW.
I HEARD MEI HUA LIKES STEVIE WONDER, TOO.
I BET THEY'D LIKE IT IF I COULD PLAY "I WISH," TOO.
IF I *TALKED* TO THEM.
I HAVEN'T TALKED TO THEM SINCE...
OH. IT'S BEEN AWHILE.
I CAN'T USE SCHOOL WORK TO JUSTIFY AVOIDING EVERYONE.
I DON'T EVEN MEAN TO, I JUST *DO* IT.
I FEEL LIKE I'M ALWAYS RUNNING SOMEWHERE, WITH NO DESTINATION.

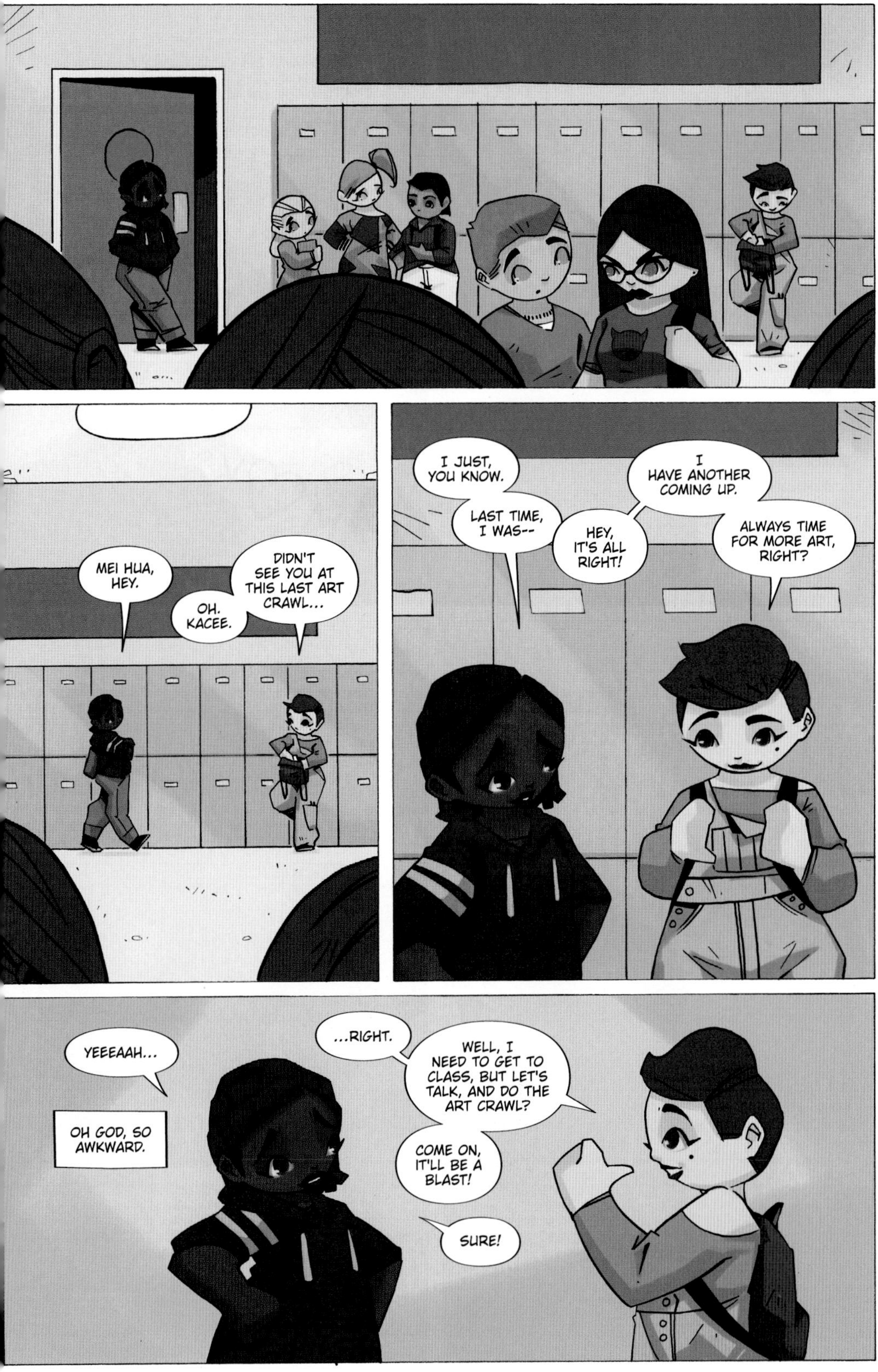
MEI HUA, HEY.
OH. KACEE.
DIDN'T SEE YOU AT THIS LAST ART CRAWL...
I JUST, YOU KNOW.
LAST TIME, I WAS--
HEY, IT'S ALL RIGHT!
I HAVE ANOTHER COMING UP.
ALWAYS TIME FOR MORE ART, RIGHT?
YEEEAAH...
OH GOD, SO AWKWARD.
...RIGHT.
WELL, I NEED TO GET TO CLASS, BUT LET'S TALK, AND DO THE ART CRAWL?
COME ON, IT'LL BE A BLAST!
SURE!

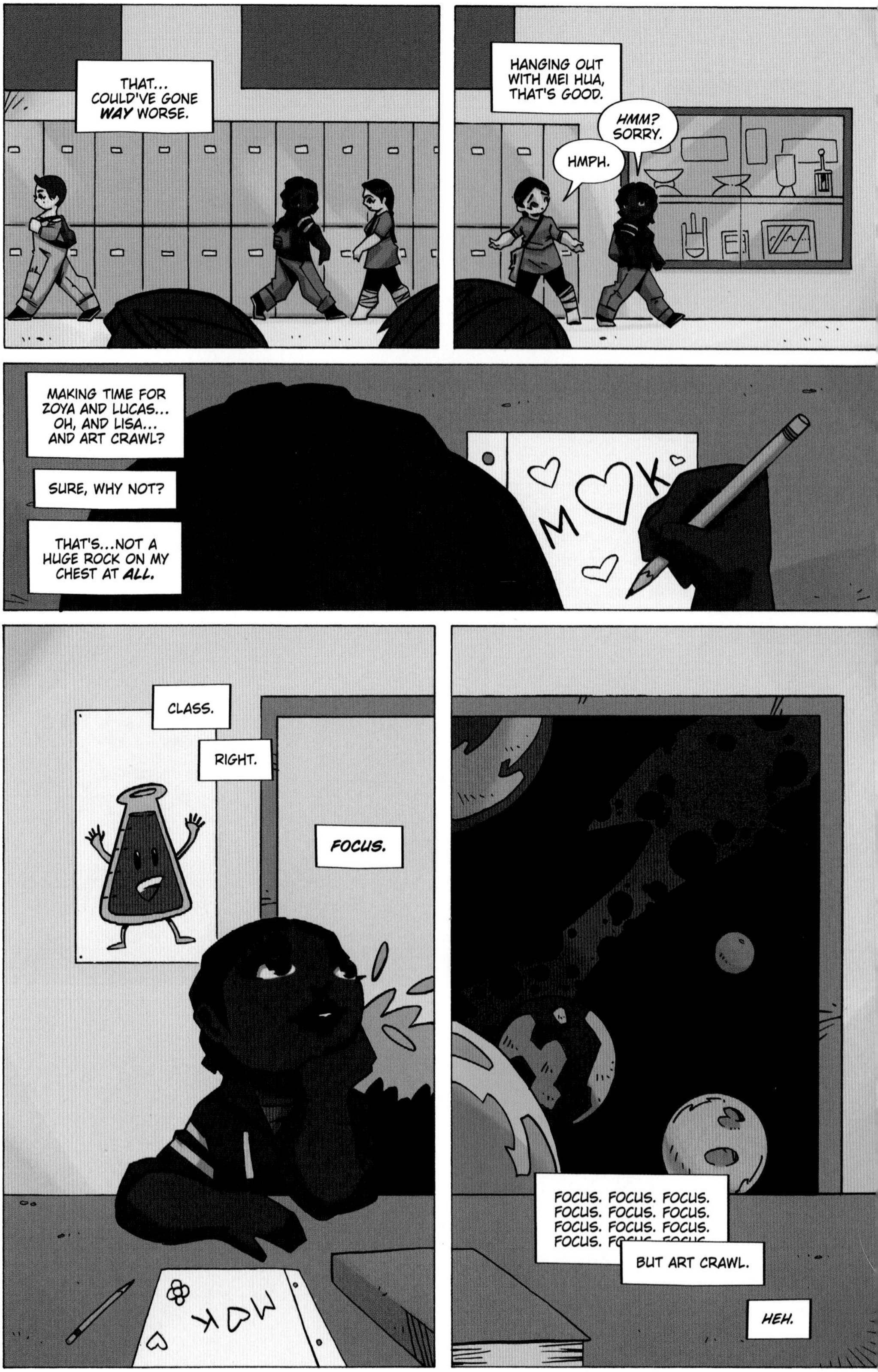
THAT... COULD'VE GONE *WAY* WORSE.
HANGING OUT WITH MEI HUA, THAT'S GOOD.
HMM? SORRY.
HMPH.
MAKING TIME FOR ZOYA AND LUCAS... OH, AND LISA... AND ART CRAWL?
SURE, WHY NOT?
THAT'S...NOT A HUGE ROCK ON MY CHEST AT *ALL.*
CLASS.
RIGHT.
FOCUS.
FOCUS. FOCUS. FOCUS.
FOCUS. FOCUS. FOCUS.
FOCUS. FOCUS. FOCUS.
FOCUS.
BUT ART CRAWL.
HEH.

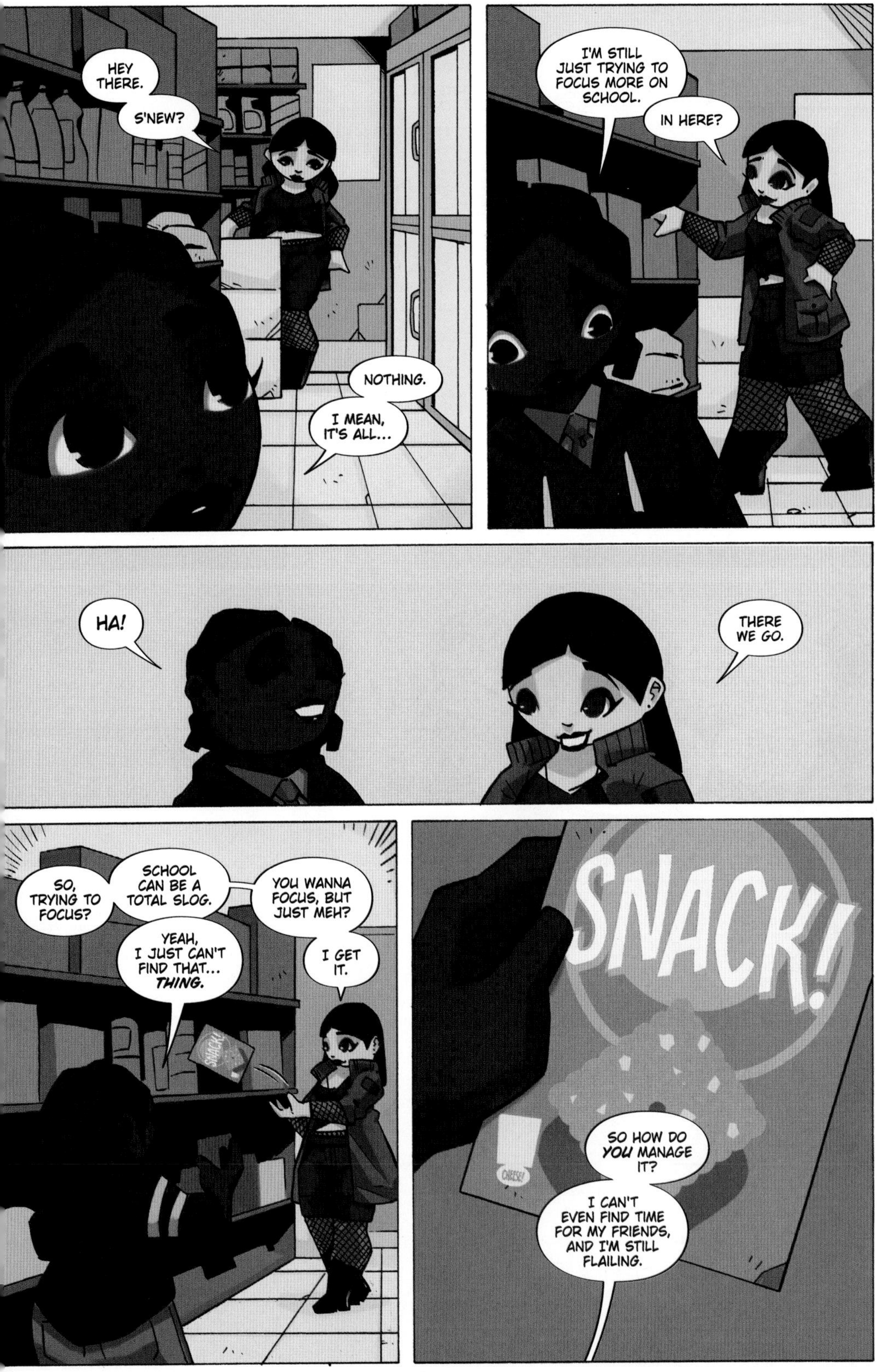
HEY THERE.
S'NEW?
NOTHING.
I MEAN, IT'S ALL...
I'M STILL JUST TRYING TO FOCUS MORE ON SCHOOL.
IN HERE?
HA!
THERE WE GO.
SO, TRYING TO FOCUS?
SCHOOL CAN BE A TOTAL SLOG.
YOU WANNA FOCUS, BUT JUST MEH?
YEAH, I JUST CAN'T FIND THAT... *THING.*
I GET IT.
SNACK!
SO HOW DO *YOU* MANAGE IT?
I CAN'T EVEN FIND TIME FOR MY FRIENDS, AND I'M STILL FLAILING.

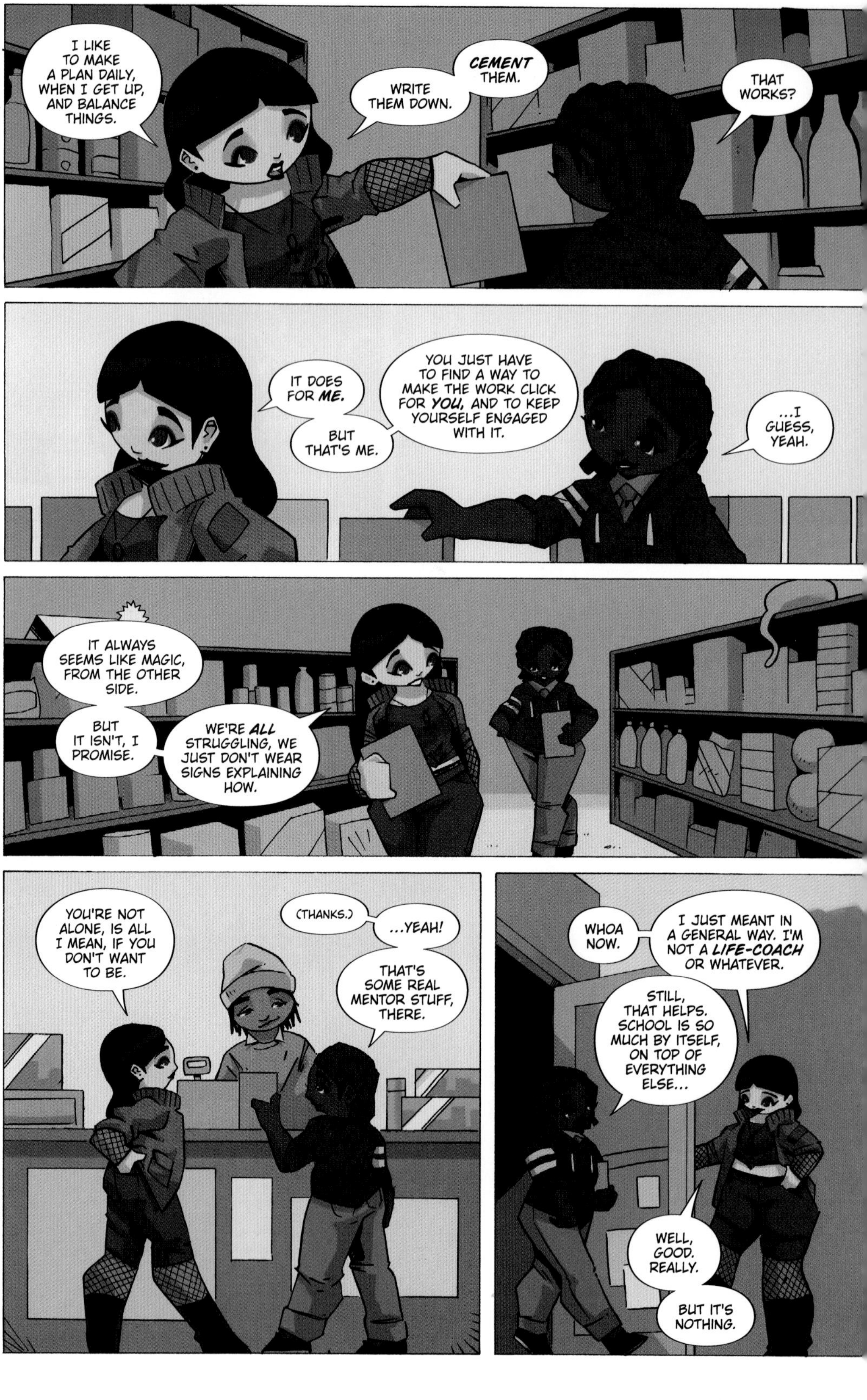
I LIKE TO MAKE A PLAN DAILY, WHEN I GET UP, AND BALANCE THINGS.
WRITE THEM DOWN.
CEMENT THEM.
THAT WORKS?
IT DOES FOR ME.
BUT THAT'S ME.
YOU JUST HAVE TO FIND A WAY TO MAKE THE WORK CLICK FOR YOU, AND TO KEEP YOURSELF ENGAGED WITH IT.
...I GUESS, YEAH.
IT ALWAYS SEEMS LIKE MAGIC, FROM THE OTHER SIDE.
BUT IT ISN'T, I PROMISE.
WE'RE ALL STRUGGLING, WE JUST DON'T WEAR SIGNS EXPLAINING HOW.
YOU'RE NOT ALONE, IS ALL I MEAN, IF YOU DON'T WANT TO BE.
(THANKS.)
...YEAH!
THAT'S SOME REAL MENTOR STUFF, THERE.
WHOA NOW.
I JUST MEANT IN A GENERAL WAY. I'M NOT A LIFE-COACH OR WHATEVER.
STILL, THAT HELPS. SCHOOL IS SO MUCH BY ITSELF, ON TOP OF EVERYTHING ELSE...
WELL, GOOD. REALLY.
BUT IT'S NOTHING.

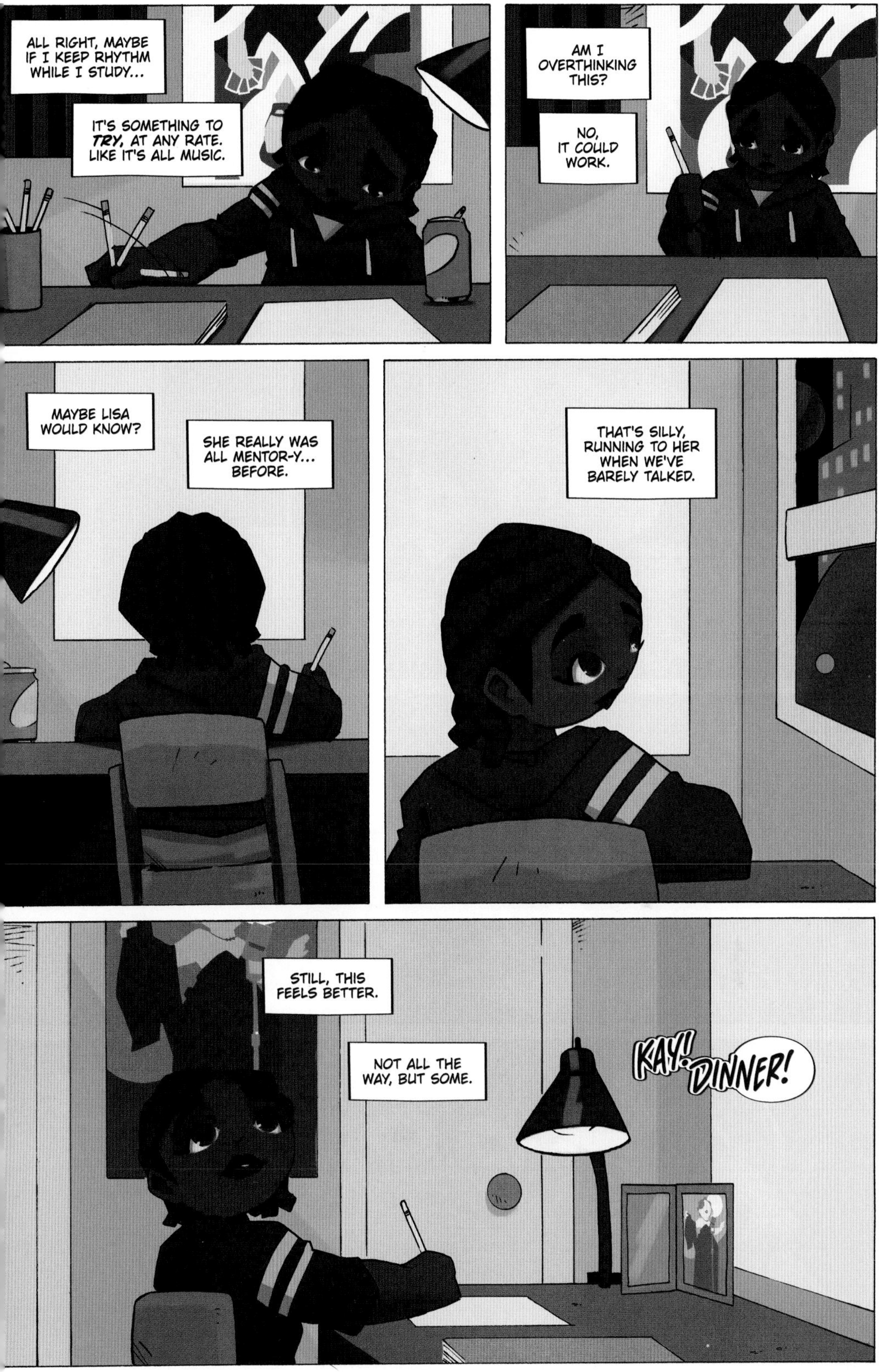
ALL RIGHT, MAYBE IF I KEEP RHYTHM WHILE I STUDY...
IT'S SOMETHING TO *TRY,* AT ANY RATE. LIKE IT'S ALL MUSIC.
AM I OVERTHINKING THIS?
NO, IT COULD WORK.
MAYBE LISA WOULD KNOW?
SHE REALLY WAS ALL MENTOR-Y... BEFORE.
THAT'S SILLY, RUNNING TO HER WHEN WE'VE BARELY TALKED.
STILL, THIS FEELS BETTER.
NOT ALL THE WAY, BUT SOME.
KAY! DINNER!

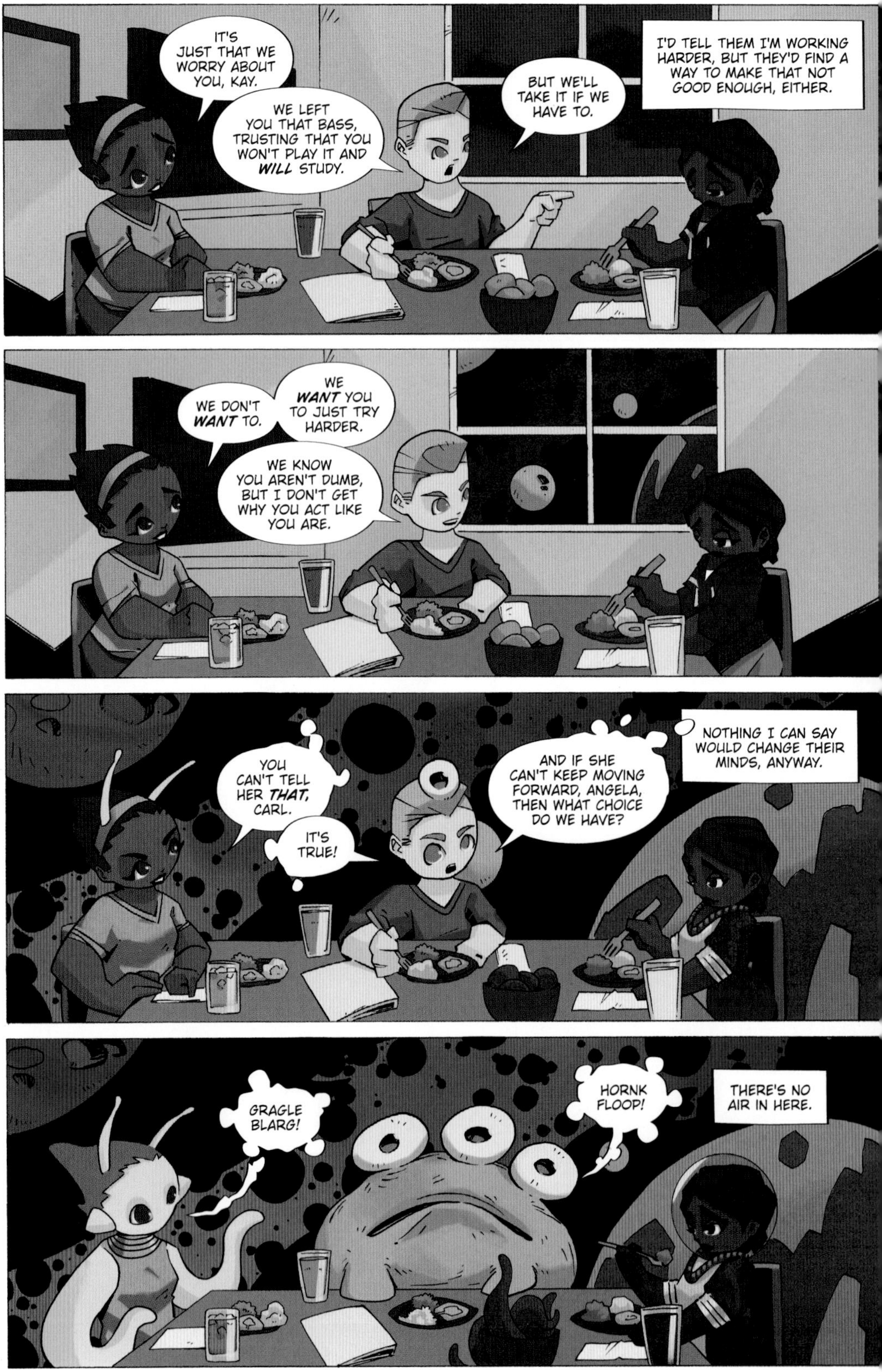
IT'S JUST THAT WE WORRY ABOUT YOU, KAY.
WE LEFT YOU THAT BASS, TRUSTING THAT YOU WON'T PLAY IT AND **WILL** STUDY.
BUT WE'LL TAKE IT IF WE HAVE TO.
I'D TELL THEM I'M WORKING HARDER, BUT THEY'D FIND A WAY TO MAKE THAT NOT GOOD ENOUGH, EITHER.
WE DON'T **WANT** TO.
WE **WANT** YOU TO JUST TRY HARDER.
WE KNOW YOU AREN'T DUMB, BUT I DON'T GET WHY YOU ACT LIKE YOU ARE.
YOU CAN'T TELL HER **THAT**, CARL.
IT'S TRUE!
AND IF SHE CAN'T KEEP MOVING FORWARD, ANGELA, THEN WHAT CHOICE DO WE HAVE?
NOTHING I CAN SAY WOULD CHANGE THEIR MINDS, ANYWAY.
GRAGLE BLARG!
HORNK FLOOP!
THERE'S NO AIR IN HERE.

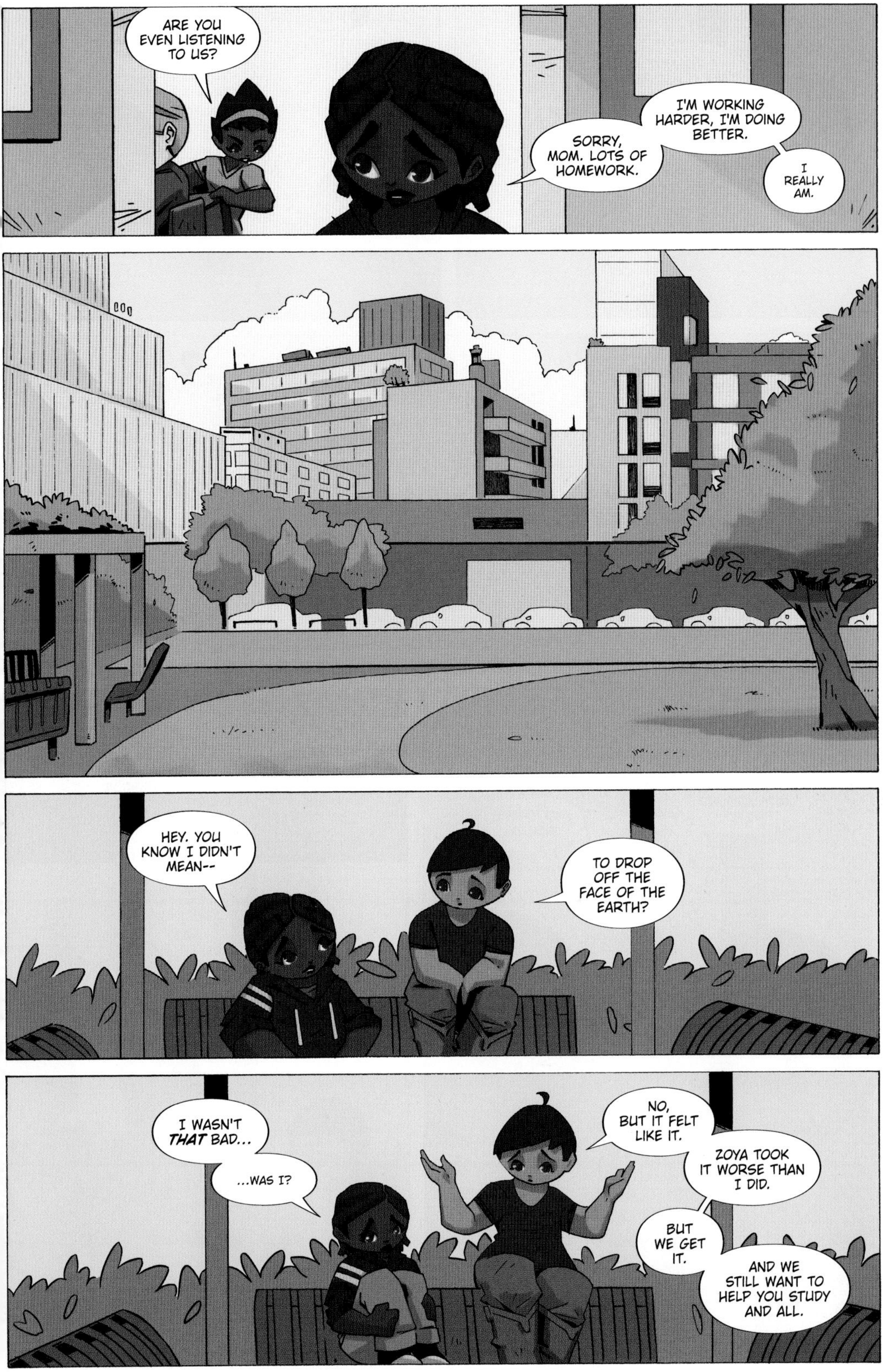
ARE YOU EVEN LISTENING TO US?
SORRY, MOM. LOTS OF HOMEWORK.
I'M WORKING HARDER, I'M DOING BETTER.
I REALLY AM.
HEY. YOU KNOW I DIDN'T MEAN--
TO DROP OFF THE FACE OF THE EARTH?
I WASN'T *THAT* BAD...
...WAS I?
NO, BUT IT FELT LIKE IT.
ZOYA TOOK IT WORSE THAN I DID.
BUT WE GET IT.
AND WE STILL WANT TO HELP YOU STUDY AND ALL.

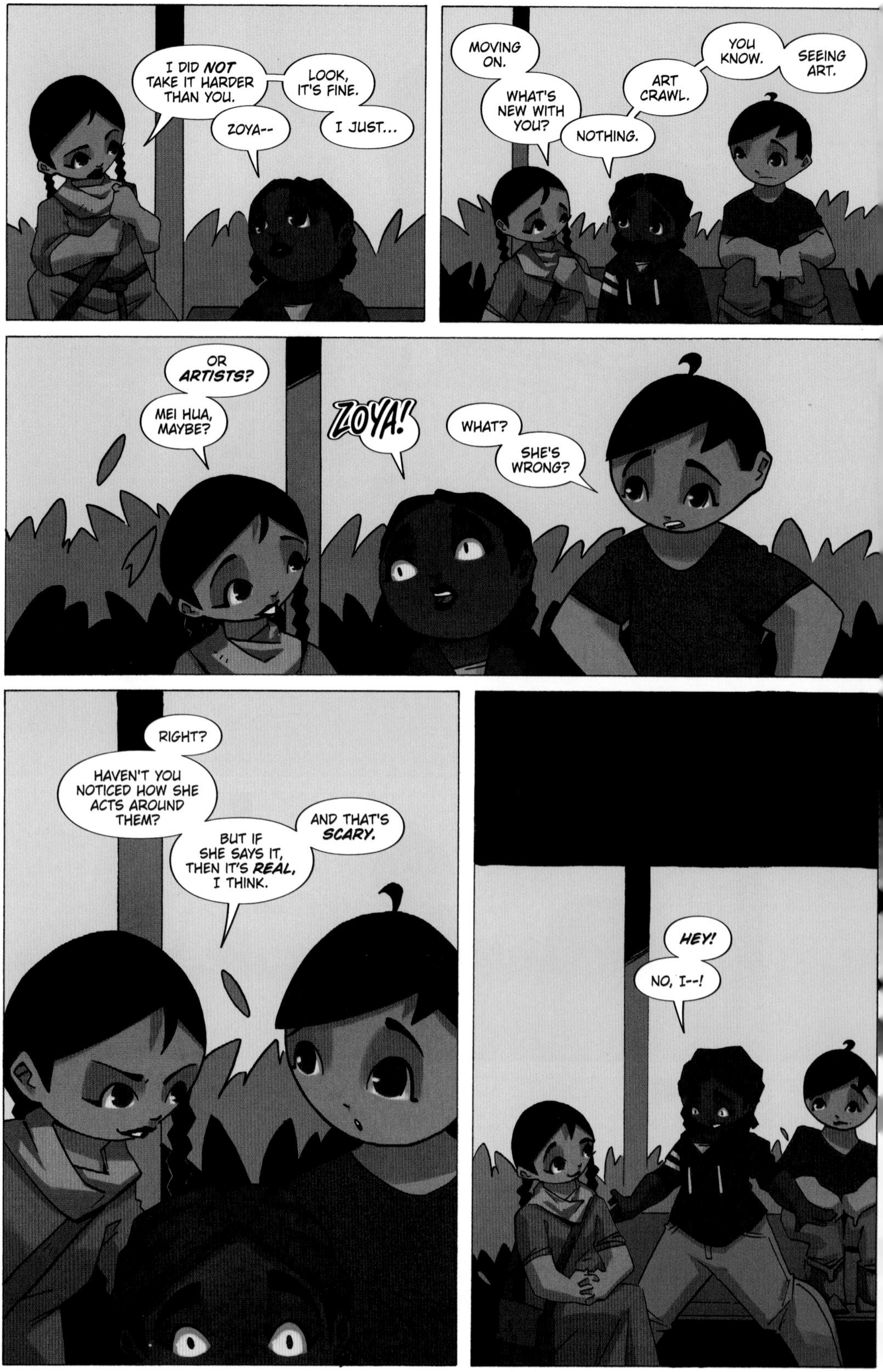
I DID NOT TAKE IT HARDER THAN YOU.
ZOYA--
LOOK, IT'S FINE.
I JUST...
MOVING ON.
WHAT'S NEW WITH YOU?
NOTHING.
ART CRAWL.
YOU KNOW.
SEEING ART.
OR ARTISTS?
MEI HUA, MAYBE?
ZOYA!
WHAT?
SHE'S WRONG?
RIGHT?
HAVEN'T YOU NOTICED HOW SHE ACTS AROUND THEM?
BUT IF SHE SAYS IT, THEN IT'S REAL, I THINK.
AND THAT'S SCARY.
HEY!
NO, I--!

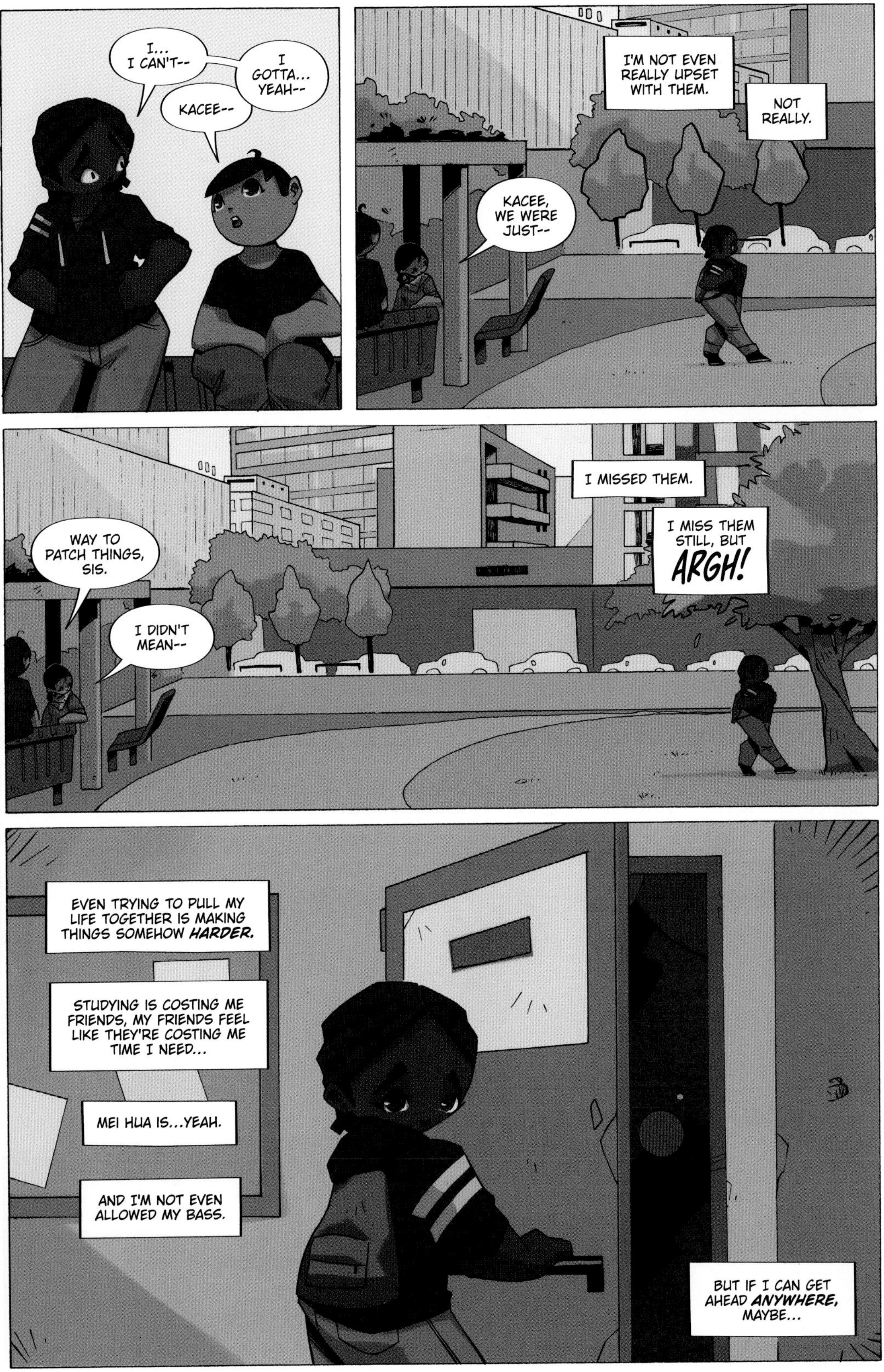
I... I CAN'T--
I GOTTA... YEAH--
KACEE--
I'M NOT EVEN REALLY UPSET WITH THEM.
NOT REALLY.
KACEE, WE WERE JUST--
I MISSED THEM.
I MISS THEM STILL, BUT ARGH!
WAY TO PATCH THINGS, SIS.
I DIDN'T MEAN--
EVEN TRYING TO PULL MY LIFE TOGETHER IS MAKING THINGS SOMEHOW HARDER.
STUDYING IS COSTING ME FRIENDS, MY FRIENDS FEEL LIKE THEY'RE COSTING ME TIME I NEED...
MEI HUA IS...YEAH.
AND I'M NOT EVEN ALLOWED MY BASS.
BUT IF I CAN GET AHEAD ANYWHERE, MAYBE...

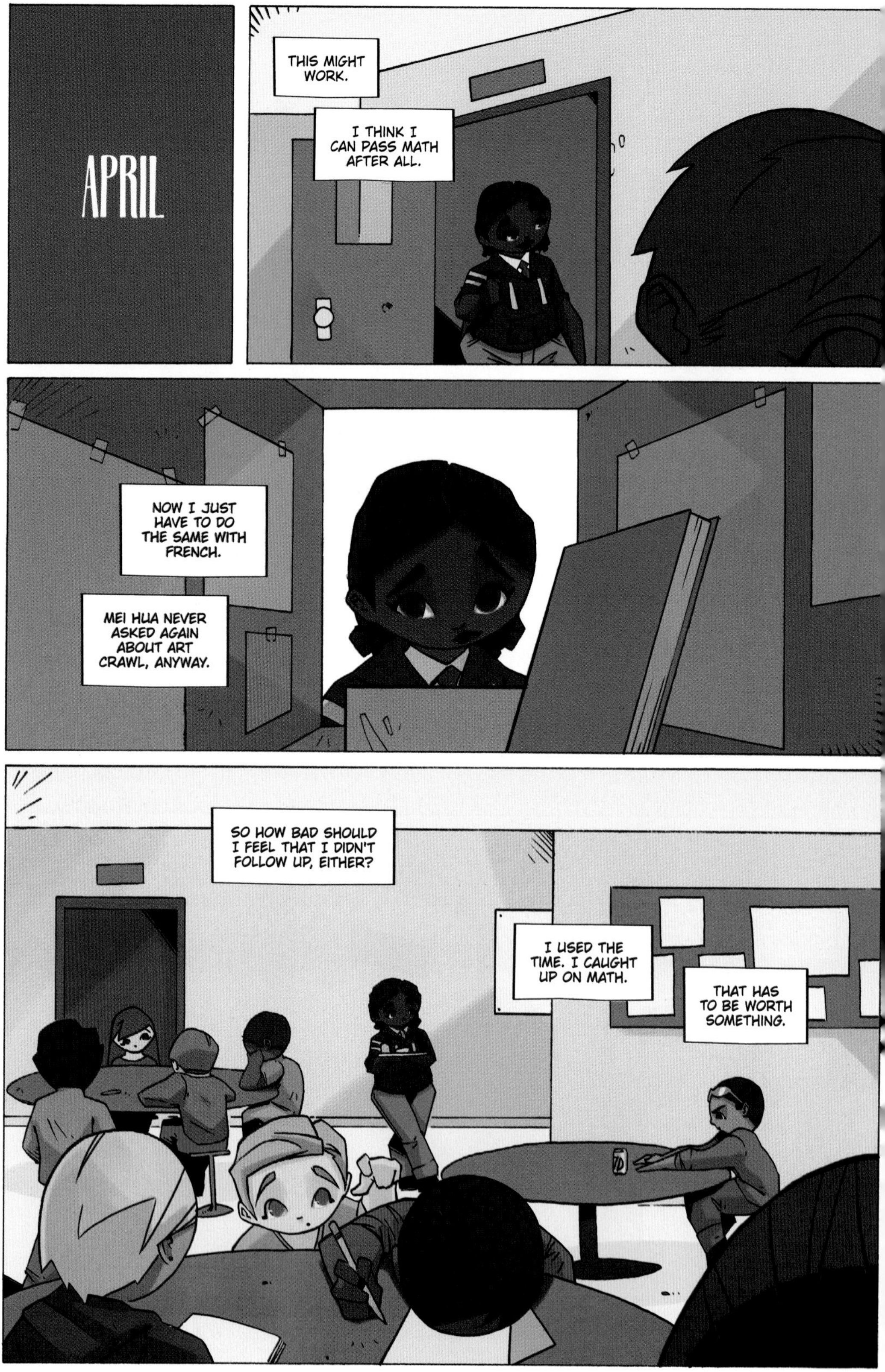
APRIL
THIS MIGHT WORK.
I THINK I CAN PASS MATH AFTER ALL.
NOW I JUST HAVE TO DO THE SAME WITH FRENCH.
MEI HUA NEVER ASKED AGAIN ABOUT ART CRAWL, ANYWAY.
SO HOW BAD SHOULD I FEEL THAT I DIDN'T FOLLOW UP, EITHER?
I USED THE TIME. I CAUGHT UP ON MATH.
THAT HAS TO BE WORTH SOMETHING.

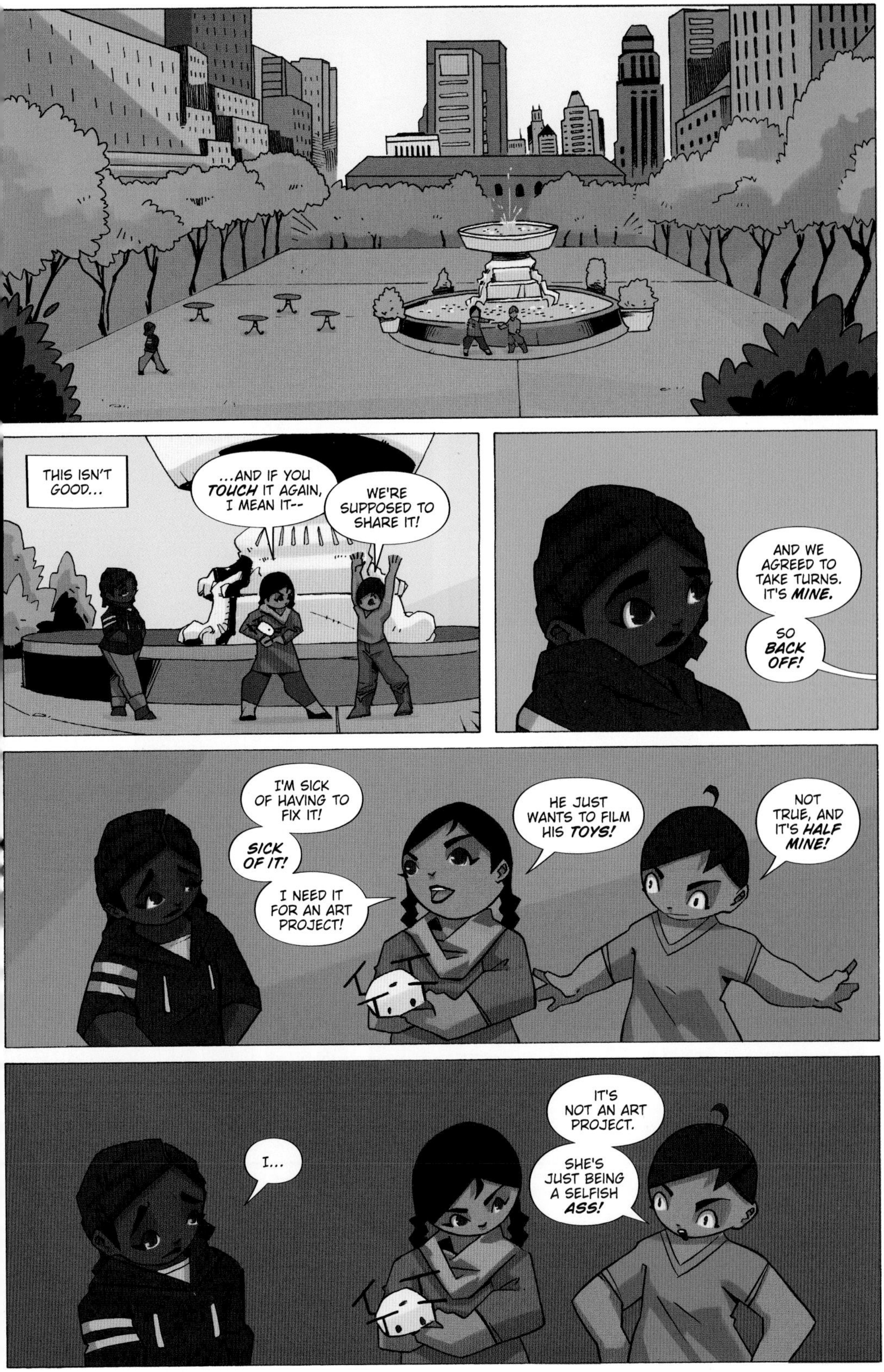
THIS ISN'T GOOD...
...AND IF YOU TOUCH IT AGAIN, I MEAN IT--
WE'RE SUPPOSED TO SHARE IT!
AND WE AGREED TO TAKE TURNS. IT'S MINE.
SO BACK OFF!
I'M SICK OF HAVING TO FIX IT!
SICK OF IT!
I NEED IT FOR AN ART PROJECT!
HE JUST WANTS TO FILM HIS TOYS!
NOT TRUE, AND IT'S HALF MINE!
I...
IT'S NOT AN ART PROJECT.
SHE'S JUST BEING A SELFISH ASS!

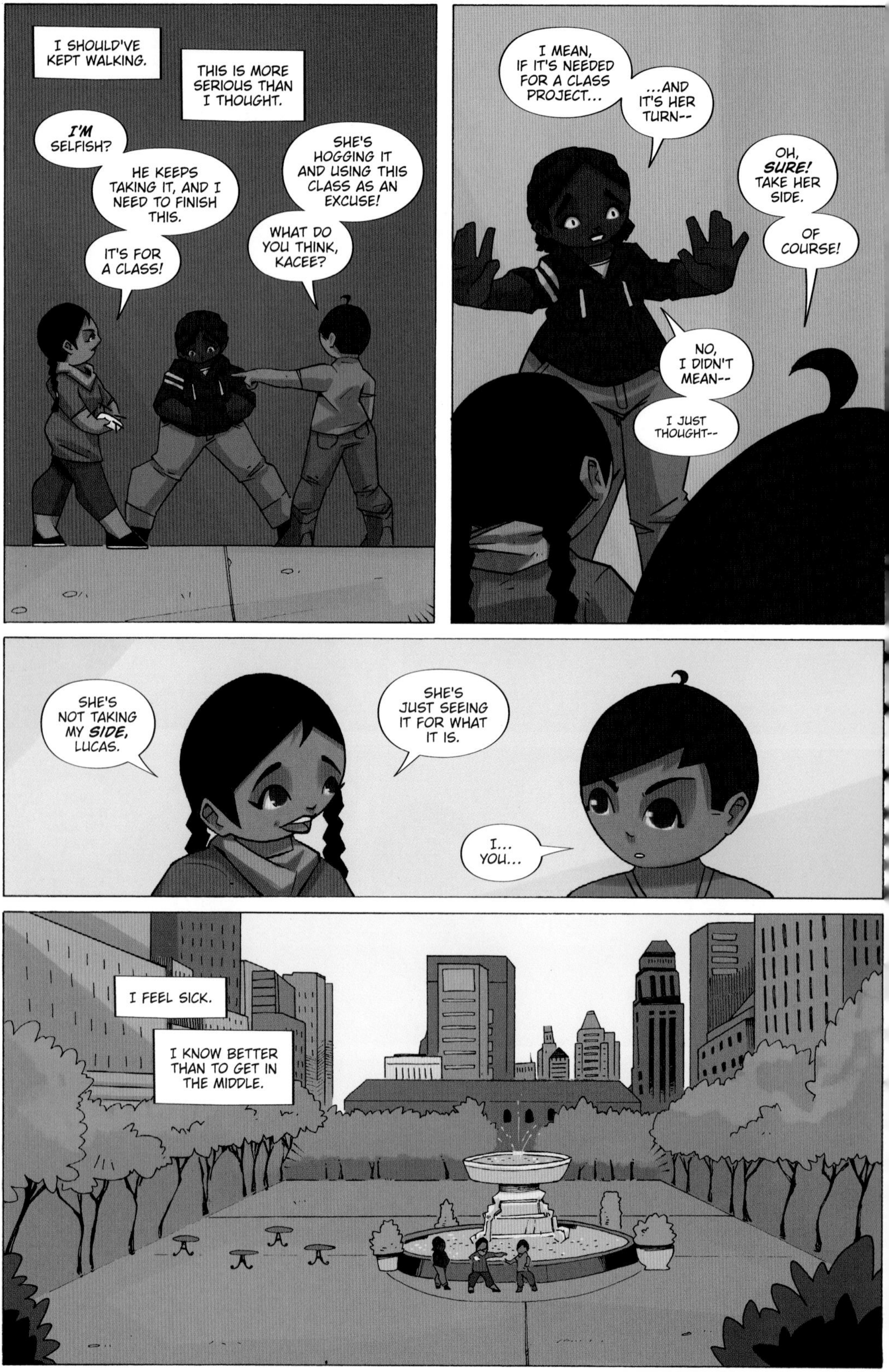
I SHOULD'VE KEPT WALKING.
THIS IS MORE SERIOUS THAN I THOUGHT.
I'M SELFISH?
HE KEEPS TAKING IT, AND I NEED TO FINISH THIS.
IT'S FOR A CLASS!
SHE'S HOGGING IT AND USING THIS CLASS AS AN EXCUSE!
WHAT DO YOU THINK, KACEE?
I MEAN, IF IT'S NEEDED FOR A CLASS PROJECT...
...AND IT'S HER TURN--
OH, SURE! TAKE HER SIDE.
OF COURSE!
NO, I DIDN'T MEAN--
I JUST THOUGHT--
SHE'S NOT TAKING MY SIDE, LUCAS.
SHE'S JUST SEEING IT FOR WHAT IT IS.
I... YOU...
I FEEL SICK.
I KNOW BETTER THAN TO GET IN THE MIDDLE.

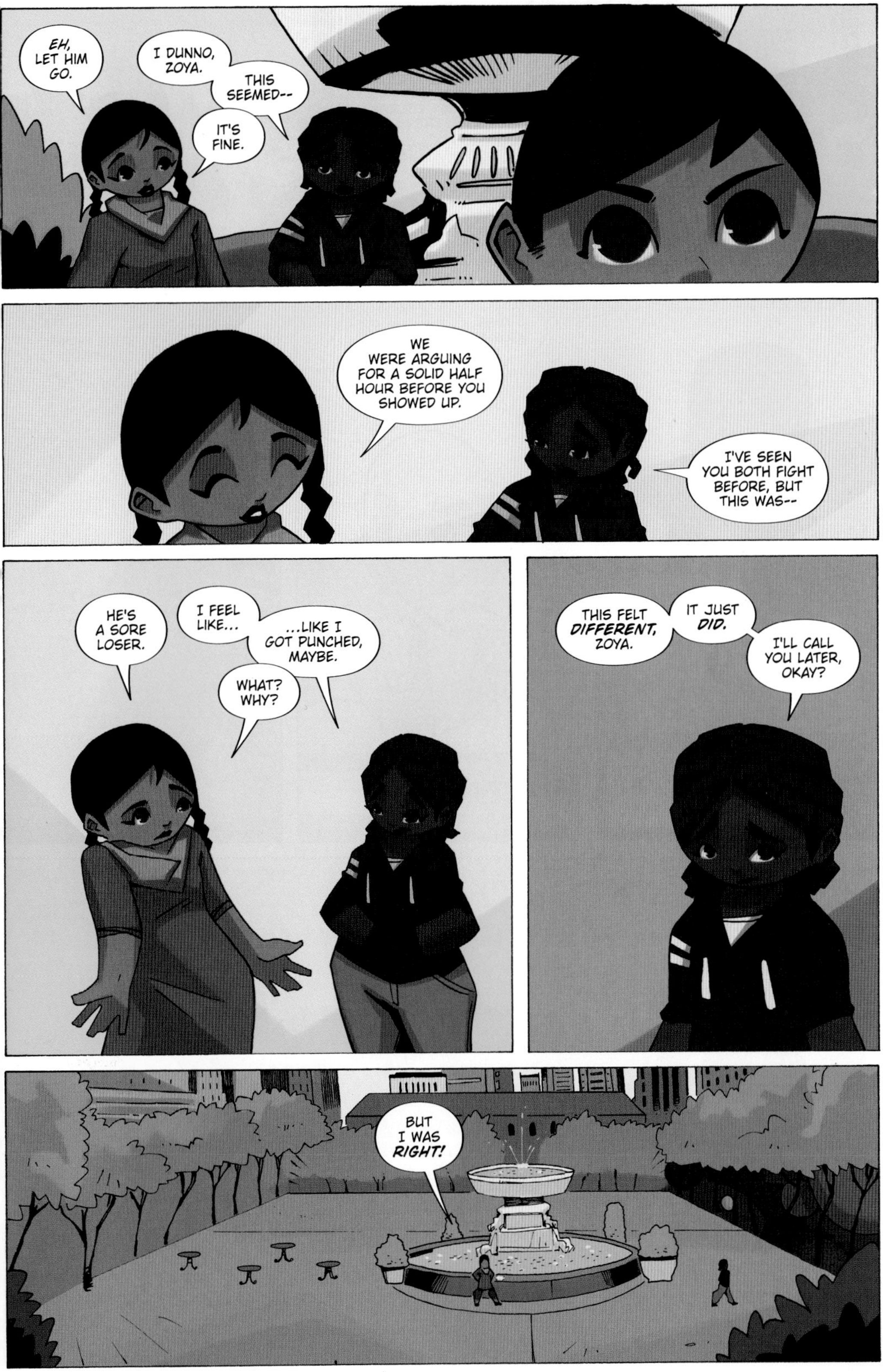

EH, LET HIM GO.
I DUNNO, ZOYA.
THIS SEEMED--
IT'S FINE.
WE WERE ARGUING FOR A SOLID HALF HOUR BEFORE YOU SHOWED UP.
I'VE SEEN YOU BOTH FIGHT BEFORE, BUT THIS WAS--
HE'S A SORE LOSER.
I FEEL LIKE...
...LIKE I GOT PUNCHED, MAYBE.
WHAT? WHY?
THIS FELT *DIFFERENT,* ZOYA.
IT JUST *DID.*
I'LL CALL YOU LATER, OKAY?
BUT I WAS *RIGHT!*

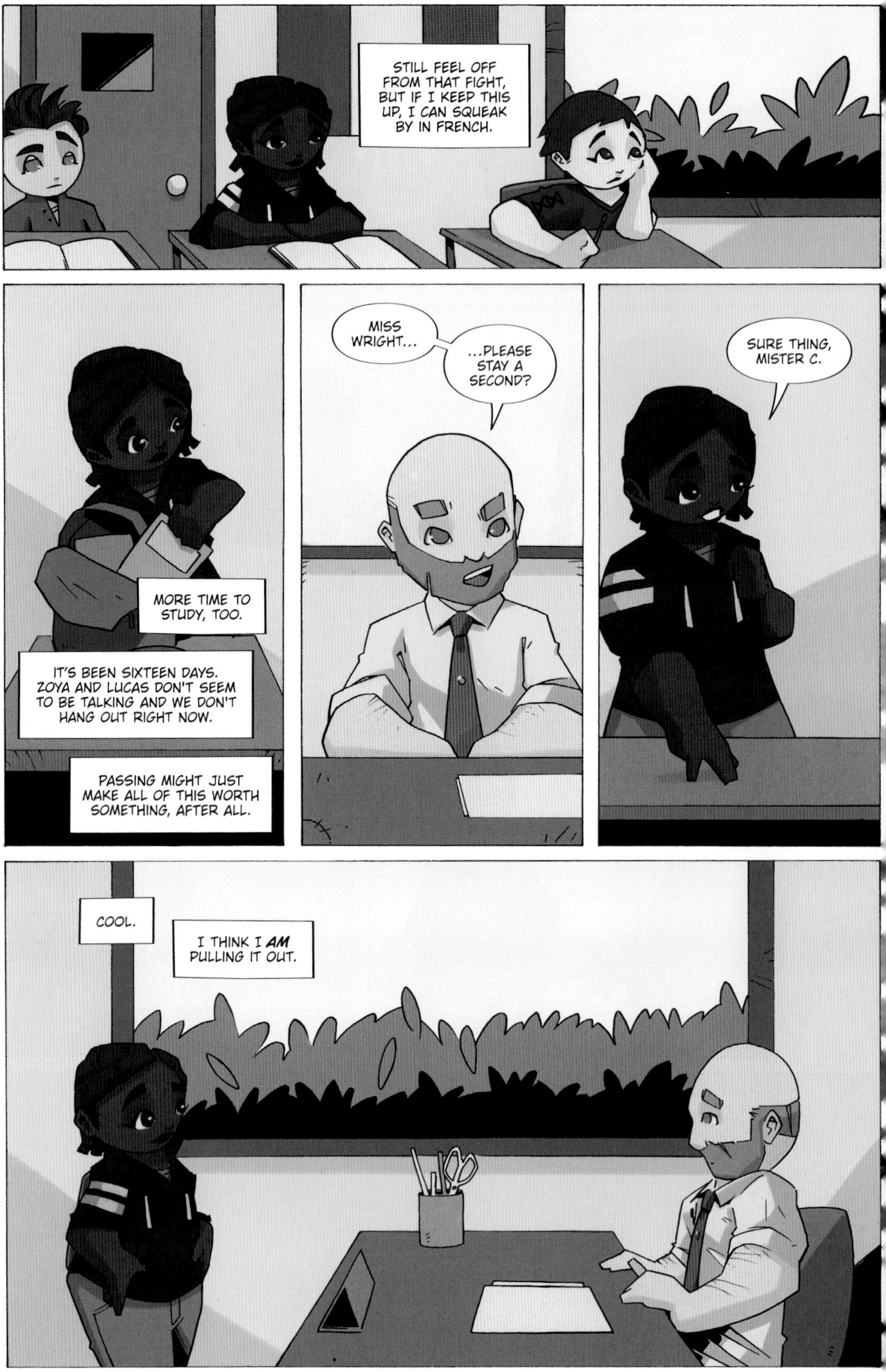
STILL FEEL OFF FROM THAT FIGHT, BUT IF I KEEP THIS UP, I CAN SQUEAK BY IN FRENCH.
MORE TIME TO STUDY, TOO.
IT'S BEEN SIXTEEN DAYS. ZOYA AND LUCAS DON'T SEEM TO BE TALKING AND WE DON'T HANG OUT RIGHT NOW.
PASSING MIGHT JUST MAKE ALL OF THIS WORTH SOMETHING, AFTER ALL.
MISS WRIGHT...
...PLEASE STAY A SECOND?
SURE THING, MISTER C.
COOL.
I THINK I *AM* PULLING IT OUT.

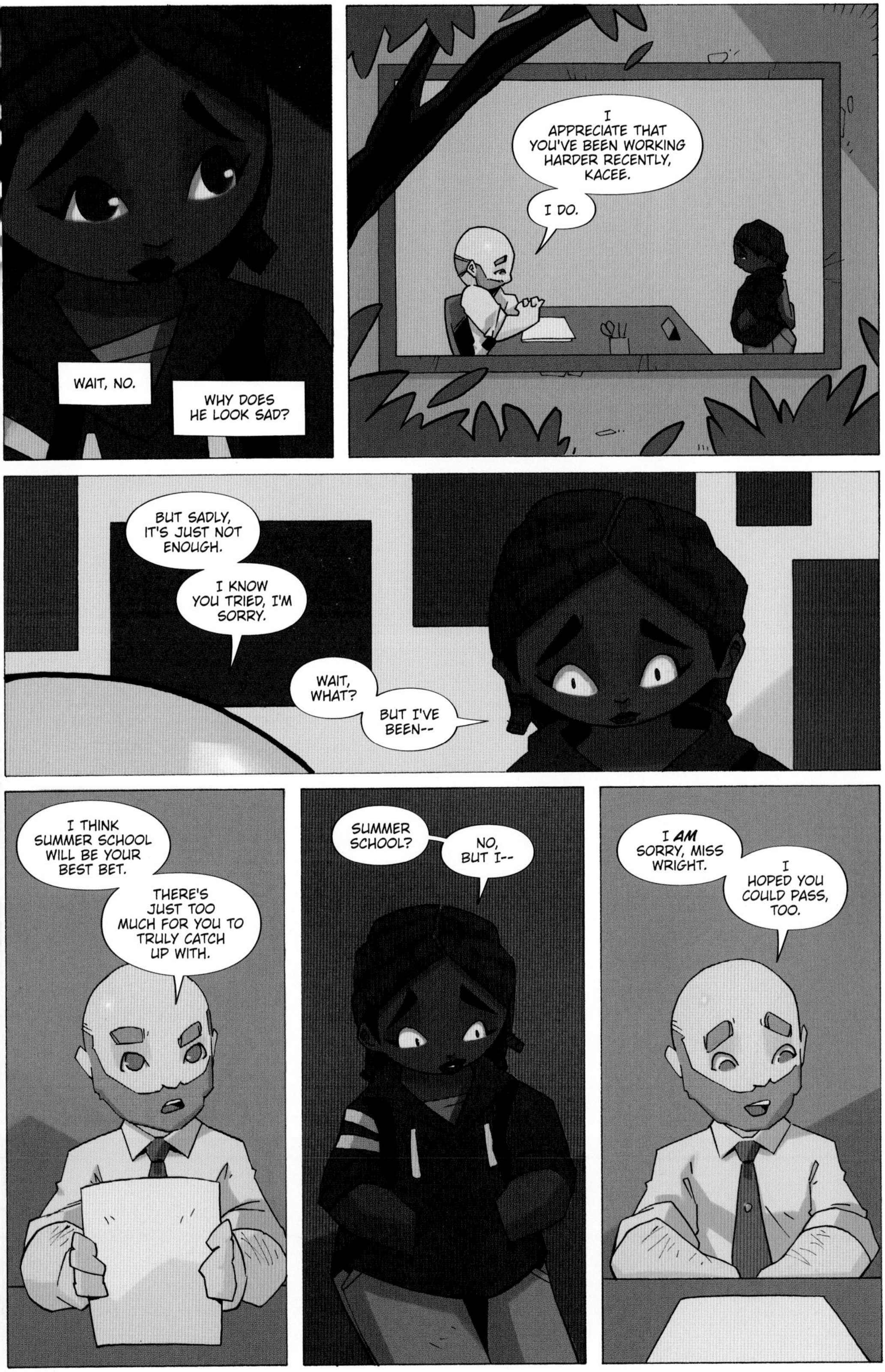
WAIT, NO.
WHY DOES HE LOOK SAD?
I APPRECIATE THAT YOU'VE BEEN WORKING HARDER RECENTLY, KACEE.
I DO.
BUT SADLY, IT'S JUST NOT ENOUGH.
I KNOW YOU TRIED, I'M SORRY.
WAIT, WHAT?
BUT I'VE BEEN--
I THINK SUMMER SCHOOL WILL BE YOUR BEST BET.
THERE'S JUST TOO MUCH FOR YOU TO TRULY CATCH UP WITH.
SUMMER SCHOOL?
NO, BUT I--
I AM SORRY, MISS WRIGHT.
I HOPED YOU COULD PASS, TOO.

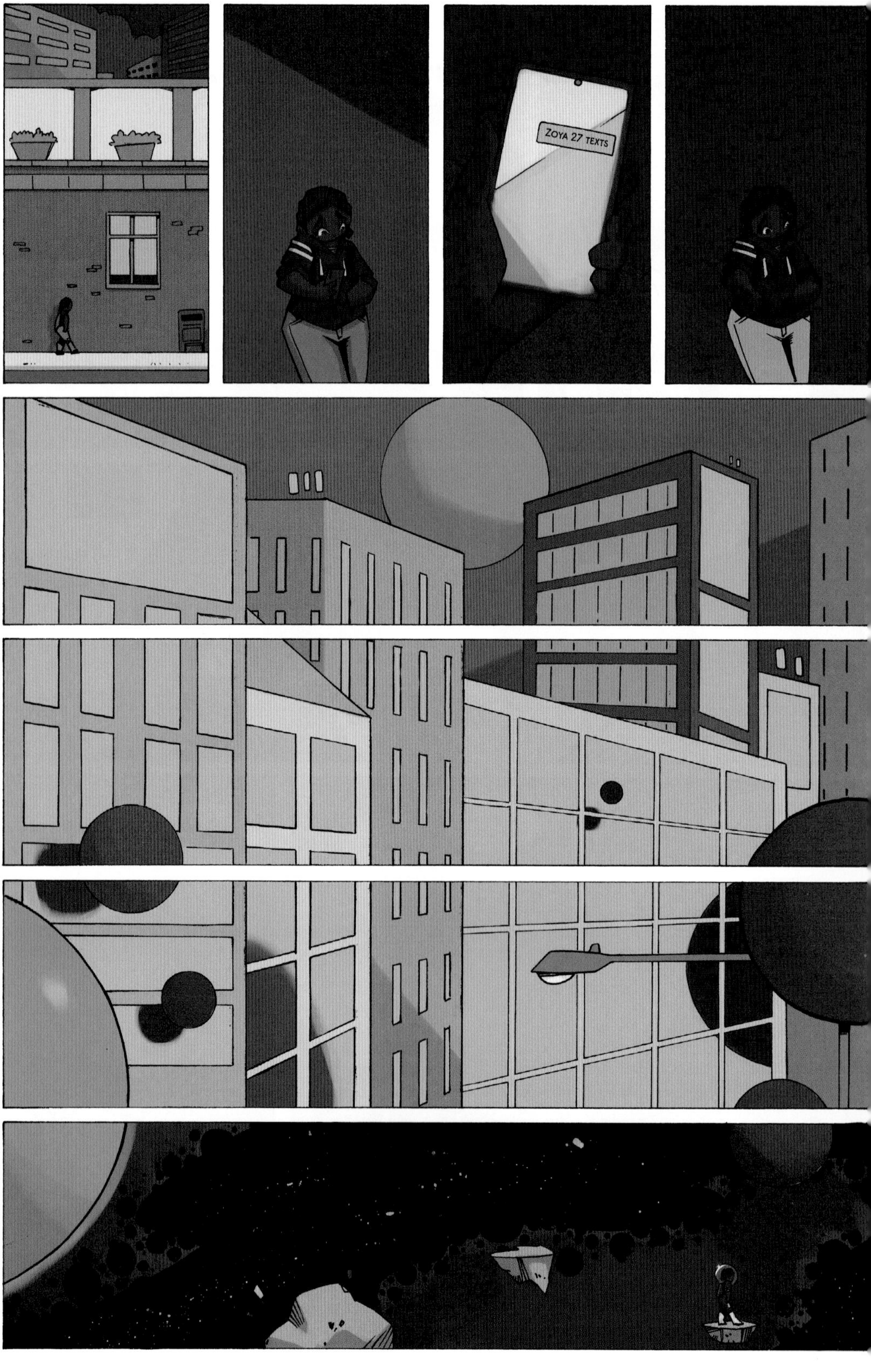
ZOYA 27 TEXTS

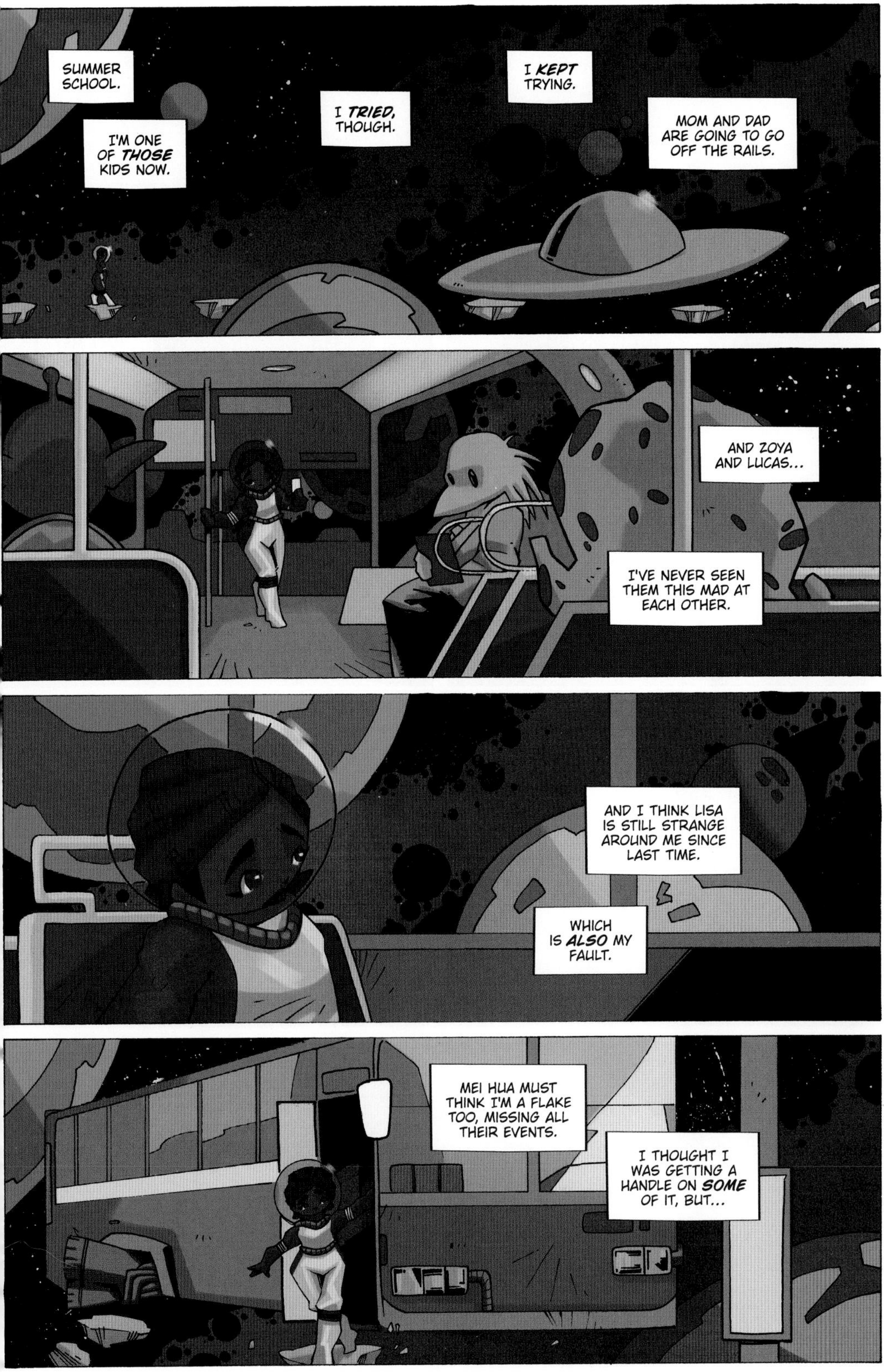
SUMMER SCHOOL.
I'M ONE OF THOSE KIDS NOW.
I TRIED, THOUGH.
I KEPT TRYING.
MOM AND DAD ARE GOING TO GO OFF THE RAILS.
AND ZOYA AND LUCAS...
I'VE NEVER SEEN THEM THIS MAD AT EACH OTHER.
AND I THINK LISA IS STILL STRANGE AROUND ME SINCE LAST TIME.
WHICH IS ALSO MY FAULT.
MEI HUA MUST THINK I'M A FLAKE TOO, MISSING ALL THEIR EVENTS.
I THOUGHT I WAS GETTING A HANDLE ON SOME OF IT, BUT...

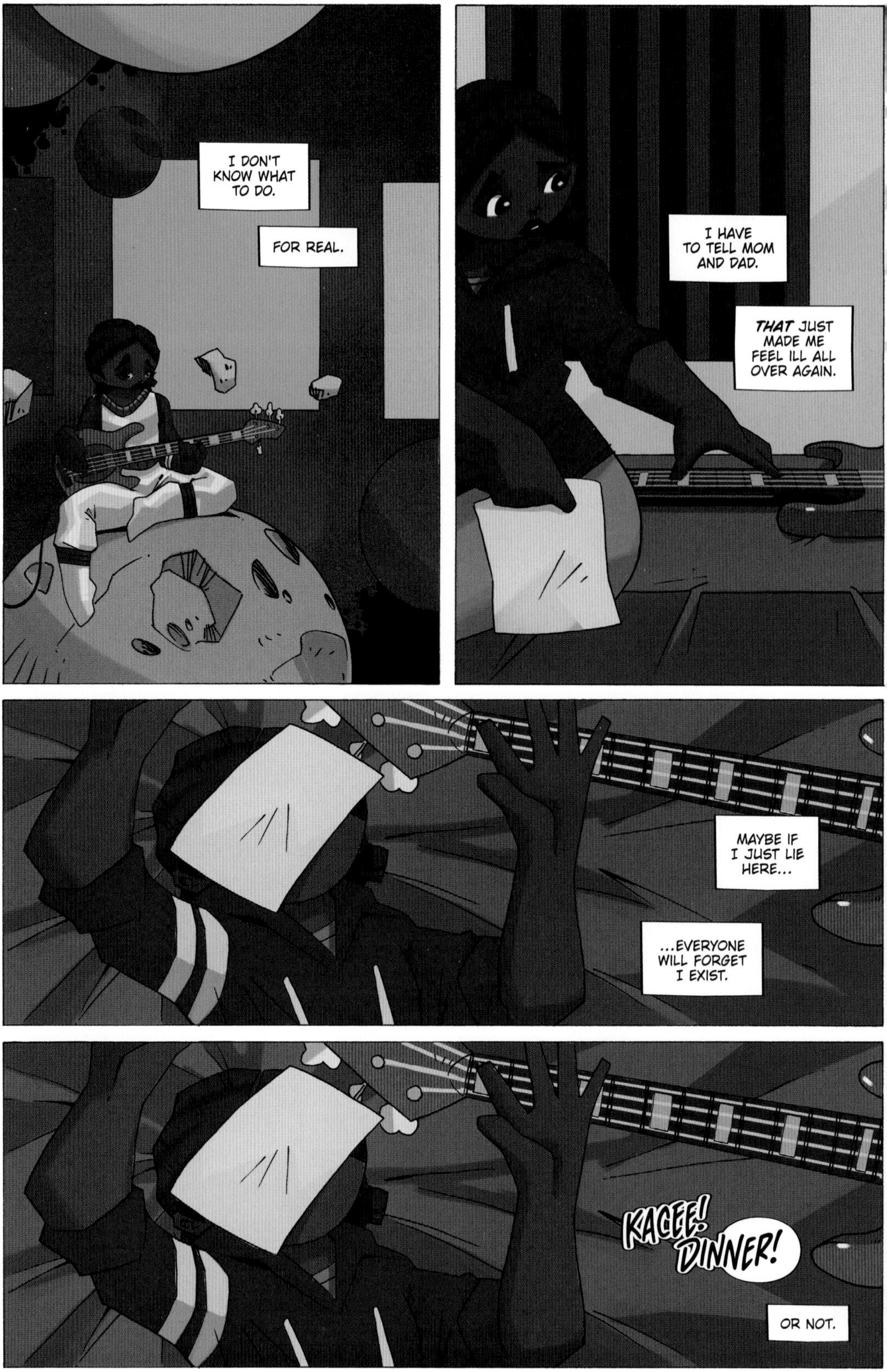
I DON'T KNOW WHAT TO DO.
FOR REAL.
I HAVE TO TELL MOM AND DAD.
THAT JUST MADE ME FEEL ILL ALL OVER AGAIN.
MAYBE IF I JUST LIE HERE...
...EVERYONE WILL FORGET I EXIST.
KACEE! DINNER!
OR NOT.

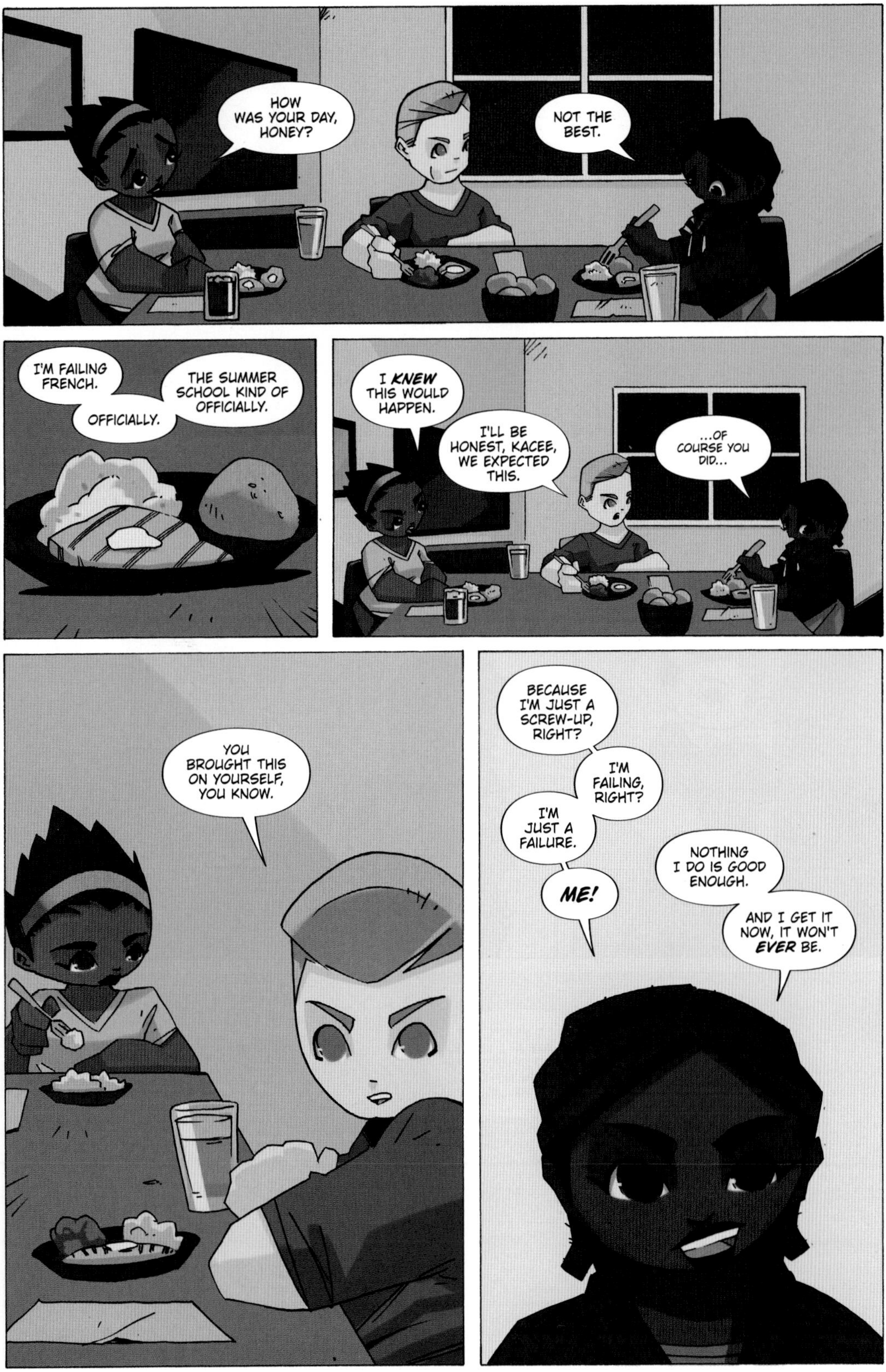
HOW WAS YOUR DAY, HONEY?
NOT THE BEST.
I'M FAILING FRENCH.
OFFICIALLY.
THE SUMMER SCHOOL KIND OF OFFICIALLY.
I *KNEW* THIS WOULD HAPPEN.
I'LL BE HONEST, KACEE, WE EXPECTED THIS.
...OF COURSE YOU DID...
YOU BROUGHT THIS ON YOURSELF, YOU KNOW.
BECAUSE I'M JUST A SCREW-UP, RIGHT?
I'M FAILING, RIGHT?
I'M JUST A FAILURE.
ME!
NOTHING I DO IS GOOD ENOUGH.
AND I GET IT NOW, IT WON'T *EVER* BE.

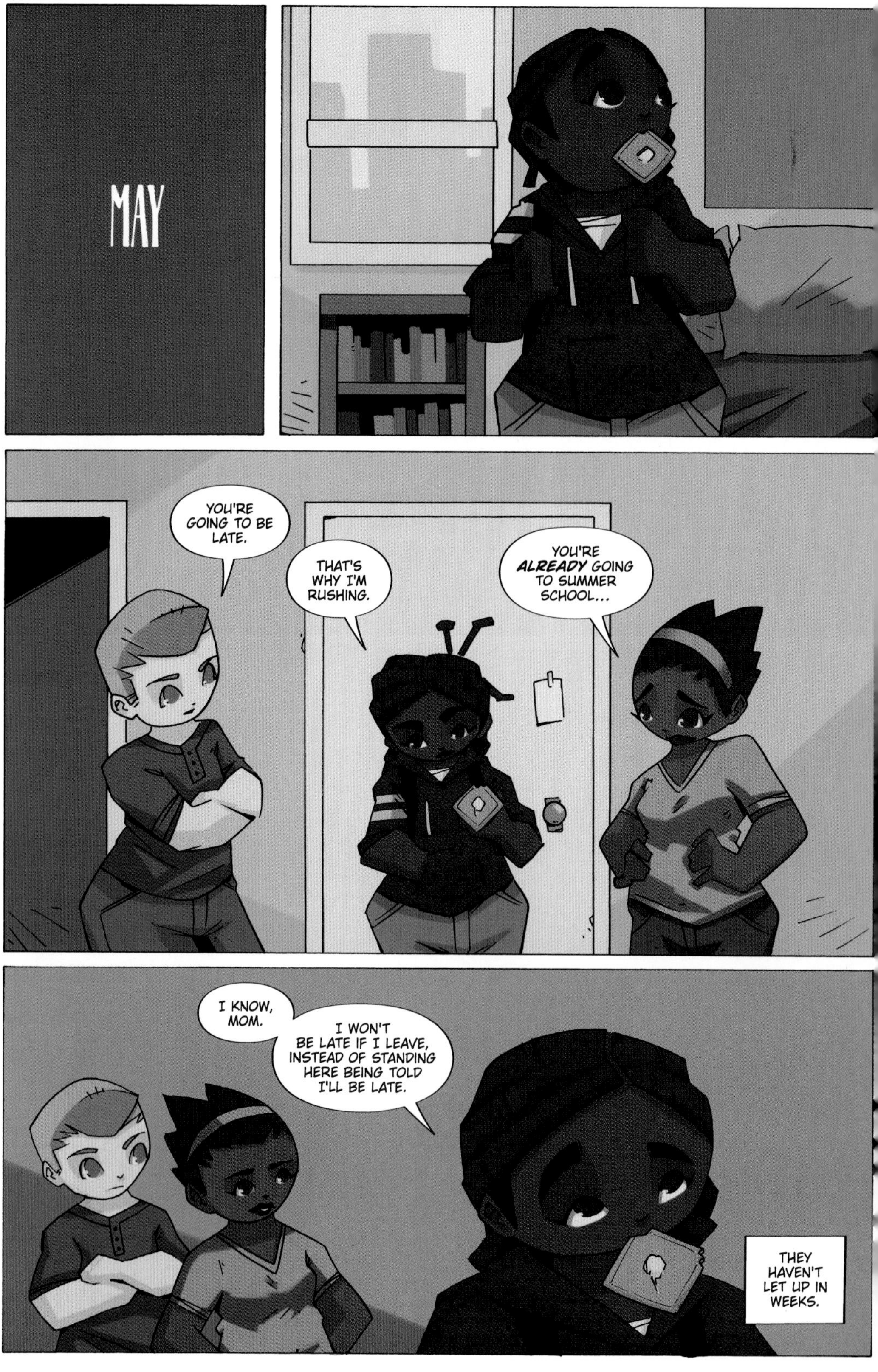
MAY
YOU'RE GOING TO BE LATE.
THAT'S WHY I'M RUSHING.
YOU'RE *ALREADY* GOING TO SUMMER SCHOOL...
I KNOW, MOM.
I WON'T BE LATE IF I LEAVE, INSTEAD OF STANDING HERE BEING TOLD I'LL BE LATE.
THEY HAVEN'T LET UP IN WEEKS.

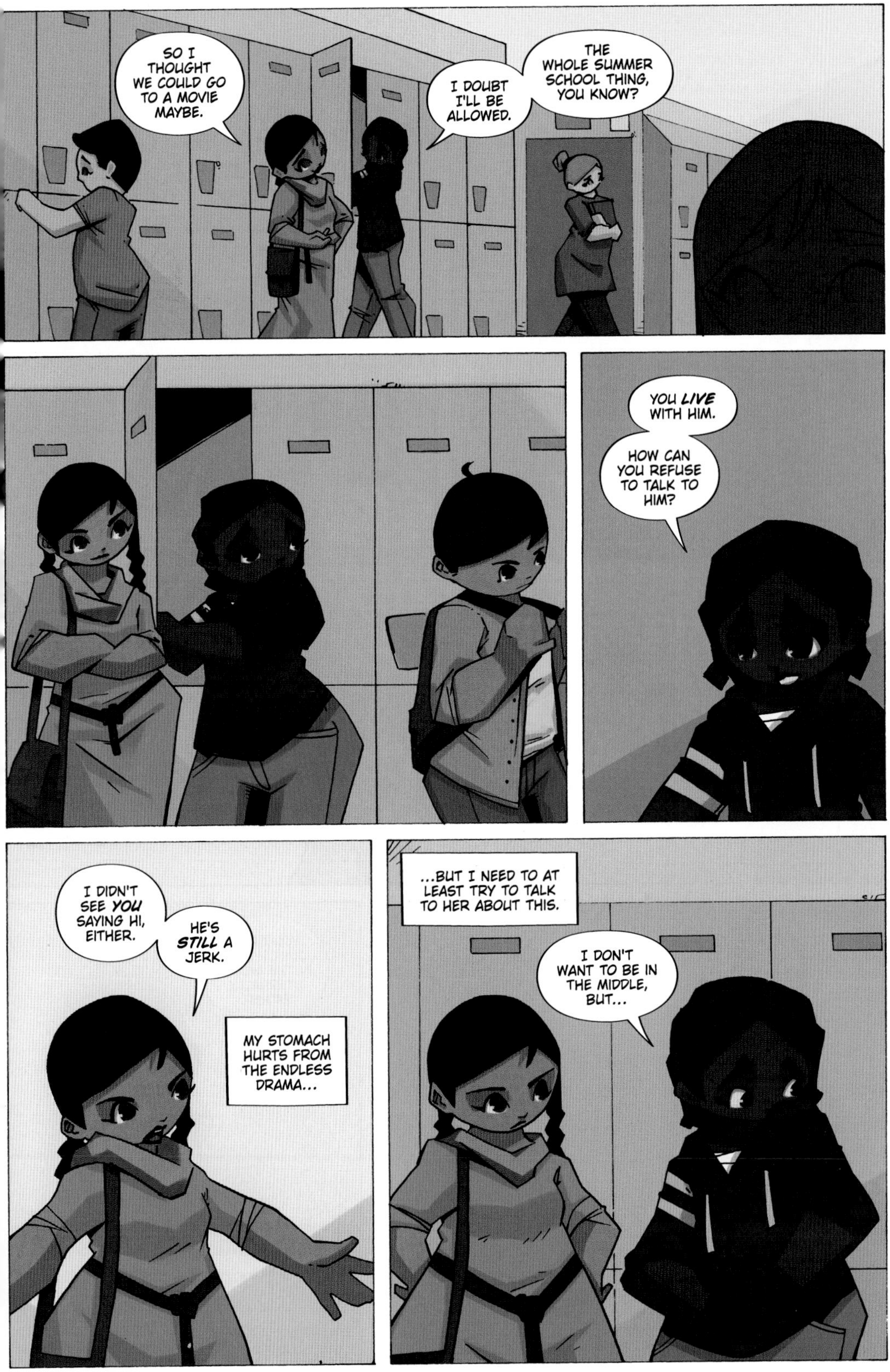

SO I THOUGHT WE COULD GO TO A MOVIE MAYBE.
I DOUBT I'LL BE ALLOWED.
THE WHOLE SUMMER SCHOOL THING, YOU KNOW?
YOU *LIVE* WITH HIM.
HOW CAN YOU REFUSE TO TALK TO HIM?
I DIDN'T SEE *YOU* SAYING HI, EITHER.
HE'S *STILL* A JERK.
MY STOMACH HURTS FROM THE ENDLESS DRAMA...
...BUT I NEED TO AT LEAST TRY TO TALK TO HER ABOUT THIS.
I DON'T WANT TO BE IN THE MIDDLE, BUT...

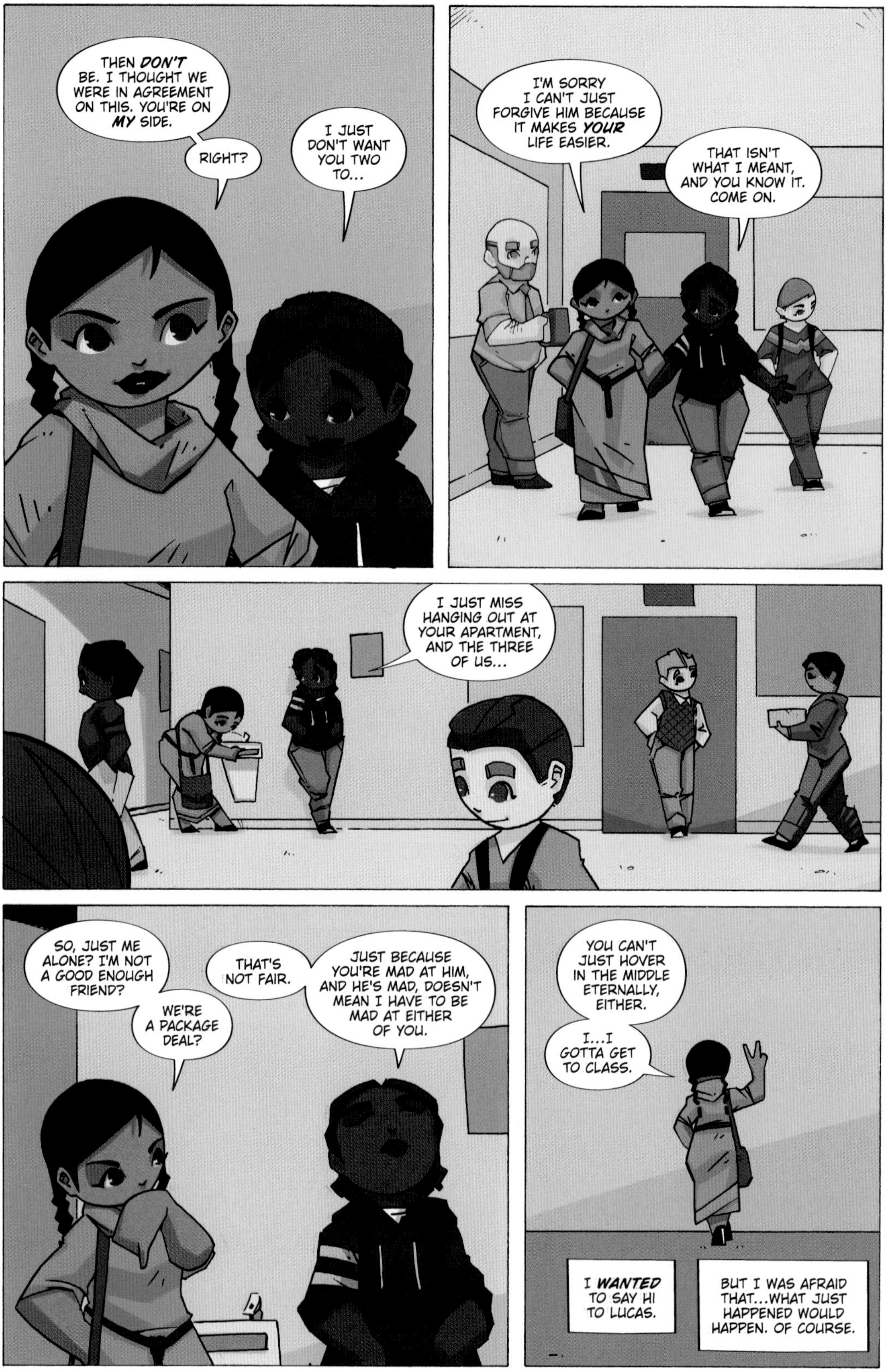

THEN *DON'T* BE. I THOUGHT WE WERE IN AGREEMENT ON THIS. YOU'RE ON *MY* SIDE.
RIGHT?
I JUST DON'T WANT YOU TWO TO...
I'M SORRY I CAN'T JUST FORGIVE HIM BECAUSE IT MAKES *YOUR* LIFE EASIER.
THAT ISN'T WHAT I MEANT, AND YOU KNOW IT. COME ON.
I JUST MISS HANGING OUT AT YOUR APARTMENT, AND THE THREE OF US...
SO, JUST ME ALONE? I'M NOT A GOOD ENOUGH FRIEND?
WE'RE A PACKAGE DEAL?
THAT'S NOT FAIR.
JUST BECAUSE YOU'RE MAD AT HIM, AND HE'S MAD, DOESN'T MEAN I HAVE TO BE MAD AT EITHER OF YOU.
YOU CAN'T JUST HOVER IN THE MIDDLE ETERNALLY, EITHER.
I...I GOTTA GET TO CLASS.
I *WANTED* TO SAY HI TO LUCAS.
BUT I WAS AFRAID THAT...WHAT JUST HAPPENED WOULD HAPPEN. OF COURSE.

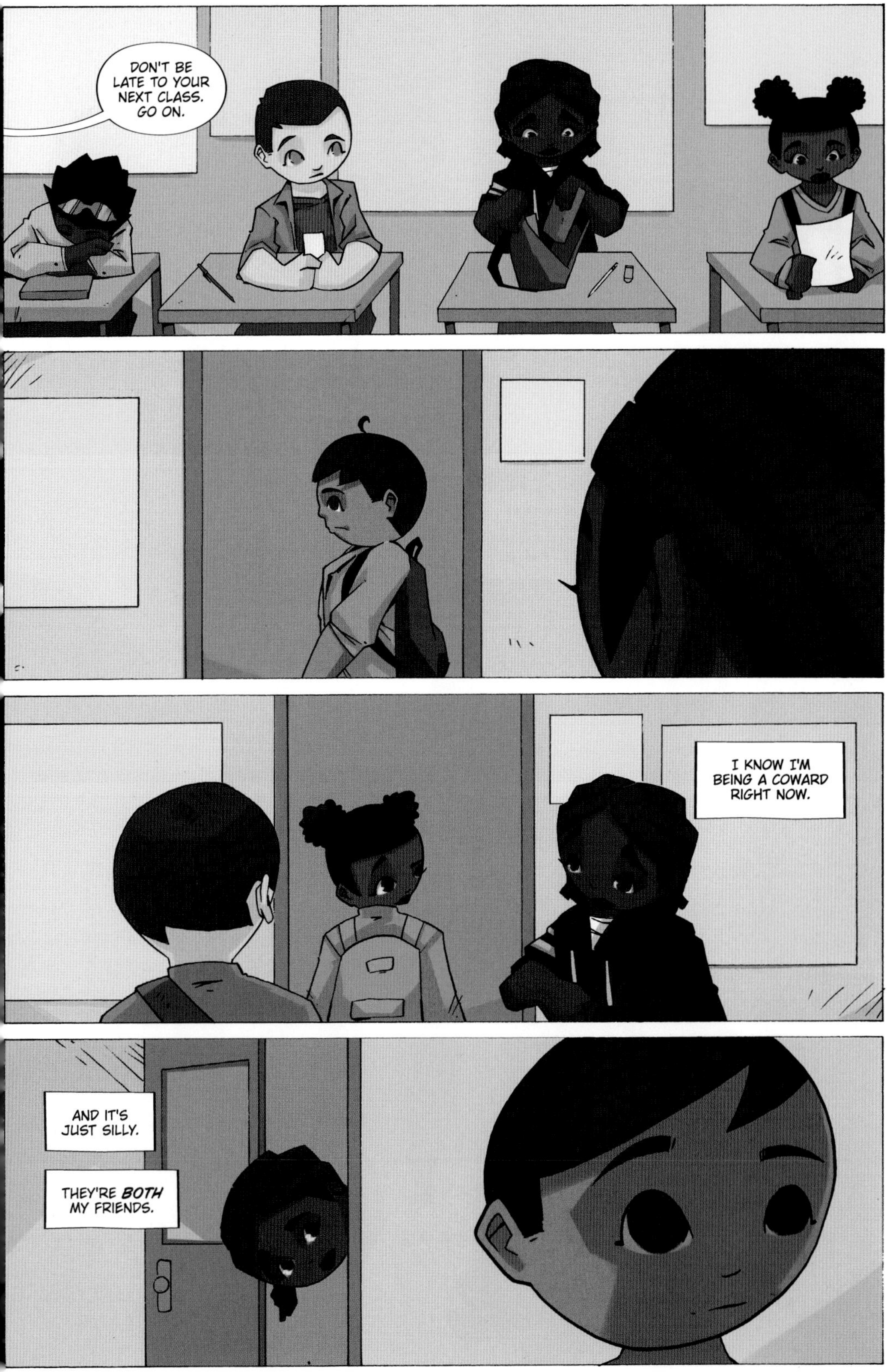

DON'T BE LATE TO YOUR NEXT CLASS. GO ON.
I KNOW I'M BEING A COWARD RIGHT NOW.
AND IT'S JUST SILLY.
THEY'RE *BOTH* MY FRIENDS.

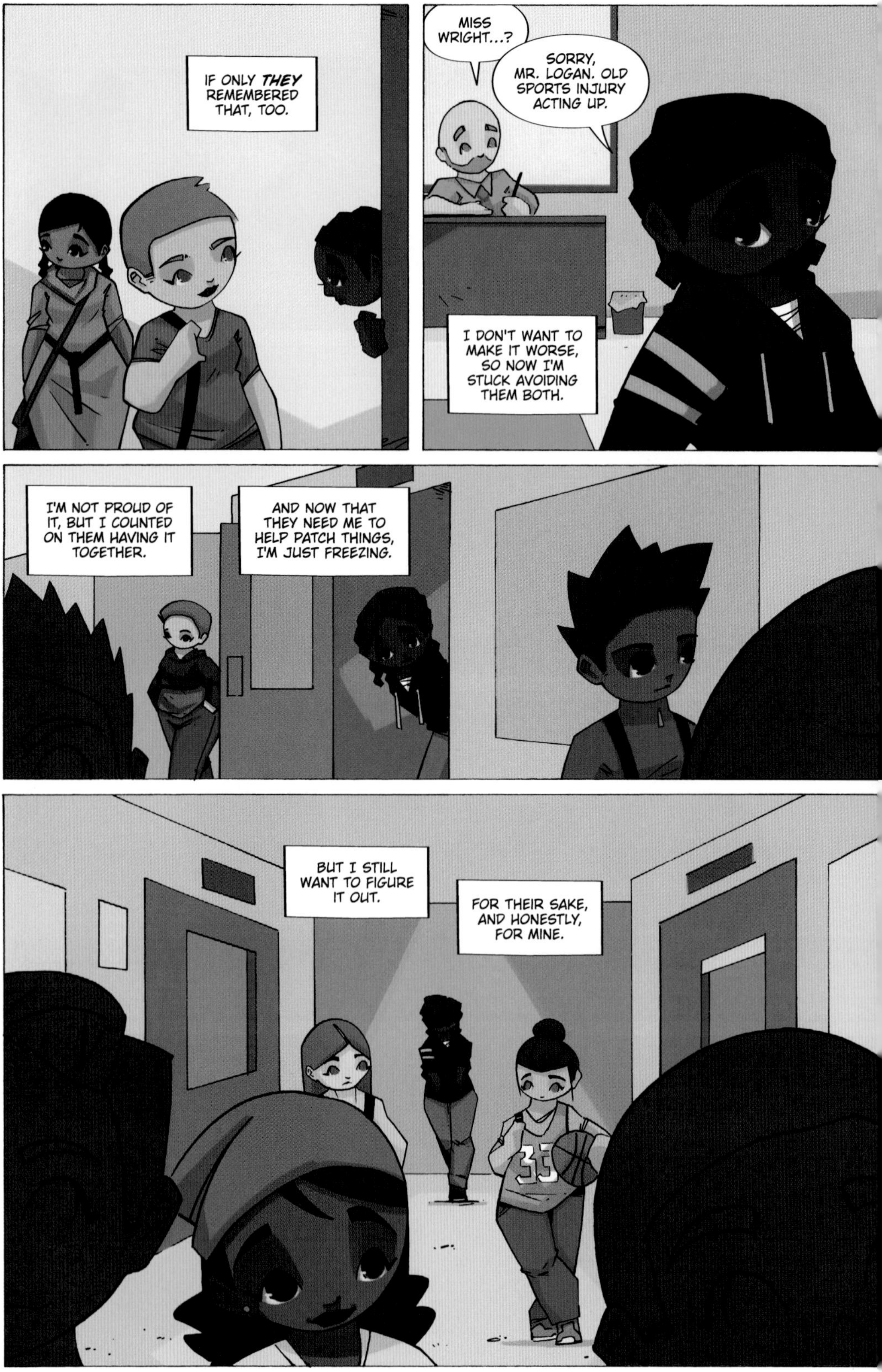
IF ONLY *THEY* REMEMBERED THAT, TOO.
MISS WRIGHT...?
SORRY, MR. LOGAN. OLD SPORTS INJURY ACTING UP.
I DON'T WANT TO MAKE IT WORSE, SO NOW I'M STUCK AVOIDING THEM BOTH.
I'M NOT PROUD OF IT, BUT I COUNTED ON THEM HAVING IT TOGETHER.
AND NOW THAT THEY NEED ME TO HELP PATCH THINGS, I'M JUST FREEZING.
BUT I STILL WANT TO FIGURE IT OUT.
FOR THEIR SAKE, AND HONESTLY, FOR MINE.
33

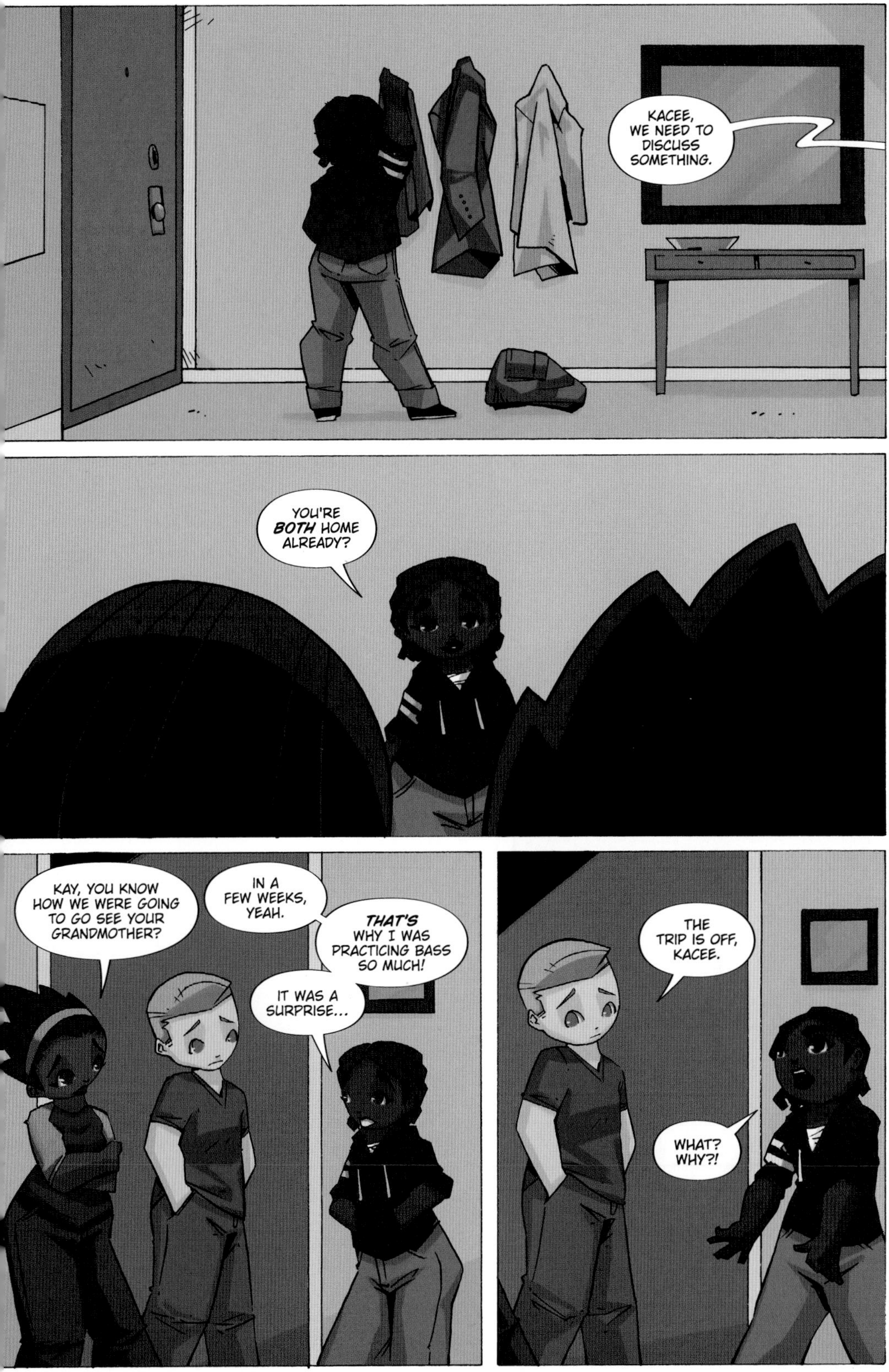
KACEE, WE NEED TO DISCUSS SOMETHING.
YOU'RE *BOTH* HOME ALREADY?
KAY, YOU KNOW HOW WE WERE GOING TO GO SEE YOUR GRANDMOTHER?
IN A FEW WEEKS, YEAH.
THAT'S WHY I WAS PRACTICING BASS SO MUCH!
IT WAS A SURPRISE...
THE TRIP IS OFF, KACEE.
WHAT? WHY?!

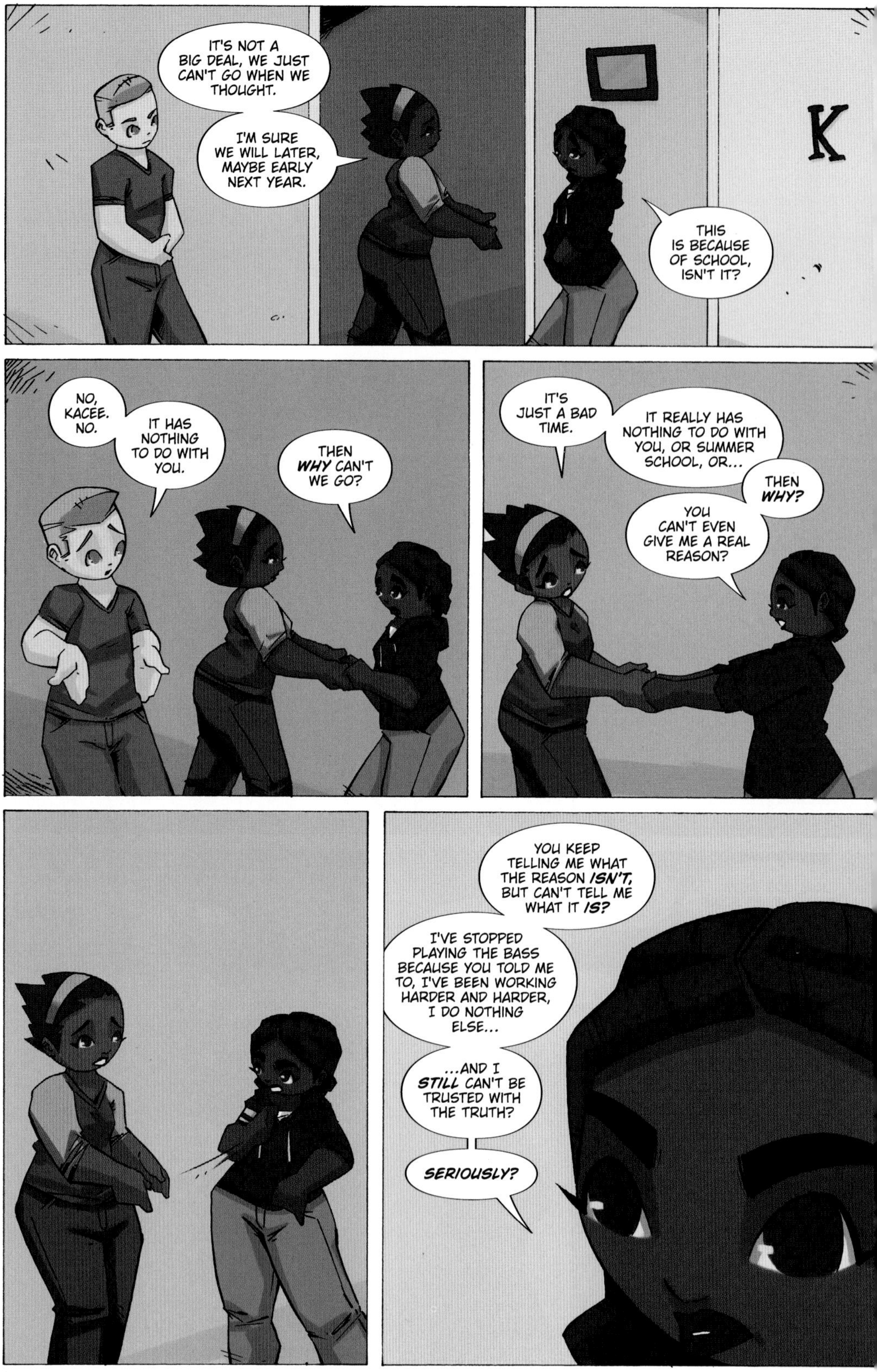
IT'S NOT A BIG DEAL, WE JUST CAN'T GO WHEN WE THOUGHT.
I'M SURE WE WILL LATER, MAYBE EARLY NEXT YEAR.
K
THIS IS BECAUSE OF SCHOOL, ISN'T IT?
NO, KACEE. NO.
IT HAS NOTHING TO DO WITH YOU.
THEN WHY CAN'T WE GO?
IT'S JUST A BAD TIME.
IT REALLY HAS NOTHING TO DO WITH YOU, OR SUMMER SCHOOL, OR...
THEN WHY?
YOU CAN'T EVEN GIVE ME A REAL REASON?
YOU KEEP TELLING ME WHAT THE REASON ISN'T, BUT CAN'T TELL ME WHAT IT IS?
I'VE STOPPED PLAYING THE BASS BECAUSE YOU TOLD ME TO, I'VE BEEN WORKING HARDER AND HARDER, I DO NOTHING ELSE...
...AND I STILL CAN'T BE TRUSTED WITH THE TRUTH?
SERIOUSLY?

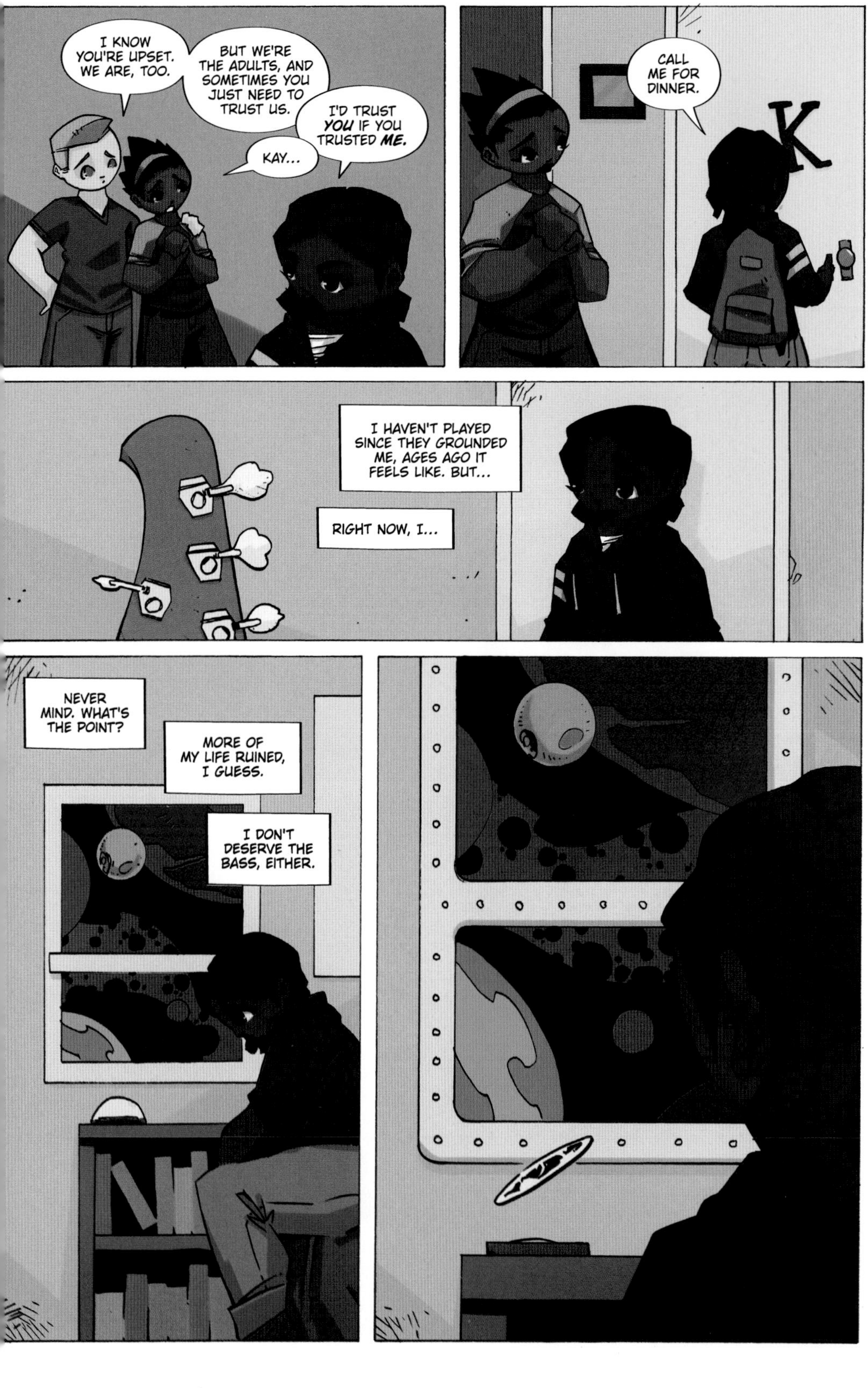

I KNOW YOU'RE UPSET. WE ARE, TOO.
BUT WE'RE THE ADULTS, AND SOMETIMES YOU JUST NEED TO TRUST US.
KAY...
I'D TRUST *YOU* IF YOU TRUSTED *ME.*
CALL ME FOR DINNER.
K
I HAVEN'T PLAYED SINCE THEY GROUNDED ME, AGES AGO IT FEELS LIKE. BUT...
RIGHT NOW, I...
NEVER MIND. WHAT'S THE POINT?
MORE OF MY LIFE RUINED, I GUESS.
I DON'T DESERVE THE BASS, EITHER.

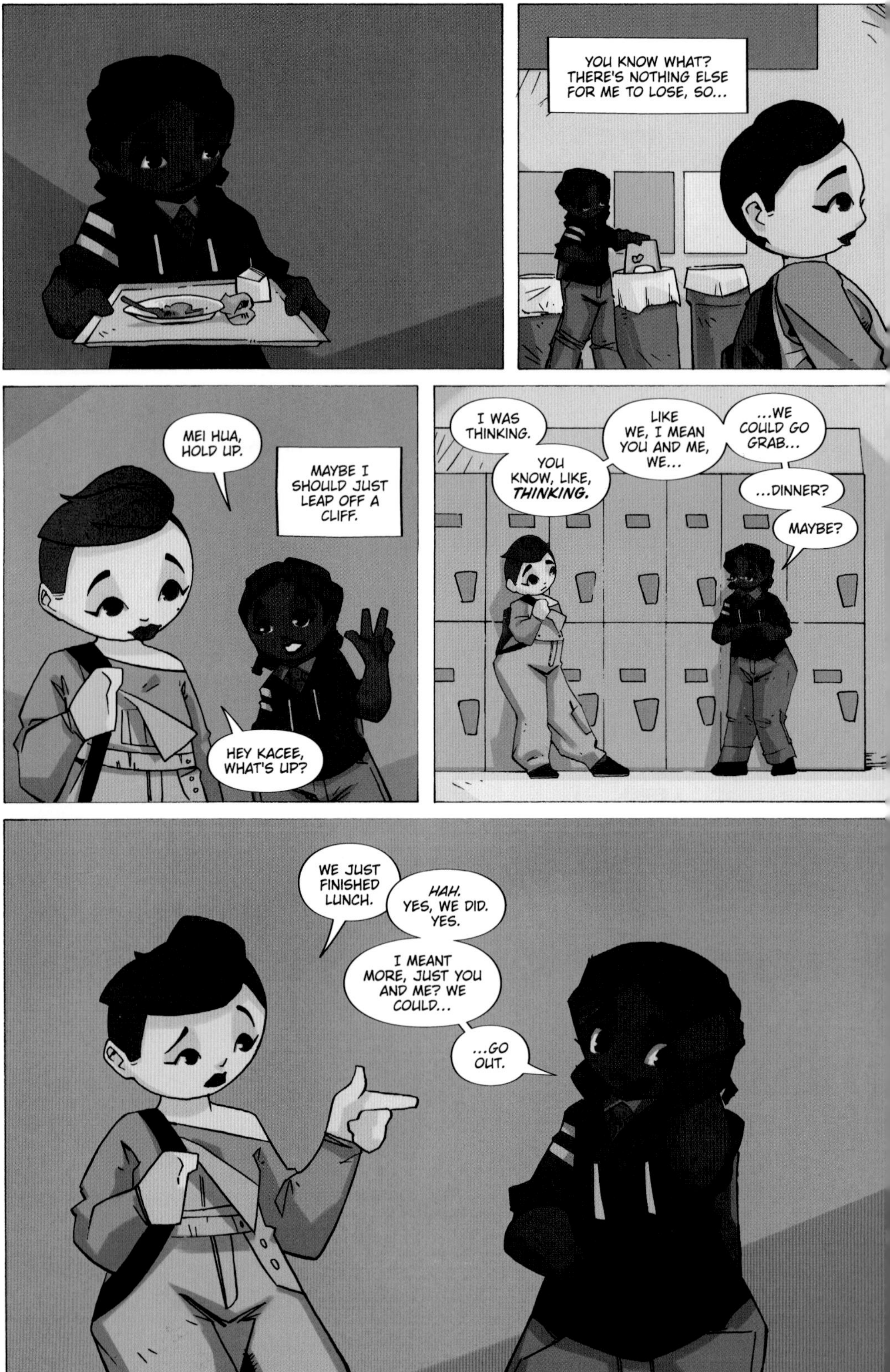
YOU KNOW WHAT? THERE'S NOTHING ELSE FOR ME TO LOSE, SO...
MEI HUA, HOLD UP.
MAYBE I SHOULD JUST LEAP OFF A CLIFF.
HEY KACEE, WHAT'S UP?
I WAS THINKING.
YOU KNOW, LIKE, *THINKING.*
LIKE WE, I MEAN YOU AND ME, WE...
...WE COULD GO GRAB...
...DINNER?
MAYBE?
WE JUST FINISHED LUNCH.
HAH. YES, WE DID. YES.
I MEANT MORE, JUST YOU AND ME? WE COULD...
...GO OUT.

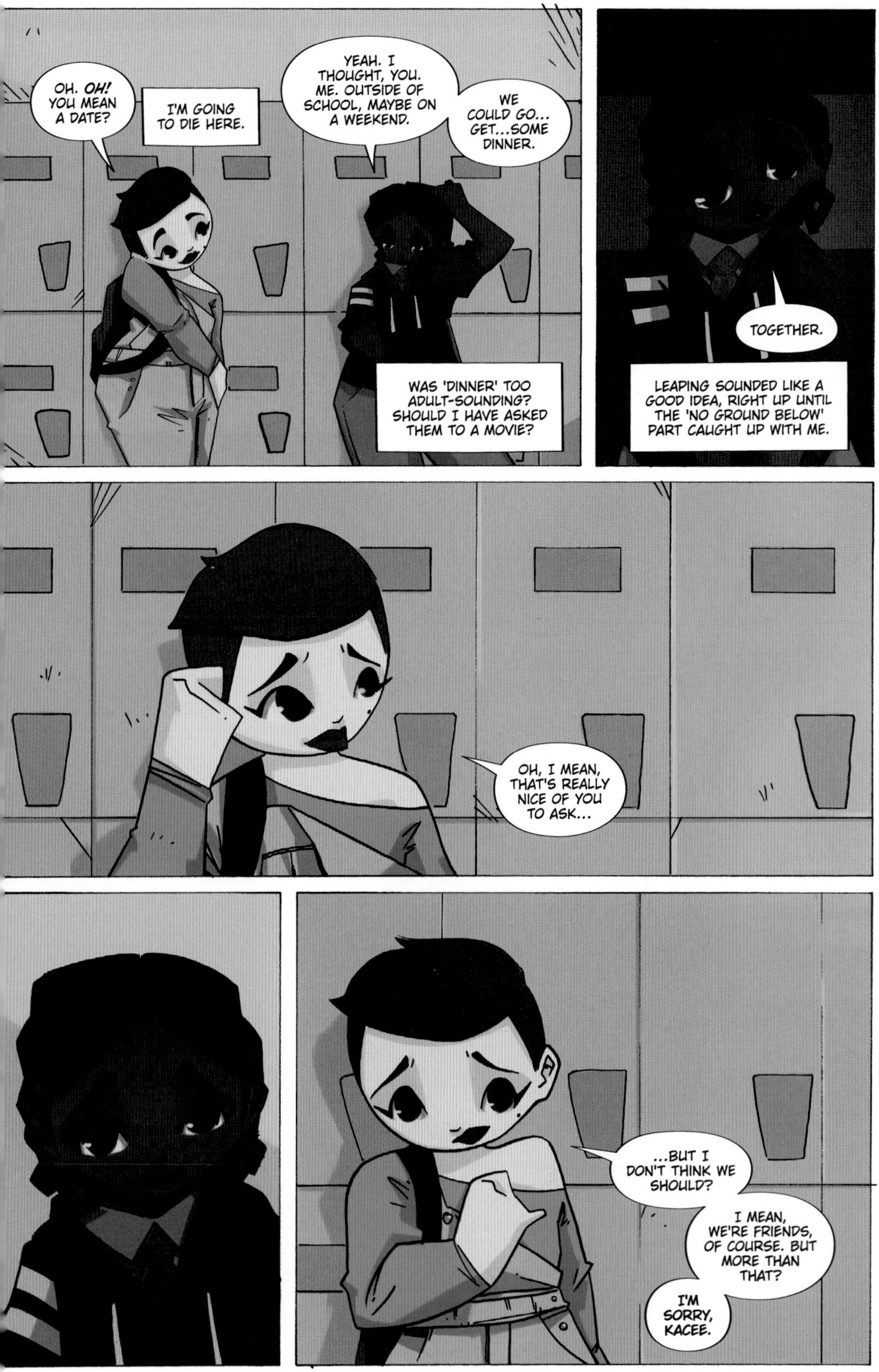
OH. OH! YOU MEAN A DATE?
I'M GOING TO DIE HERE.
YEAH. I THOUGHT, YOU. ME. OUTSIDE OF SCHOOL, MAYBE ON A WEEKEND.
WE COULD GO... GET...SOME DINNER.
WAS 'DINNER' TOO ADULT-SOUNDING? SHOULD I HAVE ASKED THEM TO A MOVIE?
TOGETHER.
LEAPING SOUNDED LIKE A GOOD IDEA, RIGHT UP UNTIL THE 'NO GROUND BELOW' PART CAUGHT UP WITH ME.
OH, I MEAN, THAT'S REALLY NICE OF YOU TO ASK...
...BUT I DON'T THINK WE SHOULD?
I MEAN, WE'RE FRIENDS, OF COURSE. BUT MORE THAN THAT?
I'M SORRY, KACEE.

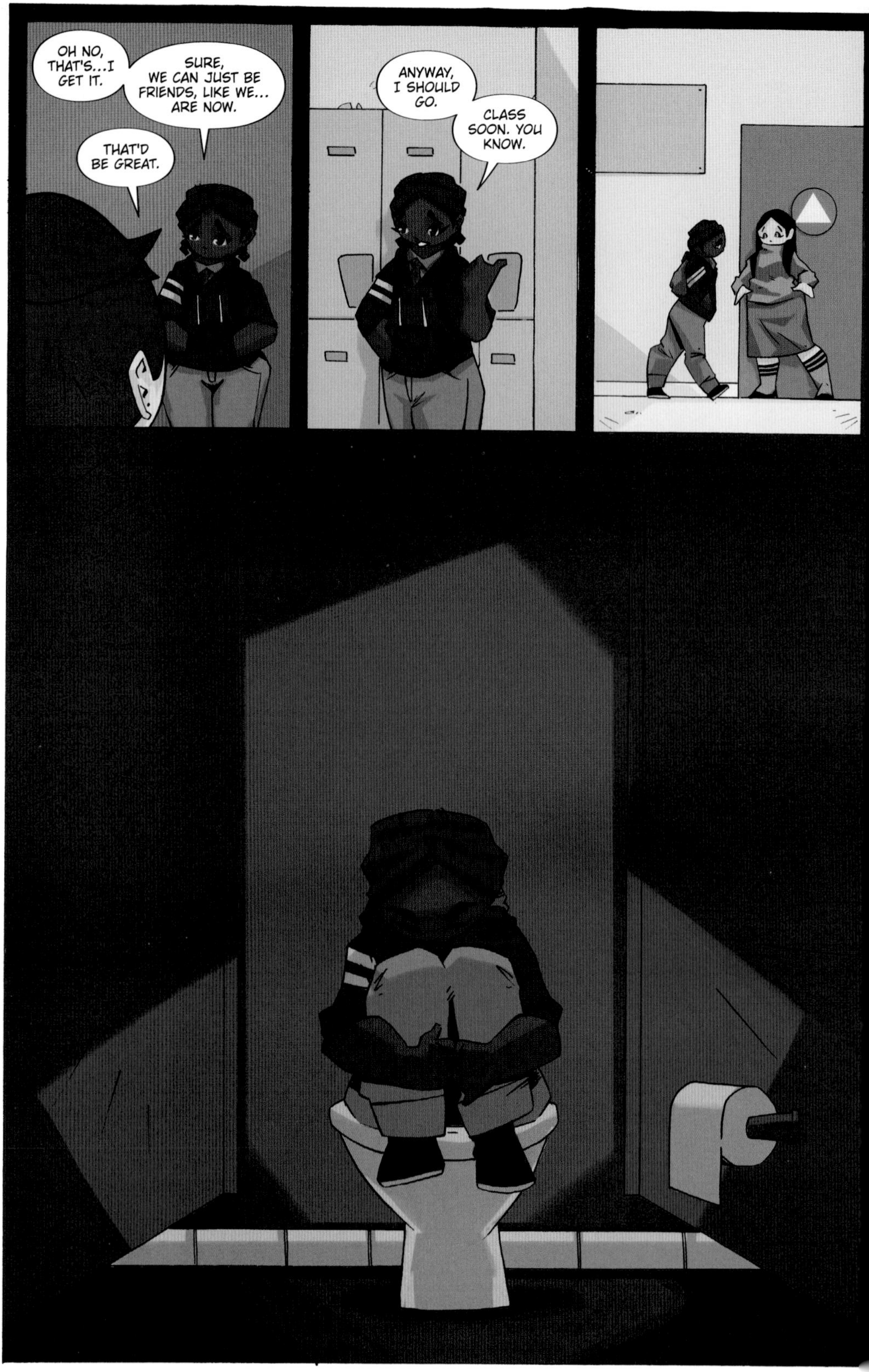
OH NO, THAT'S...I GET IT.
SURE, WE CAN JUST BE FRIENDS, LIKE WE... ARE NOW.
THAT'D BE GREAT.
ANYWAY, I SHOULD GO.
CLASS SOON. YOU KNOW.

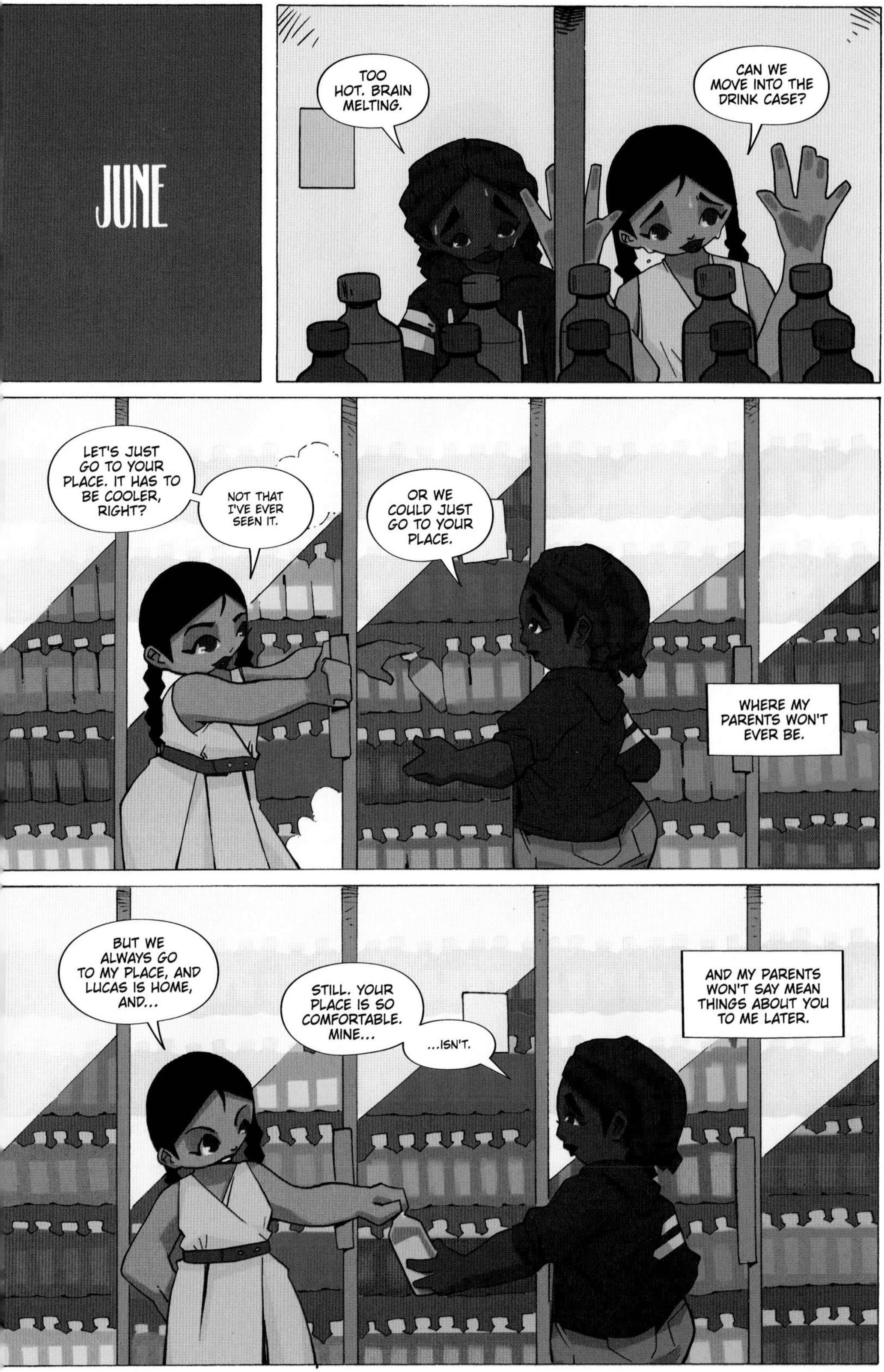
JUNE
TOO HOT. BRAIN MELTING.
CAN WE MOVE INTO THE DRINK CASE?
LET'S JUST GO TO YOUR PLACE. IT HAS TO BE COOLER, RIGHT?
NOT THAT I'VE EVER SEEN IT.
OR WE COULD JUST GO TO YOUR PLACE.
WHERE MY PARENTS WON'T EVER BE.
BUT WE ALWAYS GO TO MY PLACE, AND LUCAS IS HOME, AND...
STILL. YOUR PLACE IS SO COMFORTABLE. MINE...
...ISN'T.
AND MY PARENTS WON'T SAY MEAN THINGS ABOUT YOU TO ME LATER.

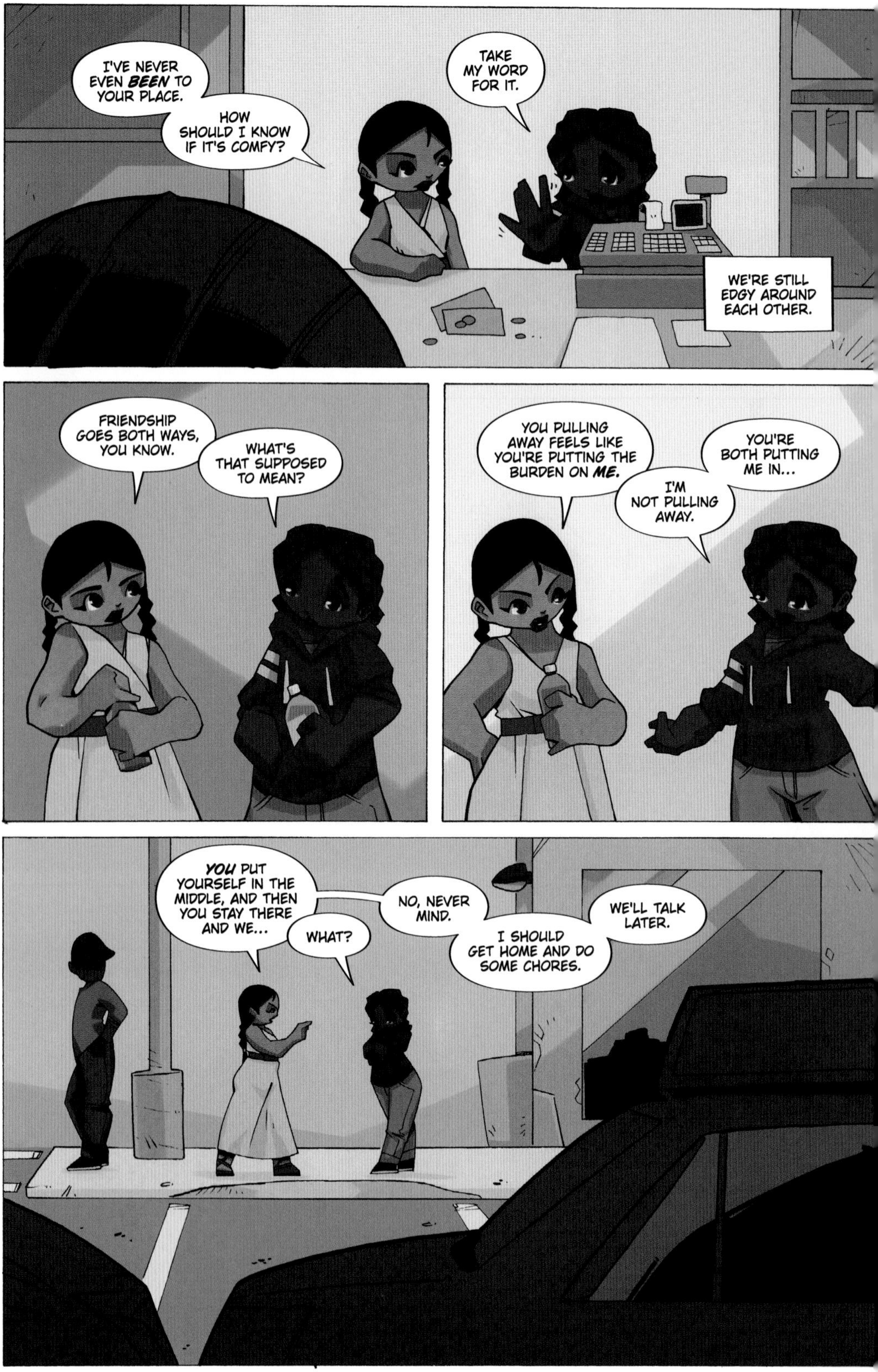
I'VE NEVER EVEN *BEEN* TO YOUR PLACE.
HOW SHOULD I KNOW IF IT'S COMFY?
TAKE MY WORD FOR IT.
WE'RE STILL EDGY AROUND EACH OTHER.
FRIENDSHIP GOES BOTH WAYS, YOU KNOW.
WHAT'S THAT SUPPOSED TO MEAN?
YOU PULLING AWAY FEELS LIKE YOU'RE PUTTING THE BURDEN ON *ME.*
I'M NOT PULLING AWAY.
YOU'RE BOTH PUTTING ME IN...
YOU PUT YOURSELF IN THE MIDDLE, AND THEN YOU STAY THERE AND WE...
WHAT?
NO, NEVER MIND.
I SHOULD GET HOME AND DO SOME CHORES.
WE'LL TALK LATER.

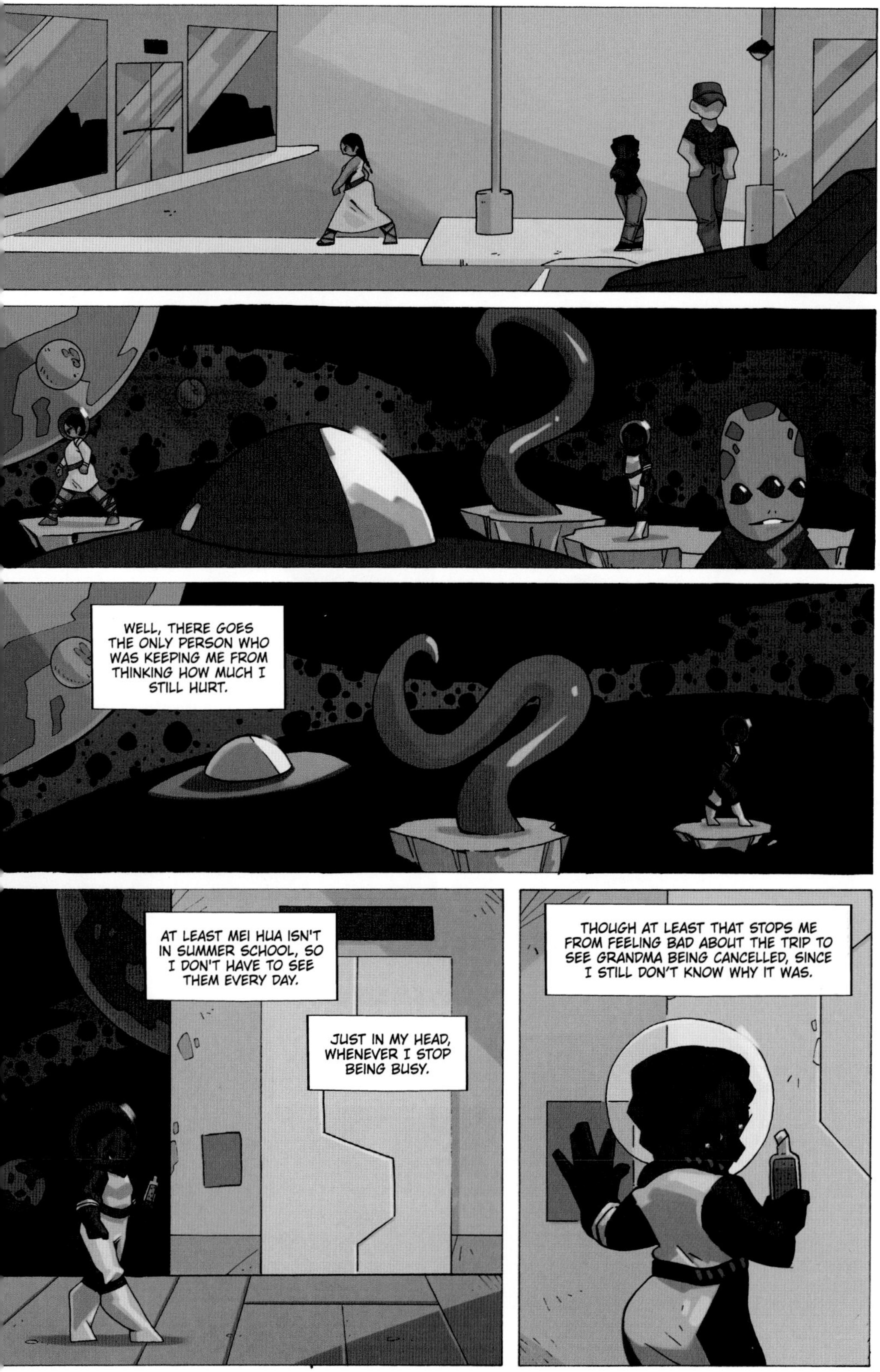
WELL, THERE GOES THE ONLY PERSON WHO WAS KEEPING ME FROM THINKING HOW MUCH I STILL HURT.
AT LEAST MEI HUA ISN'T IN SUMMER SCHOOL, SO I DON'T HAVE TO SEE THEM EVERY DAY.
JUST IN MY HEAD, WHENEVER I STOP BEING BUSY.
THOUGH AT LEAST THAT STOPS ME FROM FEELING BAD ABOUT THE TRIP TO SEE GRANDMA BEING CANCELLED, SINCE I STILL DON'T KNOW WHY IT WAS.

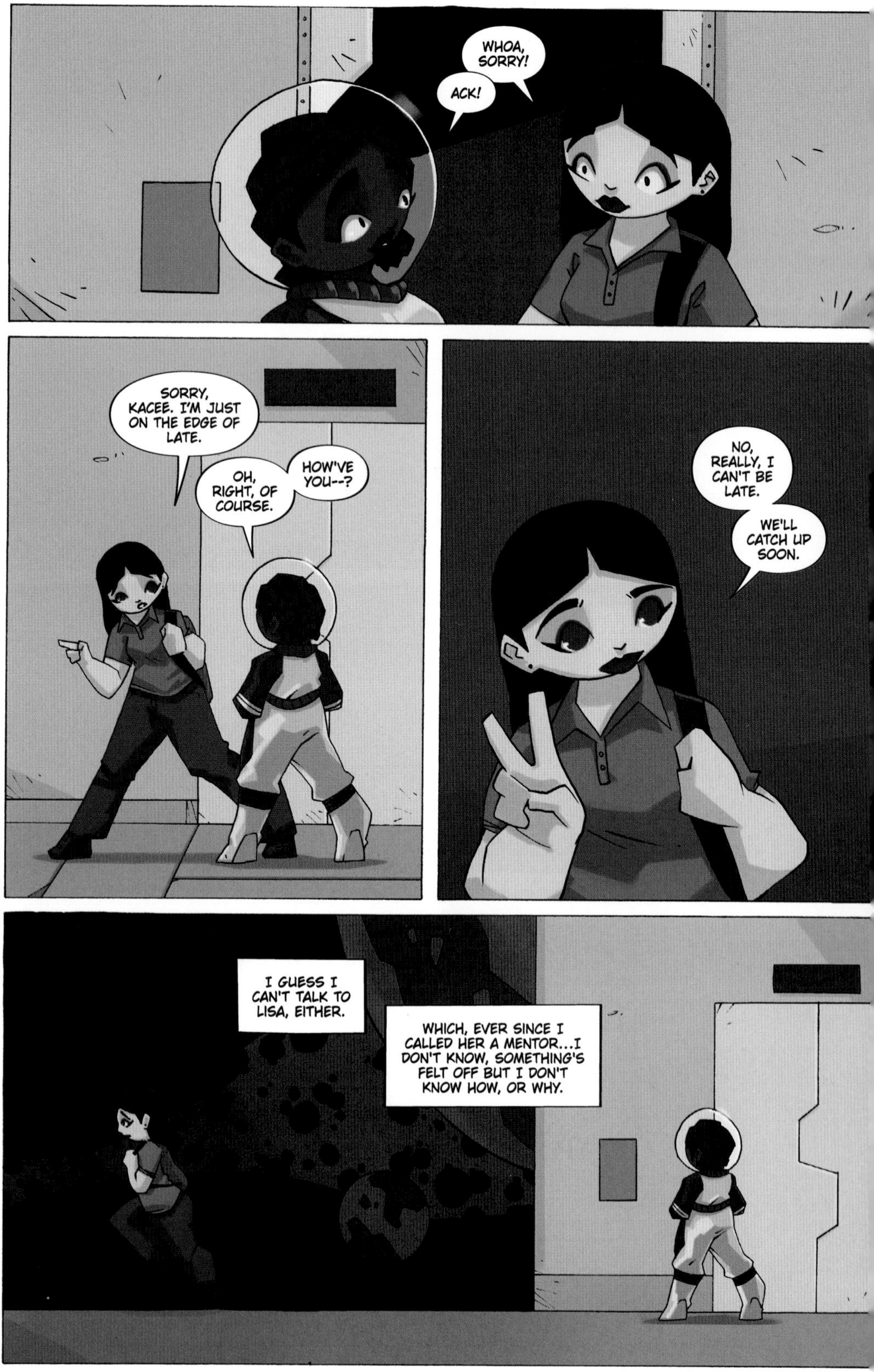
WHOA, SORRY!
ACK!
SORRY, KACEE. I'M JUST ON THE EDGE OF LATE.
OH, RIGHT, OF COURSE.
HOW'VE YOU--?
NO, REALLY, I CAN'T BE LATE.
WE'LL CATCH UP SOON.
I GUESS I CAN'T TALK TO LISA, EITHER.
WHICH, EVER SINCE I CALLED HER A MENTOR...I DON'T KNOW, SOMETHING'S FELT OFF BUT I DON'T KNOW HOW, OR WHY.

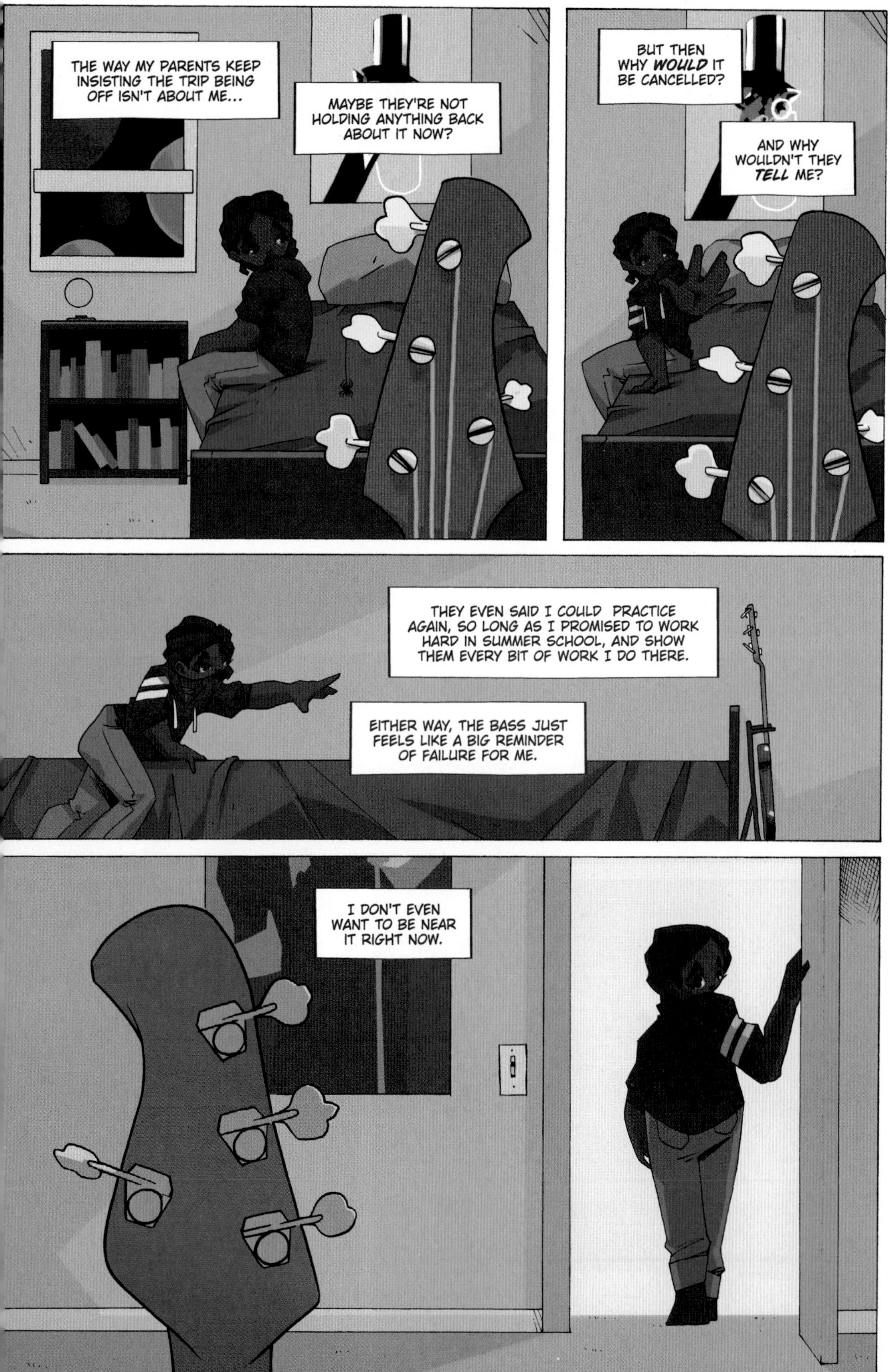
THE WAY MY PARENTS KEEP INSISTING THE TRIP BEING OFF ISN'T ABOUT ME...
MAYBE THEY'RE NOT HOLDING ANYTHING BACK ABOUT IT NOW?
BUT THEN WHY **WOULD** IT BE CANCELLED?
AND WHY WOULDN'T THEY **TELL** ME?
THEY EVEN SAID I COULD PRACTICE AGAIN, SO LONG AS I PROMISED TO WORK HARD IN SUMMER SCHOOL, AND SHOW THEM EVERY BIT OF WORK I DO THERE.
EITHER WAY, THE BASS JUST FEELS LIKE A BIG REMINDER OF FAILURE FOR ME.
I DON'T EVEN WANT TO BE NEAR IT RIGHT NOW.

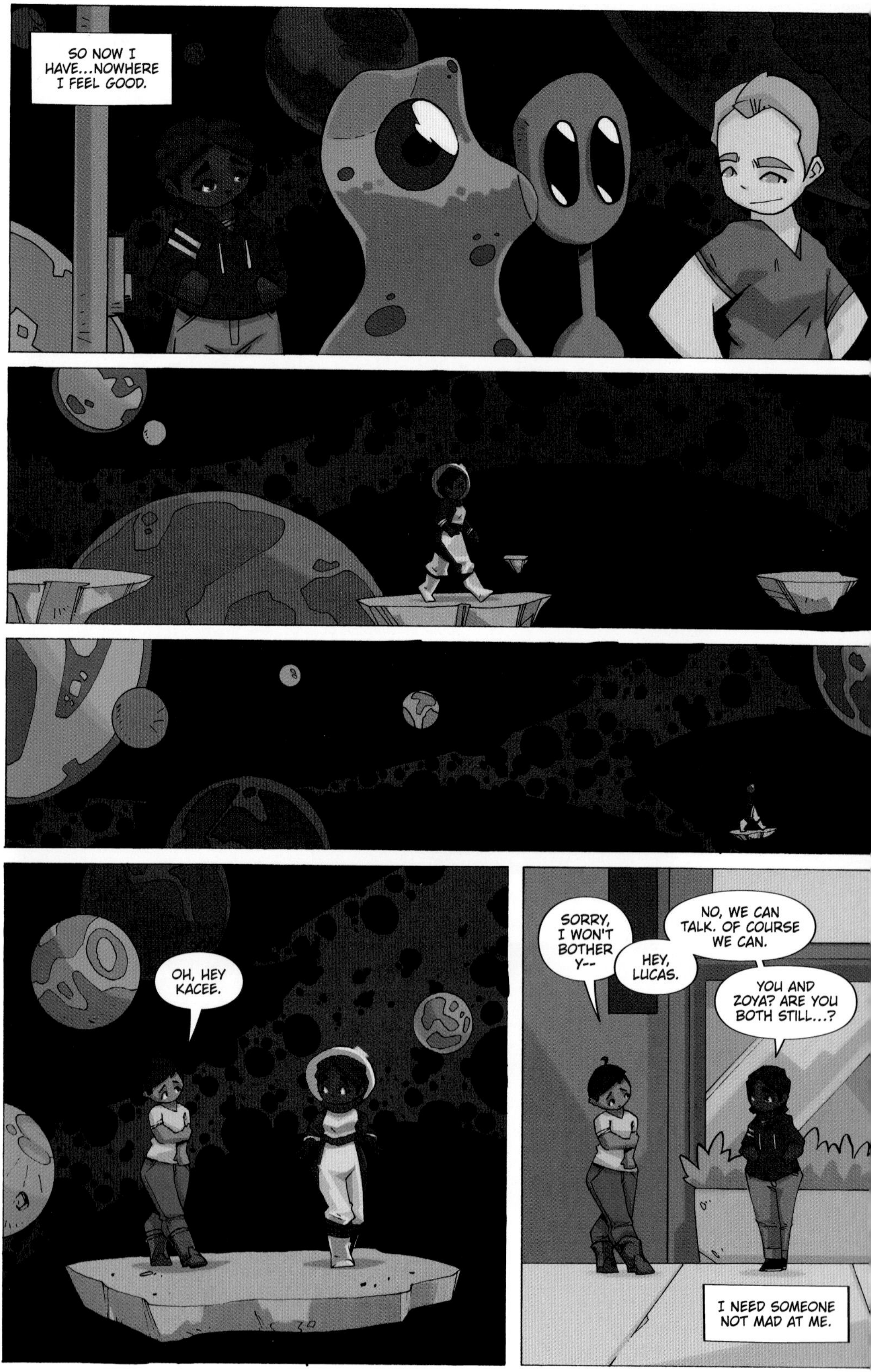
SO NOW I HAVE...NOWHERE I FEEL GOOD.
OH, HEY KACEE.
SORRY, I WON'T BOTHER Y--
HEY, LUCAS.
NO, WE CAN TALK. OF COURSE WE CAN.
YOU AND ZOYA? ARE YOU BOTH STILL...?
I NEED SOMEONE NOT MAD AT ME.

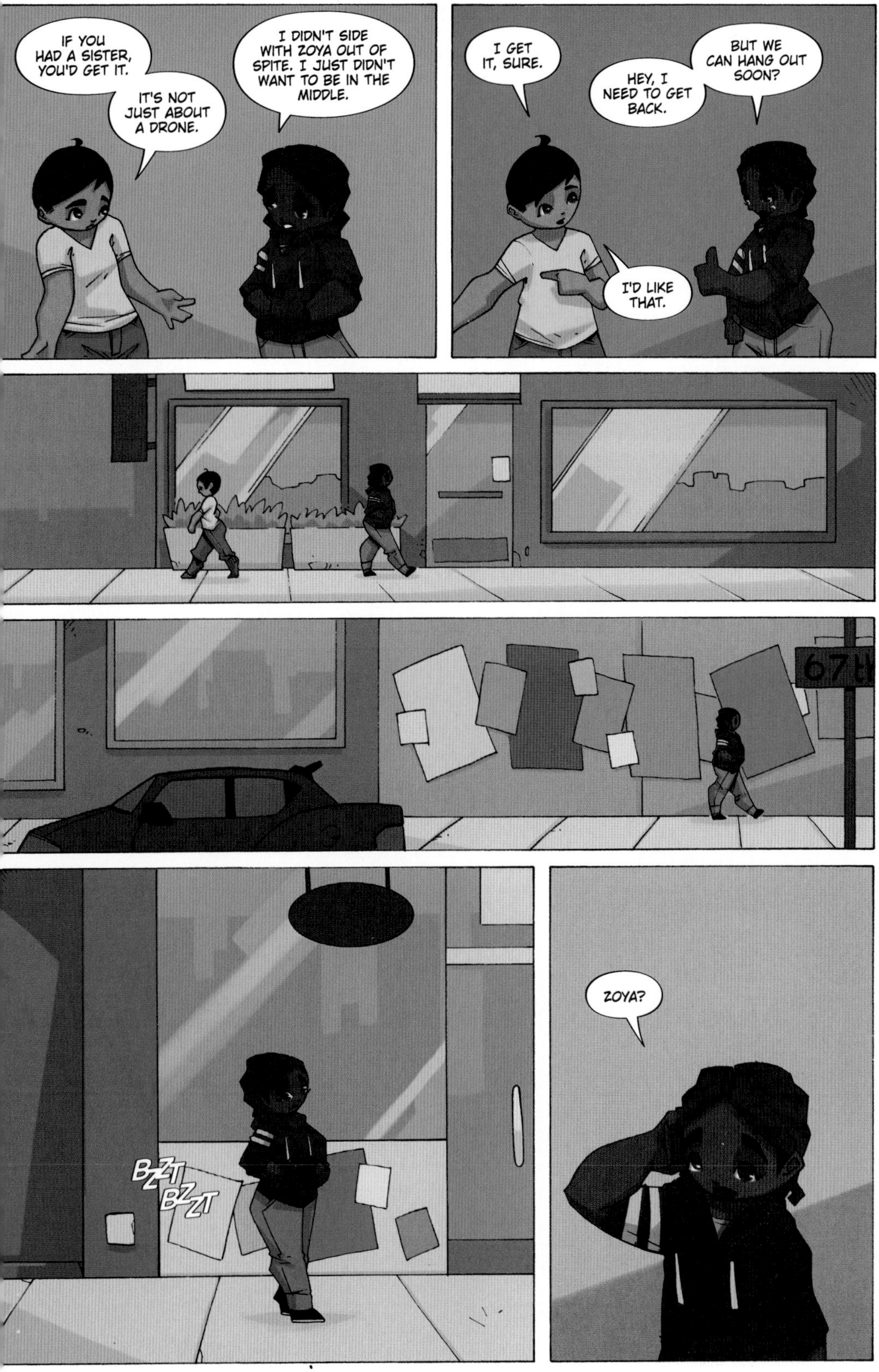
IF YOU HAD A SISTER, YOU'D GET IT.
IT'S NOT JUST ABOUT A DRONE.
I DIDN'T SIDE WITH ZOYA OUT OF SPITE. I JUST DIDN'T WANT TO BE IN THE MIDDLE.
I GET IT, SURE.
HEY, I NEED TO GET BACK.
BUT WE CAN HANG OUT SOON?
I'D LIKE THAT.
67th
BZZT BZZT
ZOYA?

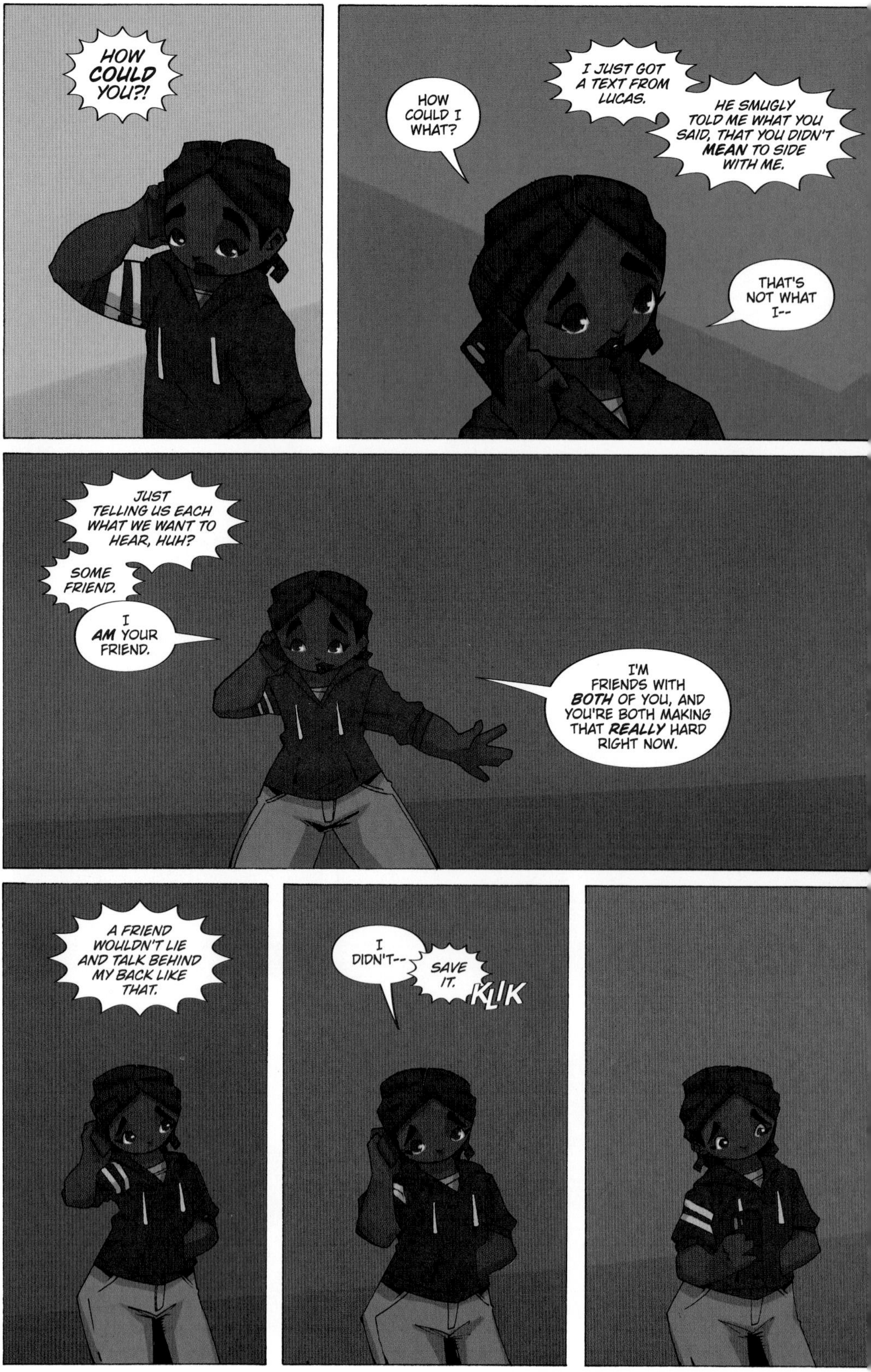
HOW COULD YOU?!
HOW COULD I WHAT?
I JUST GOT A TEXT FROM LUCAS.
HE SMUGLY TOLD ME WHAT YOU SAID, THAT YOU DIDN'T MEAN TO SIDE WITH ME.
THAT'S NOT WHAT I--
JUST TELLING US EACH WHAT WE WANT TO HEAR, HUH?
SOME FRIEND.
I AM YOUR FRIEND.
I'M FRIENDS WITH BOTH OF YOU, AND YOU'RE BOTH MAKING THAT REALLY HARD RIGHT NOW.
A FRIEND WOULDN'T LIE AND TALK BEHIND MY BACK LIKE THAT.
I DIDN'T--
SAVE IT.
KLIK

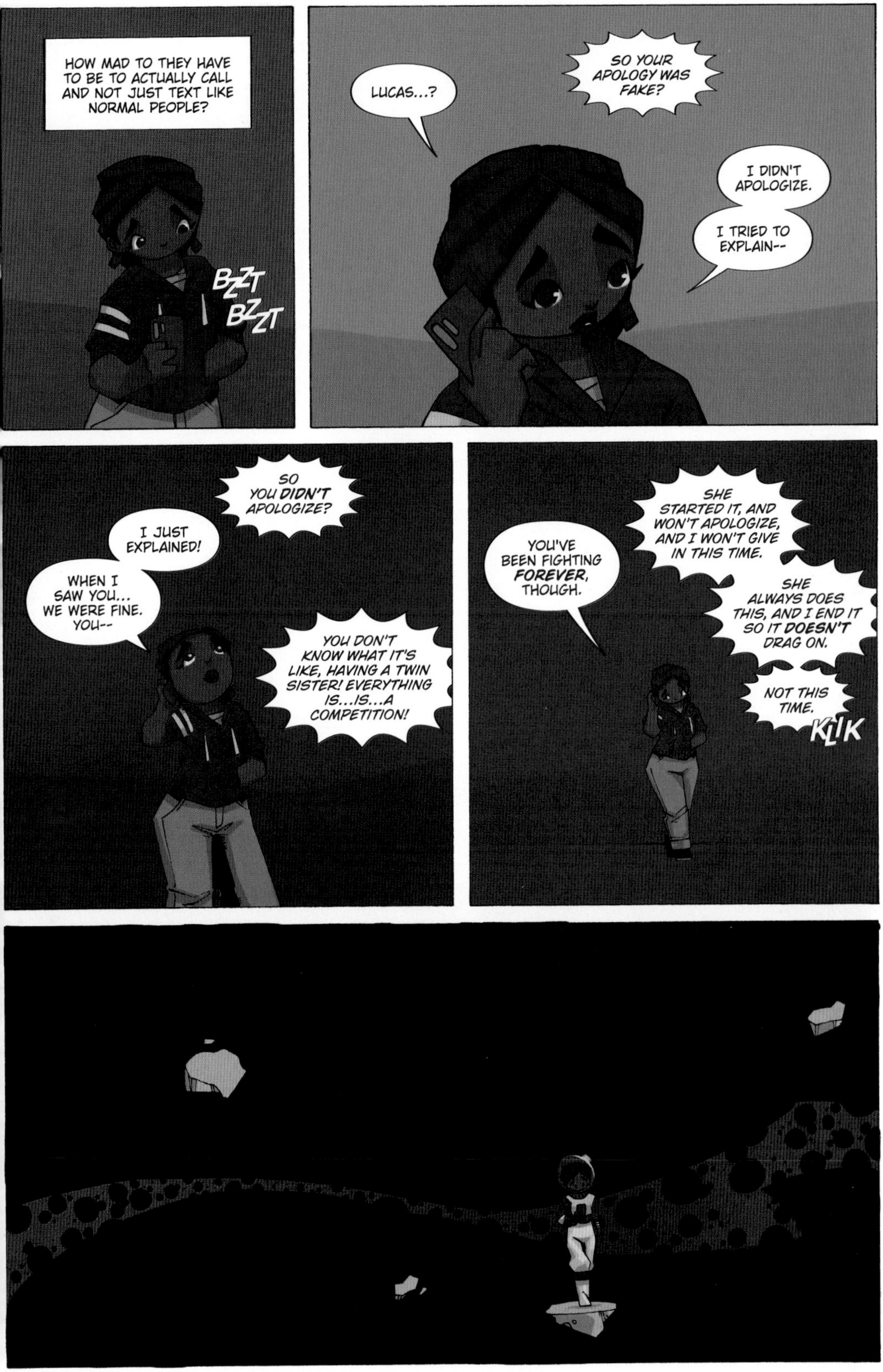
HOW MAD TO THEY HAVE TO BE TO ACTUALLY CALL AND NOT JUST TEXT LIKE NORMAL PEOPLE?
BZZT BZZT
LUCAS...?
SO YOUR APOLOGY WAS FAKE?
I DIDN'T APOLOGIZE.
I TRIED TO EXPLAIN--
SO YOU DIDN'T APOLOGIZE?
I JUST EXPLAINED!
WHEN I SAW YOU... WE WERE FINE. YOU--
YOU DON'T KNOW WHAT IT'S LIKE, HAVING A TWIN SISTER! EVERYTHING IS...IS...A COMPETITION!
YOU'VE BEEN FIGHTING FOREVER, THOUGH.
SHE STARTED IT, AND WON'T APOLOGIZE, AND I WON'T GIVE IN THIS TIME.
SHE ALWAYS DOES THIS, AND I END IT SO IT DOESN'T DRAG ON.
NOT THIS TIME.
KLIK

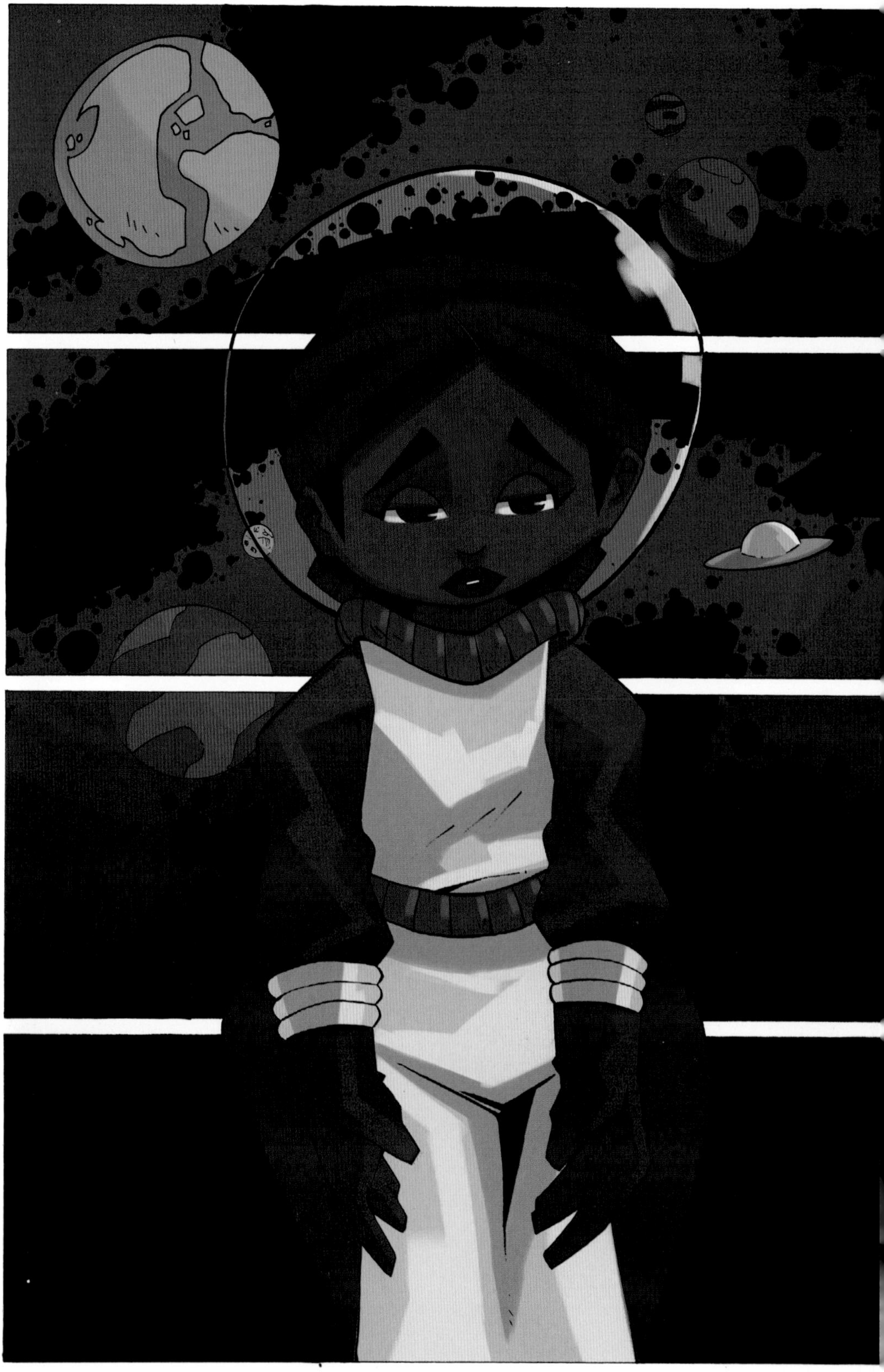

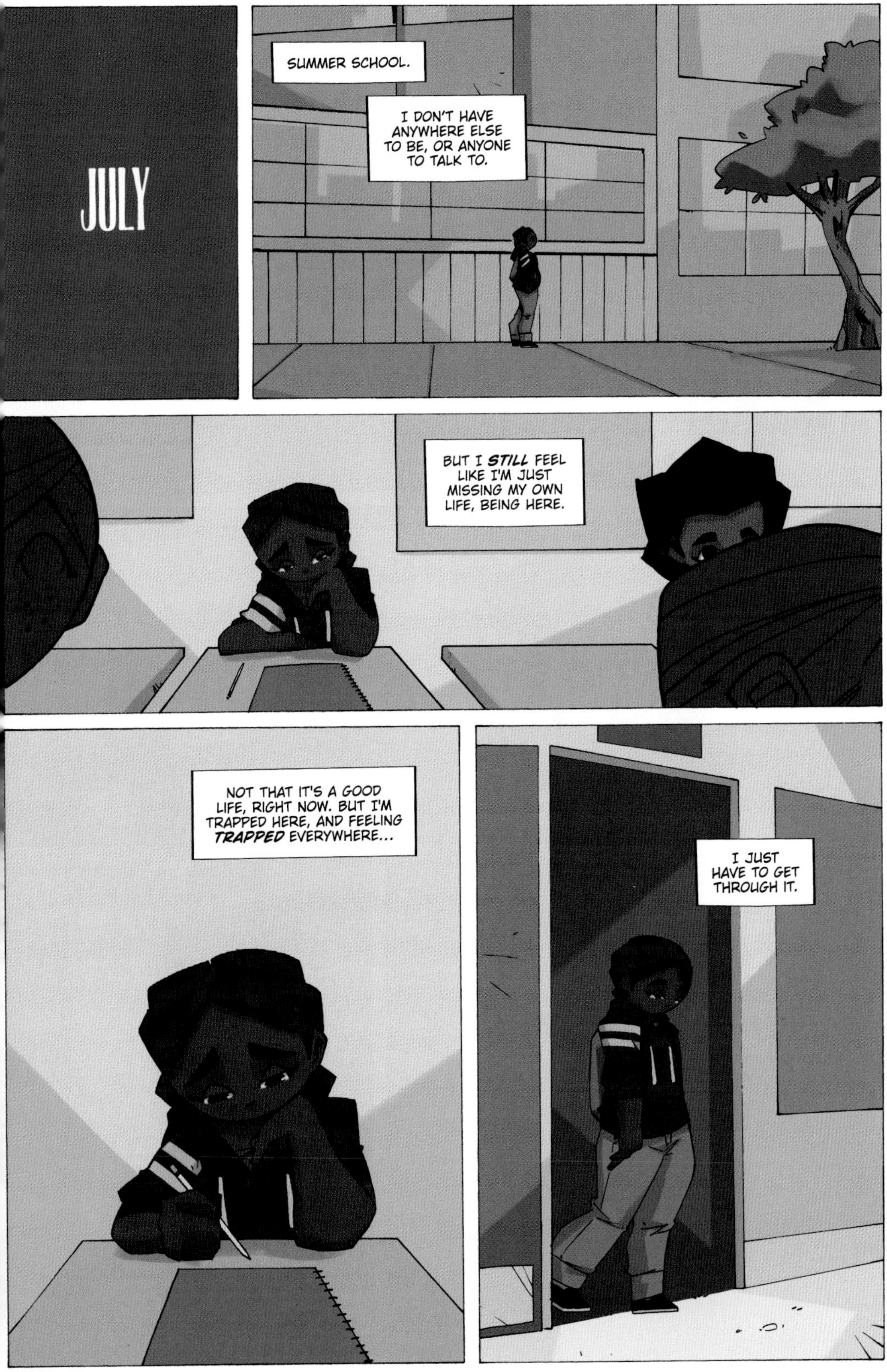
JULY
SUMMER SCHOOL.
I DON'T HAVE ANYWHERE ELSE TO BE, OR ANYONE TO TALK TO.
BUT I STILL FEEL LIKE I'M JUST MISSING MY OWN LIFE, BEING HERE.
NOT THAT IT'S A GOOD LIFE, RIGHT NOW. BUT I'M TRAPPED HERE, AND FEELING TRAPPED EVERYWHERE...
I JUST HAVE TO GET THROUGH IT.

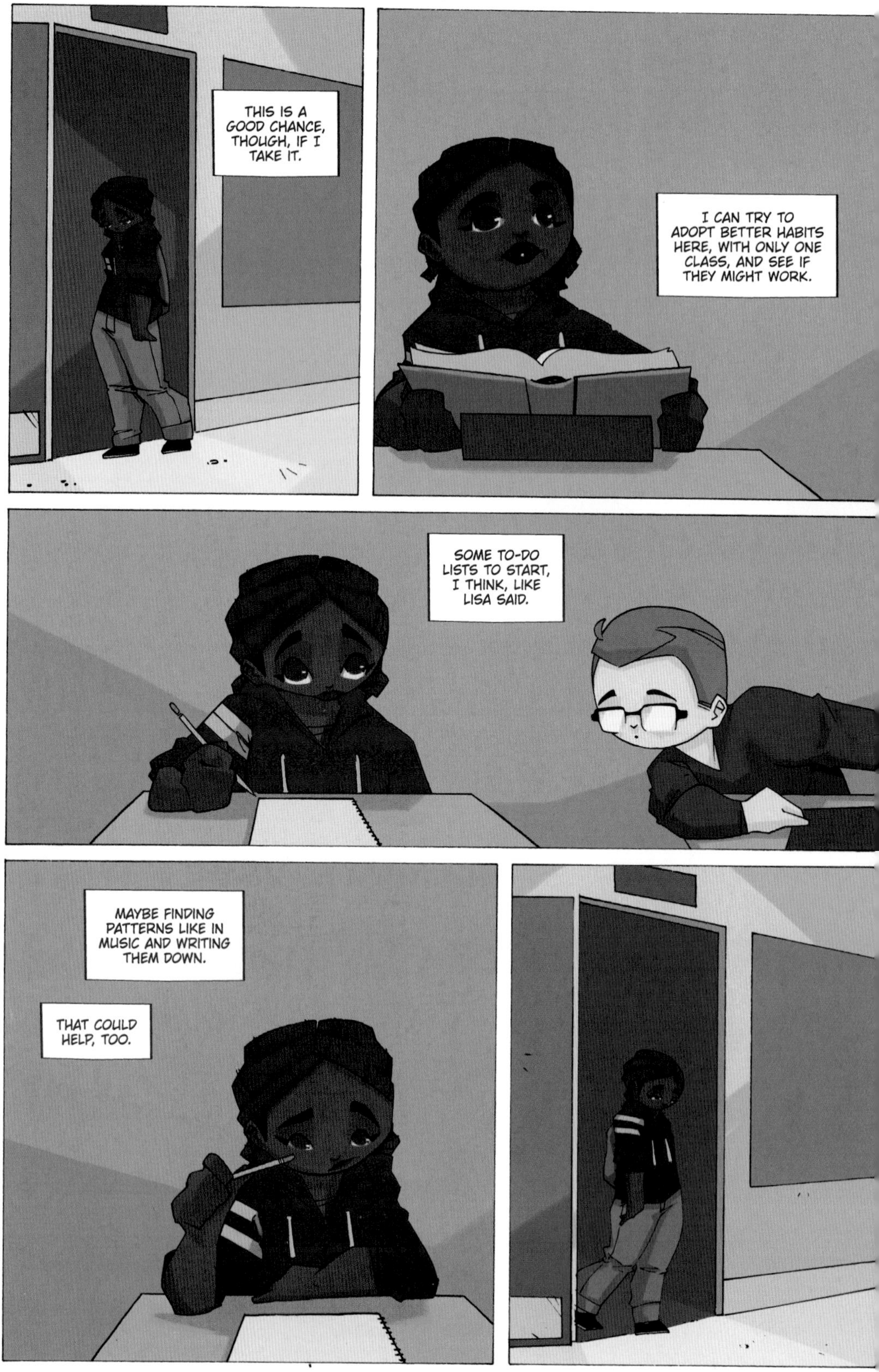
THIS IS A GOOD CHANCE, THOUGH, IF I TAKE IT.
I CAN TRY TO ADOPT BETTER HABITS HERE, WITH ONLY ONE CLASS, AND SEE IF THEY MIGHT WORK.
SOME TO-DO LISTS TO START, I THINK, LIKE LISA SAID.
MAYBE FINDING PATTERNS LIKE IN MUSIC AND WRITING THEM DOWN.
THAT COULD HELP, TOO.

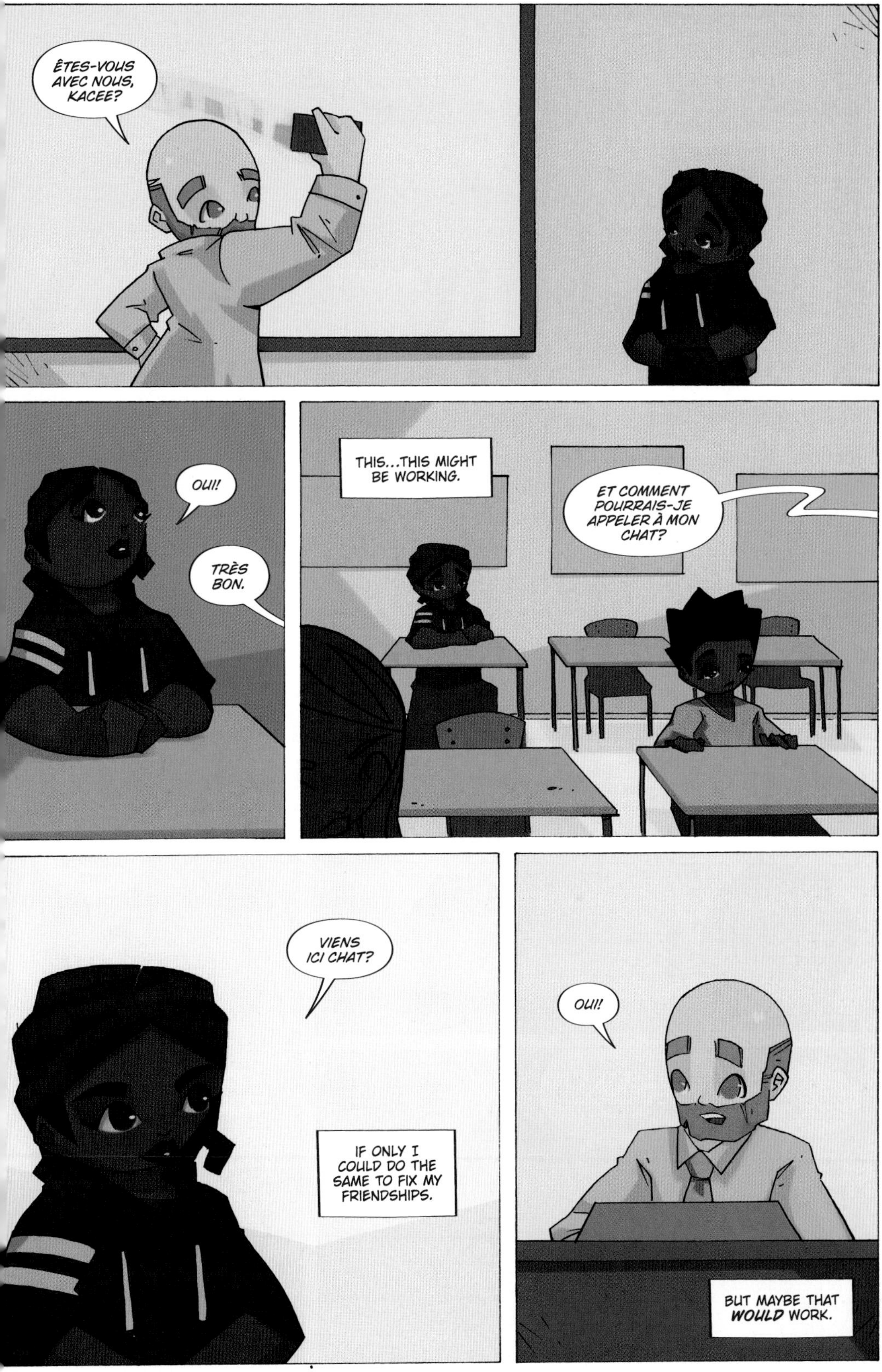
ÊTES-VOUS AVEC NOUS, KACEE?
OUI!
TRÈS BON.
THIS...THIS MIGHT BE WORKING.
ET COMMENT POURRAIS-JE APPELER À MON CHAT?
VIENS ICI CHAT?
IF ONLY I COULD DO THE SAME TO FIX MY FRIENDSHIPS.
OUI!
BUT MAYBE THAT ***WOULD*** WORK.

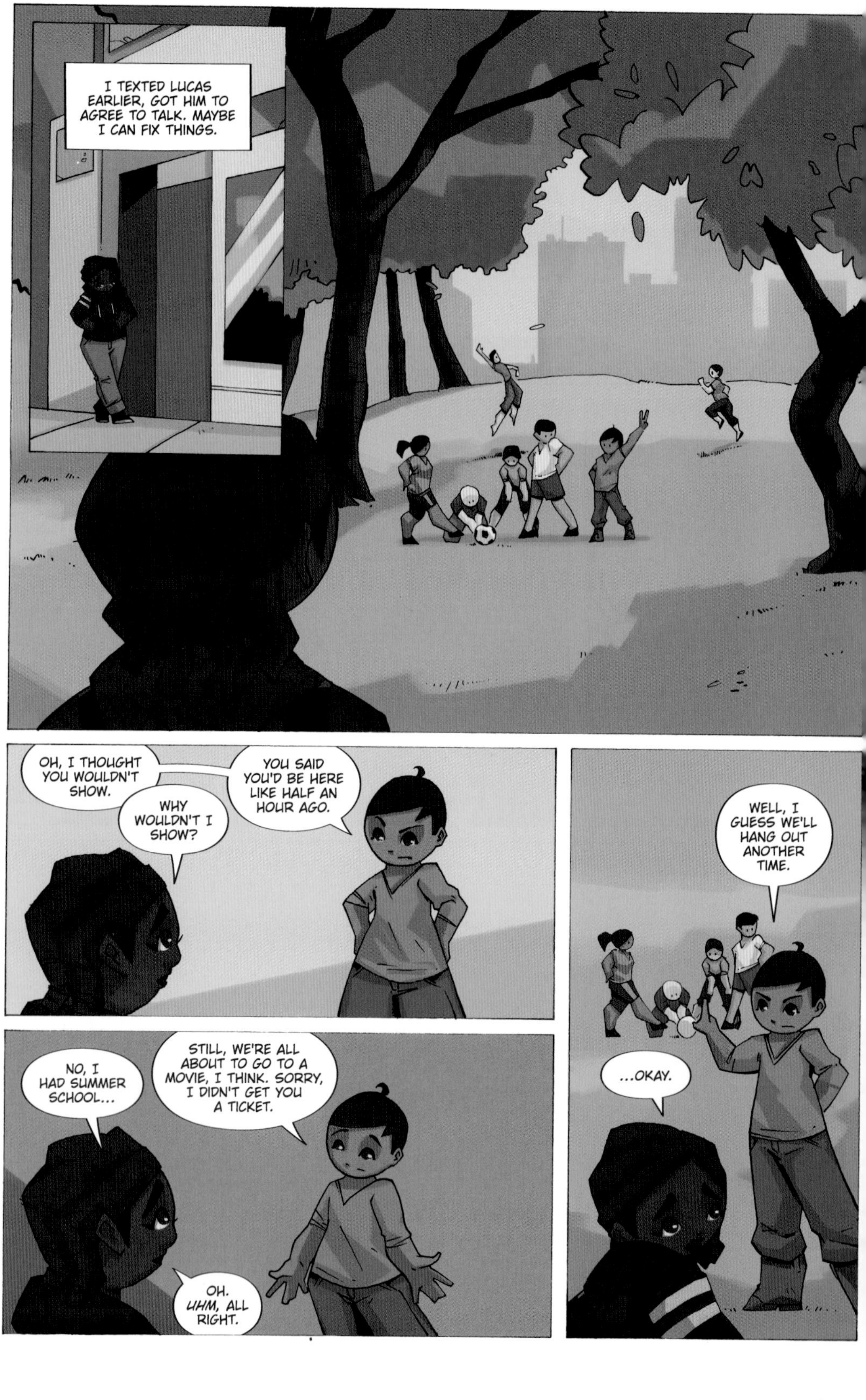
I TEXTED LUCAS EARLIER, GOT HIM TO AGREE TO TALK. MAYBE I CAN FIX THINGS.
OH, I THOUGHT YOU WOULDN'T SHOW.
YOU SAID YOU'D BE HERE LIKE HALF AN HOUR AGO.
WHY WOULDN'T I SHOW?
NO, I HAD SUMMER SCHOOL...
STILL, WE'RE ALL ABOUT TO GO TO A MOVIE, I THINK. SORRY, I DIDN'T GET YOU A TICKET.
OH. UHM, ALL RIGHT.
WELL, I GUESS WE'LL HANG OUT ANOTHER TIME.
...OKAY.

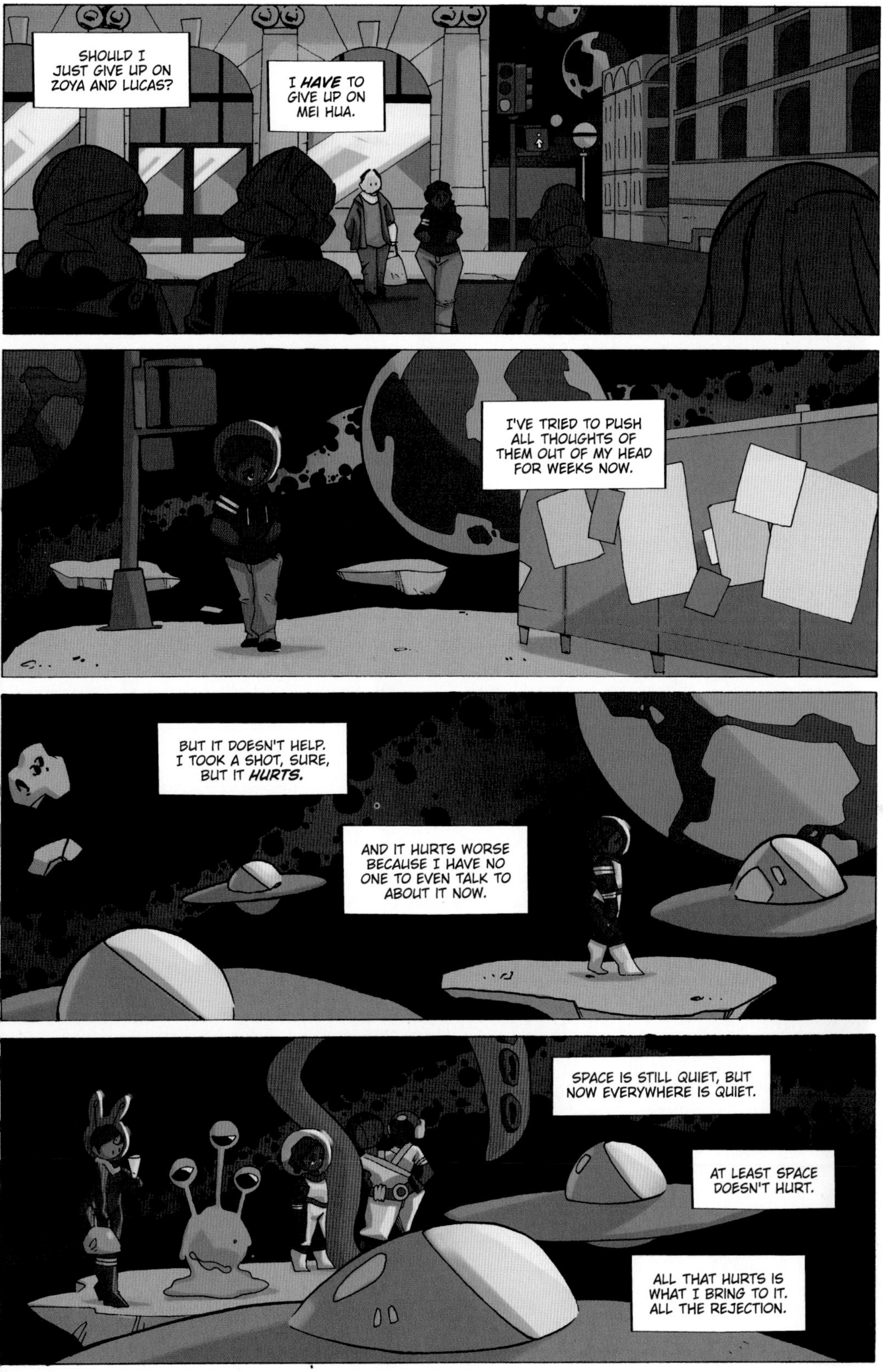
SHOULD I JUST GIVE UP ON ZOYA AND LUCAS?
I *HAVE* TO GIVE UP ON MEI HUA.
I'VE TRIED TO PUSH ALL THOUGHTS OF THEM OUT OF MY HEAD FOR WEEKS NOW.
BUT IT DOESN'T HELP. I TOOK A SHOT, SURE, BUT IT *HURTS.*
AND IT HURTS WORSE BECAUSE I HAVE NO ONE TO EVEN TALK TO ABOUT IT NOW.
SPACE IS STILL QUIET, BUT NOW EVERYWHERE IS QUIET.
AT LEAST SPACE DOESN'T HURT.
ALL THAT HURTS IS WHAT I BRING TO IT. ALL THE REJECTION.

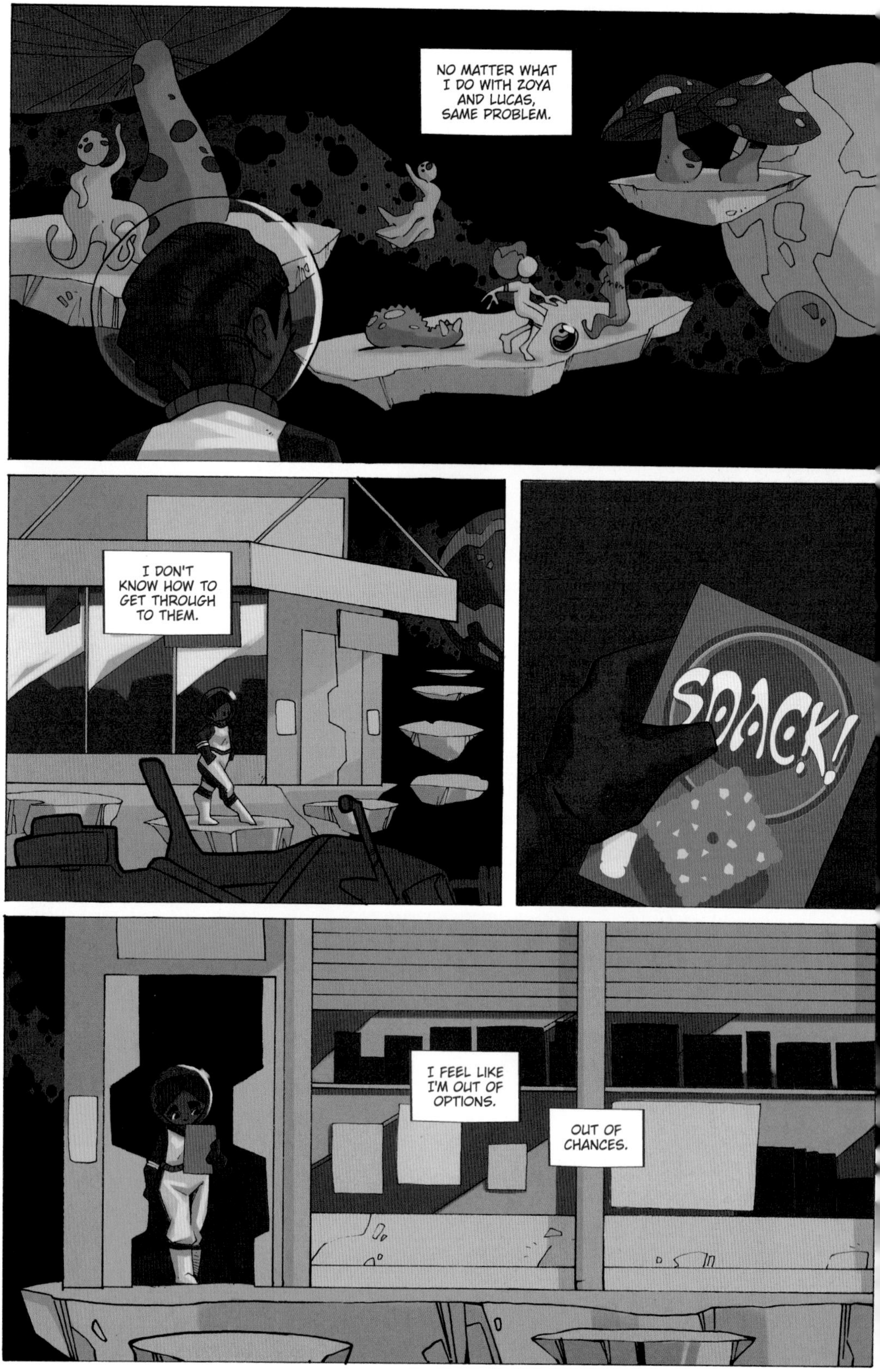
NO MATTER WHAT I DO WITH ZOYA AND LUCAS, SAME PROBLEM.
I DON'T KNOW HOW TO GET THROUGH TO THEM.
SNACK!
I FEEL LIKE I'M OUT OF OPTIONS.
OUT OF CHANCES.

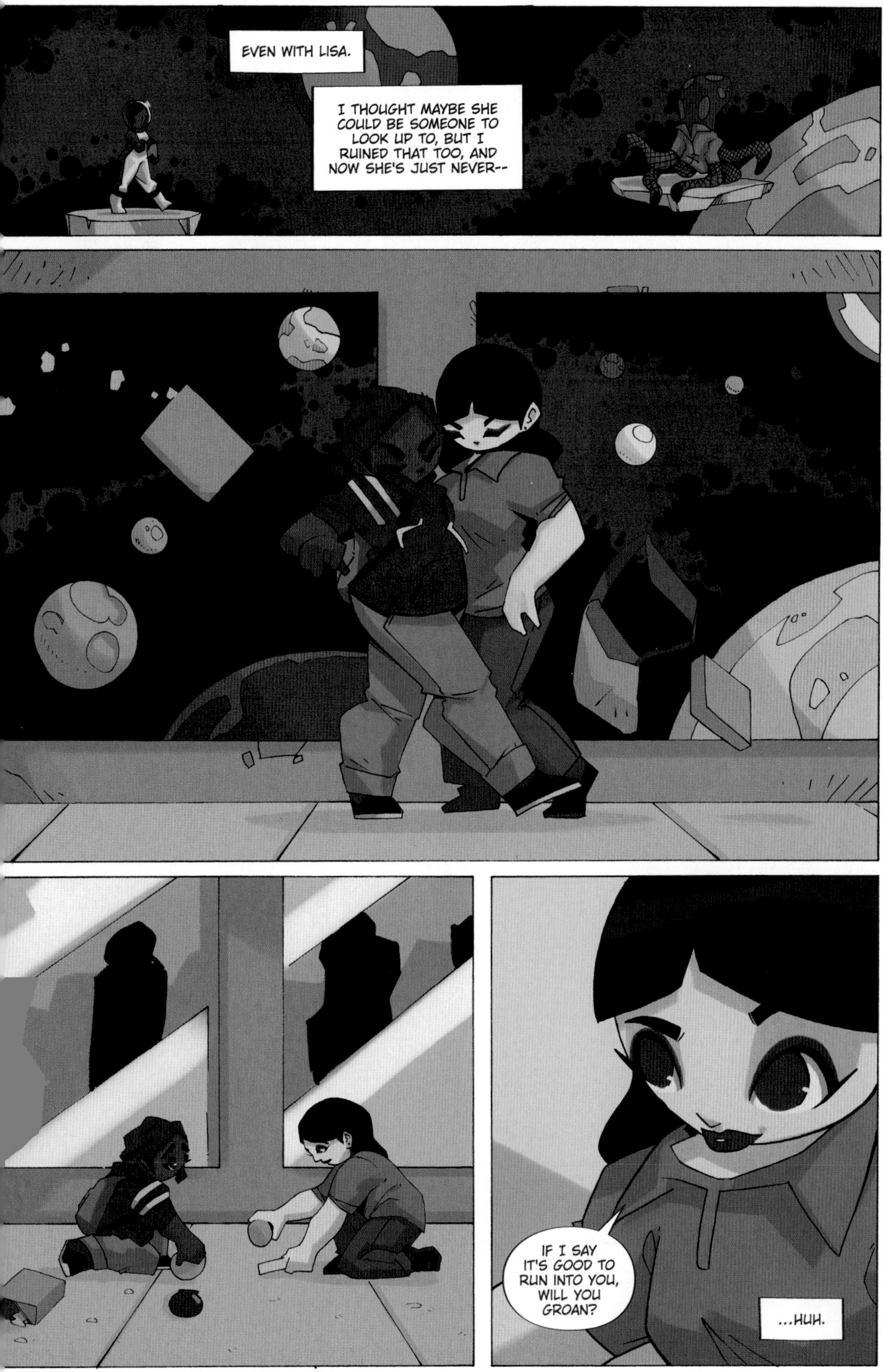
EVEN WITH LISA.
I THOUGHT MAYBE SHE COULD BE SOMEONE TO LOOK UP TO, BUT I RUINED THAT TOO, AND NOW SHE'S JUST NEVER--
IF I SAY IT'S GOOD TO RUN INTO YOU, WILL YOU GROAN?
...HUH.

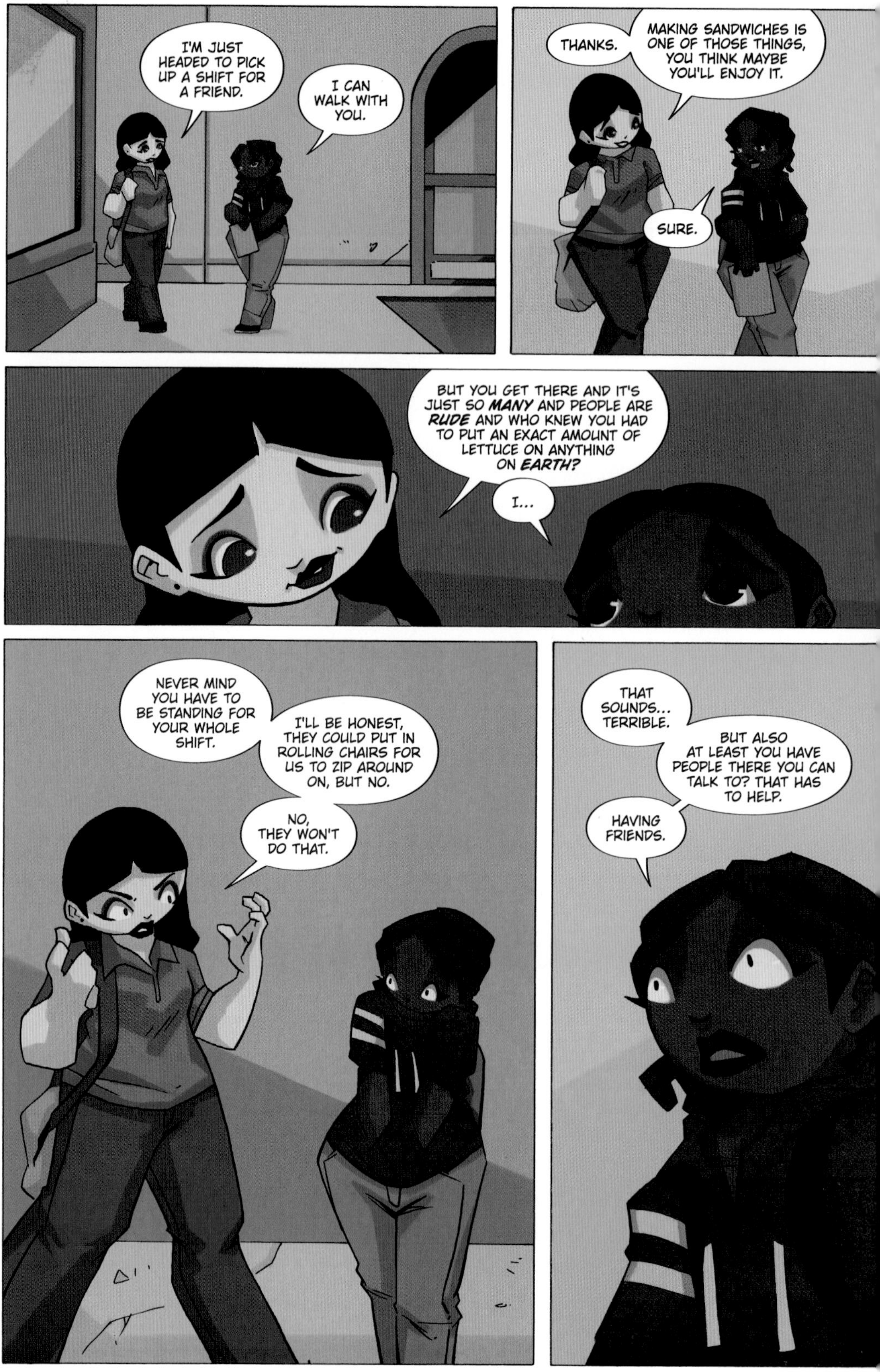
I'M JUST HEADED TO PICK UP A SHIFT FOR A FRIEND.
I CAN WALK WITH YOU.
THANKS.
MAKING SANDWICHES IS ONE OF THOSE THINGS, YOU THINK MAYBE YOU'LL ENJOY IT.
SURE.
BUT YOU GET THERE AND IT'S JUST SO MANY AND PEOPLE ARE RUDE AND WHO KNEW YOU HAD TO PUT AN EXACT AMOUNT OF LETTUCE ON ANYTHING ON EARTH?
I...
NEVER MIND YOU HAVE TO BE STANDING FOR YOUR WHOLE SHIFT.
I'LL BE HONEST, THEY COULD PUT IN ROLLING CHAIRS FOR US TO ZIP AROUND ON, BUT NO.
NO, THEY WON'T DO THAT.
THAT SOUNDS... TERRIBLE.
BUT ALSO AT LEAST YOU HAVE PEOPLE THERE YOU CAN TALK TO? THAT HAS TO HELP.
HAVING FRIENDS.

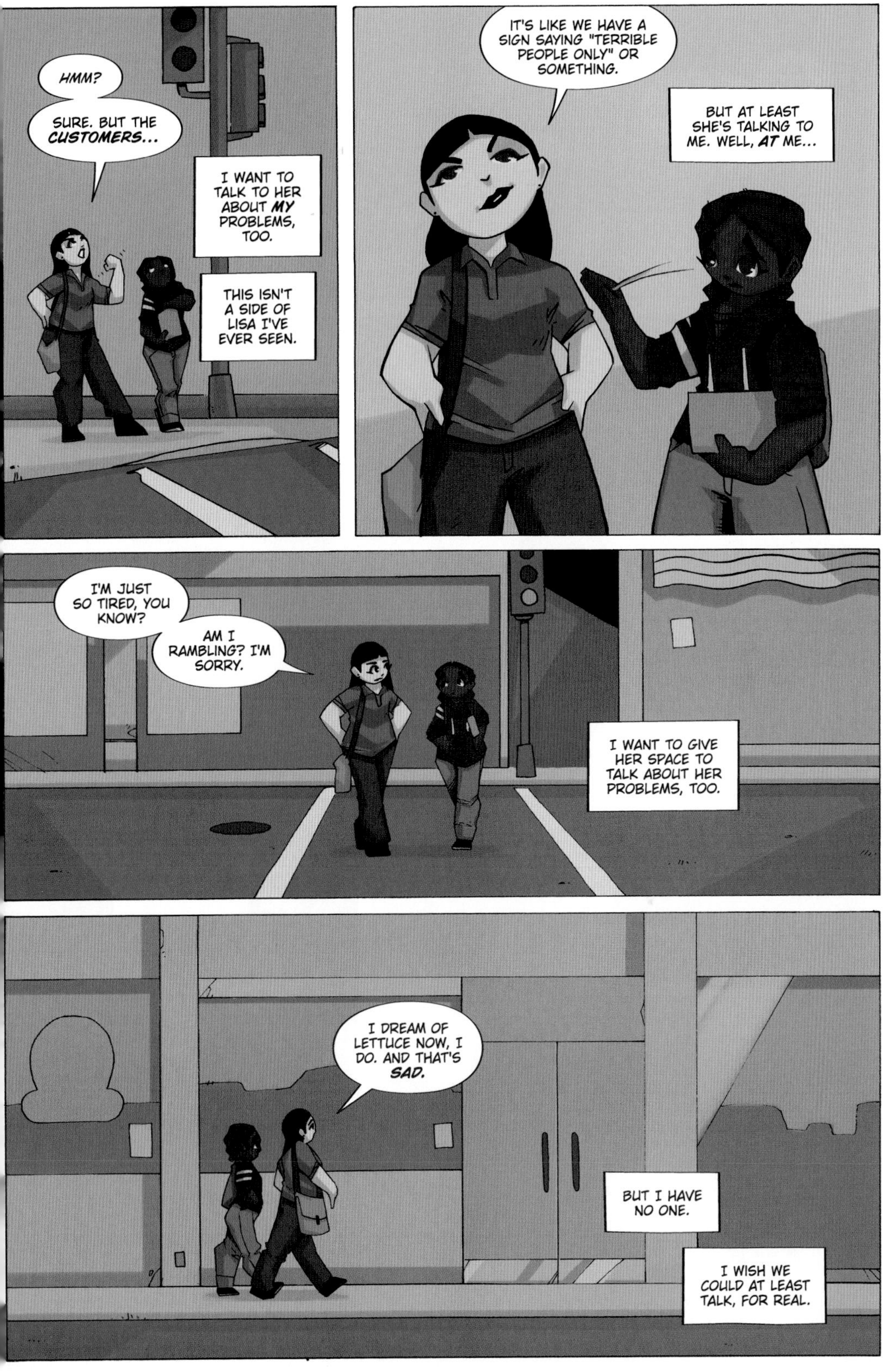
HMM?
SURE. BUT THE CUSTOMERS...
I WANT TO TALK TO HER ABOUT MY PROBLEMS, TOO.
THIS ISN'T A SIDE OF LISA I'VE EVER SEEN.
IT'S LIKE WE HAVE A SIGN SAYING "TERRIBLE PEOPLE ONLY" OR SOMETHING.
BUT AT LEAST SHE'S TALKING TO ME. WELL, AT ME...
I'M JUST SO TIRED, YOU KNOW?
AM I RAMBLING? I'M SORRY.
I WANT TO GIVE HER SPACE TO TALK ABOUT HER PROBLEMS, TOO.
I DREAM OF LETTUCE NOW, I DO. AND THAT'S SAD.
BUT I HAVE NO ONE.
I WISH WE COULD AT LEAST TALK, FOR REAL.

ALL RIGHT.

I GOTTA FACE THIS ALL AGAIN.

...OKAY. HAVE A GOOD SHIFT.

I JUST NEED *SOMETHING.*

SOMETHING THAT'S MINE, THAT'S FOR ME.

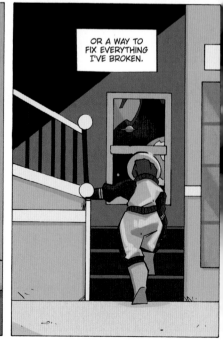

OR A WAY TO FIX EVERYTHING I'VE BROKEN.

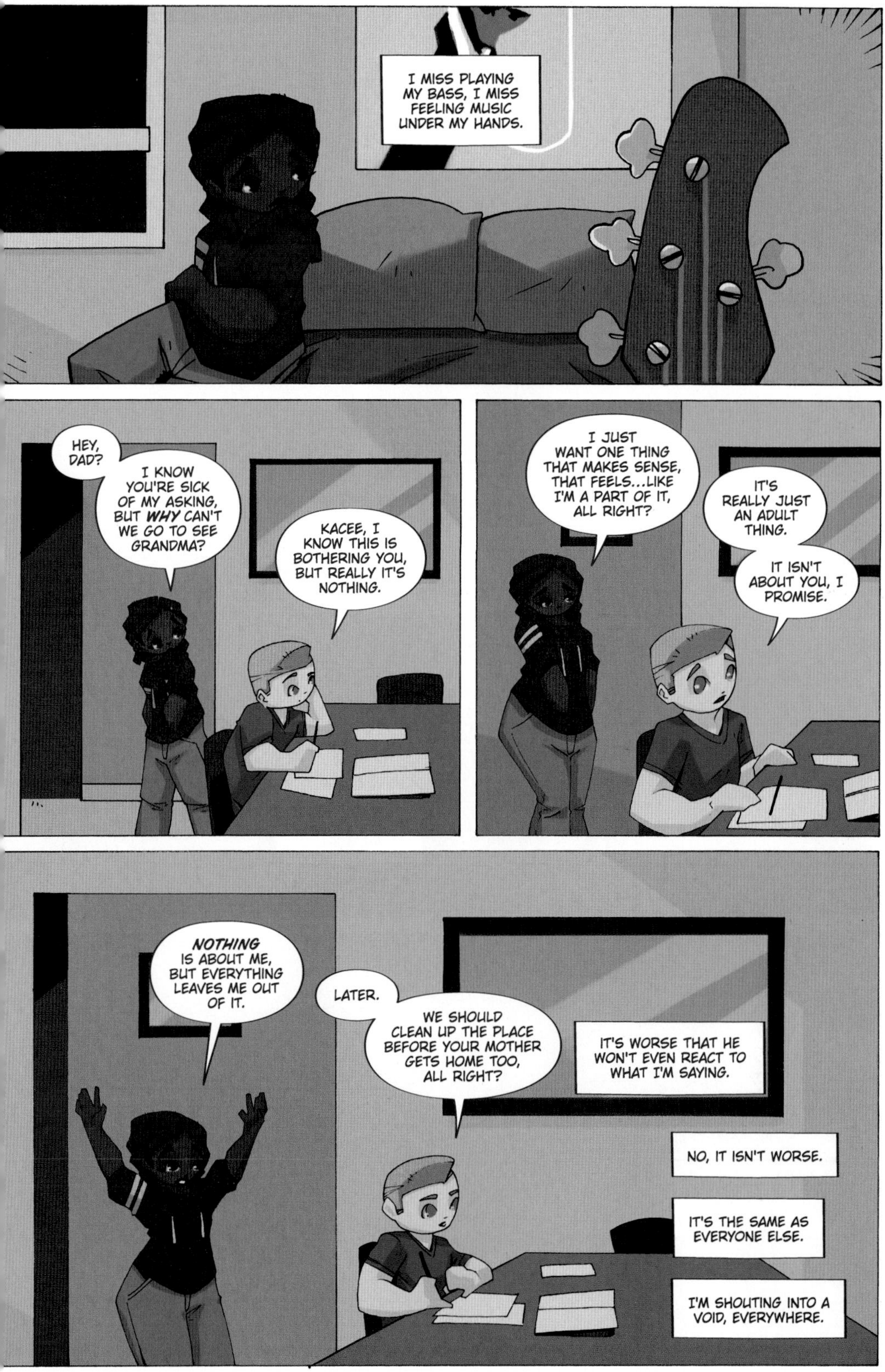
I MISS PLAYING MY BASS, I MISS FEELING MUSIC UNDER MY HANDS.
HEY, DAD?
I KNOW YOU'RE SICK OF MY ASKING, BUT *WHY* CAN'T WE GO TO SEE GRANDMA?
KACEE, I KNOW THIS IS BOTHERING YOU, BUT REALLY IT'S NOTHING.
I JUST WANT ONE THING THAT MAKES SENSE, THAT FEELS...LIKE I'M A PART OF IT, ALL RIGHT?
IT'S REALLY JUST AN ADULT THING.
IT ISN'T ABOUT YOU, I PROMISE.
NOTHING IS ABOUT ME, BUT EVERYTHING LEAVES ME OUT OF IT.
LATER.
WE SHOULD CLEAN UP THE PLACE BEFORE YOUR MOTHER GETS HOME TOO, ALL RIGHT?
IT'S WORSE THAT HE WON'T EVEN REACT TO WHAT I'M SAYING.
NO, IT ISN'T WORSE.
IT'S THE SAME AS EVERYONE ELSE.
I'M SHOUTING INTO A VOID, EVERYWHERE.

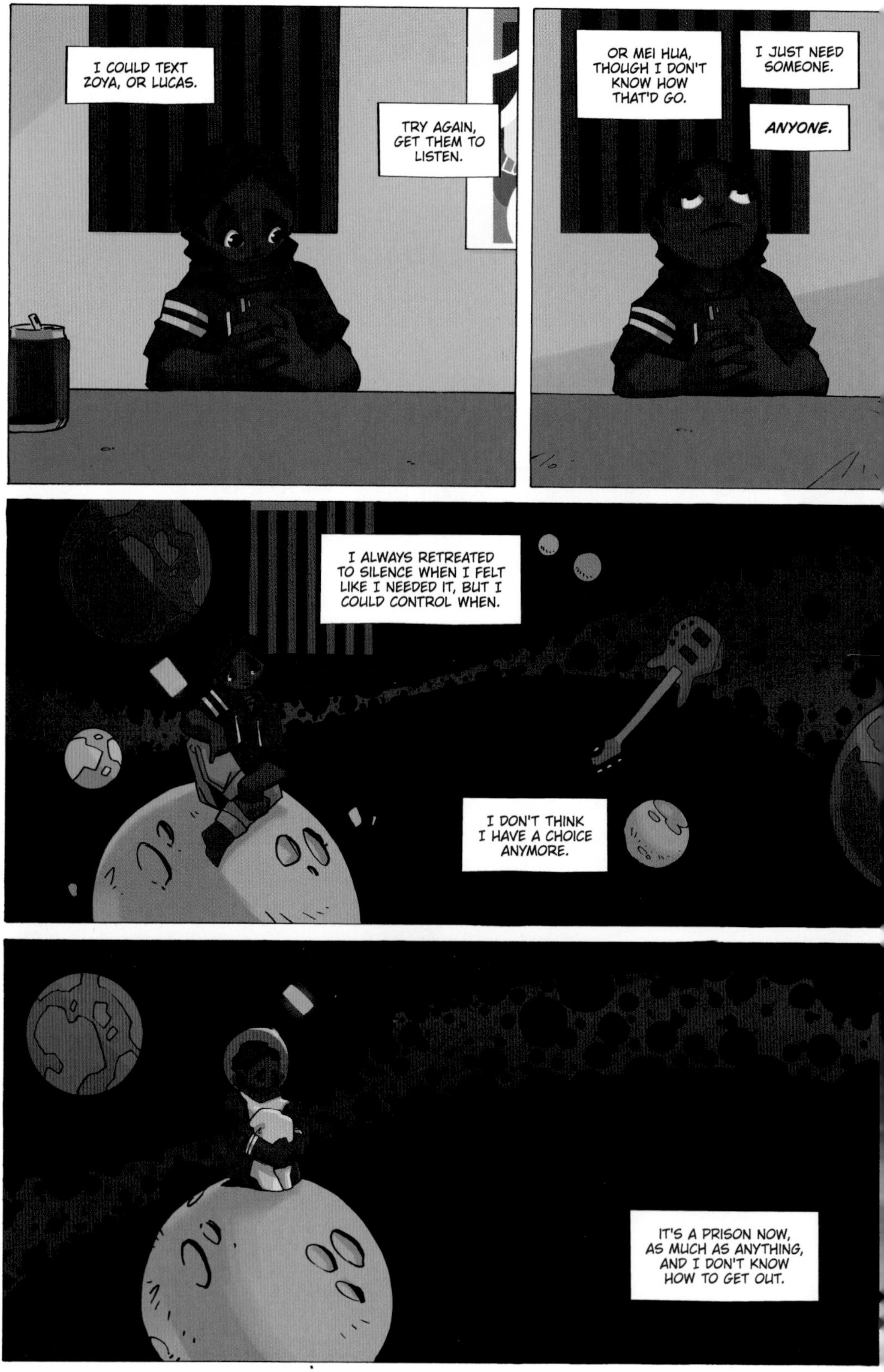
I COULD TEXT ZOYA, OR LUCAS.
TRY AGAIN, GET THEM TO LISTEN.
OR MEI HUA, THOUGH I DON'T KNOW HOW THAT'D GO.
I JUST NEED SOMEONE.
ANYONE.
I ALWAYS RETREATED TO SILENCE WHEN I FELT LIKE I NEEDED IT, BUT I COULD CONTROL WHEN.
I DON'T THINK I HAVE A CHOICE ANYMORE.
IT'S A PRISON NOW, AS MUCH AS ANYTHING, AND I DON'T KNOW HOW TO GET OUT.

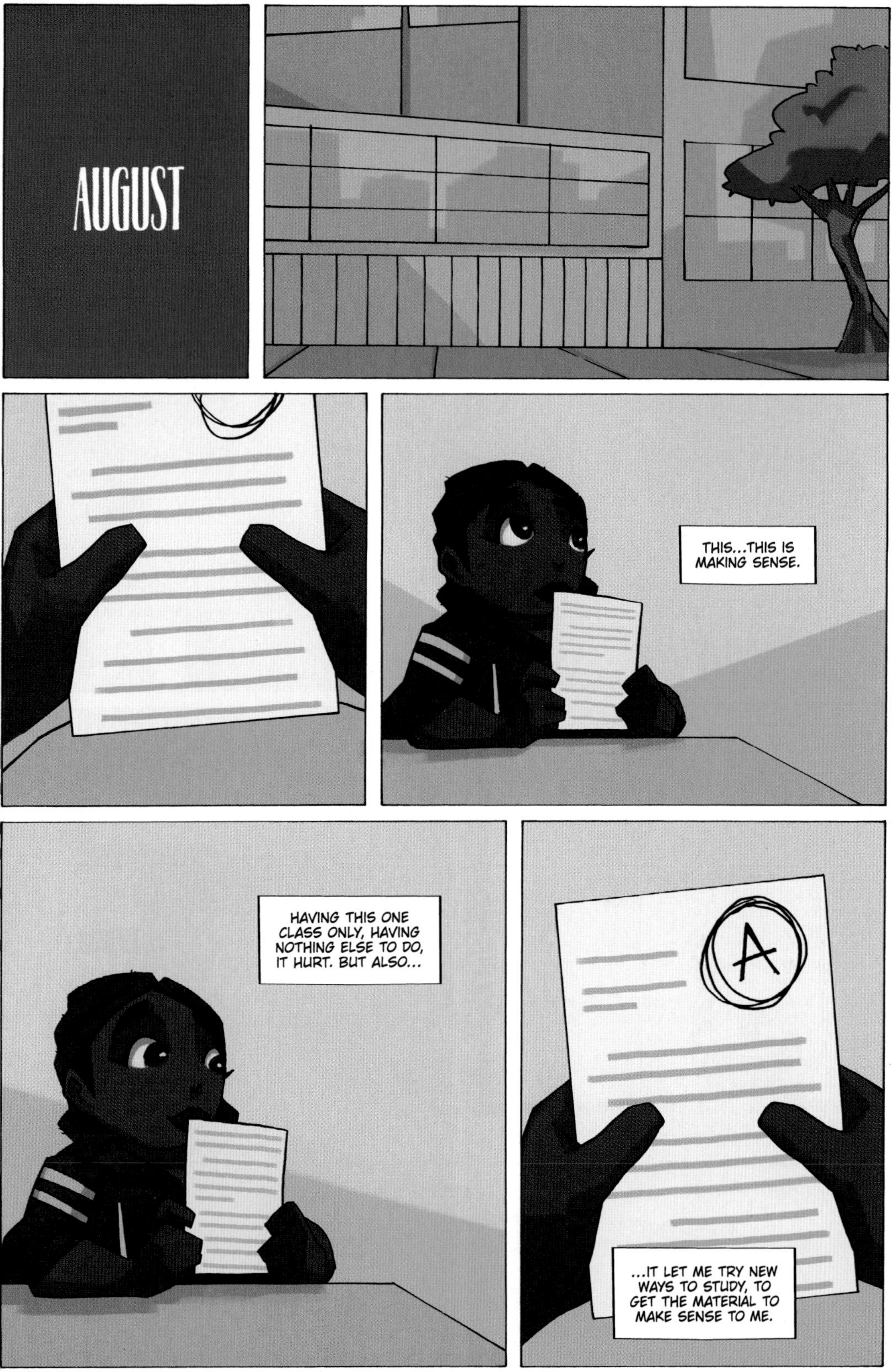
AUGUST
THIS...THIS IS MAKING SENSE.
HAVING THIS ONE CLASS ONLY, HAVING NOTHING ELSE TO DO, IT HURT. BUT ALSO...
A
...IT LET ME TRY NEW WAYS TO STUDY, TO GET THE MATERIAL TO MAKE SENSE TO ME.

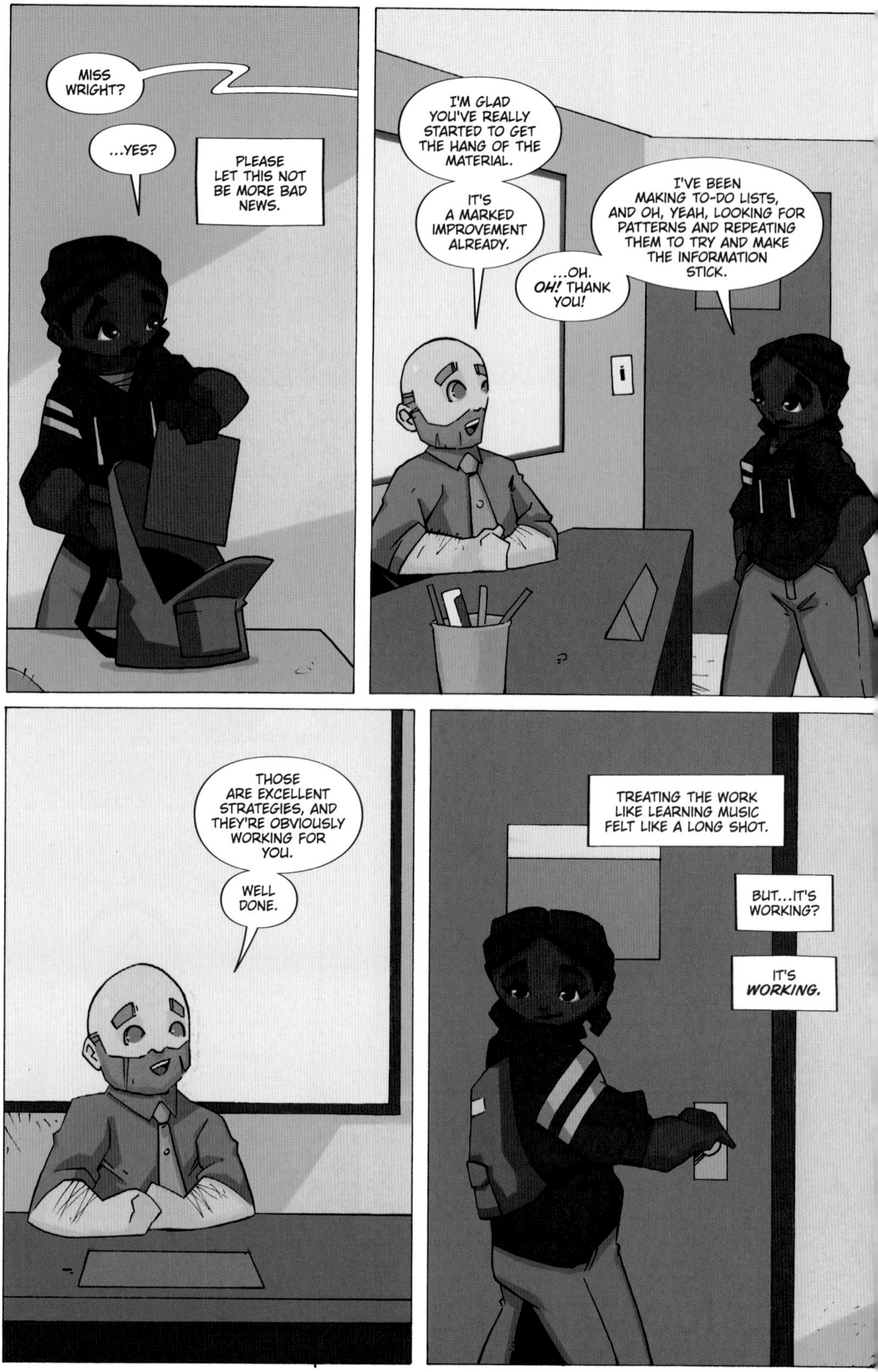
MISS WRIGHT?
...YES?
PLEASE LET THIS NOT BE MORE BAD NEWS.
I'M GLAD YOU'VE REALLY STARTED TO GET THE HANG OF THE MATERIAL.
IT'S A MARKED IMPROVEMENT ALREADY.
...OH. OH! THANK YOU!
I'VE BEEN MAKING TO-DO LISTS, AND OH, YEAH, LOOKING FOR PATTERNS AND REPEATING THEM TO TRY AND MAKE THE INFORMATION STICK.
THOSE ARE EXCELLENT STRATEGIES, AND THEY'RE OBVIOUSLY WORKING FOR YOU.
WELL DONE.
TREATING THE WORK LIKE LEARNING MUSIC FELT LIKE A LONG SHOT.
BUT...IT'S WORKING?
IT'S WORKING.

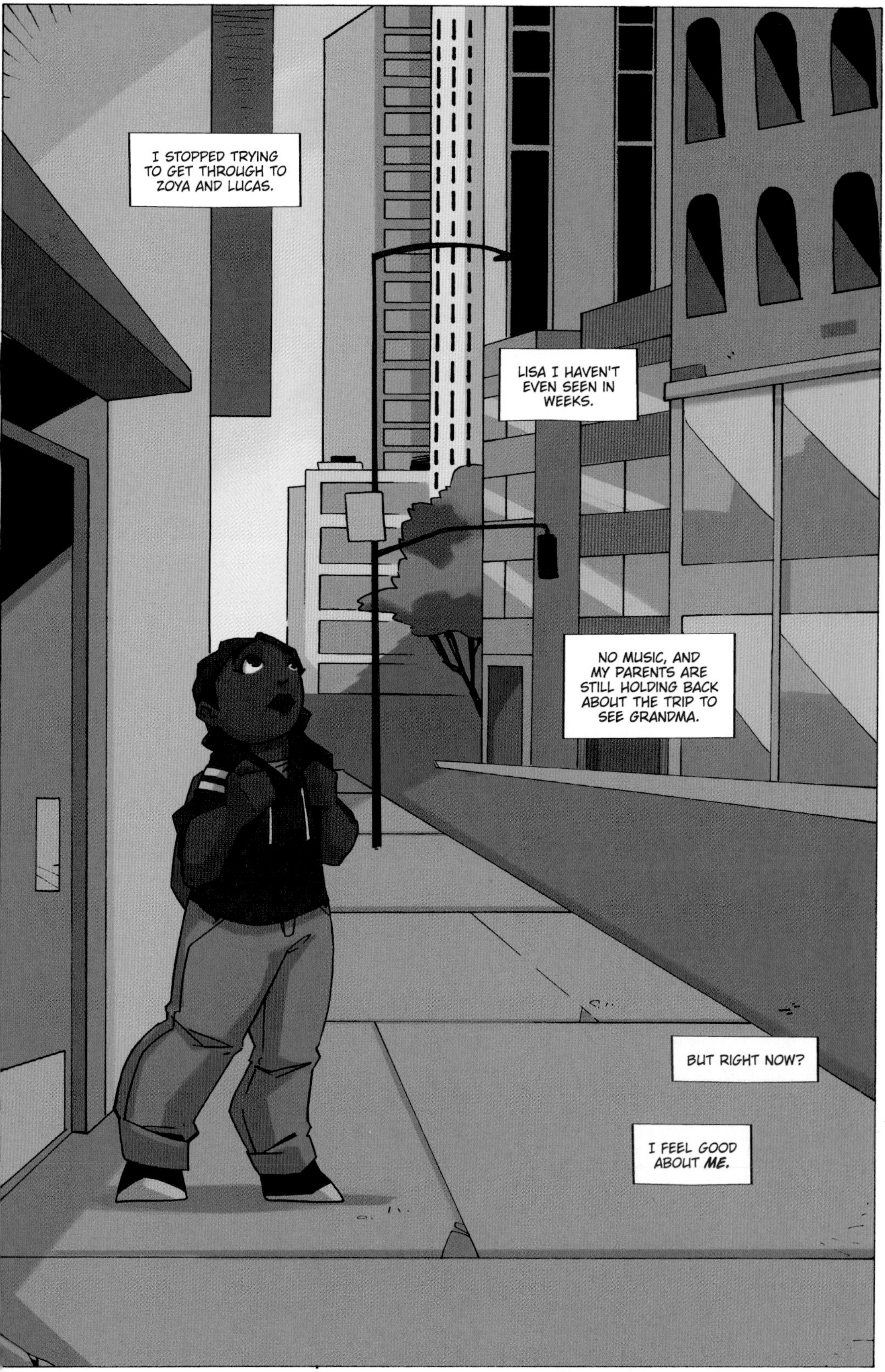
I STOPPED TRYING TO GET THROUGH TO ZOYA AND LUCAS.
LISA I HAVEN'T EVEN SEEN IN WEEKS.
NO MUSIC, AND MY PARENTS ARE STILL HOLDING BACK ABOUT THE TRIP TO SEE GRANDMA.
BUT RIGHT NOW?
I FEEL GOOD ABOUT **ME.**

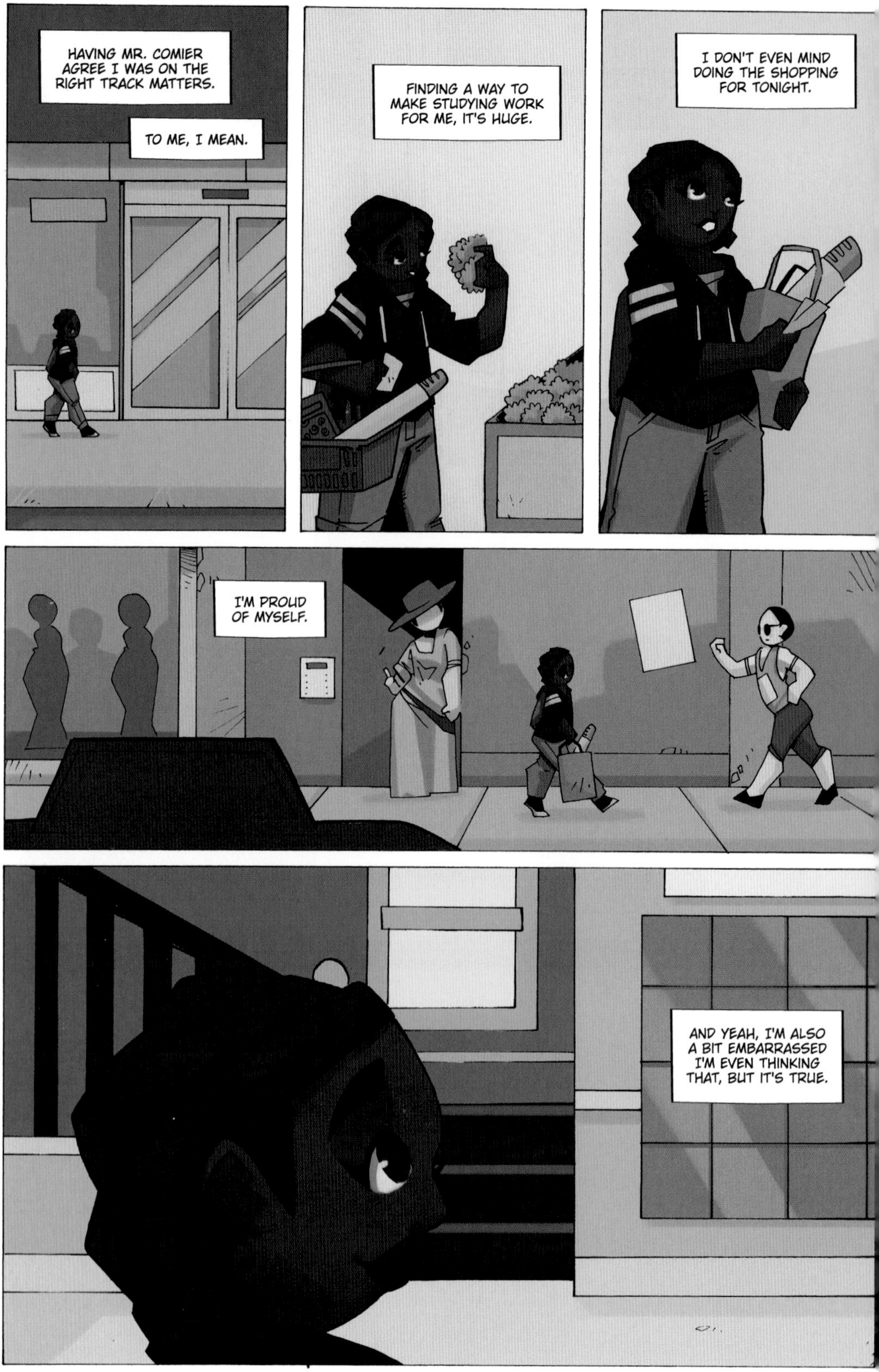
HAVING MR. COMIER AGREE I WAS ON THE RIGHT TRACK MATTERS.
TO ME, I MEAN.
FINDING A WAY TO MAKE STUDYING WORK FOR ME, IT'S HUGE.
I DON'T EVEN MIND DOING THE SHOPPING FOR TONIGHT.
I'M PROUD OF MYSELF.
AND YEAH, I'M ALSO A BIT EMBARRASSED I'M EVEN THINKING THAT, BUT IT'S TRUE.

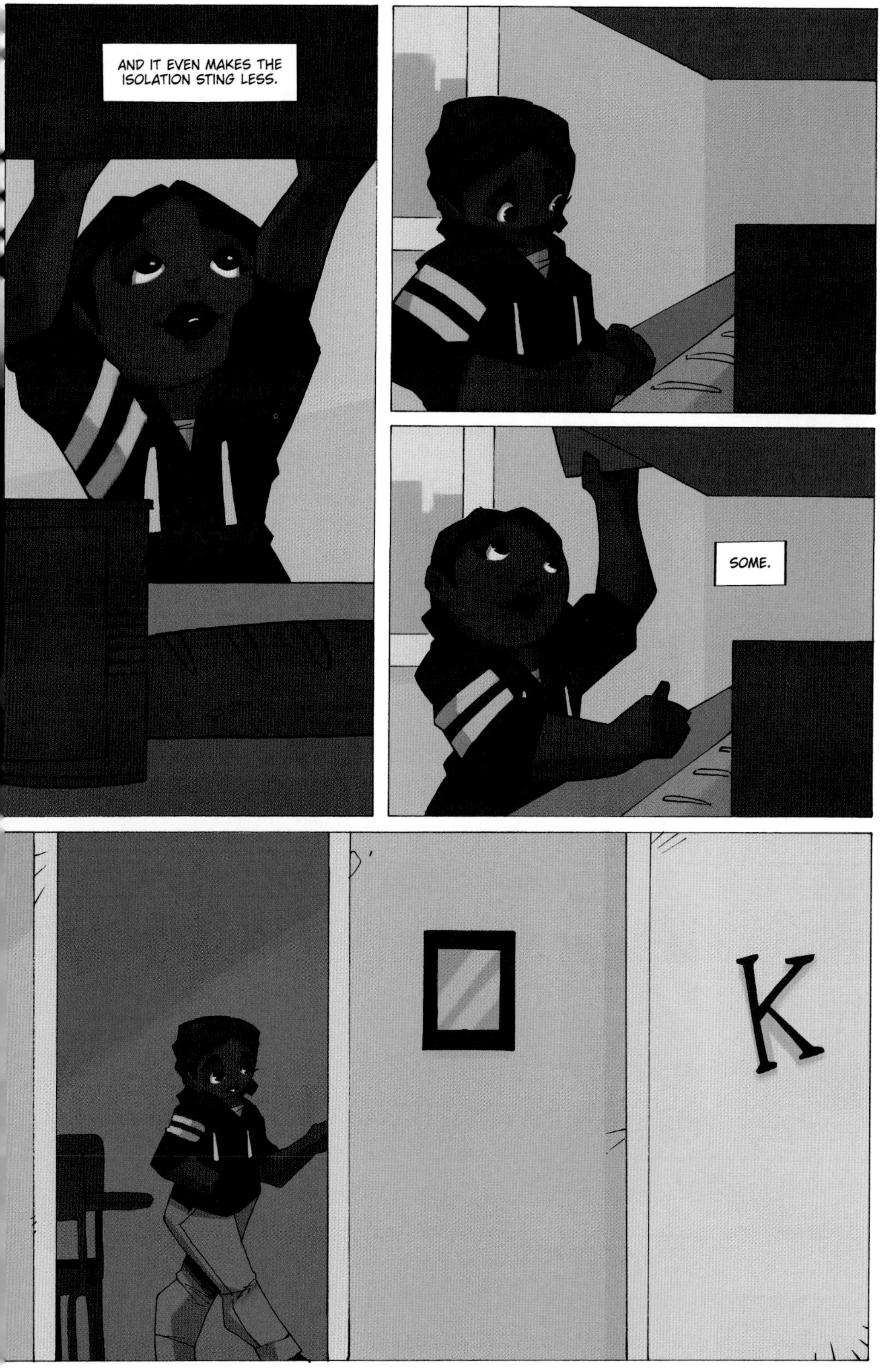
AND IT EVEN MAKES THE ISOLATION STING LESS.
SOME.
K

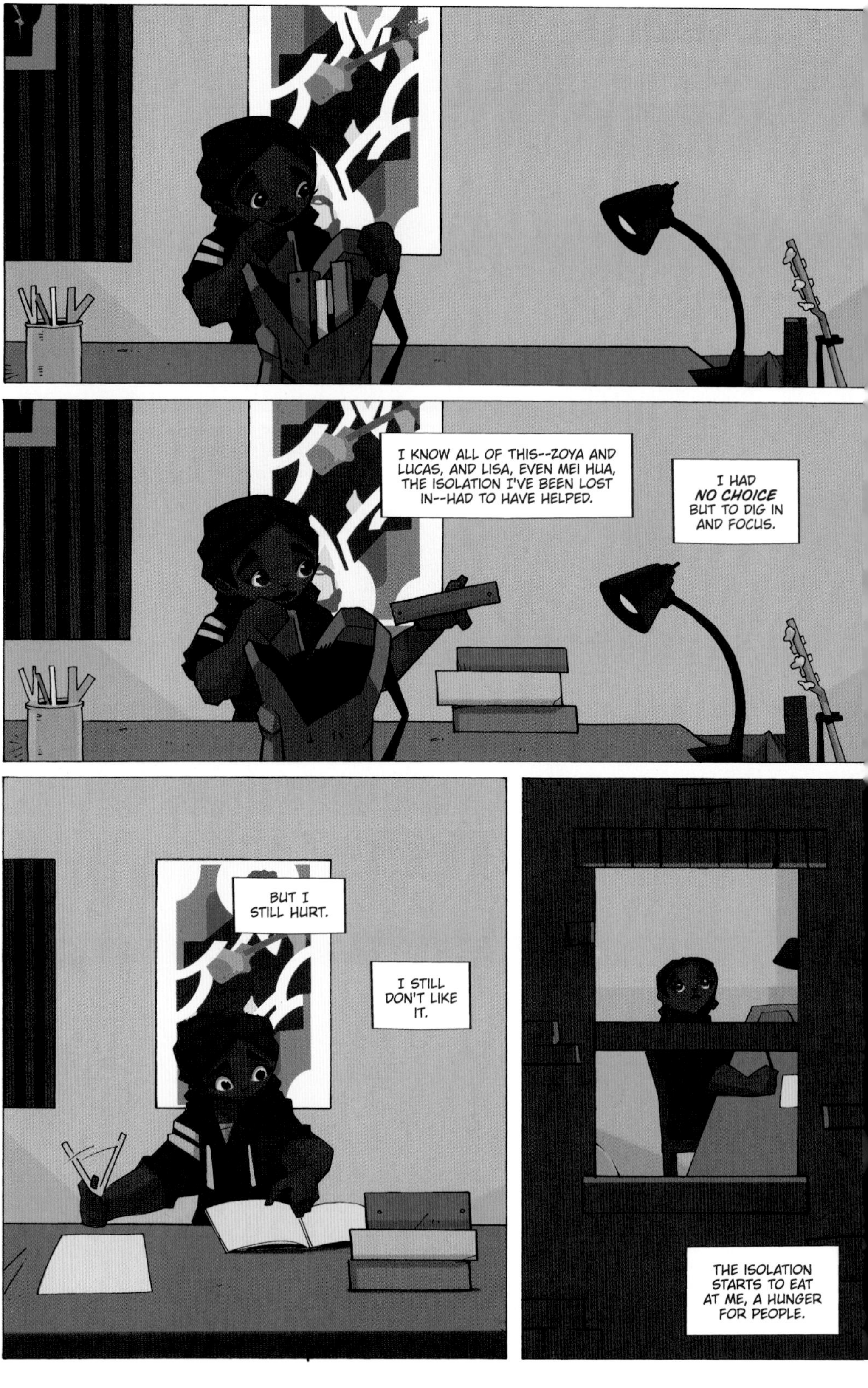

I KNOW ALL OF THIS--ZOYA AND LUCAS, AND LISA, EVEN MEI HUA, THE ISOLATION I'VE BEEN LOST IN--HAD TO HAVE HELPED.
I HAD **NO CHOICE** BUT TO DIG IN AND FOCUS.
BUT I STILL HURT.
I STILL DON'T LIKE IT.
THE ISOLATION STARTS TO EAT AT ME, A HUNGER FOR PEOPLE.

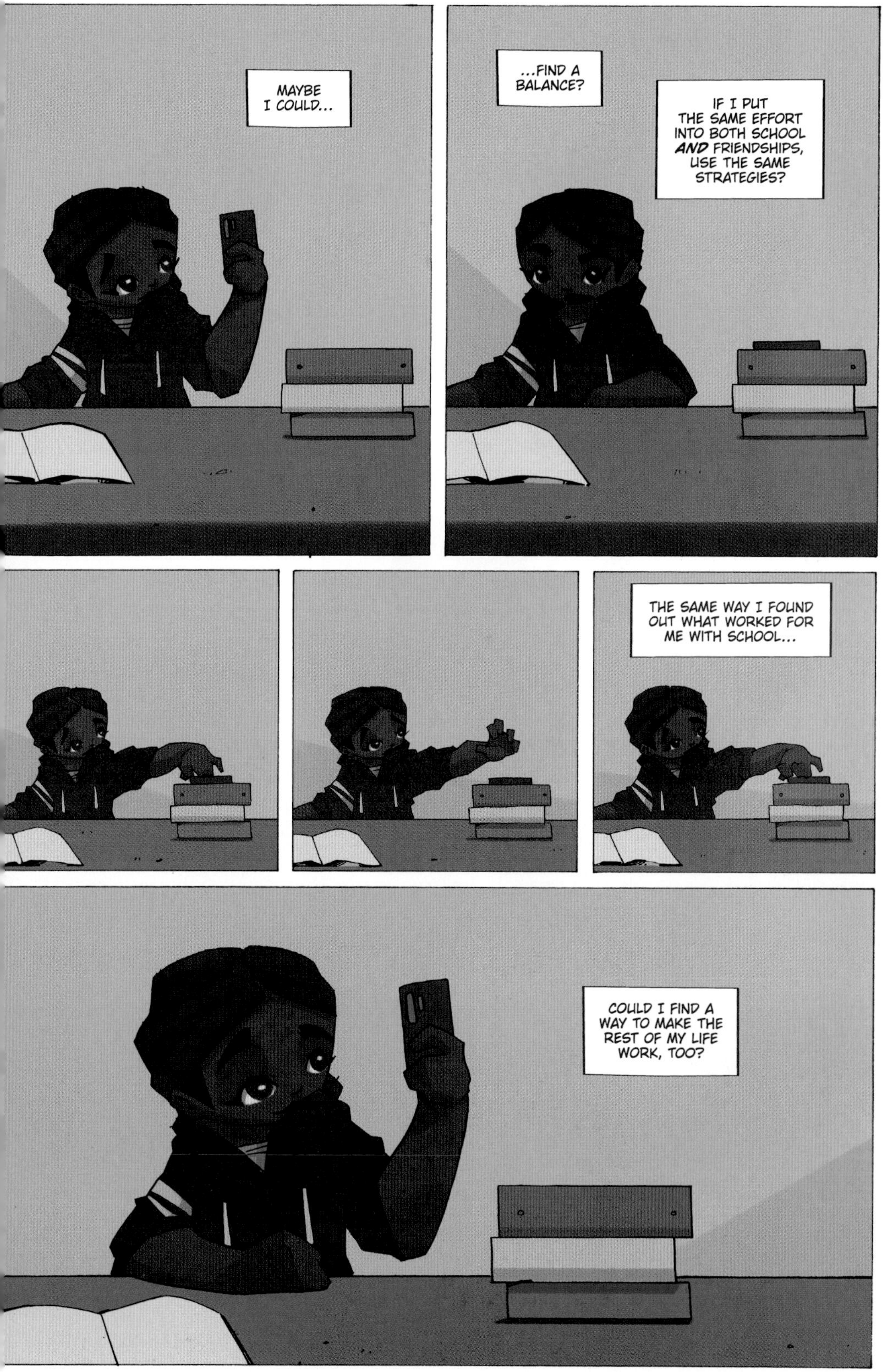
MAYBE I COULD...
...FIND A BALANCE?
IF I PUT THE SAME EFFORT INTO BOTH SCHOOL *AND* FRIENDSHIPS, USE THE SAME STRATEGIES?
THE SAME WAY I FOUND OUT WHAT WORKED FOR ME WITH SCHOOL...
COULD I FIND A WAY TO MAKE THE REST OF MY LIFE WORK, TOO?

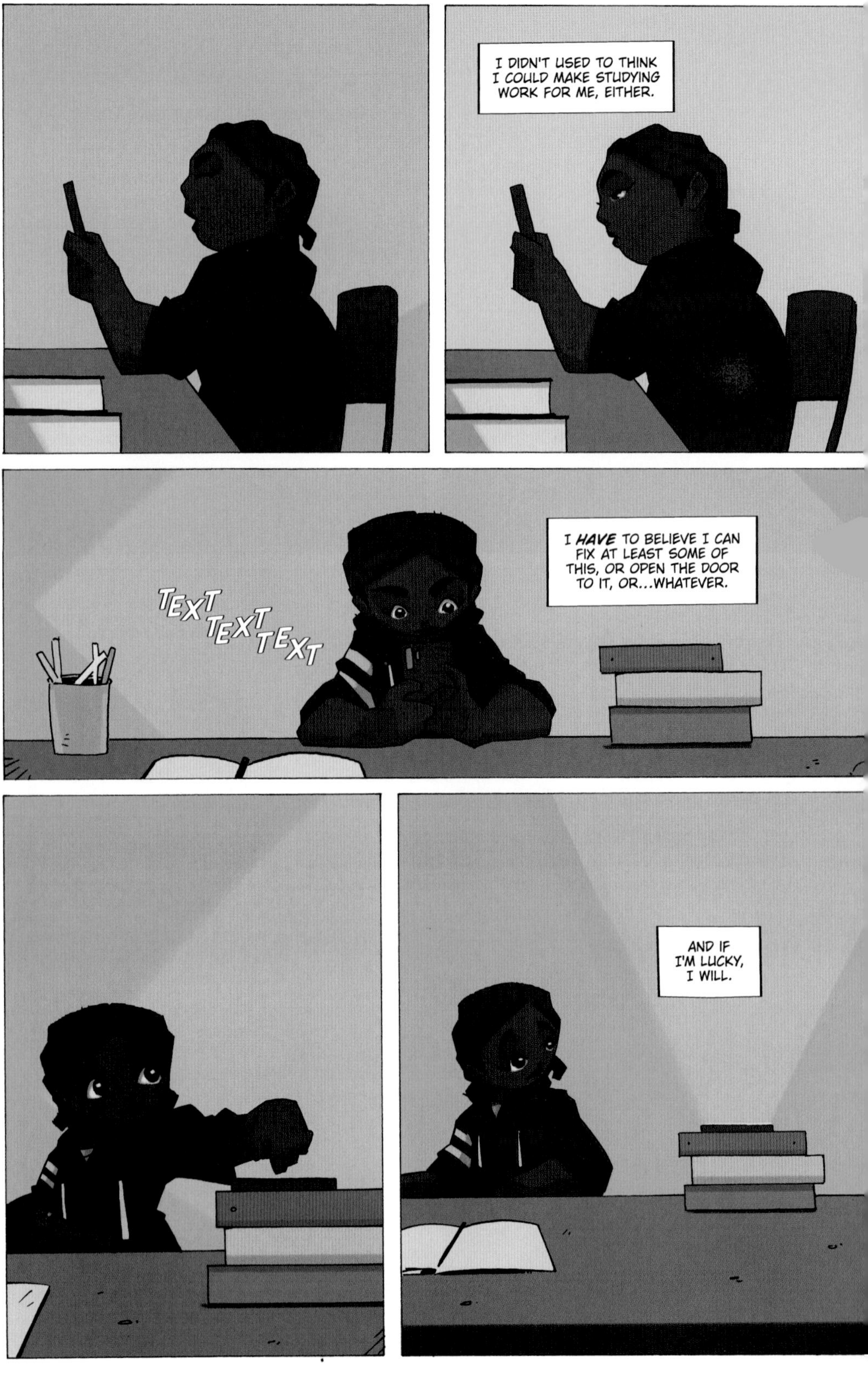
I DIDN'T USED TO THINK I COULD MAKE STUDYING WORK FOR ME, EITHER.
TEXT TEXT TEXT
I HAVE TO BELIEVE I CAN FIX AT LEAST SOME OF THIS, OR OPEN THE DOOR TO IT, OR...WHATEVER.
AND IF I'M LUCKY, I WILL.

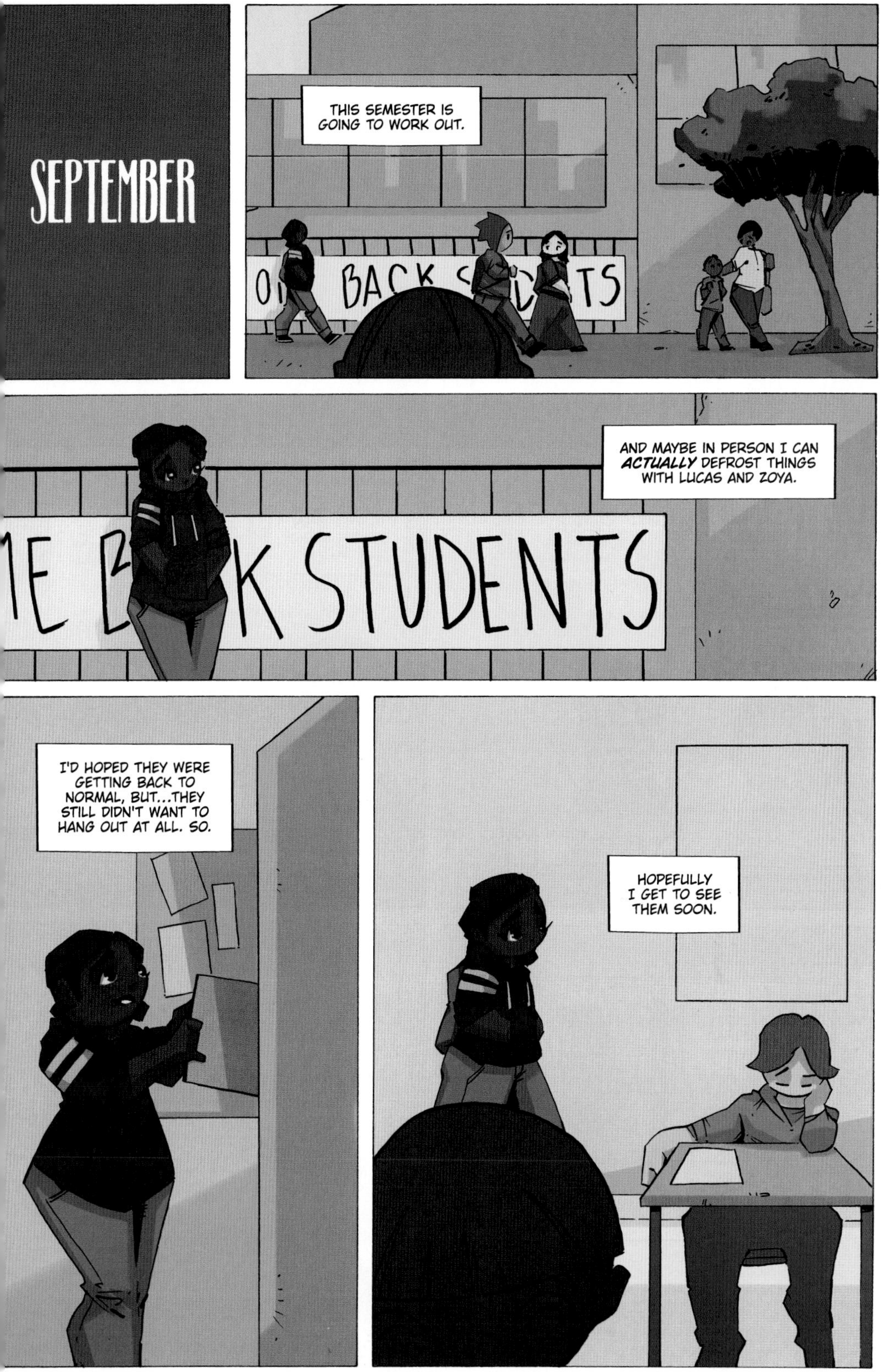
SEPTEMBER
THIS SEMESTER IS GOING TO WORK OUT.
AND MAYBE IN PERSON I CAN ACTUALLY DEFROST THINGS WITH LUCAS AND ZOYA.
I'D HOPED THEY WERE GETTING BACK TO NORMAL, BUT...THEY STILL DIDN'T WANT TO HANG OUT AT ALL. SO.
HOPEFULLY I GET TO SEE THEM SOON.

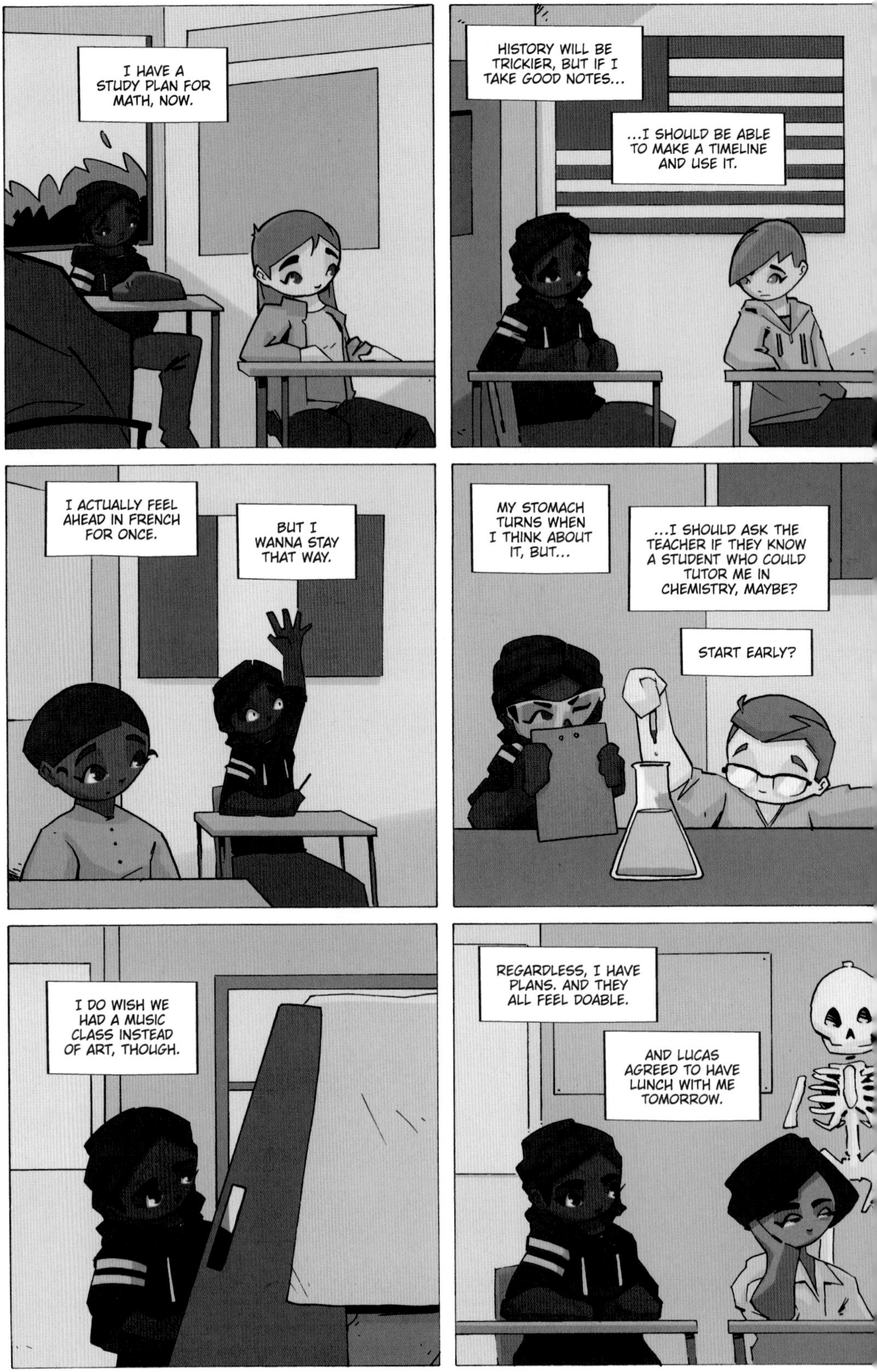
I HAVE A STUDY PLAN FOR MATH, NOW.
HISTORY WILL BE TRICKIER, BUT IF I TAKE GOOD NOTES...
...I SHOULD BE ABLE TO MAKE A TIMELINE AND USE IT.
I ACTUALLY FEEL AHEAD IN FRENCH FOR ONCE.
BUT I WANNA STAY THAT WAY.
MY STOMACH TURNS WHEN I THINK ABOUT IT, BUT...
...I SHOULD ASK THE TEACHER IF THEY KNOW A STUDENT WHO COULD TUTOR ME IN CHEMISTRY, MAYBE?
START EARLY?
I DO WISH WE HAD A MUSIC CLASS INSTEAD OF ART, THOUGH.
REGARDLESS, I HAVE PLANS. AND THEY ALL FEEL DOABLE.
AND LUCAS AGREED TO HAVE LUNCH WITH ME TOMORROW.

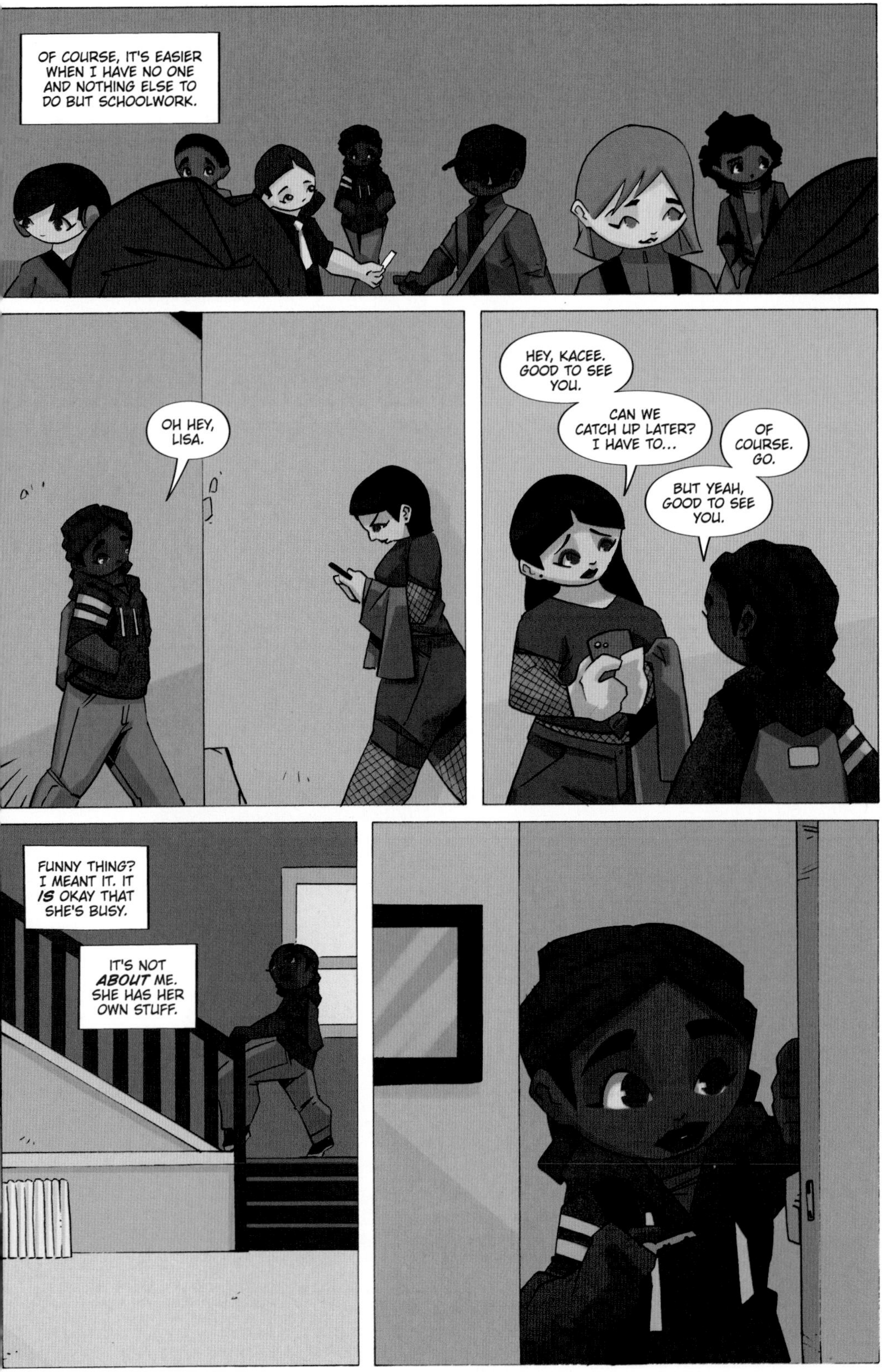
OF COURSE, IT'S EASIER WHEN I HAVE NO ONE AND NOTHING ELSE TO DO BUT SCHOOLWORK.
OH HEY, LISA.
HEY, KACEE. GOOD TO SEE YOU.
CAN WE CATCH UP LATER? I HAVE TO...
OF COURSE. GO.
BUT YEAH, GOOD TO SEE YOU.
FUNNY THING? I MEANT IT. IT *IS* OKAY THAT SHE'S BUSY.
IT'S NOT *ABOUT* ME. SHE HAS HER OWN STUFF.

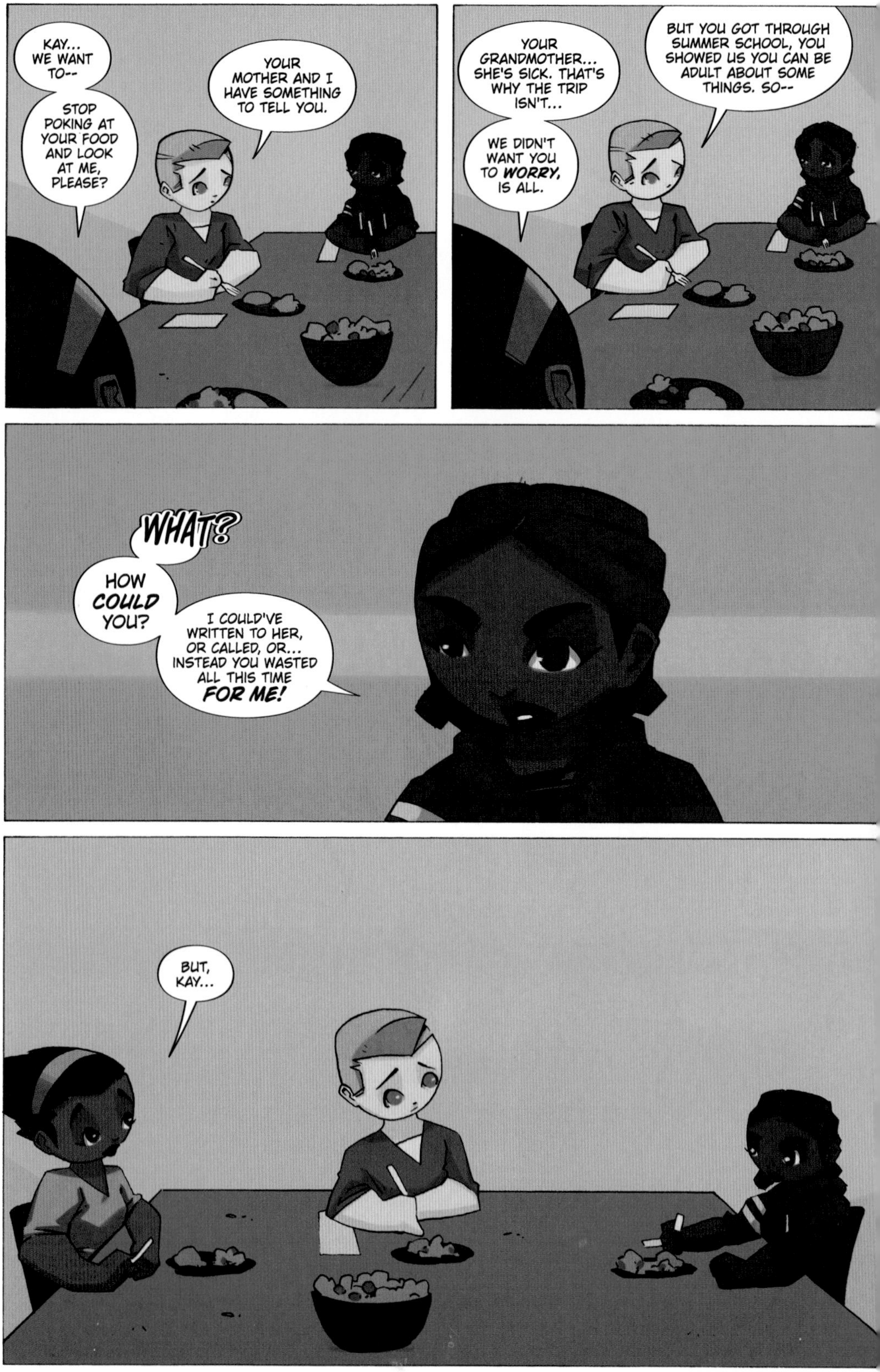
KAY... WE WANT TO--
STOP POKING AT YOUR FOOD AND LOOK AT ME, PLEASE?
YOUR MOTHER AND I HAVE SOMETHING TO TELL YOU.
YOUR GRANDMOTHER... SHE'S SICK. THAT'S WHY THE TRIP ISN'T...
WE DIDN'T WANT YOU TO WORRY, IS ALL.
BUT YOU GOT THROUGH SUMMER SCHOOL, YOU SHOWED US YOU CAN BE ADULT ABOUT SOME THINGS. SO--
WHAT?
HOW COULD YOU?
I COULD'VE WRITTEN TO HER, OR CALLED, OR... INSTEAD YOU WASTED ALL THIS TIME FOR ME!
BUT, KAY...

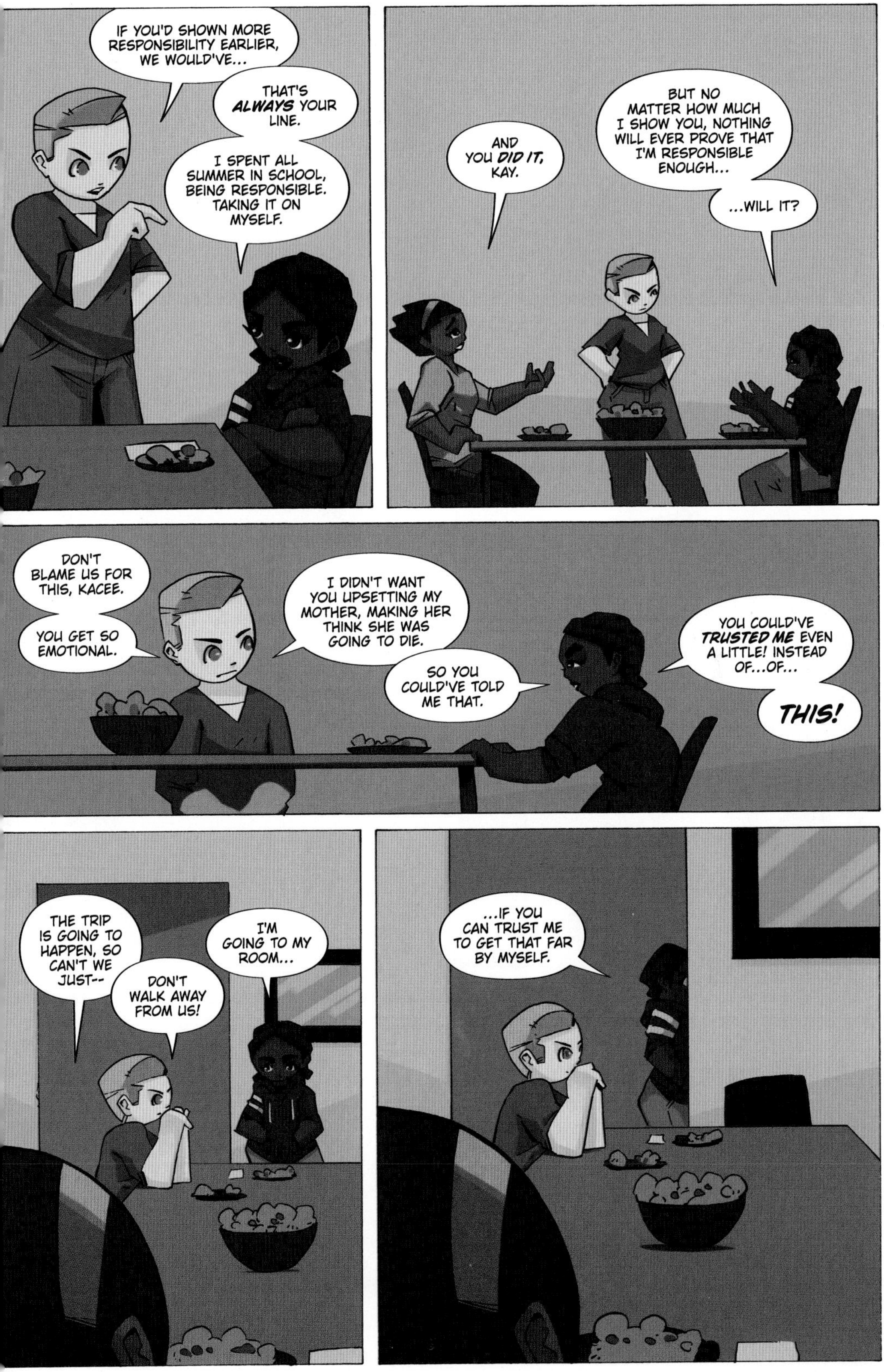
IF YOU'D SHOWN MORE RESPONSIBILITY EARLIER, WE WOULD'VE...
THAT'S *ALWAYS* YOUR LINE.
I SPENT ALL SUMMER IN SCHOOL, BEING RESPONSIBLE. TAKING IT ON MYSELF.
AND YOU *DID IT,* KAY.
BUT NO MATTER HOW MUCH I SHOW YOU, NOTHING WILL EVER PROVE THAT I'M RESPONSIBLE ENOUGH...
...WILL IT?
DON'T BLAME US FOR THIS, KACEE.
YOU GET SO EMOTIONAL.
I DIDN'T WANT YOU UPSETTING MY MOTHER, MAKING HER THINK SHE WAS GOING TO DIE.
SO YOU COULD'VE TOLD ME THAT.
YOU COULD'VE *TRUSTED ME* EVEN A LITTLE! INSTEAD OF...OF...
THIS!
THE TRIP IS GOING TO HAPPEN, SO CAN'T WE JUST--
DON'T WALK AWAY FROM US!
I'M GOING TO MY ROOM...
...IF YOU CAN TRUST ME TO GET THAT FAR BY MYSELF.

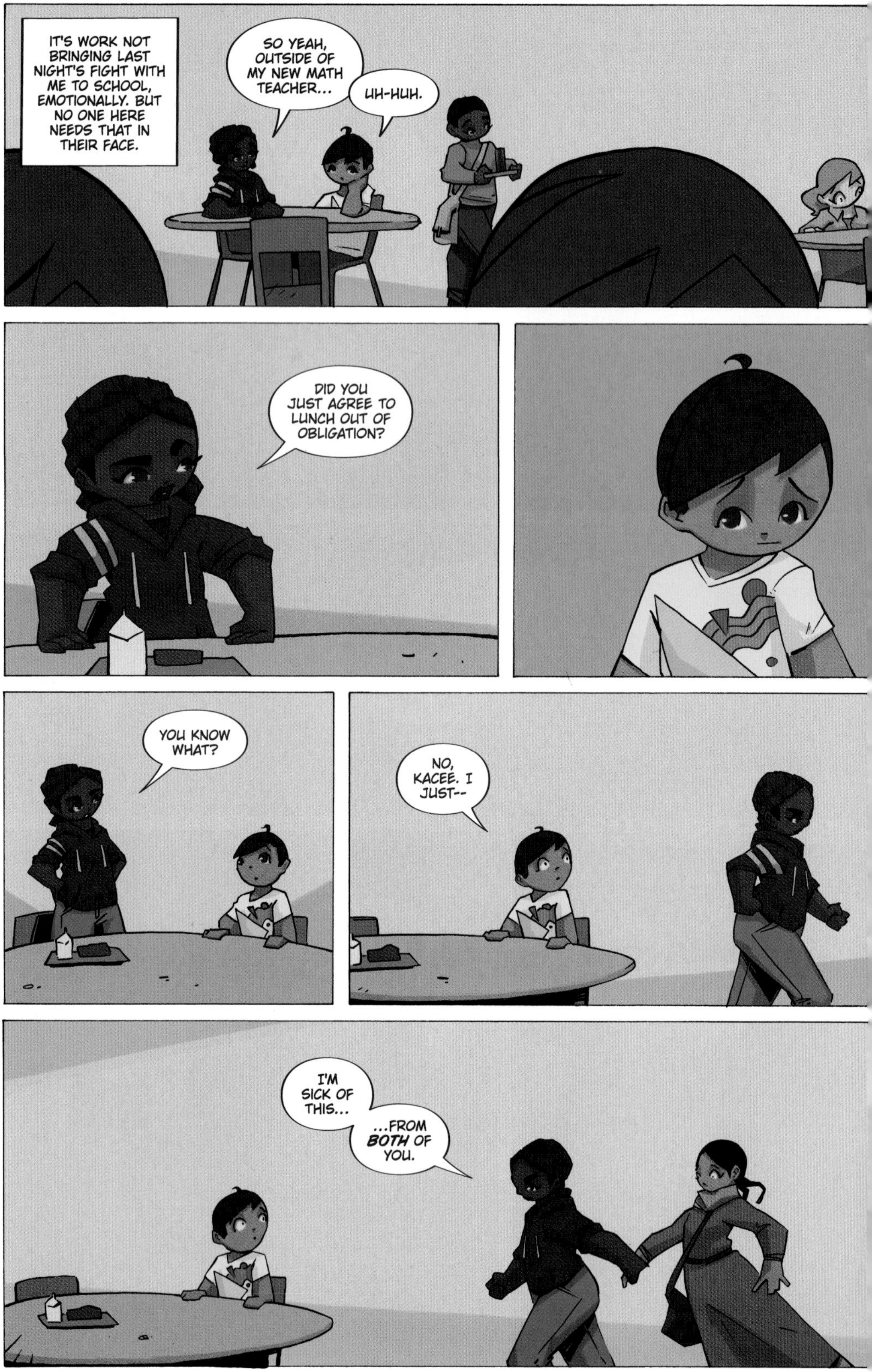
IT'S WORK NOT BRINGING LAST NIGHT'S FIGHT WITH ME TO SCHOOL, EMOTIONALLY. BUT NO ONE HERE NEEDS THAT IN THEIR FACE.
SO YEAH, OUTSIDE OF MY NEW MATH TEACHER...
UH-HUH.
DID YOU JUST AGREE TO LUNCH OUT OF OBLIGATION?
YOU KNOW WHAT?
NO, KACEE. I JUST--
I'M SICK OF THIS...
...FROM *BOTH* OF YOU.

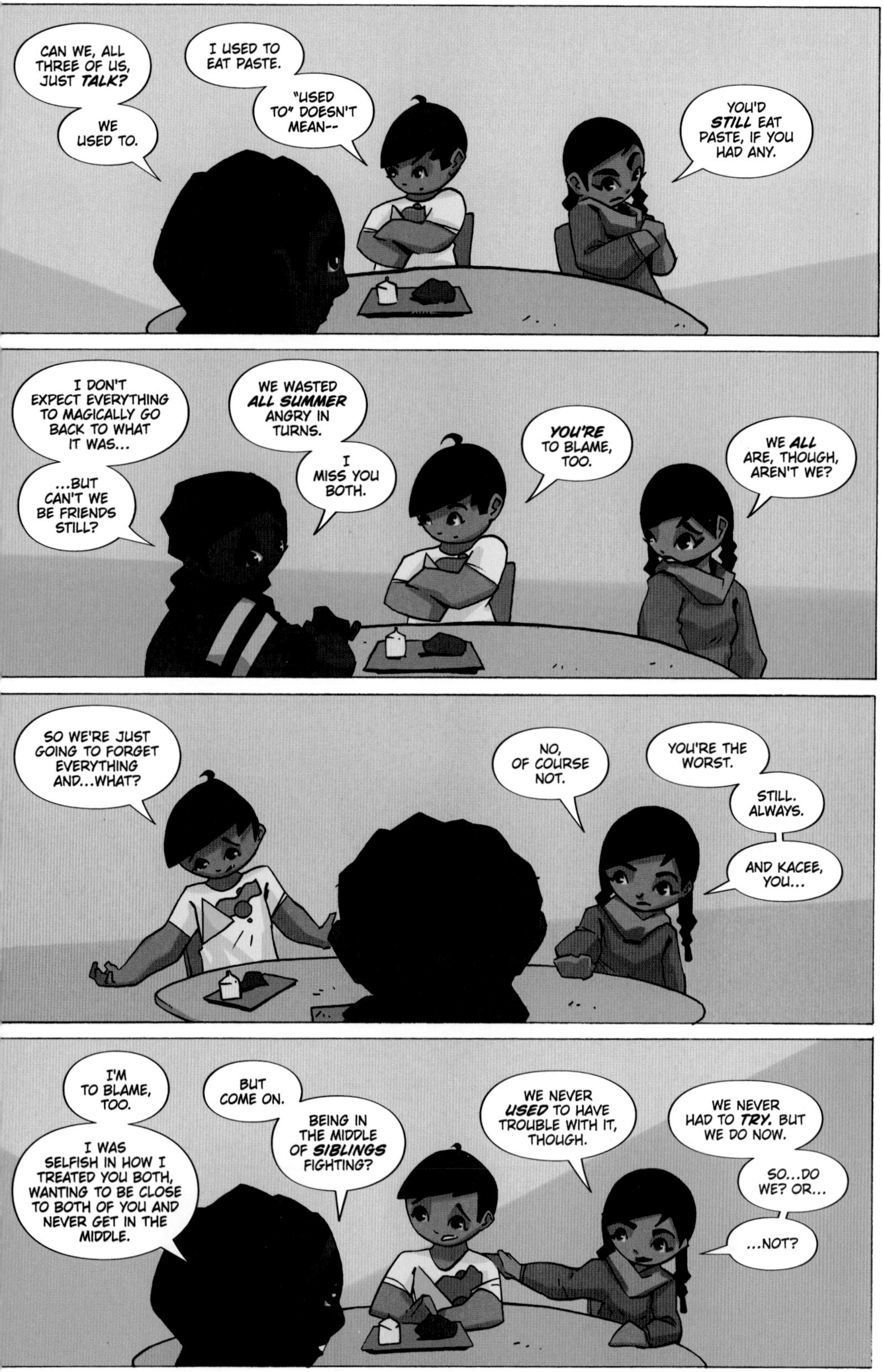

CAN WE, ALL THREE OF US, JUST *TALK?*
WE USED TO.
I USED TO EAT PASTE.
"USED TO" DOESN'T MEAN--
YOU'D *STILL* EAT PASTE, IF YOU HAD ANY.
I DON'T EXPECT EVERYTHING TO MAGICALLY GO BACK TO WHAT IT WAS...
...BUT CAN'T WE BE FRIENDS STILL?
WE WASTED *ALL SUMMER* ANGRY IN TURNS.
I MISS YOU BOTH.
YOU'RE TO BLAME, TOO.
WE *ALL* ARE, THOUGH, AREN'T WE?
SO WE'RE JUST GOING TO FORGET EVERYTHING AND...WHAT?
NO, OF COURSE NOT.
YOU'RE THE WORST.
STILL. ALWAYS.
AND KACEE, YOU...
I'M TO BLAME, TOO.
I WAS SELFISH IN HOW I TREATED YOU BOTH, WANTING TO BE CLOSE TO BOTH OF YOU AND NEVER GET IN THE MIDDLE.
BUT COME ON.
BEING IN THE MIDDLE OF *SIBLINGS* FIGHTING?
WE NEVER *USED* TO HAVE TROUBLE WITH IT, THOUGH.
WE NEVER HAD TO *TRY.* BUT WE DO NOW.
SO...DO WE? OR...
...NOT?

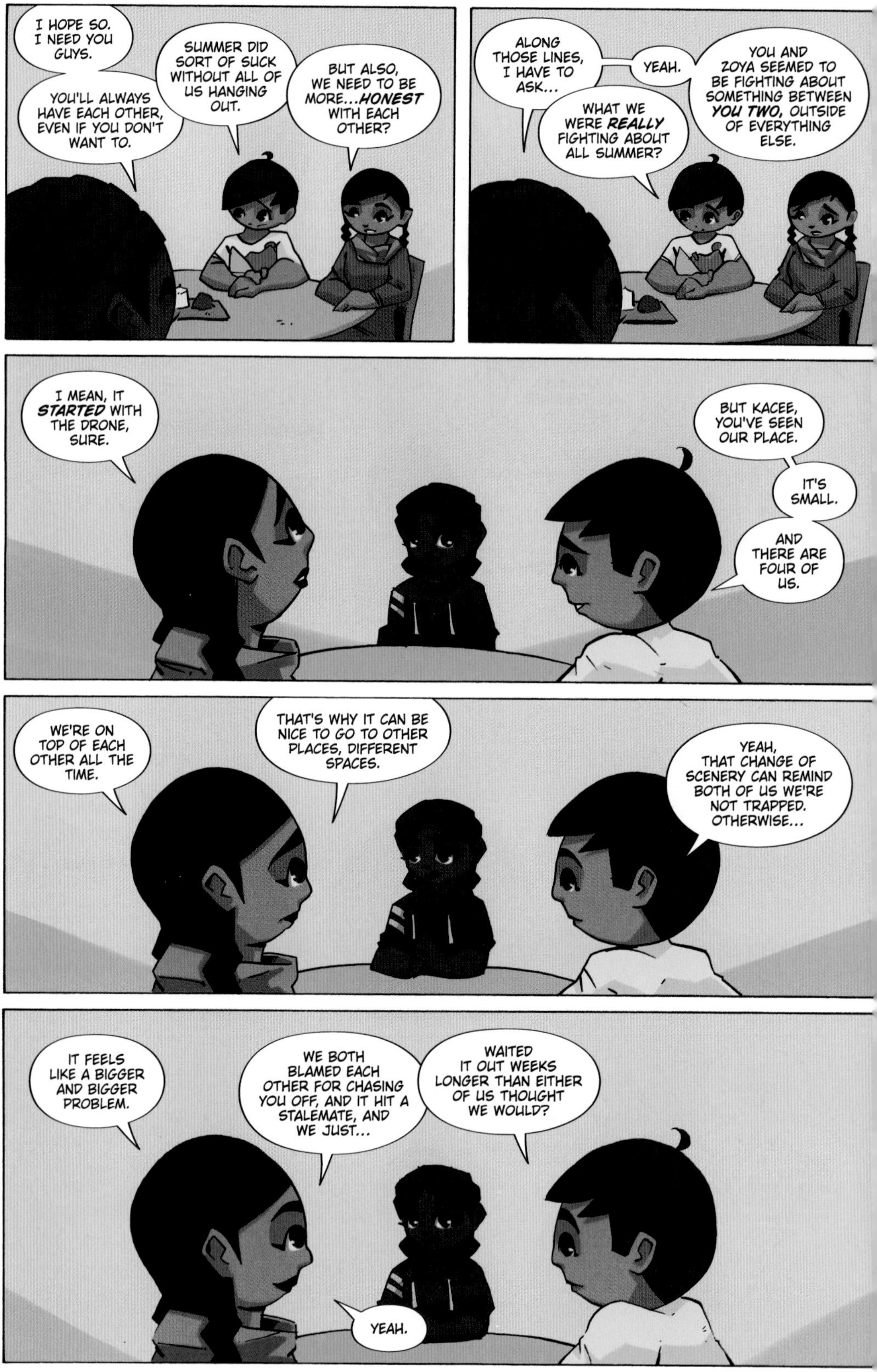
I HOPE SO. I NEED YOU GUYS.
YOU'LL ALWAYS HAVE EACH OTHER, EVEN IF YOU DON'T WANT TO.
SUMMER DID SORT OF SUCK WITHOUT ALL OF US HANGING OUT.
BUT ALSO, WE NEED TO BE MORE...**HONEST** WITH EACH OTHER?
ALONG THOSE LINES, I HAVE TO ASK...
WHAT WE WERE **REALLY** FIGHTING ABOUT ALL SUMMER?
YEAH.
YOU AND ZOYA SEEMED TO BE FIGHTING ABOUT SOMETHING BETWEEN **YOU TWO,** OUTSIDE OF EVERYTHING ELSE.
I MEAN, IT **STARTED** WITH THE DRONE, SURE.
BUT KACEE, YOU'VE SEEN OUR PLACE.
IT'S SMALL.
AND THERE ARE FOUR OF US.
WE'RE ON TOP OF EACH OTHER ALL THE TIME.
THAT'S WHY IT CAN BE NICE TO GO TO OTHER PLACES, DIFFERENT SPACES.
YEAH, THAT CHANGE OF SCENERY CAN REMIND BOTH OF US WE'RE NOT TRAPPED. OTHERWISE...
IT FEELS LIKE A BIGGER AND BIGGER PROBLEM.
WE BOTH BLAMED EACH OTHER FOR CHASING YOU OFF, AND IT HIT A STALEMATE, AND WE JUST...
WAITED IT OUT WEEKS LONGER THAN EITHER OF US THOUGHT WE WOULD?
YEAH.

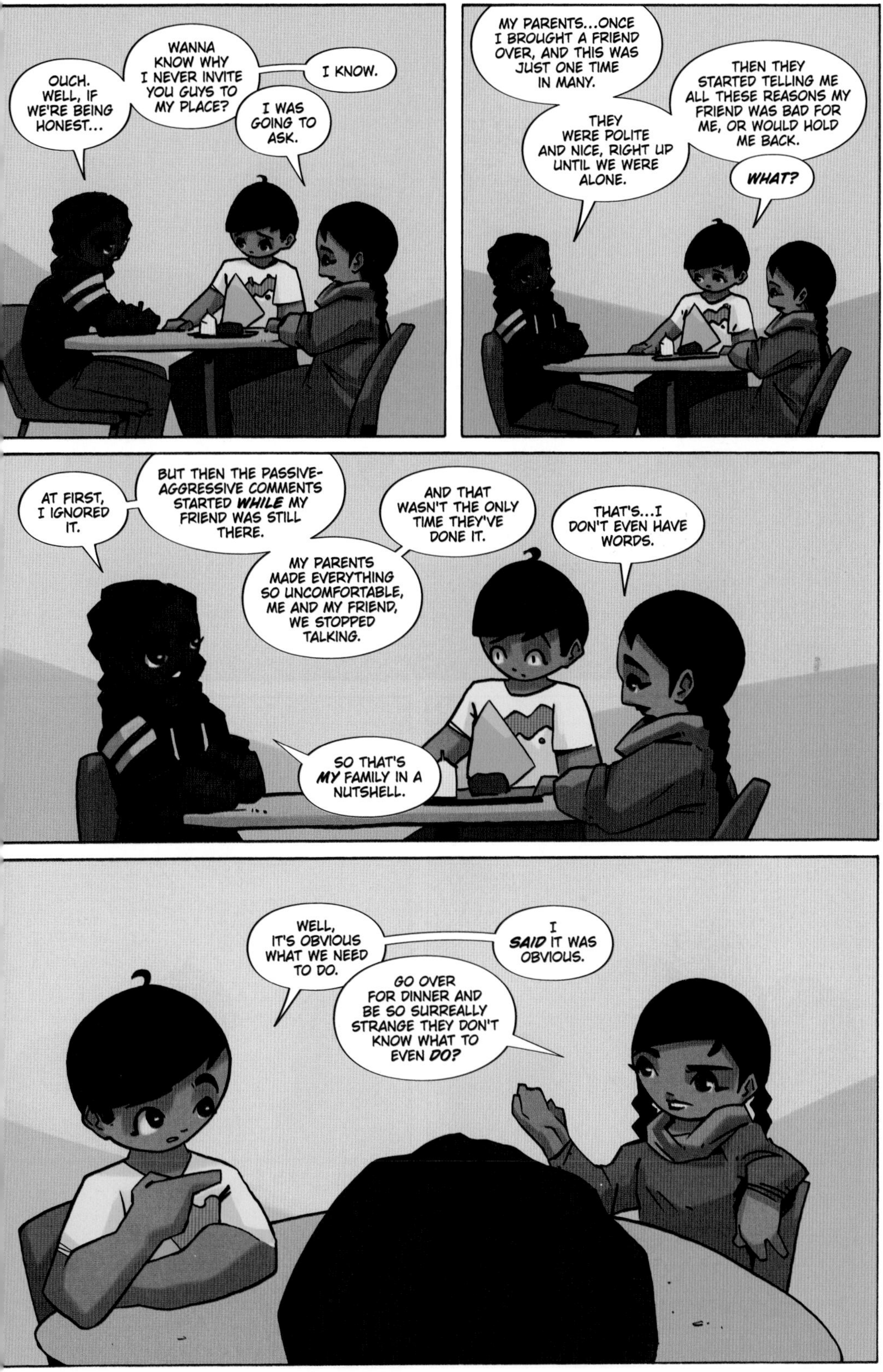
OUCH. WELL, IF WE'RE BEING HONEST...
WANNA KNOW WHY I NEVER INVITE YOU GUYS TO MY PLACE?
I KNOW.
I WAS GOING TO ASK.
MY PARENTS...ONCE I BROUGHT A FRIEND OVER, AND THIS WAS JUST ONE TIME IN MANY.
THEY WERE POLITE AND NICE, RIGHT UP UNTIL WE WERE ALONE.
THEN THEY STARTED TELLING ME ALL THESE REASONS MY FRIEND WAS BAD FOR ME, OR WOULD HOLD ME BACK.
WHAT?
AT FIRST, I IGNORED IT.
BUT THEN THE PASSIVE-AGGRESSIVE COMMENTS STARTED ***WHILE*** MY FRIEND WAS STILL THERE.
AND THAT WASN'T THE ONLY TIME THEY'VE DONE IT.
MY PARENTS MADE EVERYTHING SO UNCOMFORTABLE, ME AND MY FRIEND, WE STOPPED TALKING.
THAT'S...I DON'T EVEN HAVE WORDS.
SO THAT'S ***MY*** FAMILY IN A NUTSHELL.
WELL, IT'S OBVIOUS WHAT WE NEED TO DO.
I ***SAID*** IT WAS OBVIOUS.
GO OVER FOR DINNER AND BE SO SURREALLY STRANGE THEY DON'T KNOW WHAT TO EVEN ***DO?***

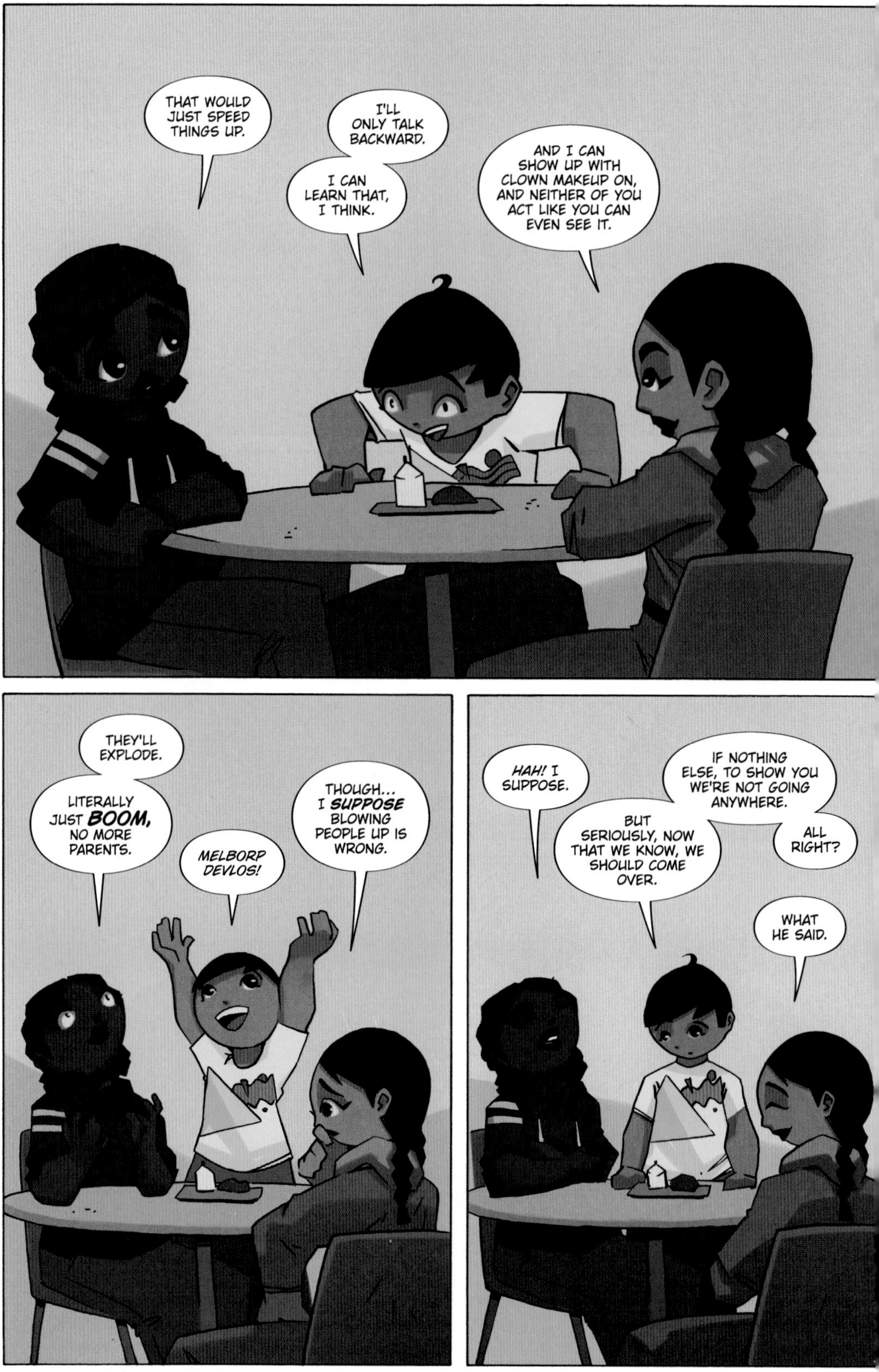
THAT WOULD JUST SPEED THINGS UP.
I'LL ONLY TALK BACKWARD.
I CAN LEARN THAT, I THINK.
AND I CAN SHOW UP WITH CLOWN MAKEUP ON, AND NEITHER OF YOU ACT LIKE YOU CAN EVEN SEE IT.
THEY'LL EXPLODE.
LITERALLY JUST BOOM, NO MORE PARENTS.
MELBORP DEVLOS!
THOUGH... I SUPPOSE BLOWING PEOPLE UP IS WRONG.
HAH! I SUPPOSE.
IF NOTHING ELSE, TO SHOW YOU WE'RE NOT GOING ANYWHERE.
BUT SERIOUSLY, NOW THAT WE KNOW, WE SHOULD COME OVER.
ALL RIGHT?
WHAT HE SAID.

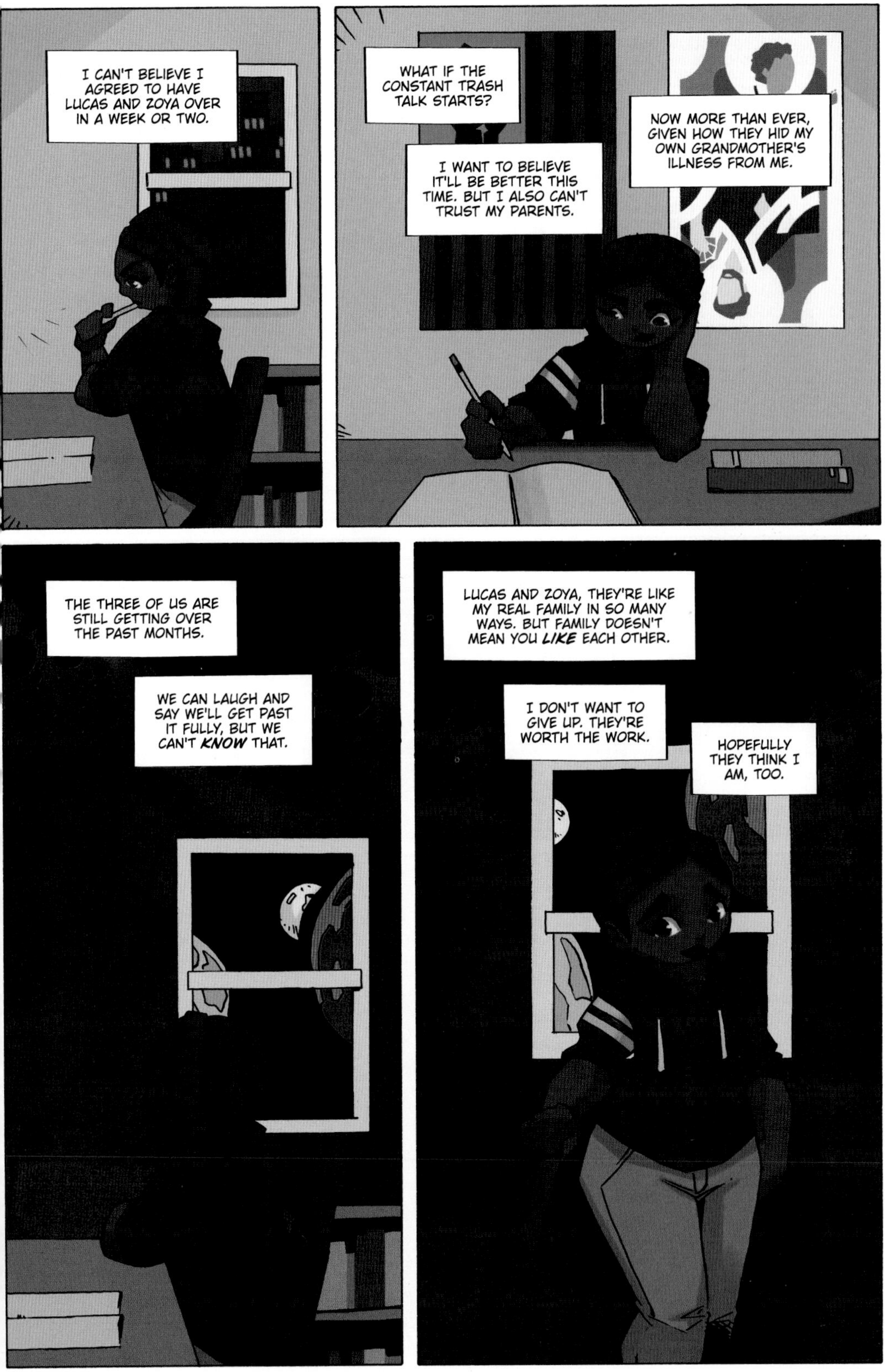
I CAN'T BELIEVE I AGREED TO HAVE LUCAS AND ZOYA OVER IN A WEEK OR TWO.
WHAT IF THE CONSTANT TRASH TALK STARTS?
I WANT TO BELIEVE IT'LL BE BETTER THIS TIME. BUT I ALSO CAN'T TRUST MY PARENTS.
NOW MORE THAN EVER, GIVEN HOW THEY HID MY OWN GRANDMOTHER'S ILLNESS FROM ME.
THE THREE OF US ARE STILL GETTING OVER THE PAST MONTHS.
WE CAN LAUGH AND SAY WE'LL GET PAST IT FULLY, BUT WE CAN'T *KNOW* THAT.
LUCAS AND ZOYA, THEY'RE LIKE MY REAL FAMILY IN SO MANY WAYS. BUT FAMILY DOESN'T MEAN YOU *LIKE* EACH OTHER.
I DON'T WANT TO GIVE UP. THEY'RE WORTH THE WORK.
HOPEFULLY THEY THINK I AM, TOO.

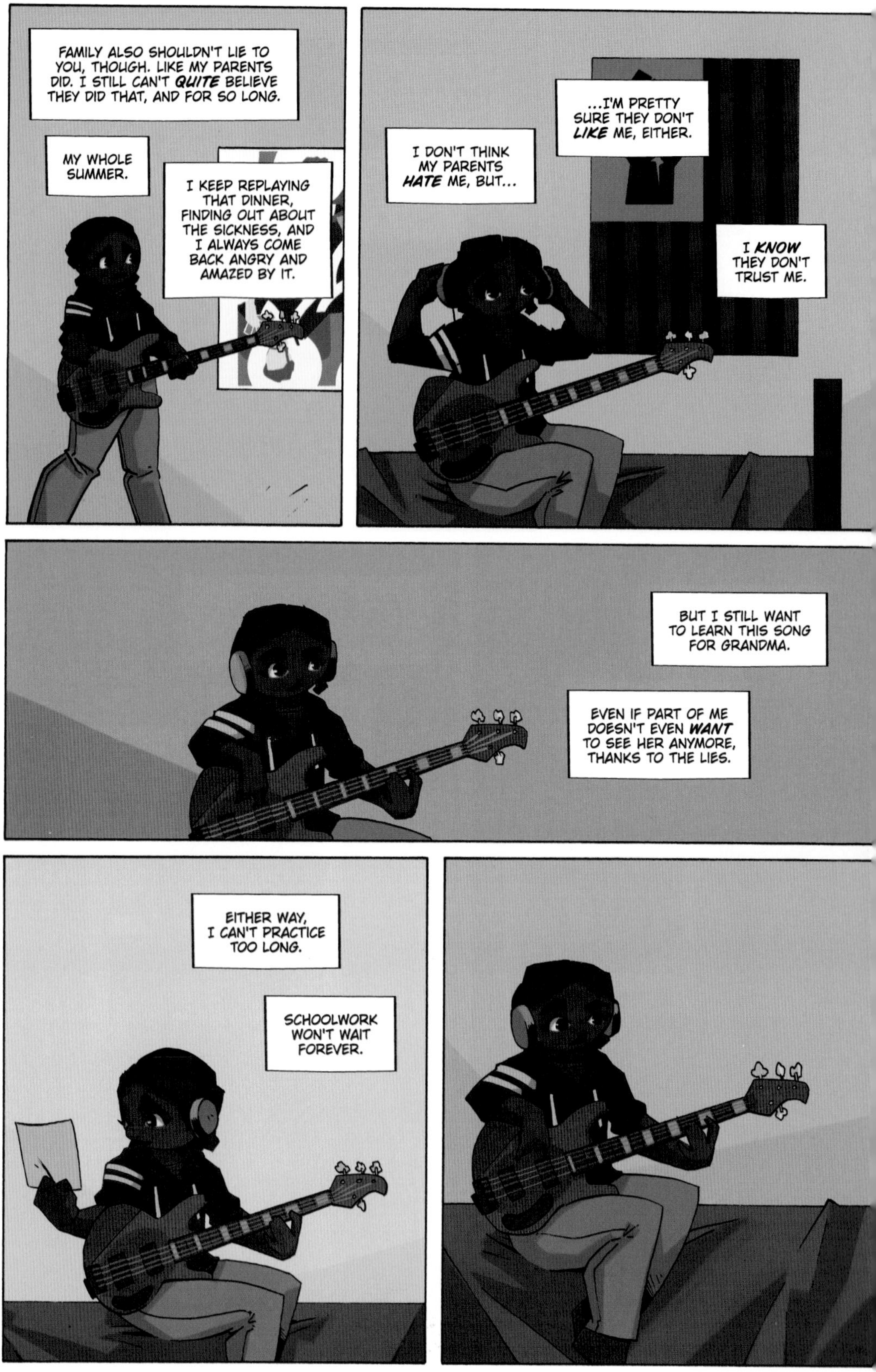
FAMILY ALSO SHOULDN'T LIE TO YOU, THOUGH. LIKE MY PARENTS DID. I STILL CAN'T *QUITE* BELIEVE THEY DID THAT, AND FOR SO LONG.
MY WHOLE SUMMER.
I KEEP REPLAYING THAT DINNER, FINDING OUT ABOUT THE SICKNESS, AND I ALWAYS COME BACK ANGRY AND AMAZED BY IT.
I DON'T THINK MY PARENTS *HATE* ME, BUT...
...I'M PRETTY SURE THEY DON'T *LIKE* ME, EITHER.
I *KNOW* THEY DON'T TRUST ME.
BUT I STILL WANT TO LEARN THIS SONG FOR GRANDMA.
EVEN IF PART OF ME DOESN'T EVEN *WANT* TO SEE HER ANYMORE, THANKS TO THE LIES.
EITHER WAY, I CAN'T PRACTICE TOO LONG.
SCHOOLWORK WON'T WAIT FOREVER.

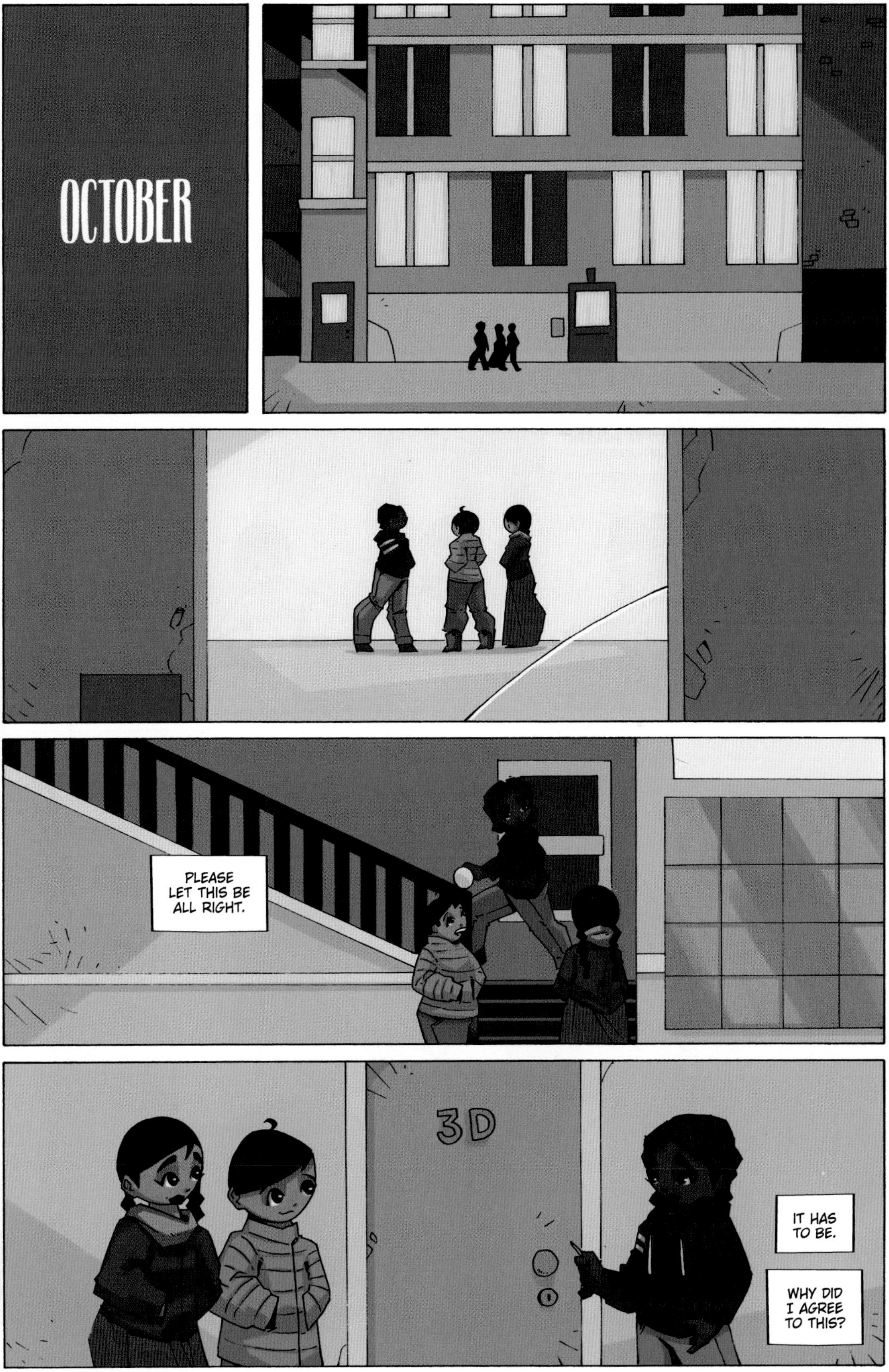
OCTOBER
PLEASE LET THIS BE ALL RIGHT.
3D
IT HAS TO BE.
WHY DID I AGREE TO THIS?

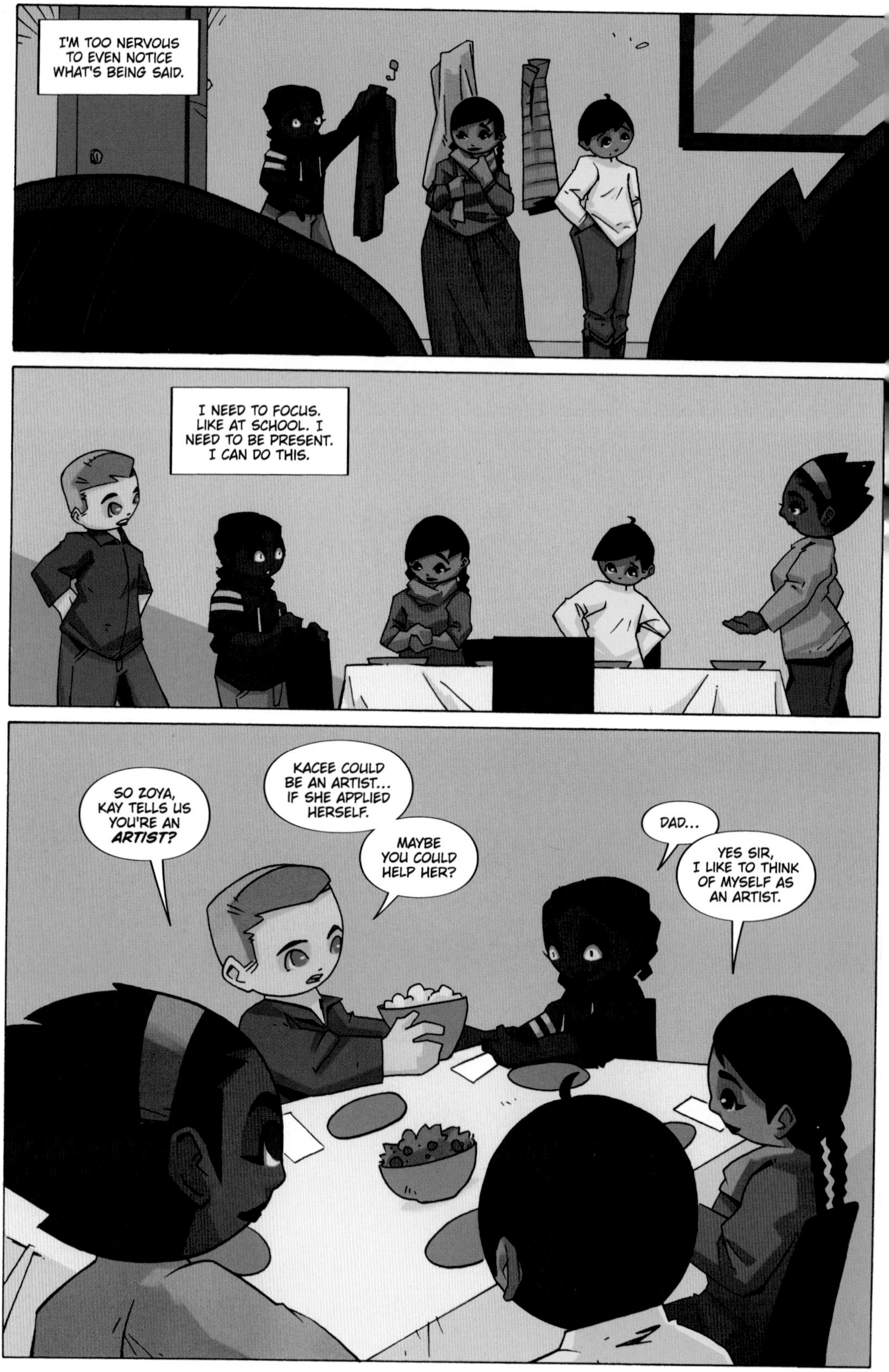
I'M TOO NERVOUS TO EVEN NOTICE WHAT'S BEING SAID.
I NEED TO FOCUS. LIKE AT SCHOOL. I NEED TO BE PRESENT. I CAN DO THIS.
SO ZOYA, KAY TELLS US YOU'RE AN *ARTIST?*
KACEE COULD BE AN ARTIST... IF SHE APPLIED HERSELF.
MAYBE YOU COULD HELP HER?
DAD...
YES SIR, I LIKE TO THINK OF MYSELF AS AN ARTIST.

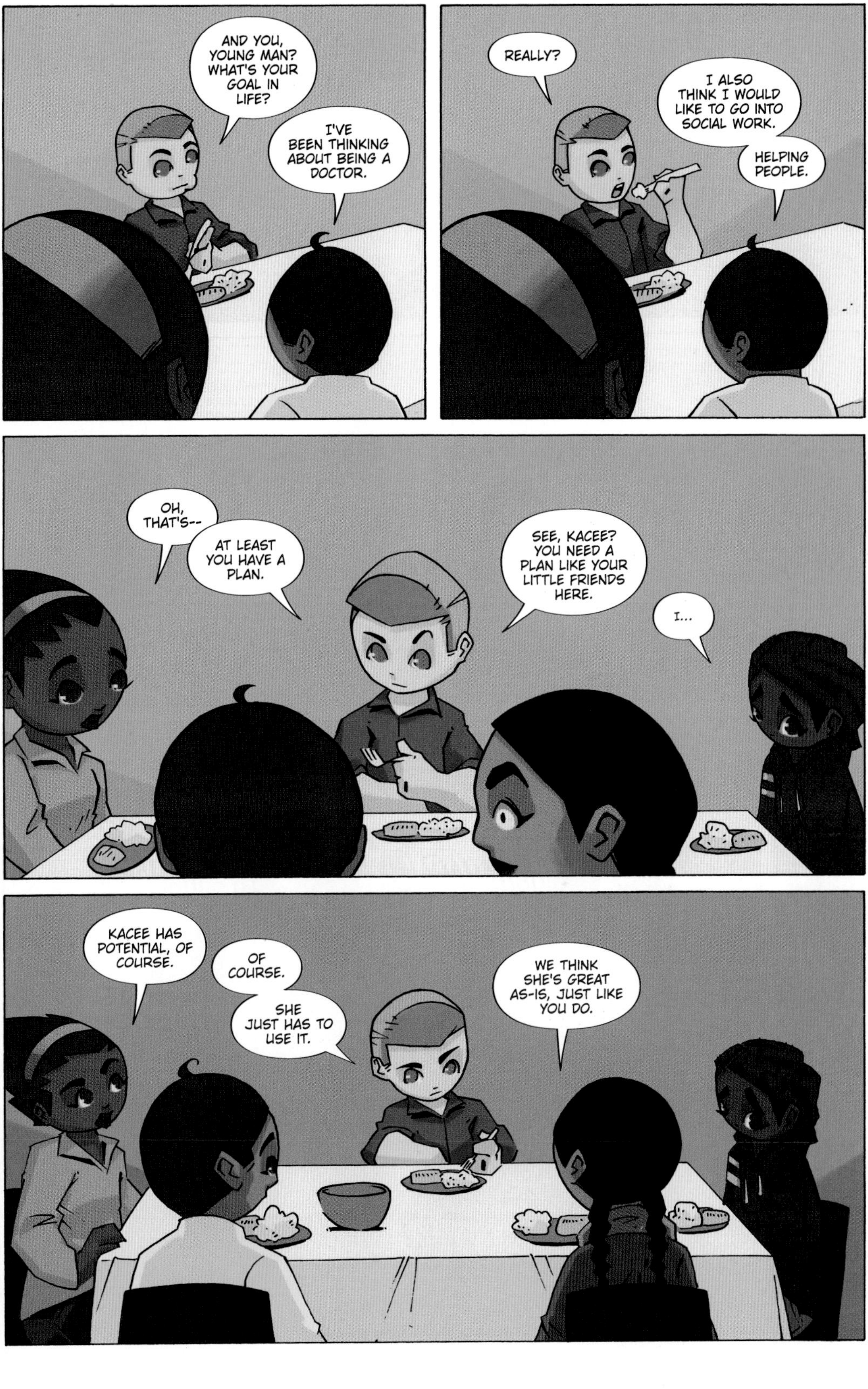
AND YOU, YOUNG MAN? WHAT'S YOUR GOAL IN LIFE?
I'VE BEEN THINKING ABOUT BEING A DOCTOR.
REALLY?
I ALSO THINK I WOULD LIKE TO GO INTO SOCIAL WORK.
HELPING PEOPLE.
OH, THAT'S--
AT LEAST YOU HAVE A PLAN.
SEE, KACEE? YOU NEED A PLAN LIKE YOUR LITTLE FRIENDS HERE.
I...
KACEE HAS POTENTIAL, OF COURSE.
OF COURSE.
SHE JUST HAS TO USE IT.
WE THINK SHE'S GREAT AS-IS, JUST LIKE YOU DO.

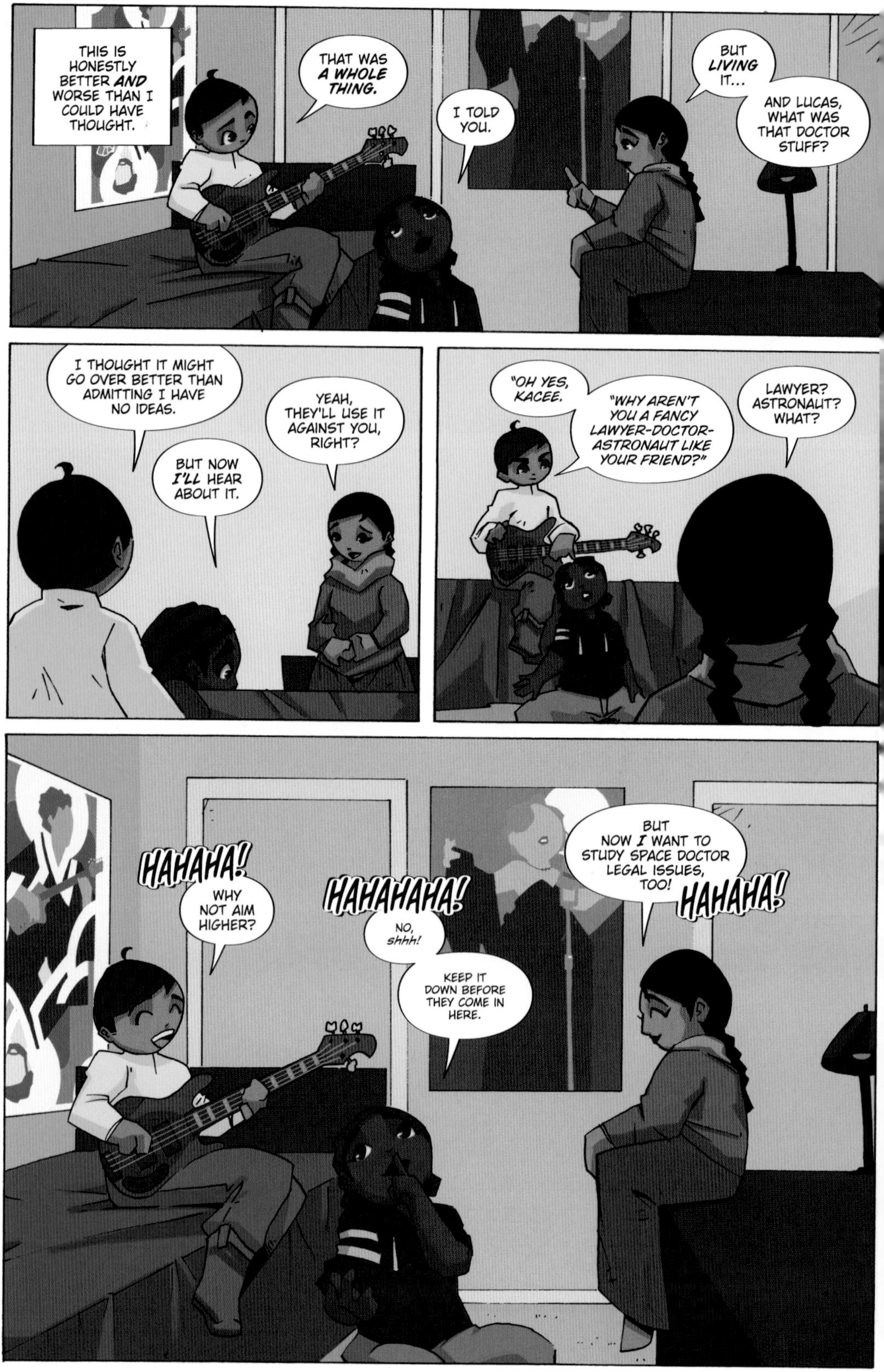
THIS IS HONESTLY BETTER AND WORSE THAN I COULD HAVE THOUGHT.
THAT WAS A WHOLE THING.
I TOLD YOU.
BUT LIVING IT...
AND LUCAS, WHAT WAS THAT DOCTOR STUFF?
I THOUGHT IT MIGHT GO OVER BETTER THAN ADMITTING I HAVE NO IDEAS.
BUT NOW I'LL HEAR ABOUT IT.
YEAH, THEY'LL USE IT AGAINST YOU, RIGHT?
"OH YES, KACEE.
"WHY AREN'T YOU A FANCY LAWYER-DOCTOR-ASTRONAUT LIKE YOUR FRIEND?"
LAWYER? ASTRONAUT? WHAT?
HAHAHA!
WHY NOT AIM HIGHER?
HAHAHAHA!
NO, shhh!
KEEP IT DOWN BEFORE THEY COME IN HERE.
BUT NOW I WANT TO STUDY SPACE DOCTOR LEGAL ISSUES, TOO!
HAHAHA!

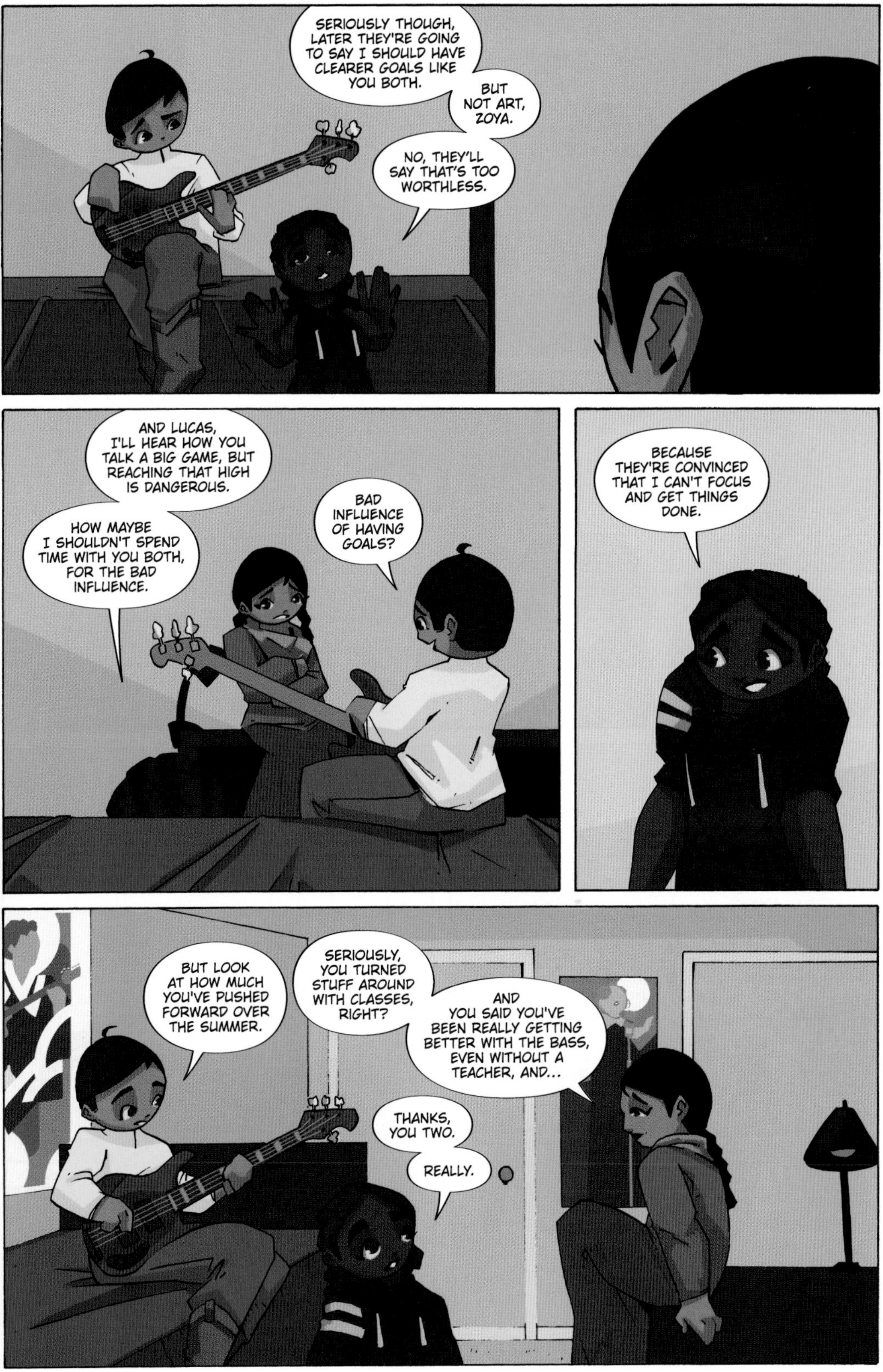
SERIOUSLY THOUGH, LATER THEY'RE GOING TO SAY I SHOULD HAVE CLEARER GOALS LIKE YOU BOTH.
BUT NOT ART, ZOYA.
NO, THEY'LL SAY THAT'S TOO WORTHLESS.
AND LUCAS, I'LL HEAR HOW YOU TALK A BIG GAME, BUT REACHING THAT HIGH IS DANGEROUS.
HOW MAYBE I SHOULDN'T SPEND TIME WITH YOU BOTH, FOR THE BAD INFLUENCE.
BAD INFLUENCE OF HAVING GOALS?
BECAUSE THEY'RE CONVINCED THAT I CAN'T FOCUS AND GET THINGS DONE.
BUT LOOK AT HOW MUCH YOU'VE PUSHED FORWARD OVER THE SUMMER.
SERIOUSLY, YOU TURNED STUFF AROUND WITH CLASSES, RIGHT?
AND YOU SAID YOU'VE BEEN REALLY GETTING BETTER WITH THE BASS, EVEN WITHOUT A TEACHER, AND...
THANKS, YOU TWO.
REALLY.

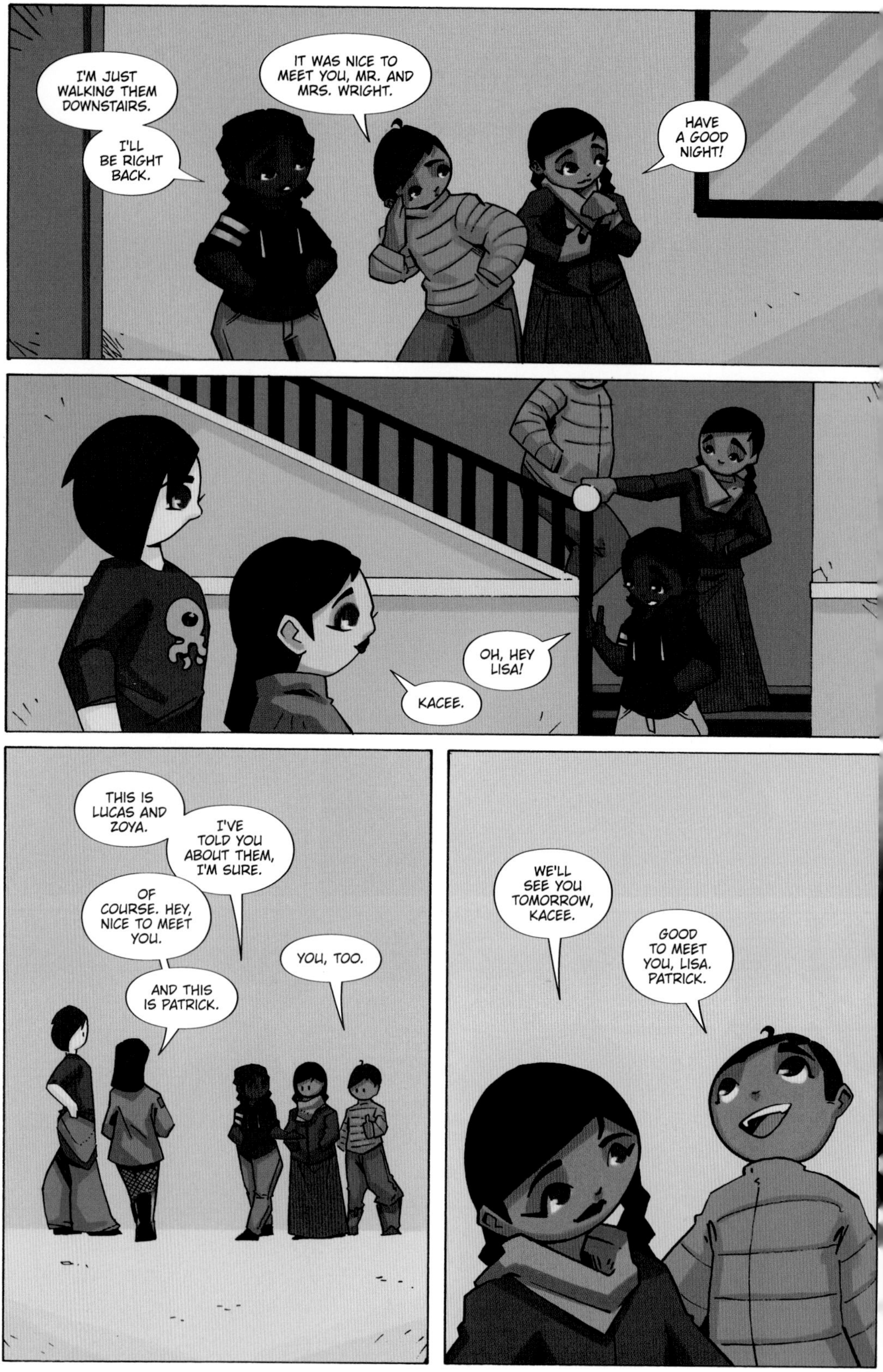
I'M JUST WALKING THEM DOWNSTAIRS.
I'LL BE RIGHT BACK.
IT WAS NICE TO MEET YOU, MR. AND MRS. WRIGHT.
HAVE A GOOD NIGHT!
OH, HEY LISA!
KACEE.
THIS IS LUCAS AND ZOYA.
I'VE TOLD YOU ABOUT THEM, I'M SURE.
OF COURSE. HEY, NICE TO MEET YOU.
YOU, TOO.
AND THIS IS PATRICK.
WE'LL SEE YOU TOMORROW, KACEE.
GOOD TO MEET YOU, LISA. PATRICK.

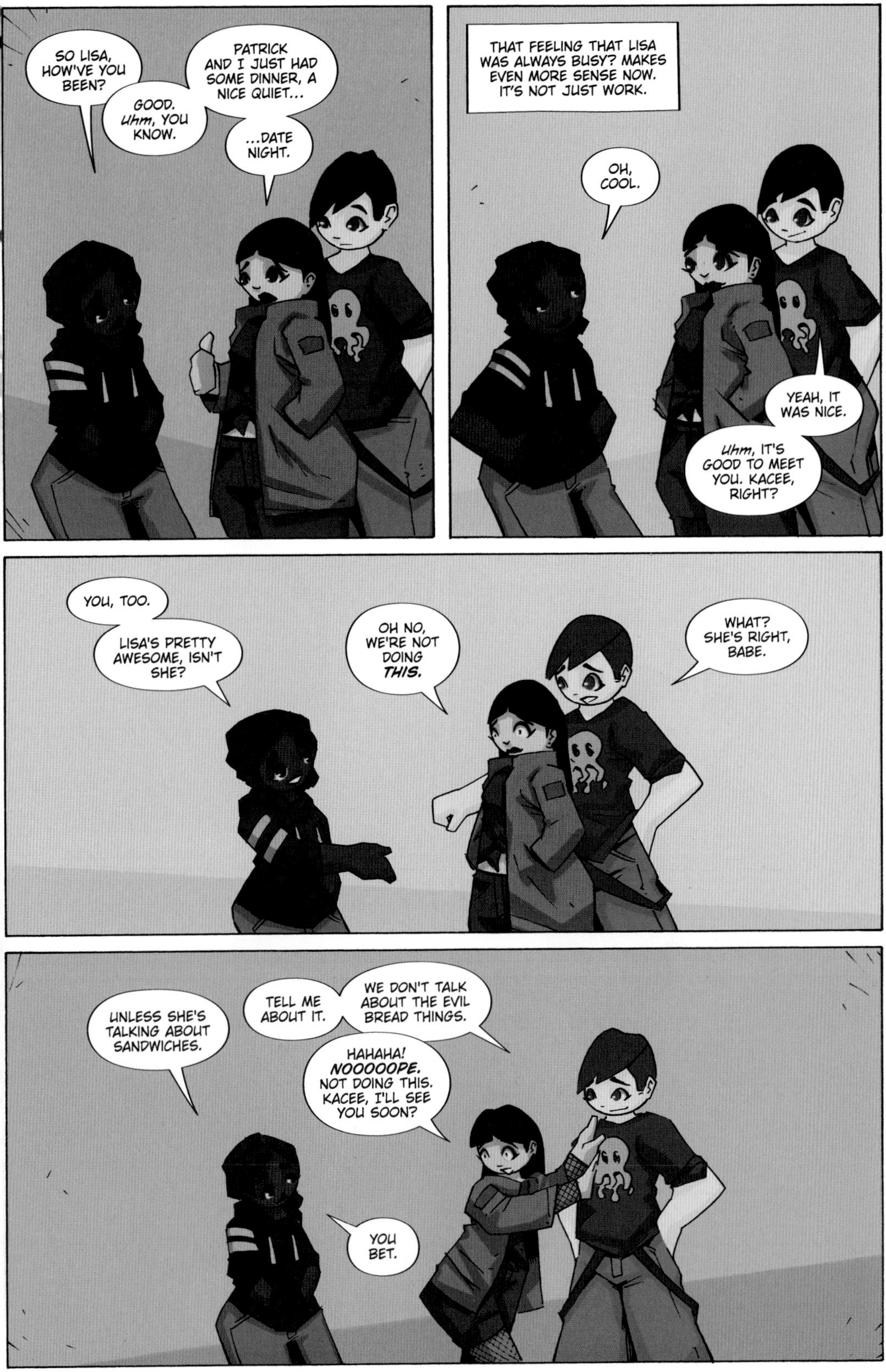
SO LISA, HOW'VE YOU BEEN?
GOOD. *Uhm*, YOU KNOW.
PATRICK AND I JUST HAD SOME DINNER, A NICE QUIET...
...DATE NIGHT.
THAT FEELING THAT LISA WAS ALWAYS BUSY? MAKES EVEN MORE SENSE NOW. IT'S NOT JUST WORK.
OH, COOL.
YEAH, IT WAS NICE.
Uhm, IT'S GOOD TO MEET YOU. KACEE, RIGHT?
YOU, TOO.
LISA'S PRETTY AWESOME, ISN'T SHE?
OH NO, WE'RE NOT DOING ***THIS.***
WHAT? SHE'S RIGHT, BABE.
UNLESS SHE'S TALKING ABOUT SANDWICHES.
TELL ME ABOUT IT.
WE DON'T TALK ABOUT THE EVIL BREAD THINGS.
HAHAHA! ***NOOOOOPE.*** NOT DOING THIS. KACEE, I'LL SEE YOU SOON?
YOU BET.

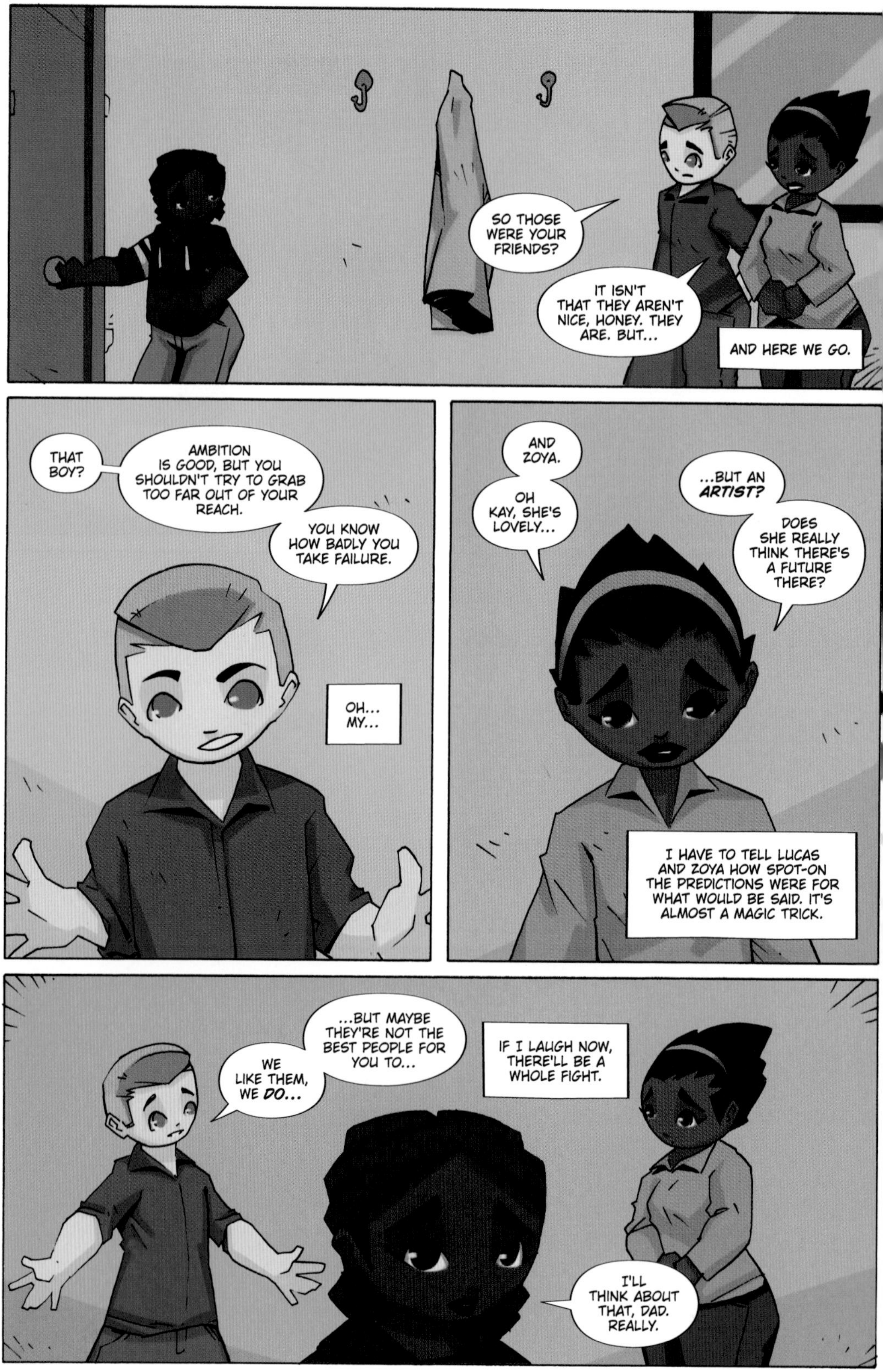
SO THOSE WERE YOUR FRIENDS?
IT ISN'T THAT THEY AREN'T NICE, HONEY. THEY ARE. BUT...
AND HERE WE GO.
THAT BOY?
AMBITION IS GOOD, BUT YOU SHOULDN'T TRY TO GRAB TOO FAR OUT OF YOUR REACH.
YOU KNOW HOW BADLY YOU TAKE FAILURE.
OH... MY...
AND ZOYA.
OH KAY, SHE'S LOVELY...
...BUT AN *ARTIST?*
DOES SHE REALLY THINK THERE'S A FUTURE THERE?
I HAVE TO TELL LUCAS AND ZOYA HOW SPOT-ON THE PREDICTIONS WERE FOR WHAT WOULD BE SAID. IT'S ALMOST A MAGIC TRICK.
WE LIKE THEM, WE *DO...*
...BUT MAYBE THEY'RE NOT THE BEST PEOPLE FOR YOU TO...
IF I LAUGH NOW, THERE'LL BE A WHOLE FIGHT.
I'LL THINK ABOUT THAT, DAD. REALLY.

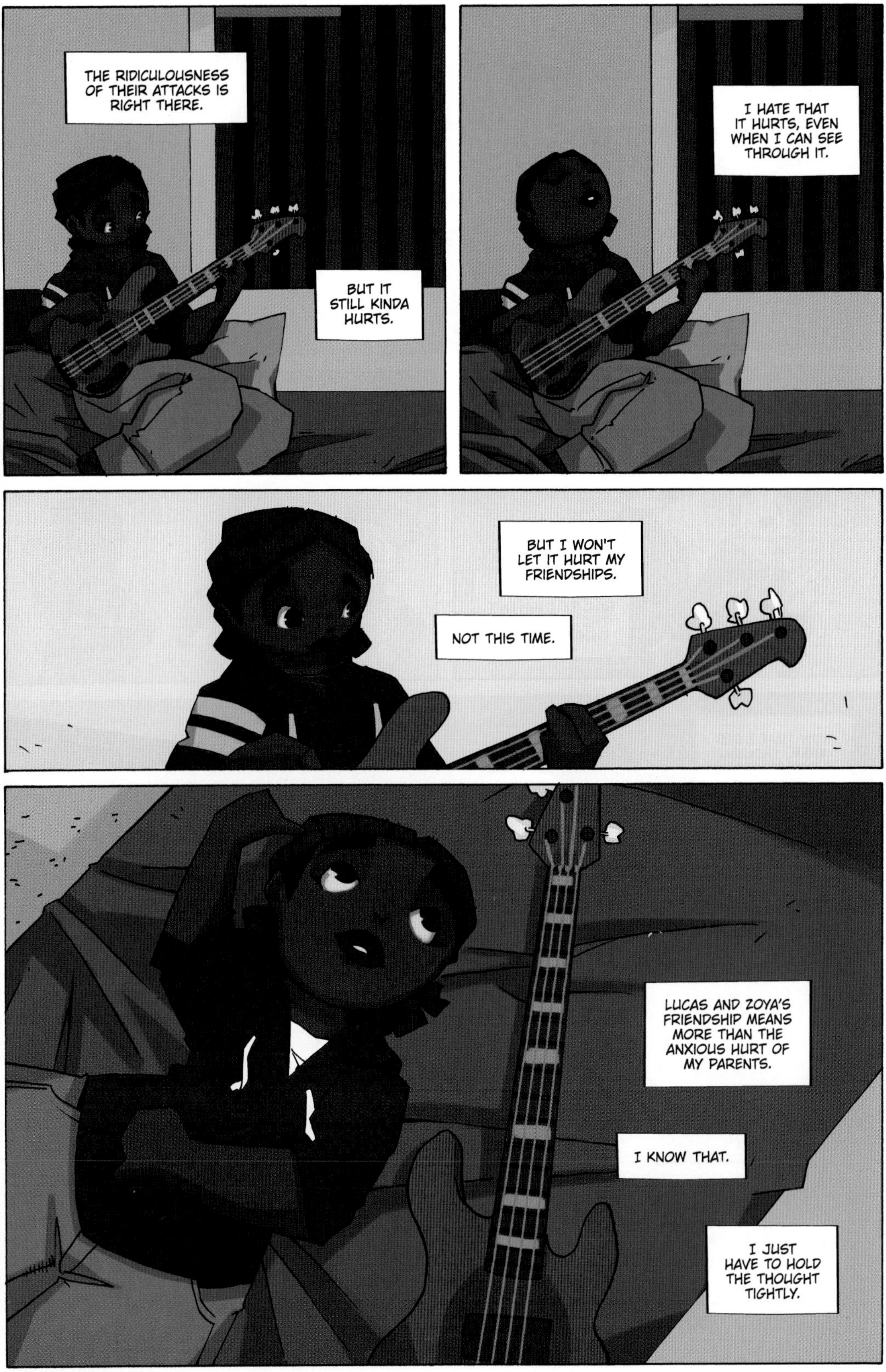
THE RIDICULOUSNESS OF THEIR ATTACKS IS RIGHT THERE.
BUT IT STILL KINDA HURTS.
I HATE THAT IT HURTS, EVEN WHEN I CAN SEE THROUGH IT.
BUT I WON'T LET IT HURT MY FRIENDSHIPS.
NOT THIS TIME.
LUCAS AND ZOYA'S FRIENDSHIP MEANS MORE THAN THE ANXIOUS HURT OF MY PARENTS.
I KNOW THAT.
I JUST HAVE TO HOLD THE THOUGHT TIGHTLY.

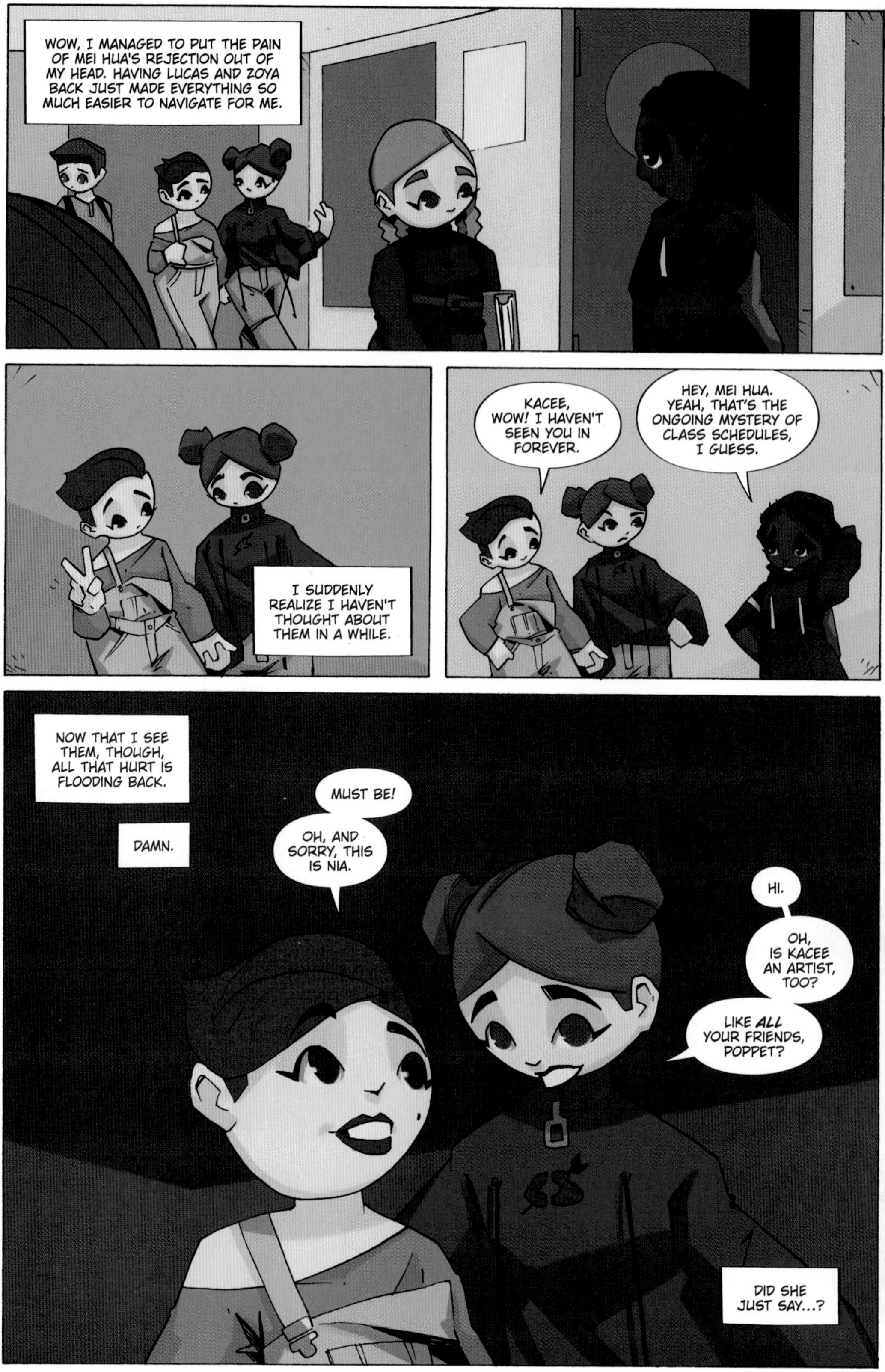
WOW, I MANAGED TO PUT THE PAIN OF MEI HUA'S REJECTION OUT OF MY HEAD. HAVING LUCAS AND ZOYA BACK JUST MADE EVERYTHING SO MUCH EASIER TO NAVIGATE FOR ME.
I SUDDENLY REALIZE I HAVEN'T THOUGHT ABOUT THEM IN A WHILE.
KACEE, WOW! I HAVEN'T SEEN YOU IN FOREVER.
HEY, MEI HUA. YEAH, THAT'S THE ONGOING MYSTERY OF CLASS SCHEDULES, I GUESS.
NOW THAT I SEE THEM, THOUGH, ALL THAT HURT IS FLOODING BACK.
DAMN.
MUST BE!
OH, AND SORRY, THIS IS NIA.
HI.
OH, IS KACEE AN ARTIST, TOO?
LIKE ALL YOUR FRIENDS, POPPET?
DID SHE JUST SAY...?

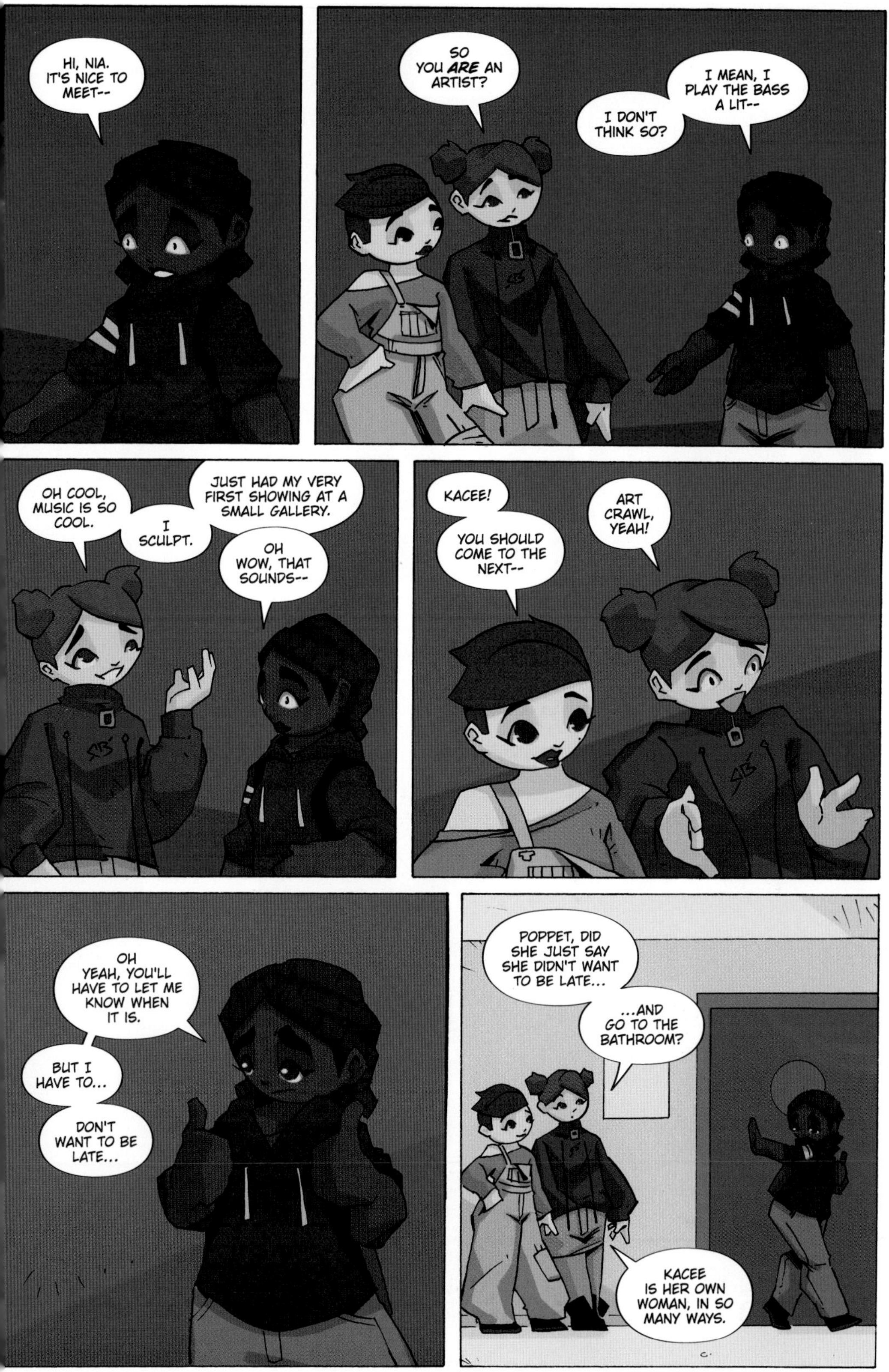
HI, NIA. IT'S NICE TO MEET--
SO YOU **ARE** AN ARTIST?
I DON'T THINK SO?
I MEAN, I PLAY THE BASS A LIT--
OH COOL, MUSIC IS SO COOL.
I SCULPT.
JUST HAD MY VERY FIRST SHOWING AT A SMALL GALLERY.
OH WOW, THAT SOUNDS--
KACEE!
YOU SHOULD COME TO THE NEXT--
ART CRAWL, YEAH!
OH YEAH, YOU'LL HAVE TO LET ME KNOW WHEN IT IS.
BUT I HAVE TO...
DON'T WANT TO BE LATE...
POPPET, DID SHE JUST SAY SHE DIDN'T WANT TO BE LATE...
...AND GO TO THE BATHROOM?
KACEE IS HER OWN WOMAN, IN SO MANY WAYS.

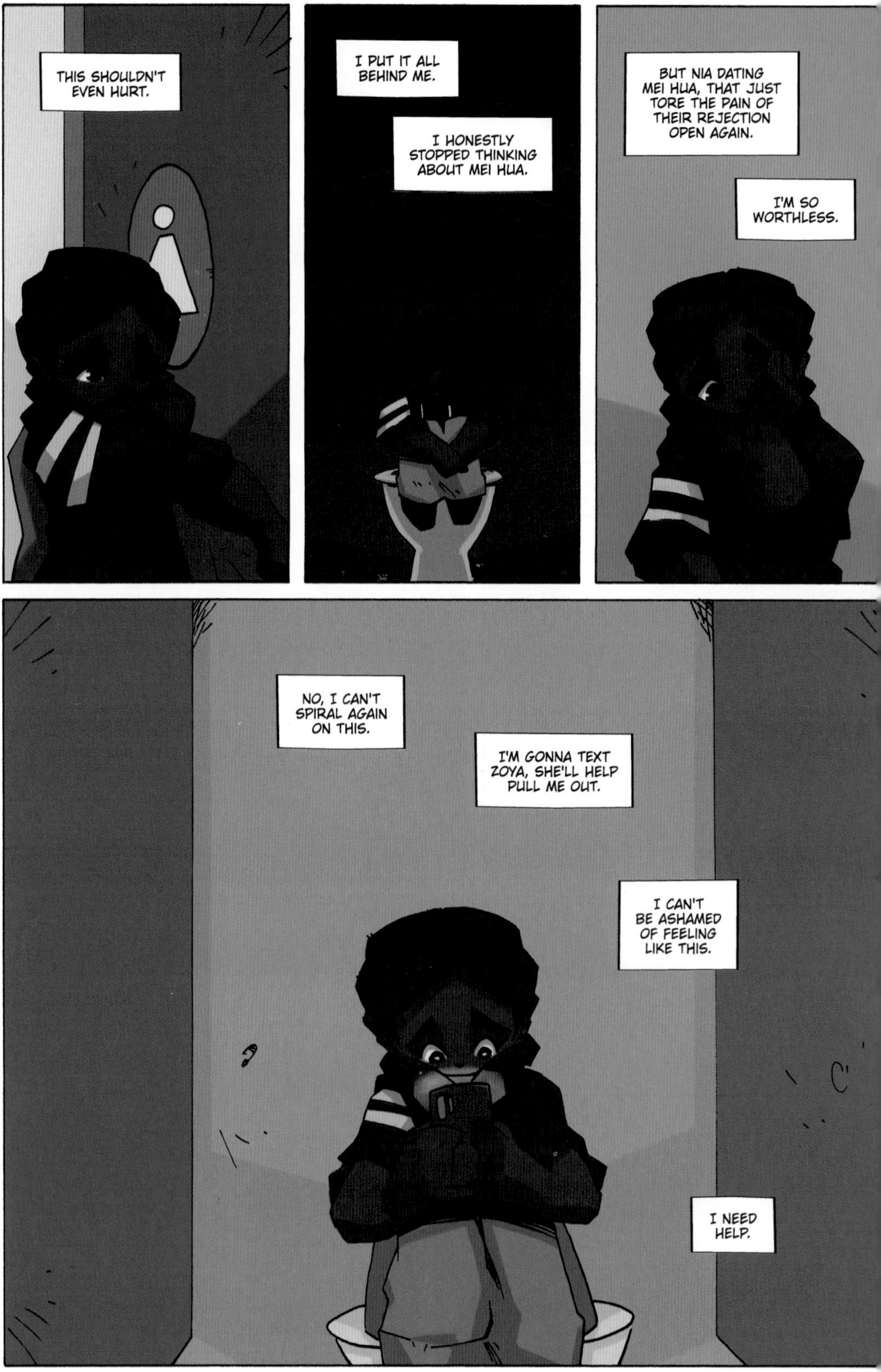
THIS SHOULDN'T EVEN HURT.
I PUT IT ALL BEHIND ME.
I HONESTLY STOPPED THINKING ABOUT MEI HUA.
BUT NIA DATING MEI HUA, THAT JUST TORE THE PAIN OF THEIR REJECTION OPEN AGAIN.
I'M SO WORTHLESS.
NO, I CAN'T SPIRAL AGAIN ON THIS.
I'M GONNA TEXT ZOYA, SHE'LL HELP PULL ME OUT.
I CAN'T BE ASHAMED OF FEELING LIKE THIS.
I NEED HELP.

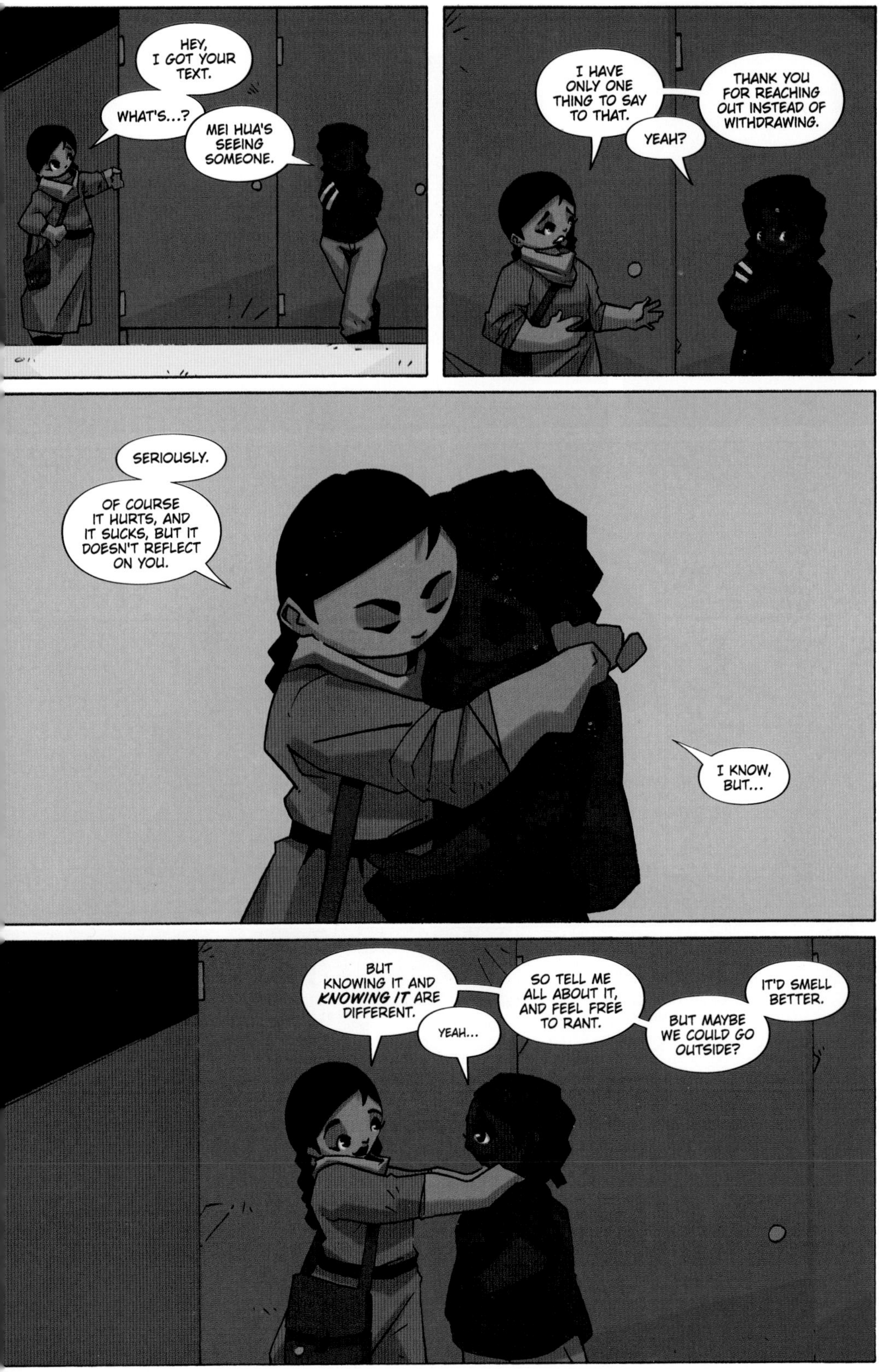
HEY, I GOT YOUR TEXT.
WHAT'S...?
MEI HUA'S SEEING SOMEONE.
I HAVE ONLY ONE THING TO SAY TO THAT.
YEAH?
THANK YOU FOR REACHING OUT INSTEAD OF WITHDRAWING.
SERIOUSLY.
OF COURSE IT HURTS, AND IT SUCKS, BUT IT DOESN'T REFLECT ON YOU.
I KNOW, BUT...
BUT KNOWING IT AND *KNOWING IT* ARE DIFFERENT.
YEAH...
SO TELL ME ALL ABOUT IT, AND FEEL FREE TO RANT.
BUT MAYBE WE COULD GO OUTSIDE?
IT'D SMELL BETTER.

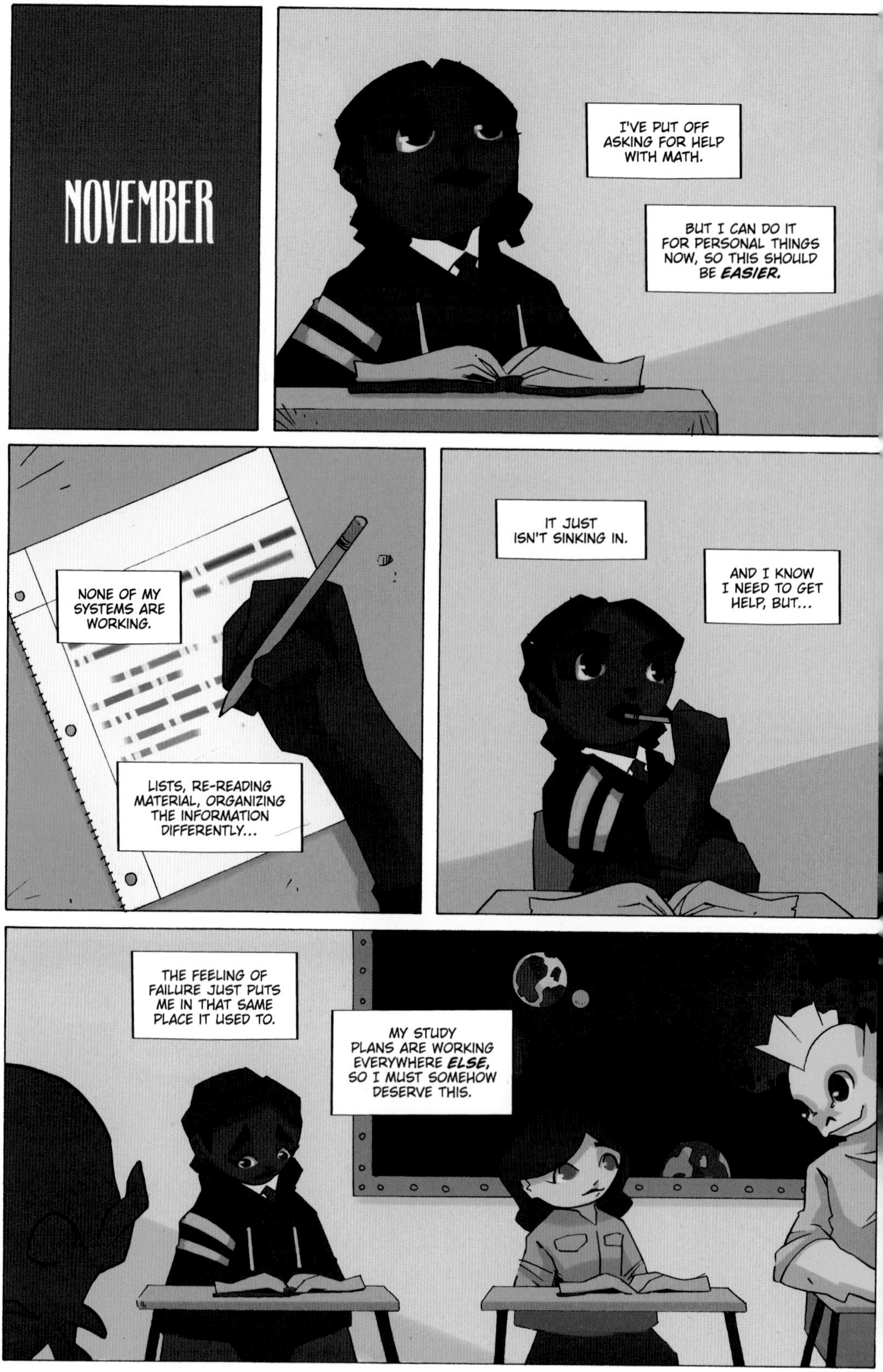
NOVEMBER
I'VE PUT OFF ASKING FOR HELP WITH MATH.
BUT I CAN DO IT FOR PERSONAL THINGS NOW, SO THIS SHOULD BE *EASIER.*
NONE OF MY SYSTEMS ARE WORKING.
LISTS, RE-READING MATERIAL, ORGANIZING THE INFORMATION DIFFERENTLY...
IT JUST ISN'T SINKING IN.
AND I KNOW I NEED TO GET HELP, BUT...
THE FEELING OF FAILURE JUST PUTS ME IN THAT SAME PLACE IT USED TO.
MY STUDY PLANS ARE WORKING EVERYWHERE *ELSE,* SO I MUST SOMEHOW DESERVE THIS.

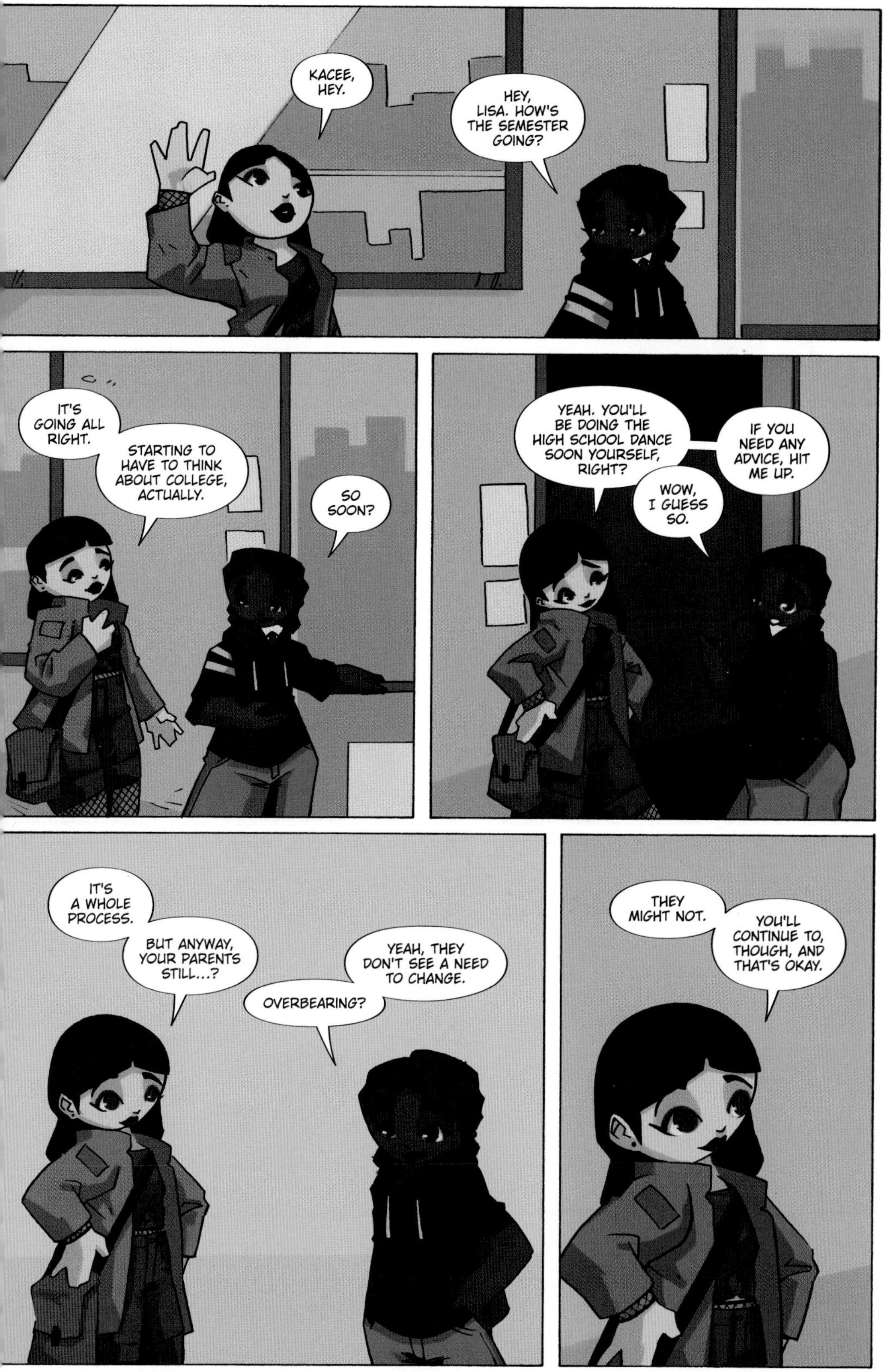
KACEE, HEY.
HEY, LISA. HOW'S THE SEMESTER GOING?
IT'S GOING ALL RIGHT.
STARTING TO HAVE TO THINK ABOUT COLLEGE, ACTUALLY.
SO SOON?
YEAH. YOU'LL BE DOING THE HIGH SCHOOL DANCE SOON YOURSELF, RIGHT?
WOW, I GUESS SO.
IF YOU NEED ANY ADVICE, HIT ME UP.
IT'S A WHOLE PROCESS.
BUT ANYWAY, YOUR PARENTS STILL...?
OVERBEARING?
YEAH, THEY DON'T SEE A NEED TO CHANGE.
THEY MIGHT NOT.
YOU'LL CONTINUE TO, THOUGH, AND THAT'S OKAY.

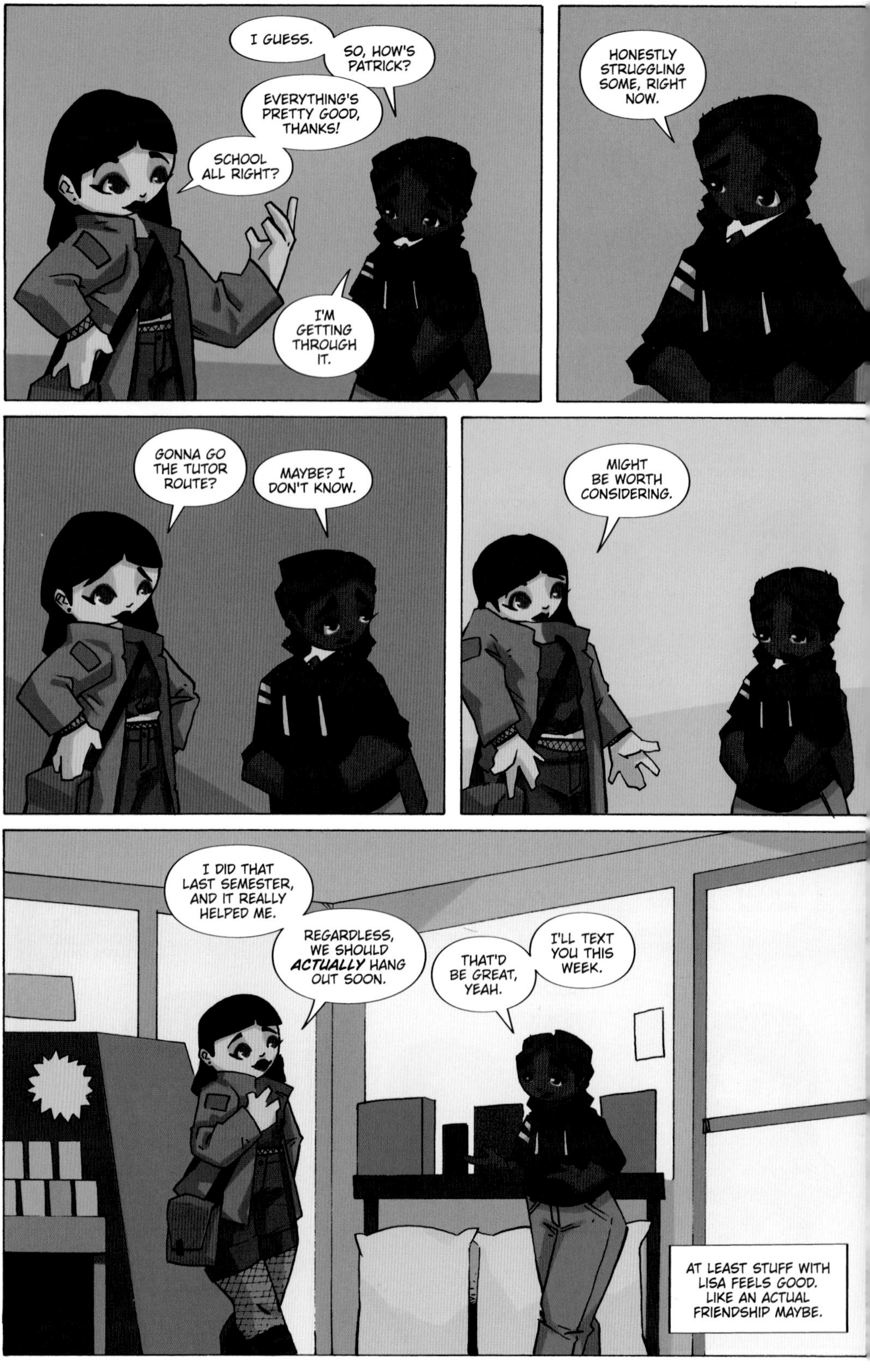
I GUESS.
SO, HOW'S PATRICK?
EVERYTHING'S PRETTY GOOD, THANKS!
SCHOOL ALL RIGHT?
I'M GETTING THROUGH IT.
HONESTLY STRUGGLING SOME, RIGHT NOW.
GONNA GO THE TUTOR ROUTE?
MAYBE? I DON'T KNOW.
MIGHT BE WORTH CONSIDERING.
I DID THAT LAST SEMESTER, AND IT REALLY HELPED ME.
REGARDLESS, WE SHOULD *ACTUALLY* HANG OUT SOON.
THAT'D BE GREAT, YEAH.
I'LL TEXT YOU THIS WEEK.
AT LEAST STUFF WITH LISA FEELS GOOD. LIKE AN ACTUAL FRIENDSHIP MAYBE.

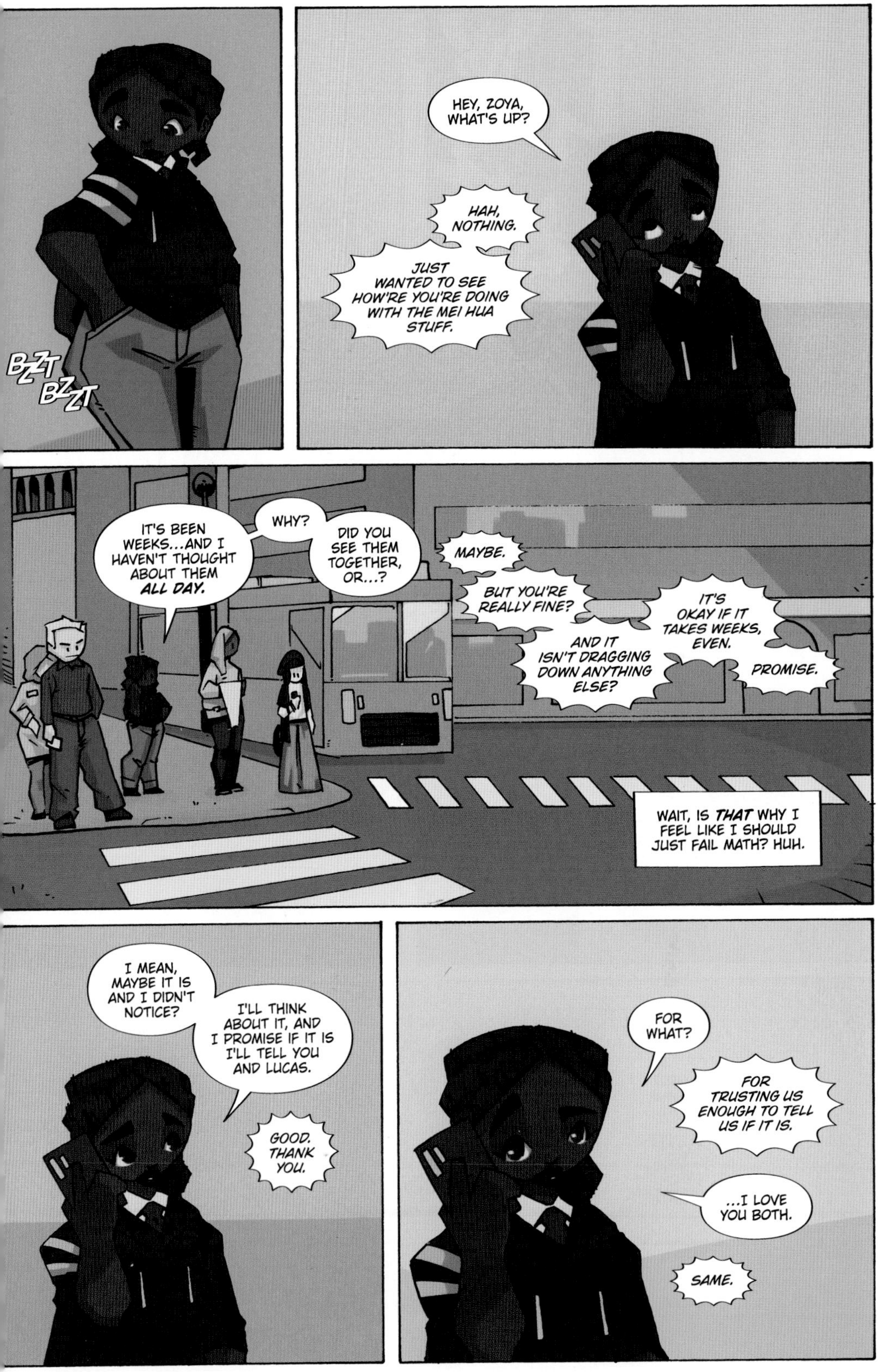
BZZT BZZT
HEY, ZOYA, WHAT'S UP?
HAH, NOTHING.
JUST WANTED TO SEE HOW'RE YOU'RE DOING WITH THE MEI HUA STUFF.
IT'S BEEN WEEKS...AND I HAVEN'T THOUGHT ABOUT THEM ALL DAY.
WHY?
DID YOU SEE THEM TOGETHER, OR...?
MAYBE.
BUT YOU'RE REALLY FINE?
AND IT ISN'T DRAGGING DOWN ANYTHING ELSE?
IT'S OKAY IF IT TAKES WEEKS, EVEN.
PROMISE.
WAIT, IS THAT WHY I FEEL LIKE I SHOULD JUST FAIL MATH? HUH.
I MEAN, MAYBE IT IS AND I DIDN'T NOTICE?
I'LL THINK ABOUT IT, AND I PROMISE IF IT IS I'LL TELL YOU AND LUCAS.
GOOD. THANK YOU.
FOR WHAT?
FOR TRUSTING US ENOUGH TO TELL US IF IT IS.
...I LOVE YOU BOTH.
SAME.

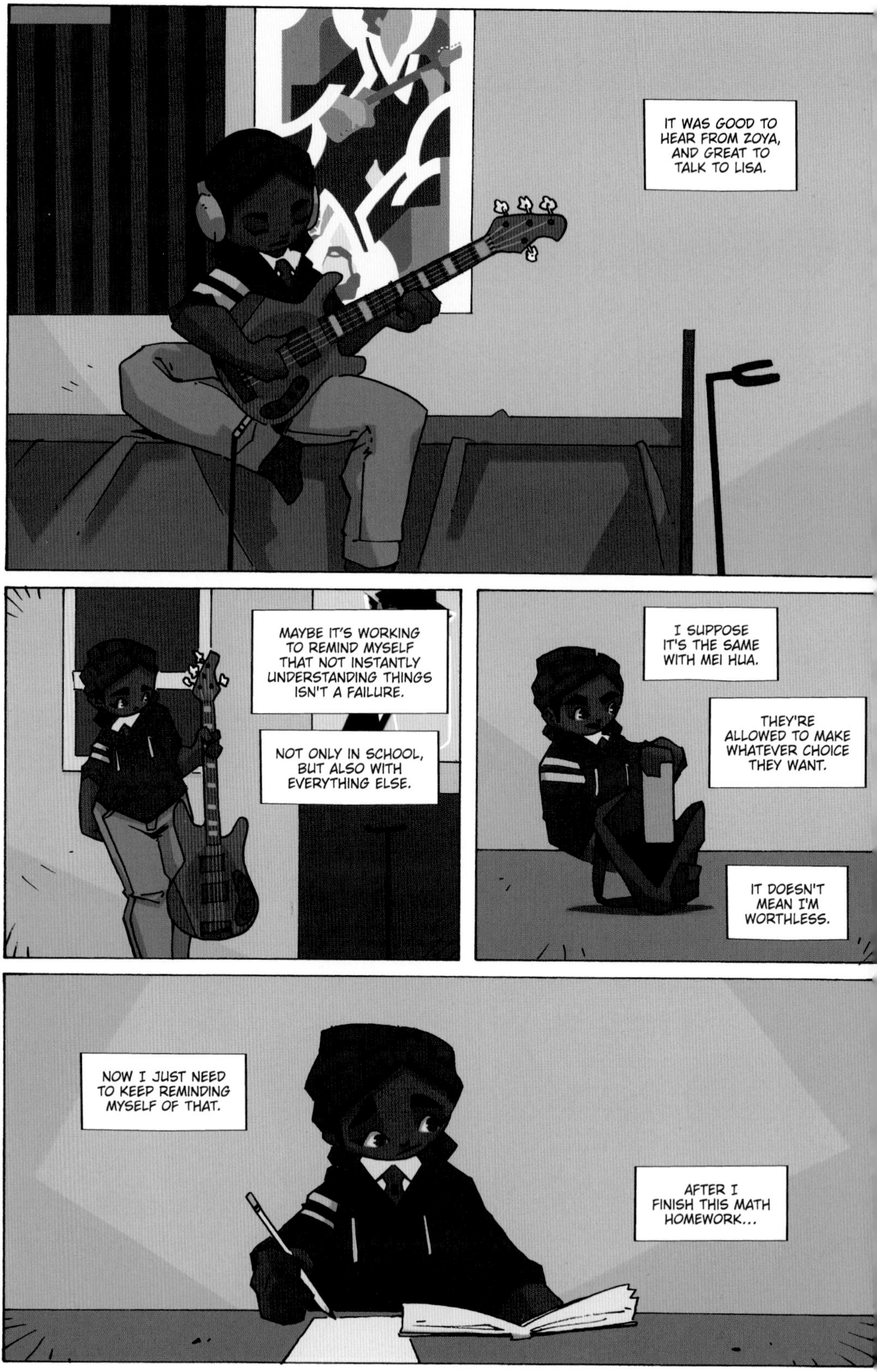
IT WAS GOOD TO HEAR FROM ZOYA, AND GREAT TO TALK TO LISA.
MAYBE IT'S WORKING TO REMIND MYSELF THAT NOT INSTANTLY UNDERSTANDING THINGS ISN'T A FAILURE.
NOT ONLY IN SCHOOL, BUT ALSO WITH EVERYTHING ELSE.
I SUPPOSE IT'S THE SAME WITH MEI HUA.
THEY'RE ALLOWED TO MAKE WHATEVER CHOICE THEY WANT.
IT DOESN'T MEAN I'M WORTHLESS.
NOW I JUST NEED TO KEEP REMINDING MYSELF OF THAT.
AFTER I FINISH THIS MATH HOMEWORK...

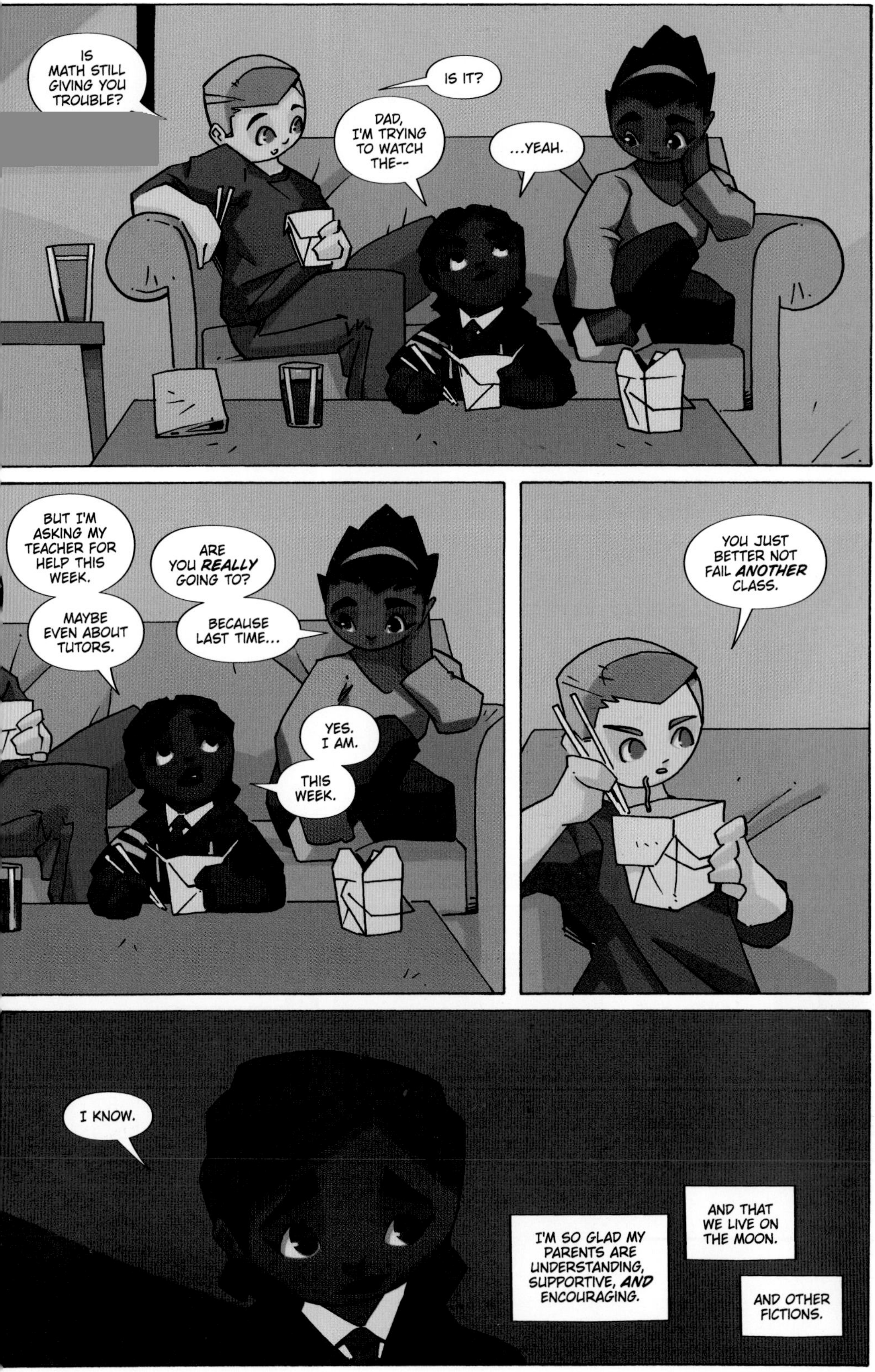
IS MATH STILL GIVING YOU TROUBLE?
IS IT?
DAD, I'M TRYING TO WATCH THE--
...YEAH.
BUT I'M ASKING MY TEACHER FOR HELP THIS WEEK.
MAYBE EVEN ABOUT TUTORS.
ARE YOU *REALLY* GOING TO?
BECAUSE LAST TIME...
YES. I AM.
THIS WEEK.
YOU JUST BETTER NOT FAIL *ANOTHER* CLASS.
I KNOW.
I'M SO GLAD MY PARENTS ARE UNDERSTANDING, SUPPORTIVE, *AND* ENCOURAGING.
AND THAT WE LIVE ON THE MOON.
AND OTHER FICTIONS.

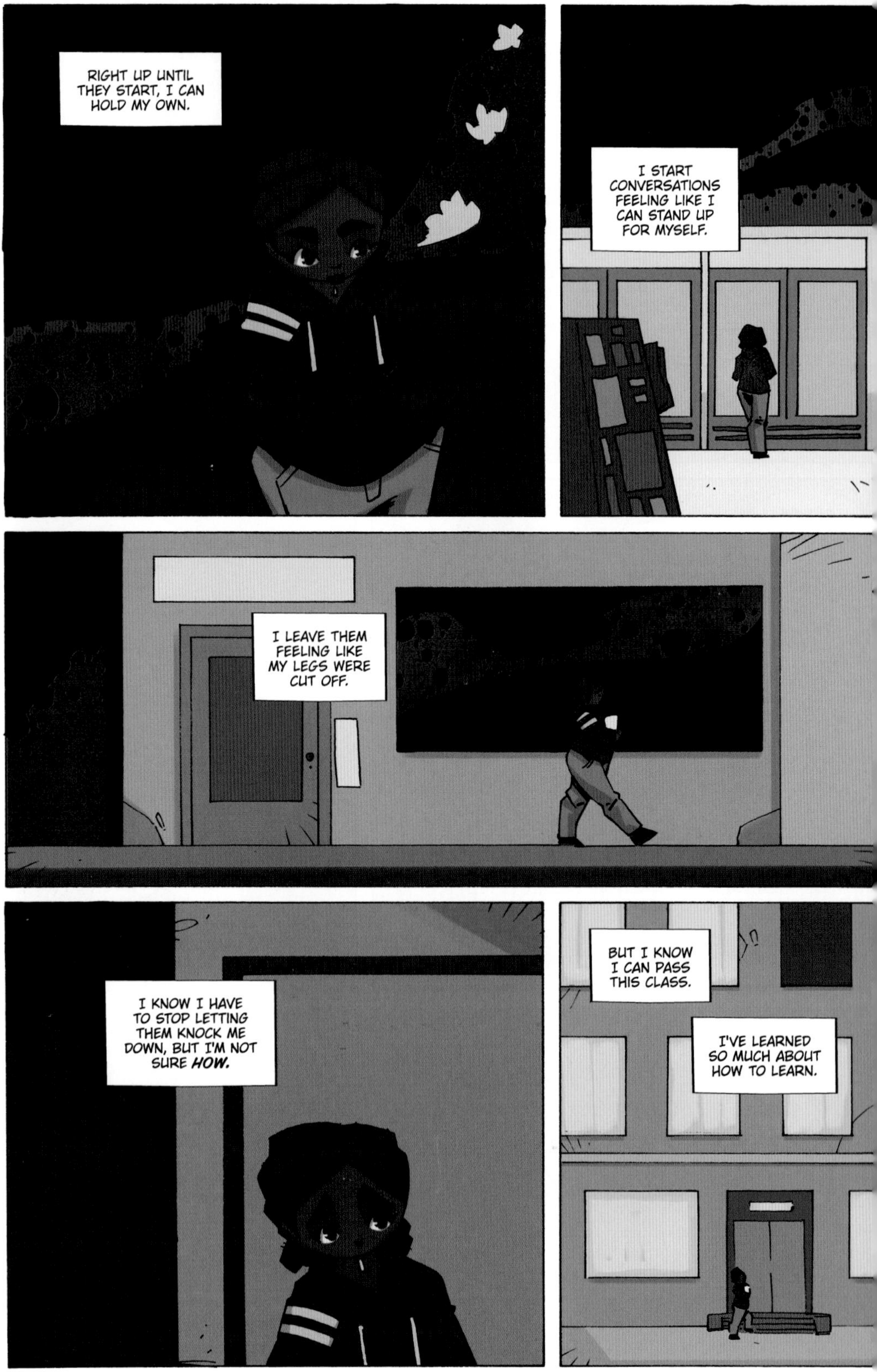
RIGHT UP UNTIL THEY START, I CAN HOLD MY OWN.
I START CONVERSATIONS FEELING LIKE I CAN STAND UP FOR MYSELF.
I LEAVE THEM FEELING LIKE MY LEGS WERE CUT OFF.
I KNOW I HAVE TO STOP LETTING THEM KNOCK ME DOWN, BUT I'M NOT SURE *HOW.*
BUT I KNOW I CAN PASS THIS CLASS.
I'VE LEARNED SO MUCH ABOUT HOW TO LEARN.

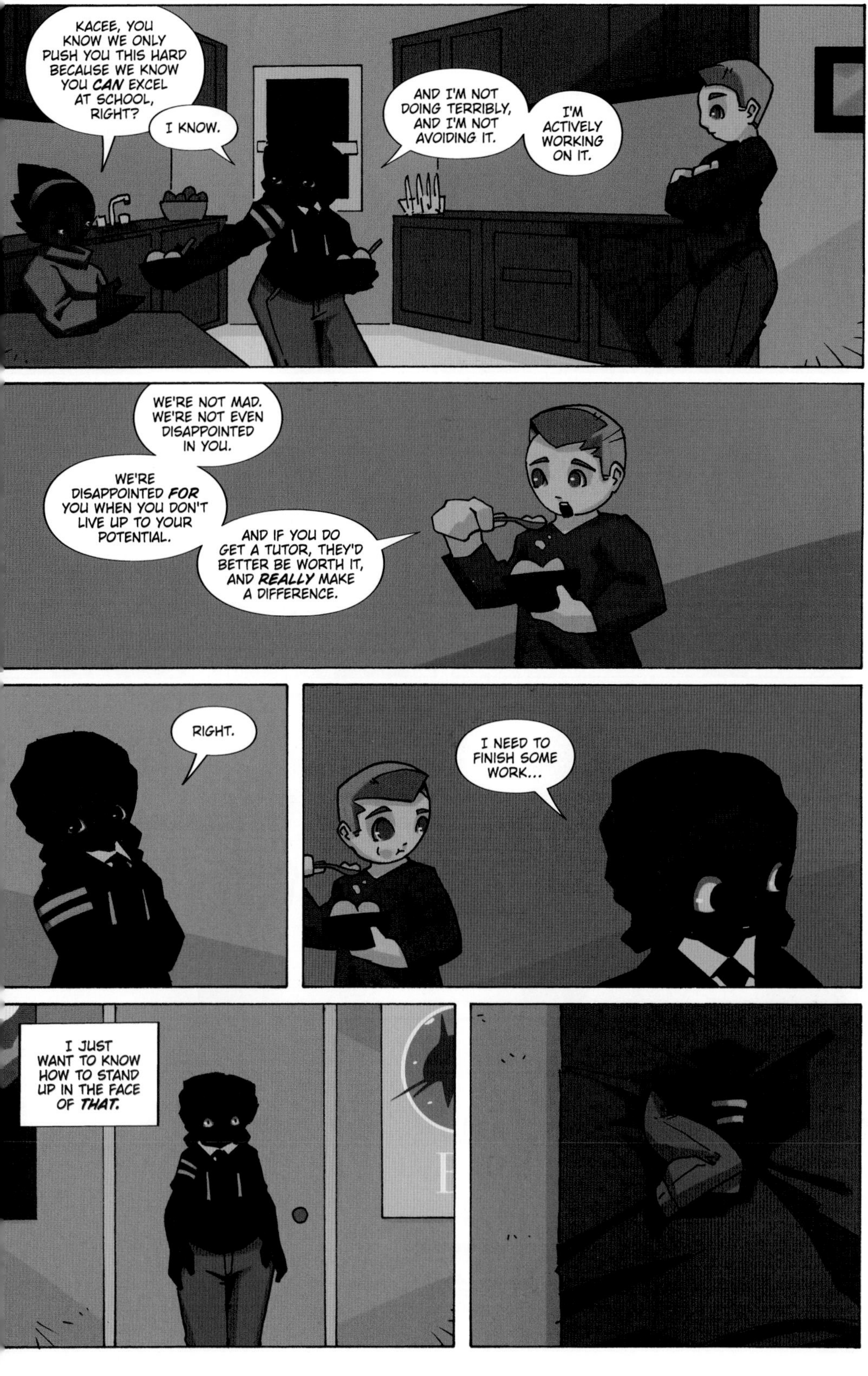
KACEE, YOU KNOW WE ONLY PUSH YOU THIS HARD BECAUSE WE KNOW YOU *CAN* EXCEL AT SCHOOL, RIGHT?
I KNOW.
AND I'M NOT DOING TERRIBLY, AND I'M NOT AVOIDING IT.
I'M ACTIVELY WORKING ON IT.
WE'RE NOT MAD. WE'RE NOT EVEN DISAPPOINTED IN YOU.
WE'RE DISAPPOINTED *FOR* YOU WHEN YOU DON'T LIVE UP TO YOUR POTENTIAL.
AND IF YOU DO GET A TUTOR, THEY'D BETTER BE WORTH IT, AND *REALLY* MAKE A DIFFERENCE.
RIGHT.
I NEED TO FINISH SOME WORK...
I JUST WANT TO KNOW HOW TO STAND UP IN THE FACE OF *THAT.*

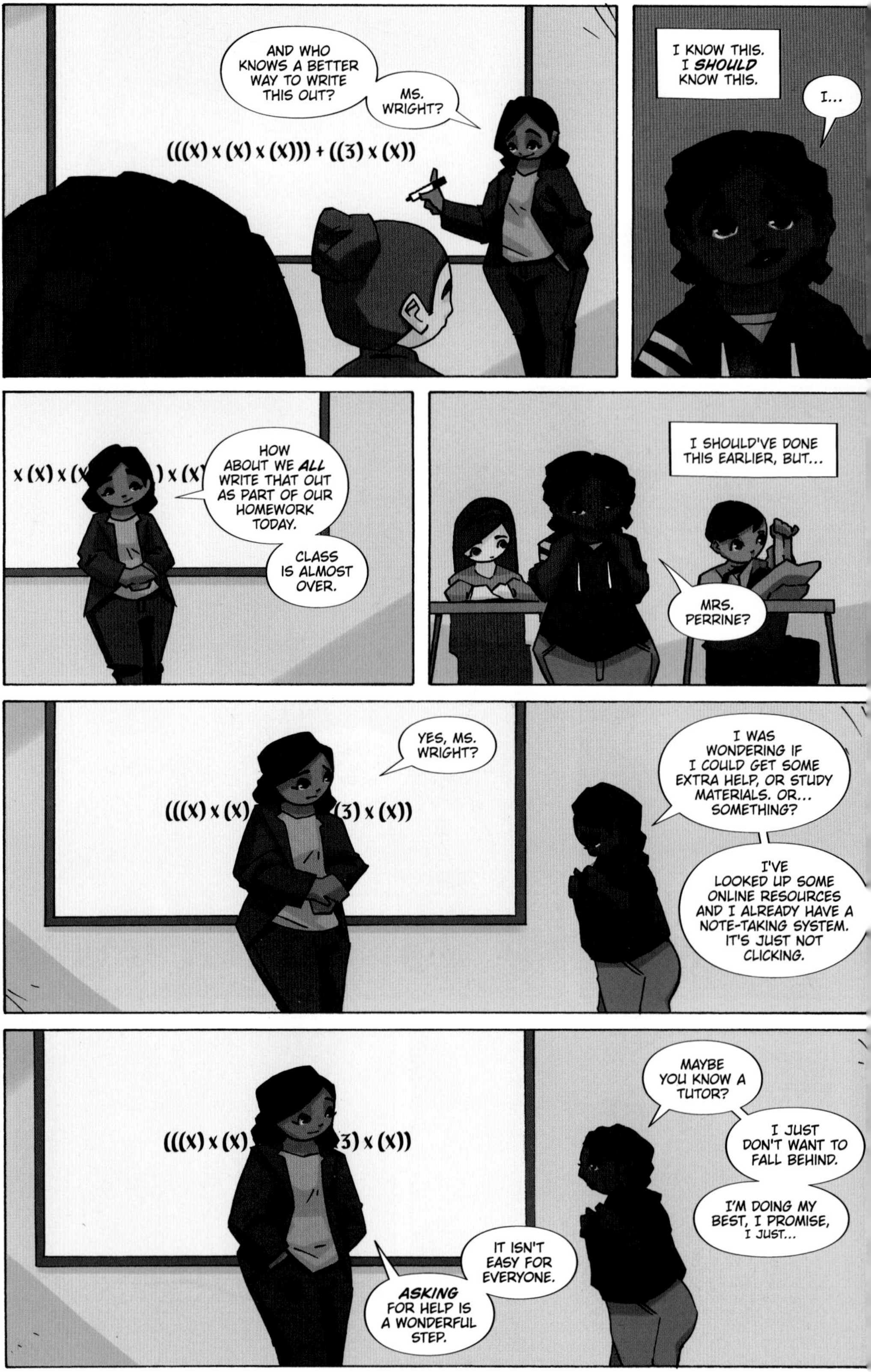

AND WHO KNOWS A BETTER WAY TO WRITE THIS OUT?
MS. WRIGHT?
(((X) x (X) x (X))) + ((3) x (X))
I KNOW THIS. I SHOULD KNOW THIS.
I...
HOW ABOUT WE ALL WRITE THAT OUT AS PART OF OUR HOMEWORK TODAY.
CLASS IS ALMOST OVER.
I SHOULD'VE DONE THIS EARLIER, BUT...
MRS. PERRINE?
YES, MS. WRIGHT?
I WAS WONDERING IF I COULD GET SOME EXTRA HELP, OR STUDY MATERIALS. OR... SOMETHING?
I'VE LOOKED UP SOME ONLINE RESOURCES AND I ALREADY HAVE A NOTE-TAKING SYSTEM. IT'S JUST NOT CLICKING.
MAYBE YOU KNOW A TUTOR?
I JUST DON'T WANT TO FALL BEHIND.
I'M DOING MY BEST, I PROMISE, I JUST...
IT ISN'T EASY FOR EVERYONE.
ASKING FOR HELP IS A WONDERFUL STEP.

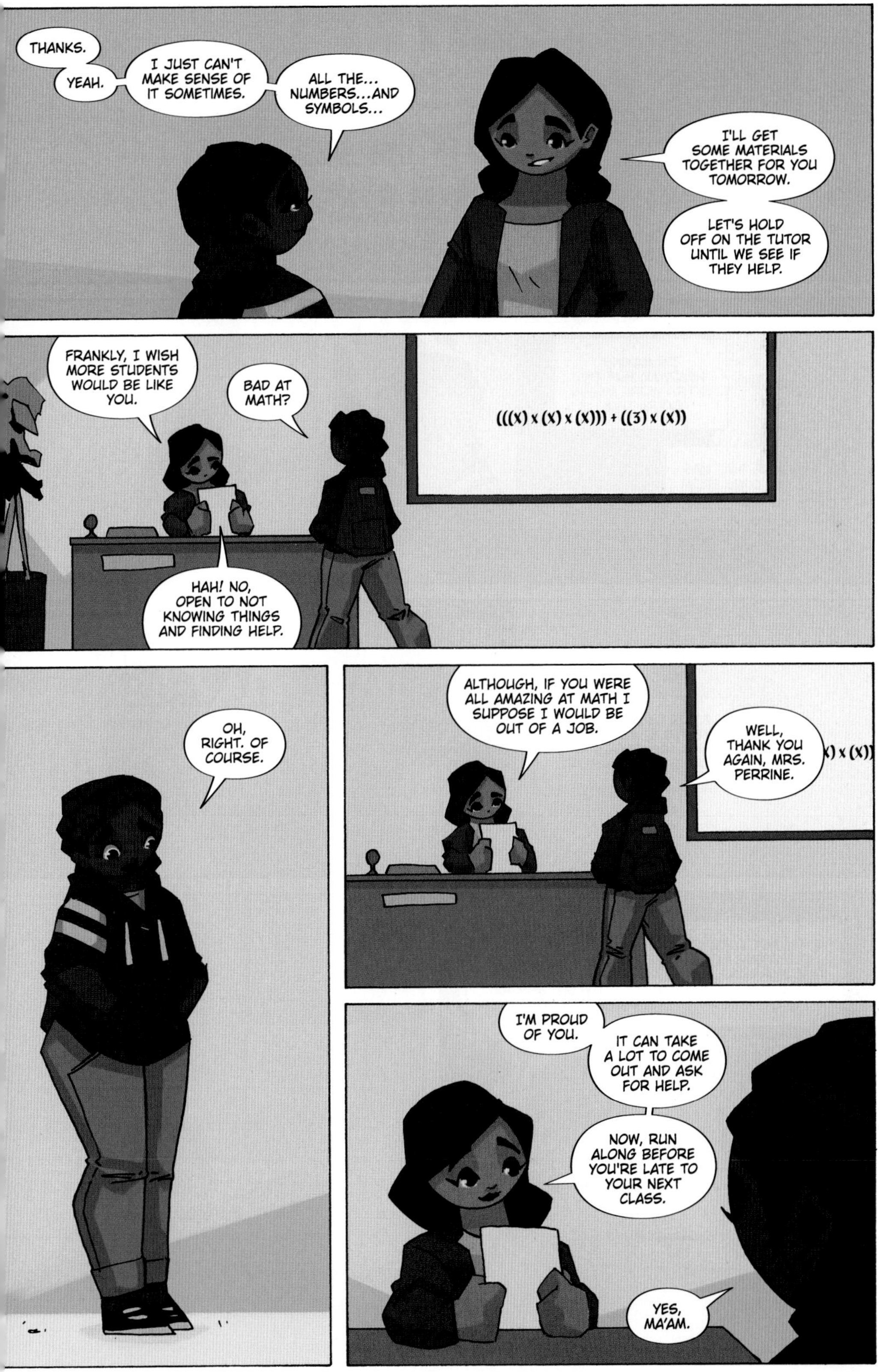
THANKS.
YEAH.
I JUST CAN'T MAKE SENSE OF IT SOMETIMES.
ALL THE... NUMBERS...AND SYMBOLS...
I'LL GET SOME MATERIALS TOGETHER FOR YOU TOMORROW.
LET'S HOLD OFF ON THE TUTOR UNTIL WE SEE IF THEY HELP.
FRANKLY, I WISH MORE STUDENTS WOULD BE LIKE YOU.
BAD AT MATH?
(((X) x (X) x (X))) + ((3) x (X))
HAH! NO, OPEN TO NOT KNOWING THINGS AND FINDING HELP.
OH, RIGHT. OF COURSE.
ALTHOUGH, IF YOU WERE ALL AMAZING AT MATH I SUPPOSE I WOULD BE OUT OF A JOB.
WELL, THANK YOU AGAIN, MRS. PERRINE.
I'M PROUD OF YOU.
IT CAN TAKE A LOT TO COME OUT AND ASK FOR HELP.
NOW, RUN ALONG BEFORE YOU'RE LATE TO YOUR NEXT CLASS.
YES, MA'AM.

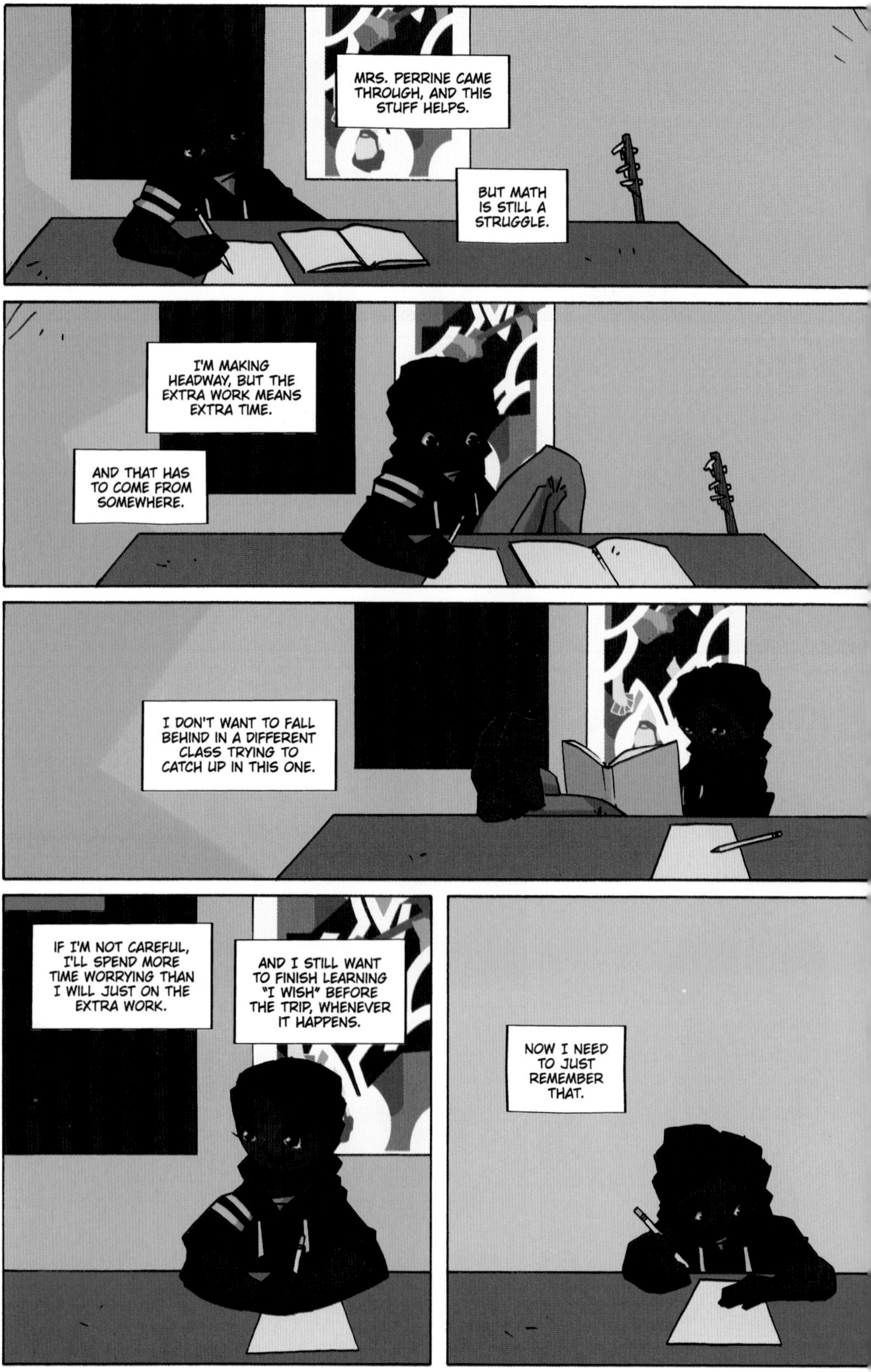
MRS. PERRINE CAME THROUGH, AND THIS STUFF HELPS.
BUT MATH IS STILL A STRUGGLE.
I'M MAKING HEADWAY, BUT THE EXTRA WORK MEANS EXTRA TIME.
AND THAT HAS TO COME FROM SOMEWHERE.
I DON'T WANT TO FALL BEHIND IN A DIFFERENT CLASS TRYING TO CATCH UP IN THIS ONE.
IF I'M NOT CAREFUL, I'LL SPEND MORE TIME WORRYING THAN I WILL JUST ON THE EXTRA WORK.
AND I STILL WANT TO FINISH LEARNING "I WISH" BEFORE THE TRIP, WHENEVER IT HAPPENS.
NOW I NEED TO JUST REMEMBER THAT.

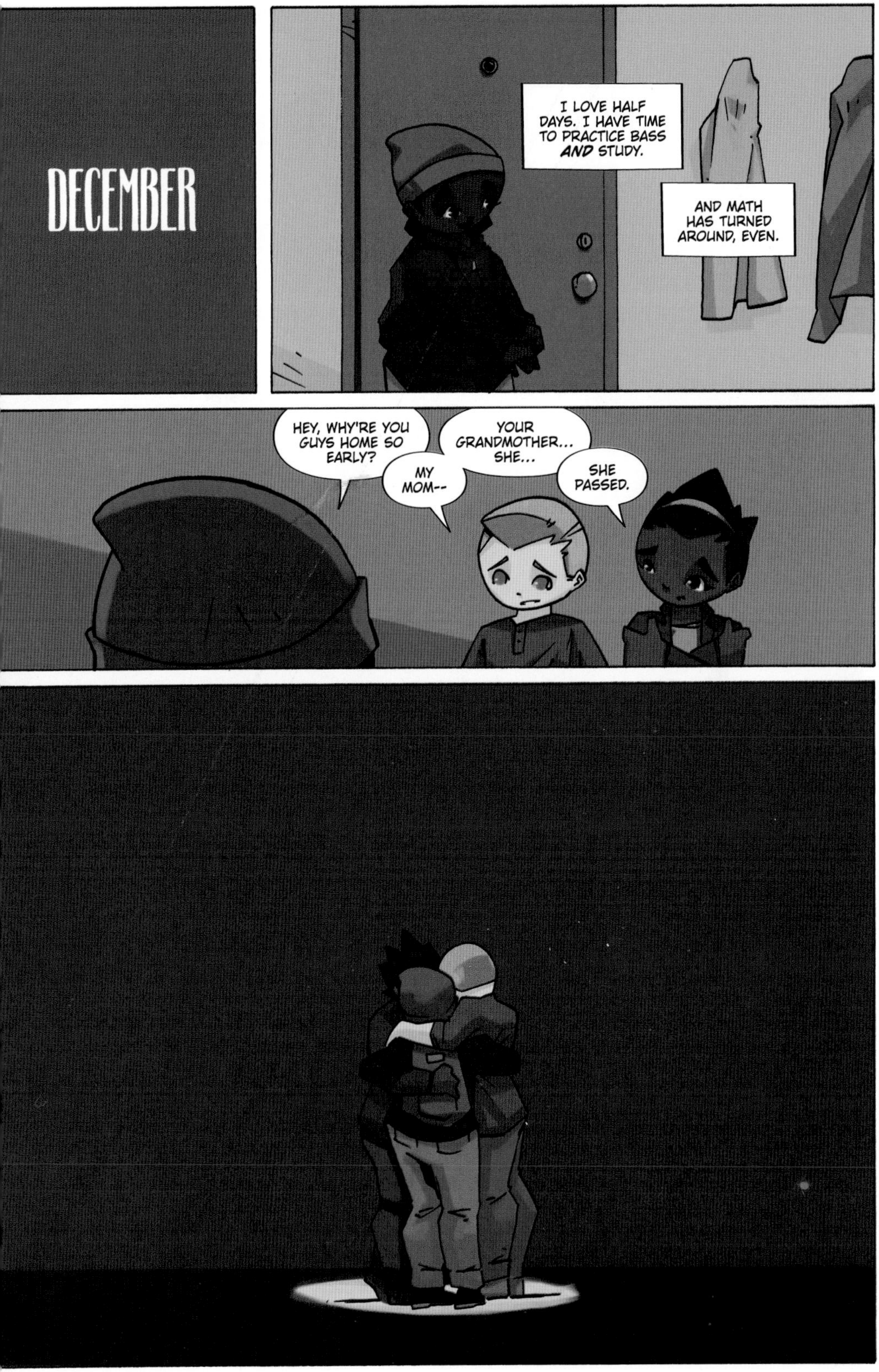
DECEMBER
I LOVE HALF DAYS. I HAVE TIME TO PRACTICE BASS *AND* STUDY.
AND MATH HAS TURNED AROUND, EVEN.
HEY, WHY'RE YOU GUYS HOME SO EARLY?
MY MOM--
YOUR GRANDMOTHER... SHE...
SHE PASSED.

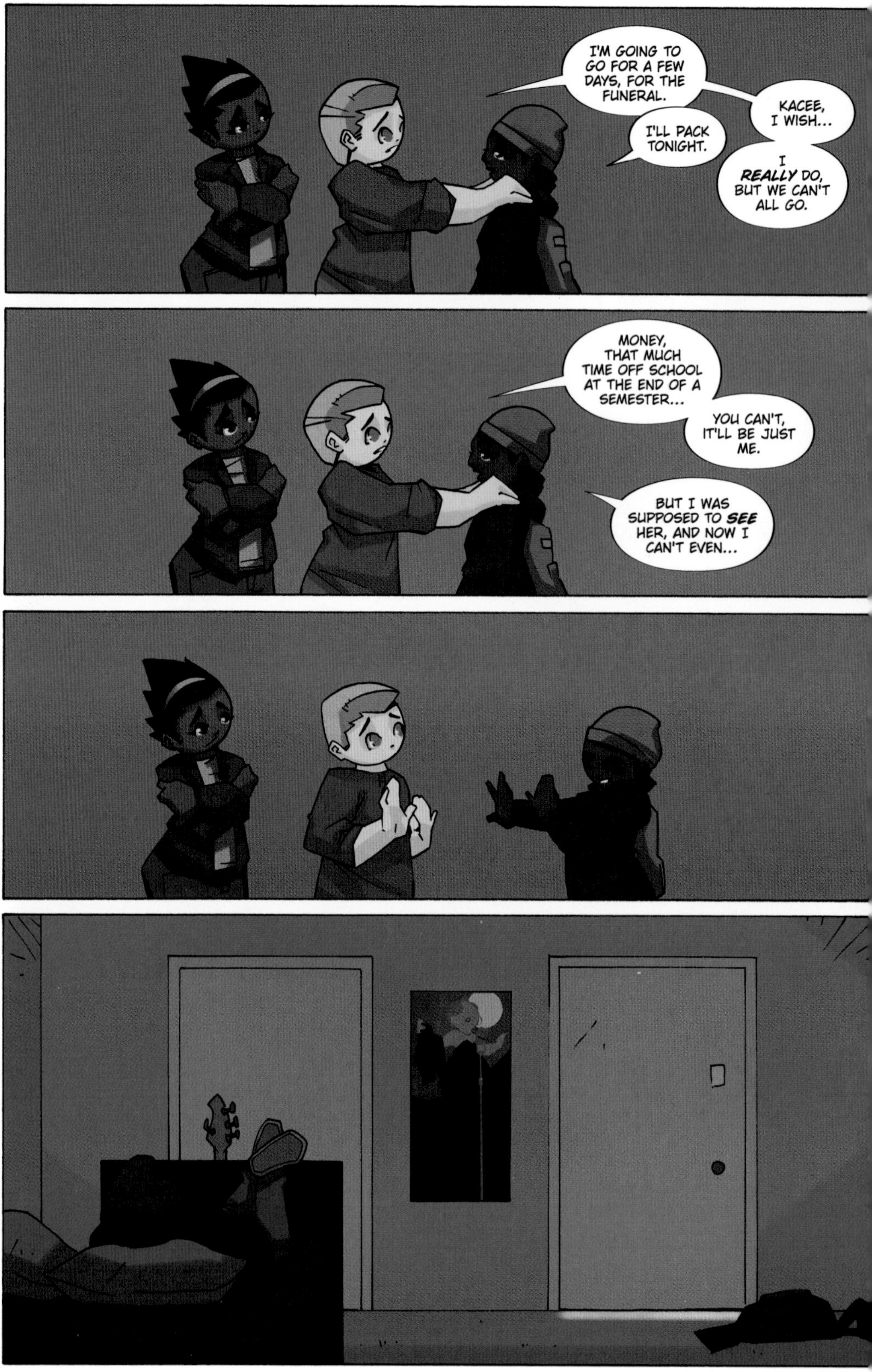
I'M GOING TO GO FOR A FEW DAYS, FOR THE FUNERAL.
I'LL PACK TONIGHT.
KACEE, I WISH...
I REALLY DO, BUT WE CAN'T ALL GO.
MONEY, THAT MUCH TIME OFF SCHOOL AT THE END OF A SEMESTER...
YOU CAN'T, IT'LL BE JUST ME.
BUT I WAS SUPPOSED TO SEE HER, AND NOW I CAN'T EVEN...

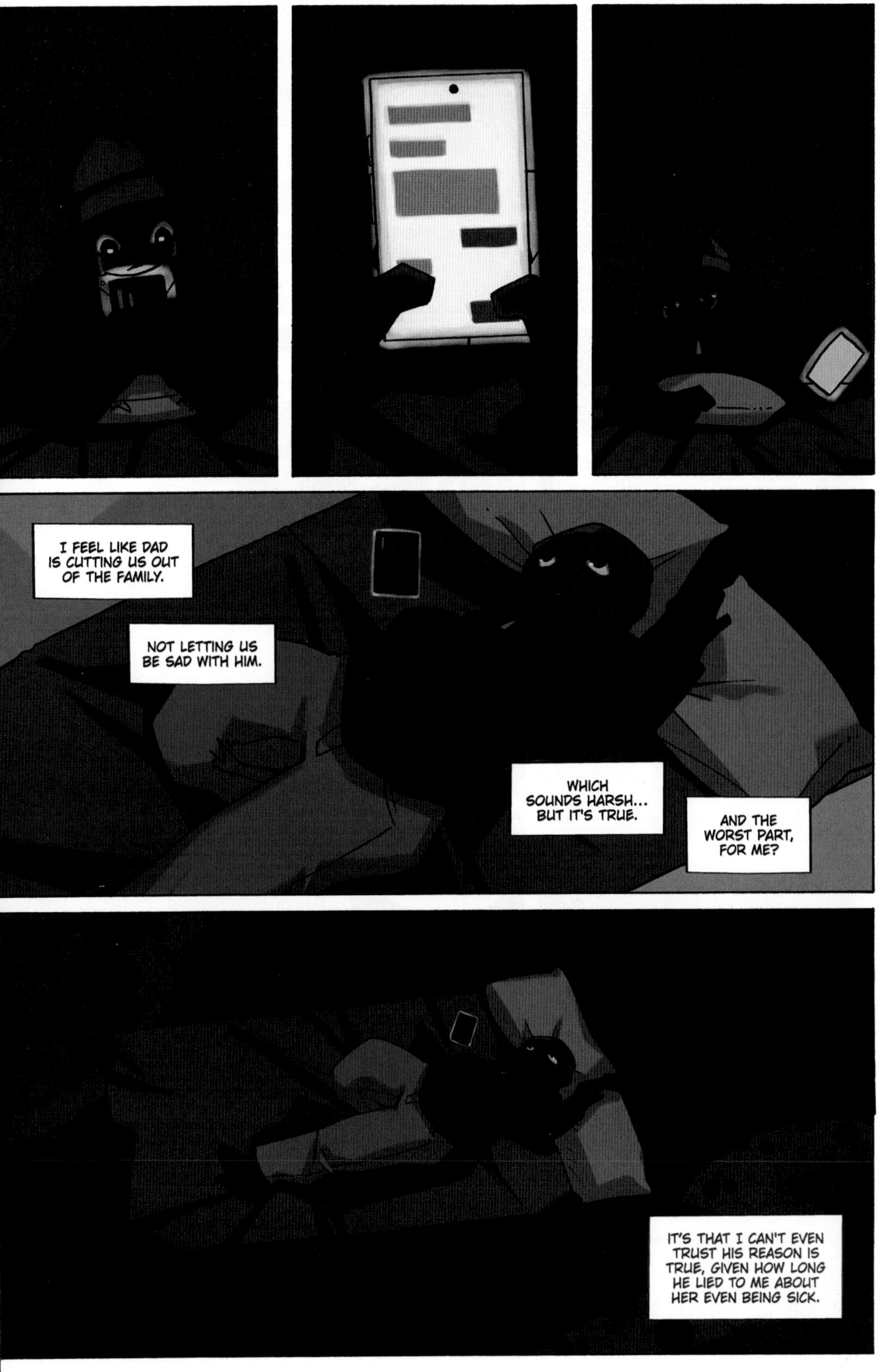
I FEEL LIKE DAD IS CUTTING US OUT OF THE FAMILY.
NOT LETTING US BE SAD WITH HIM.
WHICH SOUNDS HARSH... BUT IT'S TRUE.
AND THE WORST PART, FOR ME?
IT'S THAT I CAN'T EVEN TRUST HIS REASON IS TRUE, GIVEN HOW LONG HE LIED TO ME ABOUT HER EVEN BEING SICK.

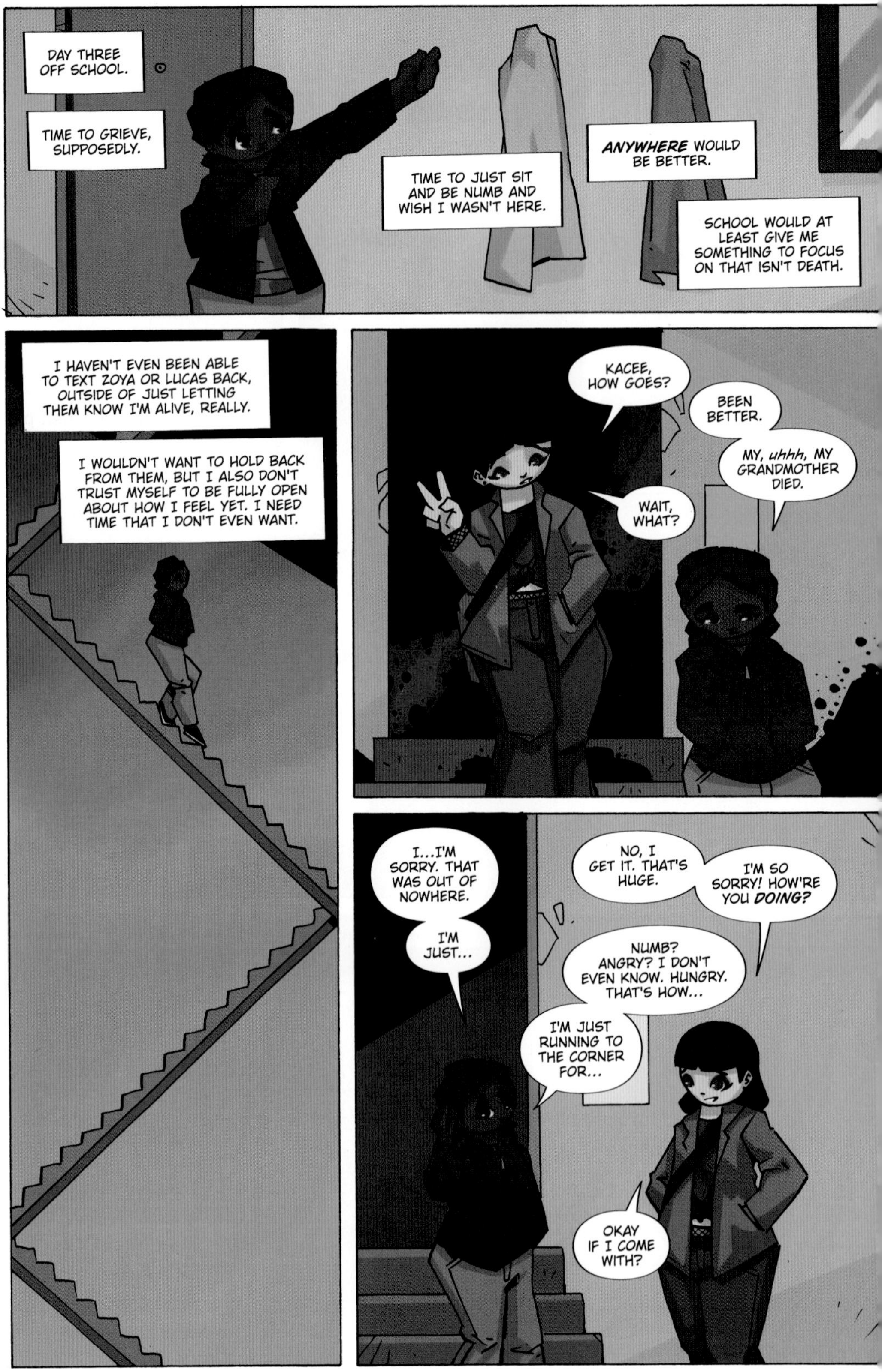
DAY THREE OFF SCHOOL.
TIME TO GRIEVE, SUPPOSEDLY.
TIME TO JUST SIT AND BE NUMB AND WISH I WASN'T HERE.
ANYWHERE WOULD BE BETTER.
SCHOOL WOULD AT LEAST GIVE ME SOMETHING TO FOCUS ON THAT ISN'T DEATH.
I HAVEN'T EVEN BEEN ABLE TO TEXT ZOYA OR LUCAS BACK, OUTSIDE OF JUST LETTING THEM KNOW I'M ALIVE, REALLY.
I WOULDN'T WANT TO HOLD BACK FROM THEM, BUT I ALSO DON'T TRUST MYSELF TO BE FULLY OPEN ABOUT HOW I FEEL YET. I NEED TIME THAT I DON'T EVEN WANT.
KACEE, HOW GOES?
BEEN BETTER.
MY, *uhhh*, MY GRANDMOTHER DIED.
WAIT, WHAT?
I...I'M SORRY. THAT WAS OUT OF NOWHERE.
I'M JUST...
NO, I GET IT. THAT'S HUGE.
I'M SO SORRY! HOW'RE YOU *DOING?*
NUMB? ANGRY? I DON'T EVEN KNOW. HUNGRY. THAT'S HOW...
I'M JUST RUNNING TO THE CORNER FOR...
OKAY IF I COME WITH?

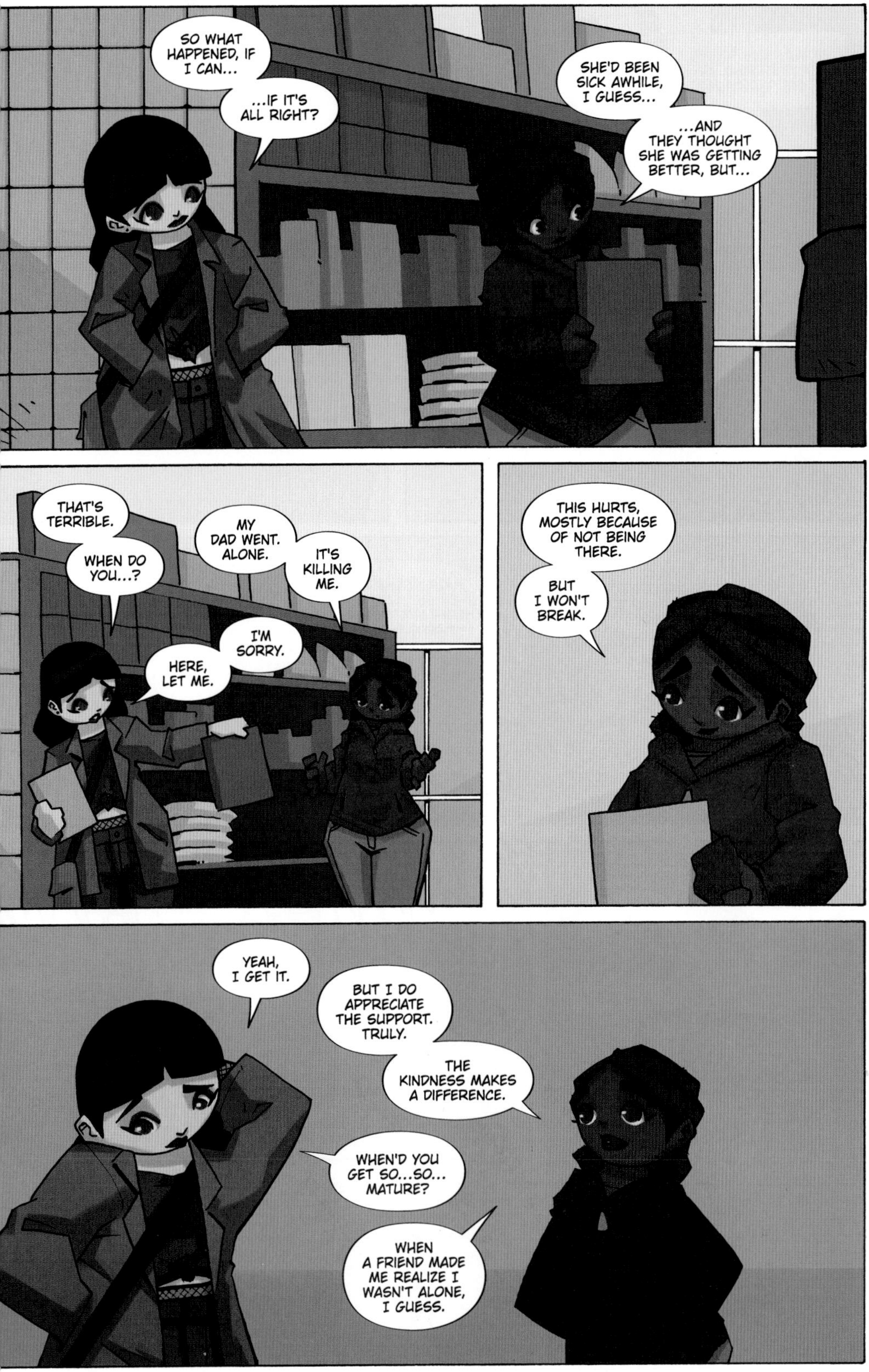
SO WHAT HAPPENED, IF I CAN...
...IF IT'S ALL RIGHT?
SHE'D BEEN SICK AWHILE, I GUESS...
...AND THEY THOUGHT SHE WAS GETTING BETTER, BUT...
THAT'S TERRIBLE.
WHEN DO YOU...?
MY DAD WENT. ALONE.
IT'S KILLING ME.
I'M SORRY.
HERE, LET ME.
THIS HURTS, MOSTLY BECAUSE OF NOT BEING THERE.
BUT I WON'T BREAK.
YEAH, I GET IT.
BUT I DO APPRECIATE THE SUPPORT. TRULY.
THE KINDNESS MAKES A DIFFERENCE.
WHEN'D YOU GET SO...SO... MATURE?
WHEN A FRIEND MADE ME REALIZE I WASN'T ALONE, I GUESS.

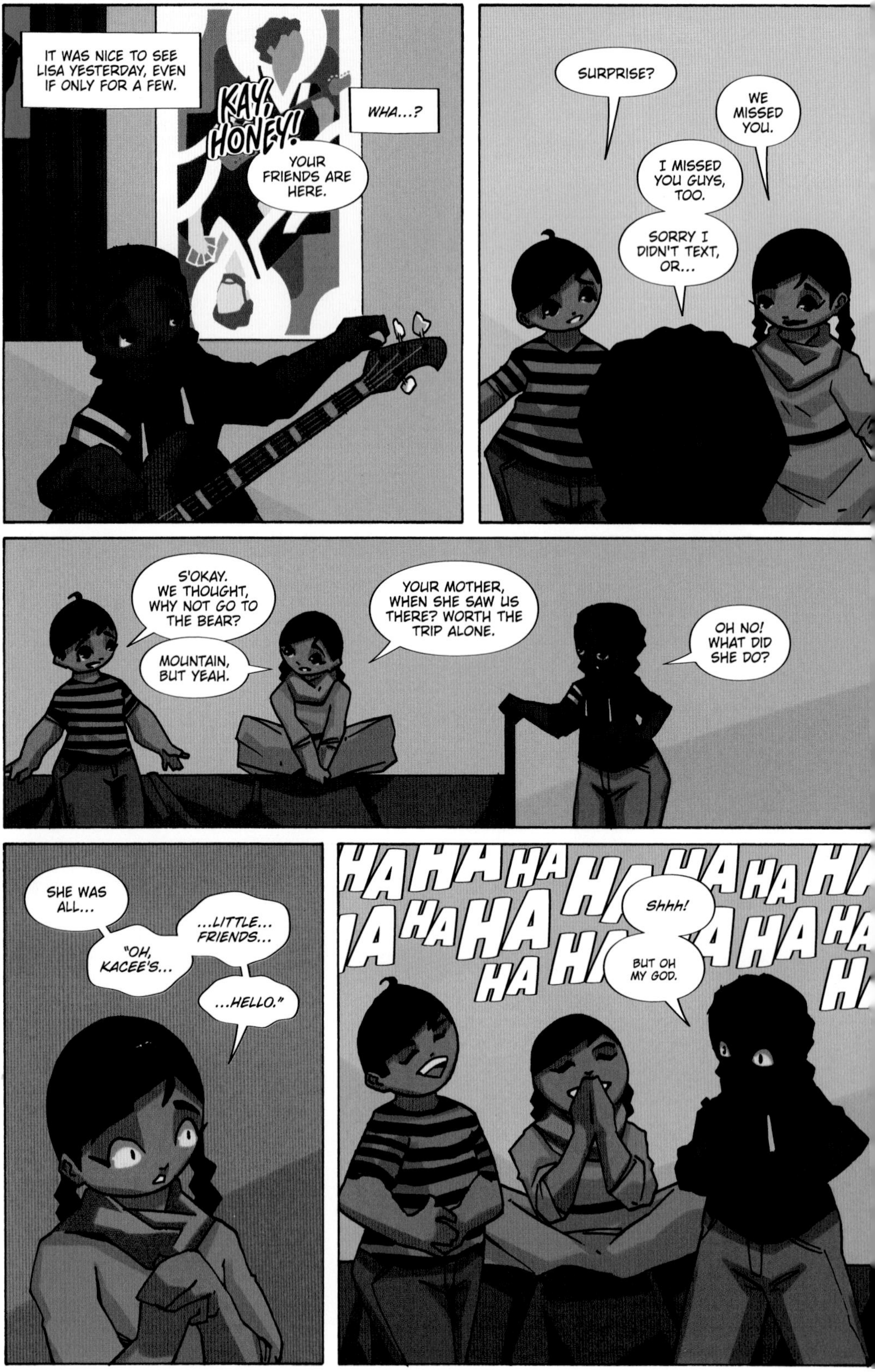

IT WAS NICE TO SEE LISA YESTERDAY, EVEN IF ONLY FOR A FEW.
KAY, HONEY!
YOUR FRIENDS ARE HERE.
WHA...?
SURPRISE?
WE MISSED YOU.
I MISSED YOU GUYS, TOO.
SORRY I DIDN'T TEXT, OR...
S'OKAY. WE THOUGHT, WHY NOT GO TO THE BEAR?
MOUNTAIN, BUT YEAH.
YOUR MOTHER, WHEN SHE SAW US THERE? WORTH THE TRIP ALONE.
OH NO! WHAT DID SHE DO?
SHE WAS ALL...
"OH, KACEE'S...
...LITTLE... FRIENDS...
...HELLO."
HA HA HA HA HA HA HA HA HA
HA HA HA HA HA HA HA HA
Shhh!
BUT OH MY GOD.

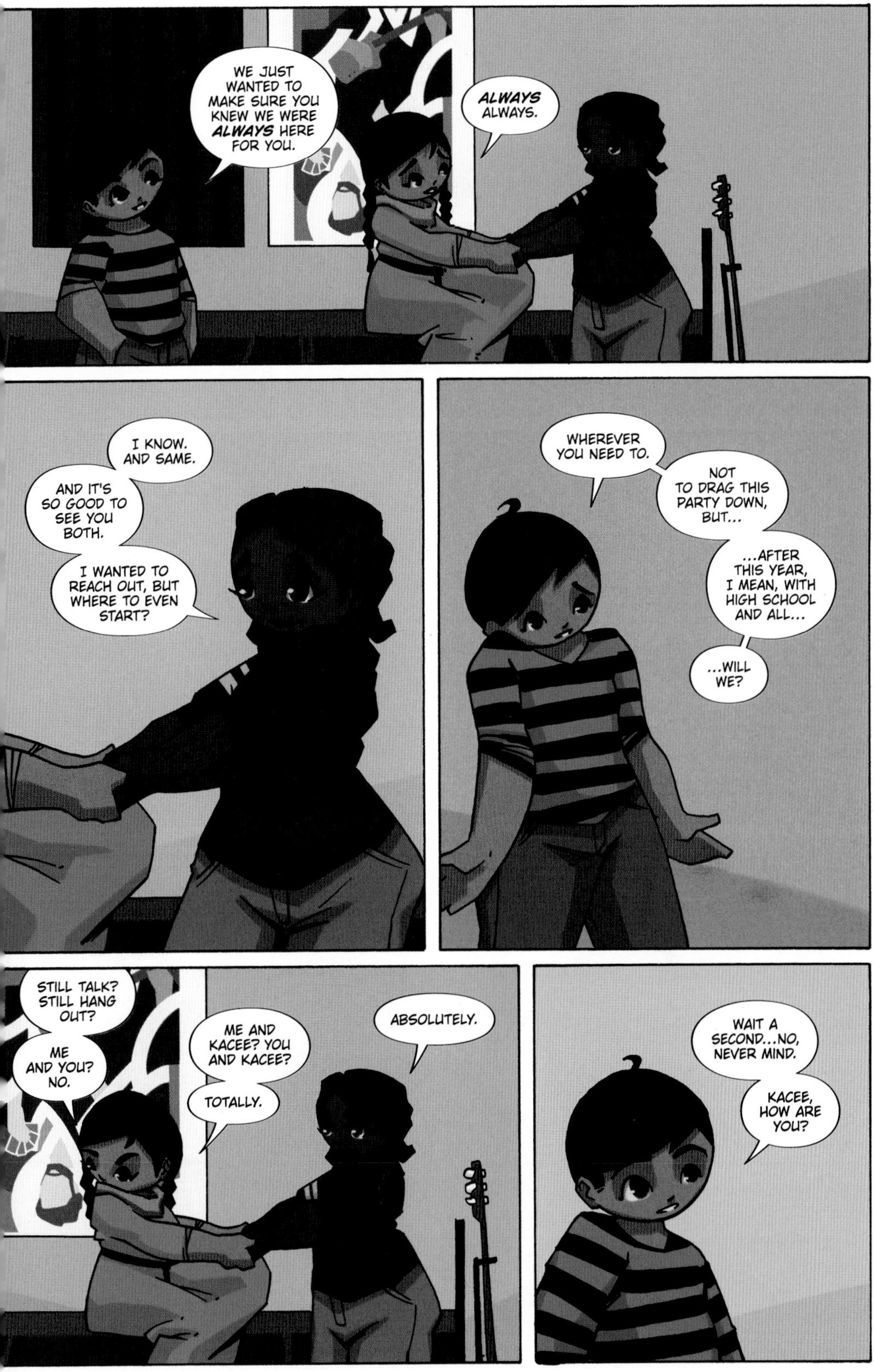
WE JUST WANTED TO MAKE SURE YOU KNEW WE WERE ***ALWAYS*** HERE FOR YOU.
ALWAYS ALWAYS.
I KNOW. AND SAME.
AND IT'S SO GOOD TO SEE YOU BOTH.
I WANTED TO REACH OUT, BUT WHERE TO EVEN START?
WHEREVER YOU NEED TO.
NOT TO DRAG THIS PARTY DOWN, BUT...
...AFTER THIS YEAR, I MEAN, WITH HIGH SCHOOL AND ALL...
...WILL WE?
STILL TALK? STILL HANG OUT?
ME AND YOU? NO.
ME AND KACEE? YOU AND KACEE?
TOTALLY.
ABSOLUTELY.
WAIT A SECOND...NO, NEVER MIND.
KACEE, HOW ARE YOU?

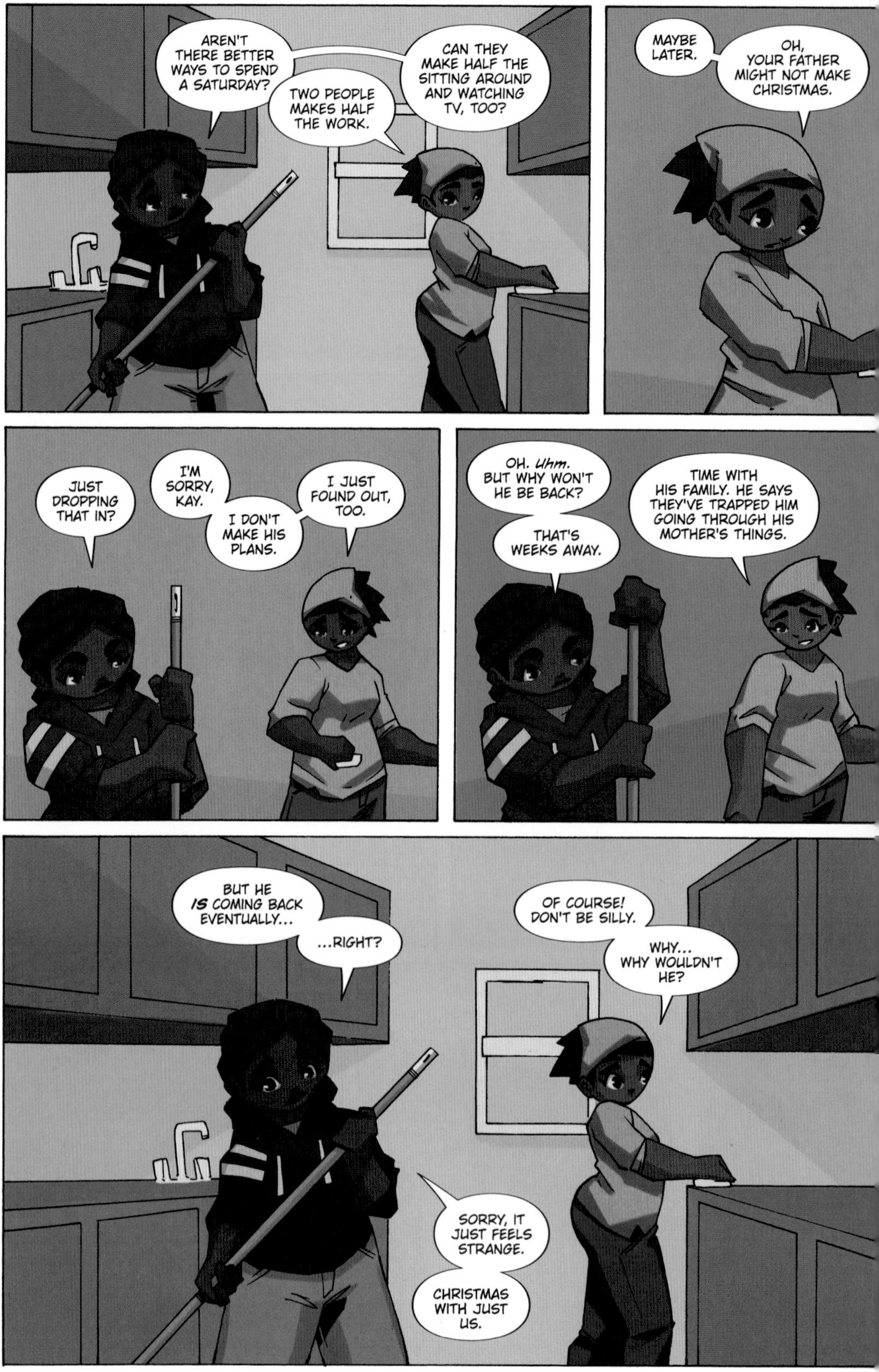
AREN'T THERE BETTER WAYS TO SPEND A SATURDAY?
TWO PEOPLE MAKES HALF THE WORK.
CAN THEY MAKE HALF THE SITTING AROUND AND WATCHING TV, TOO?
MAYBE LATER.
OH, YOUR FATHER MIGHT NOT MAKE CHRISTMAS.
JUST DROPPING THAT IN?
I'M SORRY, KAY.
I DON'T MAKE HIS PLANS.
I JUST FOUND OUT, TOO.
OH. *Uhm.* BUT WHY WON'T HE BE BACK?
THAT'S WEEKS AWAY.
TIME WITH HIS FAMILY. HE SAYS THEY'VE TRAPPED HIM GOING THROUGH HIS MOTHER'S THINGS.
BUT HE *IS* COMING BACK EVENTUALLY...
...RIGHT?
OF COURSE! DON'T BE SILLY.
WHY... WHY WOULDN'T HE?
SORRY, IT JUST FEELS STRANGE.
CHRISTMAS WITH JUST US.

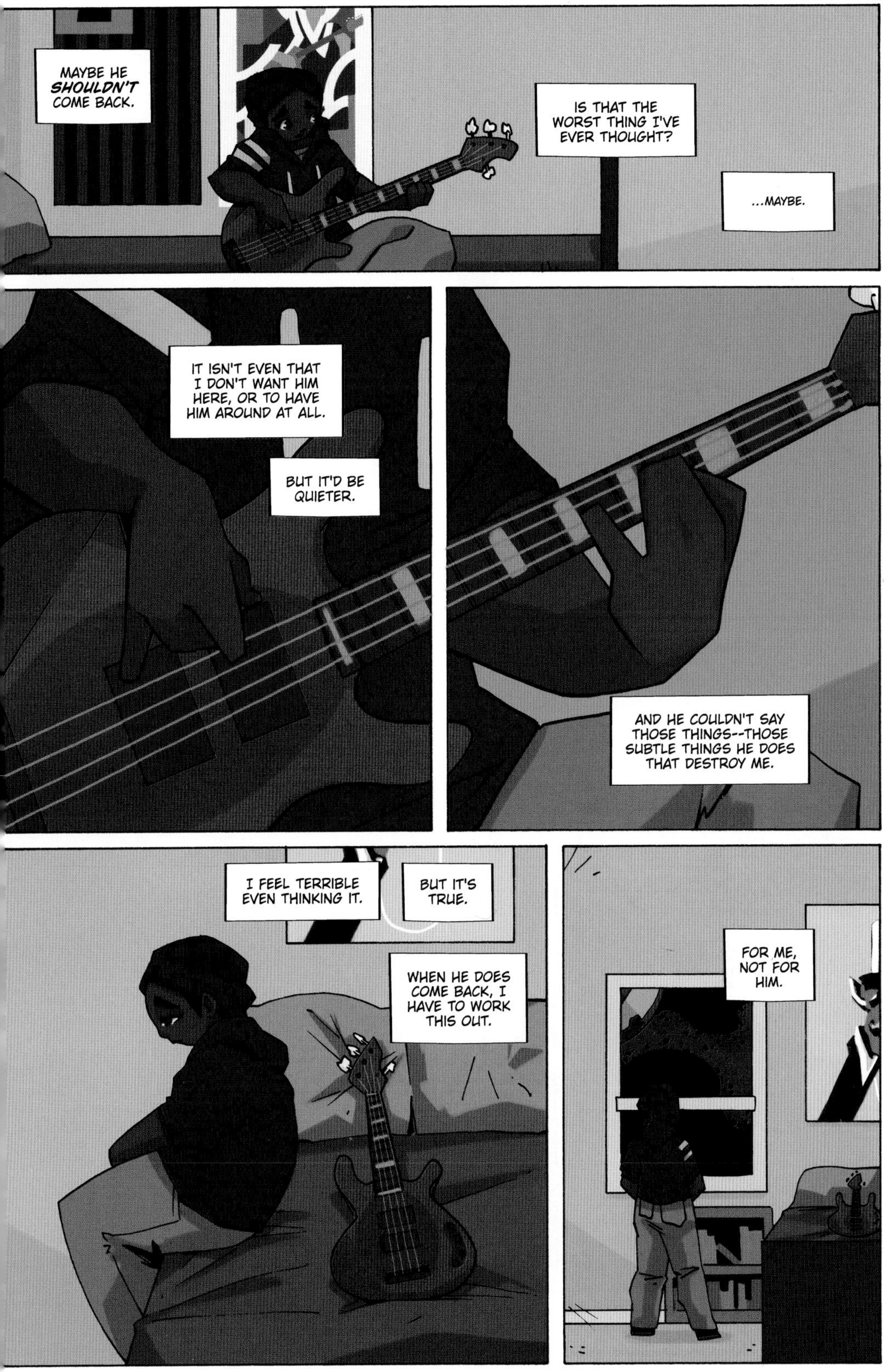
MAYBE HE *SHOULDN'T* COME BACK.
IS THAT THE WORST THING I'VE EVER THOUGHT?
...MAYBE.
IT ISN'T EVEN THAT I DON'T WANT HIM HERE, OR TO HAVE HIM AROUND AT ALL.
BUT IT'D BE QUIETER.
AND HE COULDN'T SAY THOSE THINGS--THOSE SUBTLE THINGS HE DOES THAT DESTROY ME.
I FEEL TERRIBLE EVEN THINKING IT.
BUT IT'S TRUE.
WHEN HE DOES COME BACK, I HAVE TO WORK THIS OUT.
FOR ME, NOT FOR HIM.

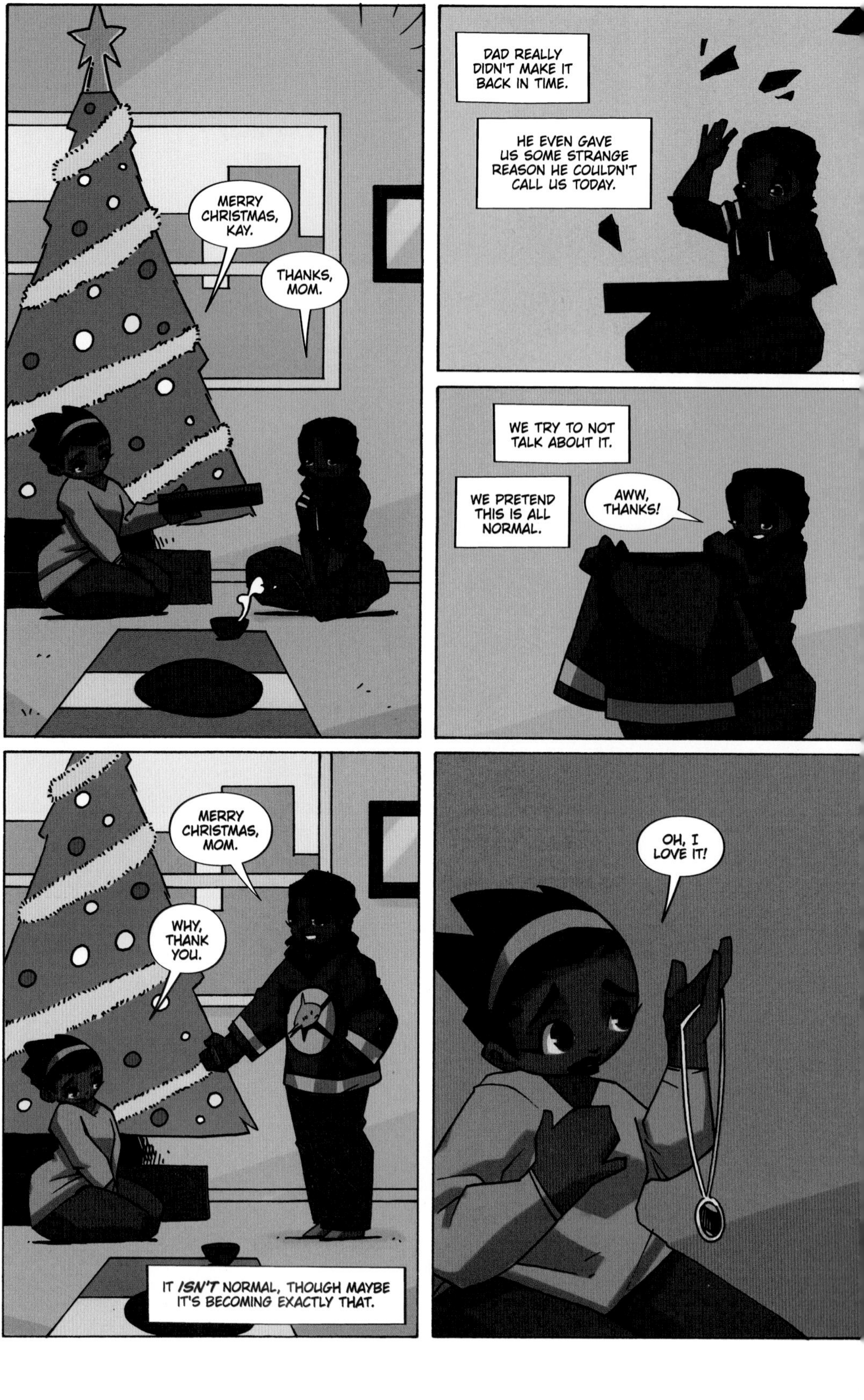
MERRY CHRISTMAS, KAY.
THANKS, MOM.
DAD REALLY DIDN'T MAKE IT BACK IN TIME.
HE EVEN GAVE US SOME STRANGE REASON HE COULDN'T CALL US TODAY.
WE TRY TO NOT TALK ABOUT IT.
WE PRETEND THIS IS ALL NORMAL.
AWW, THANKS!
MERRY CHRISTMAS, MOM.
WHY, THANK YOU.
IT ISN'T NORMAL, THOUGH MAYBE IT'S BECOMING EXACTLY THAT.
OH, I LOVE IT!

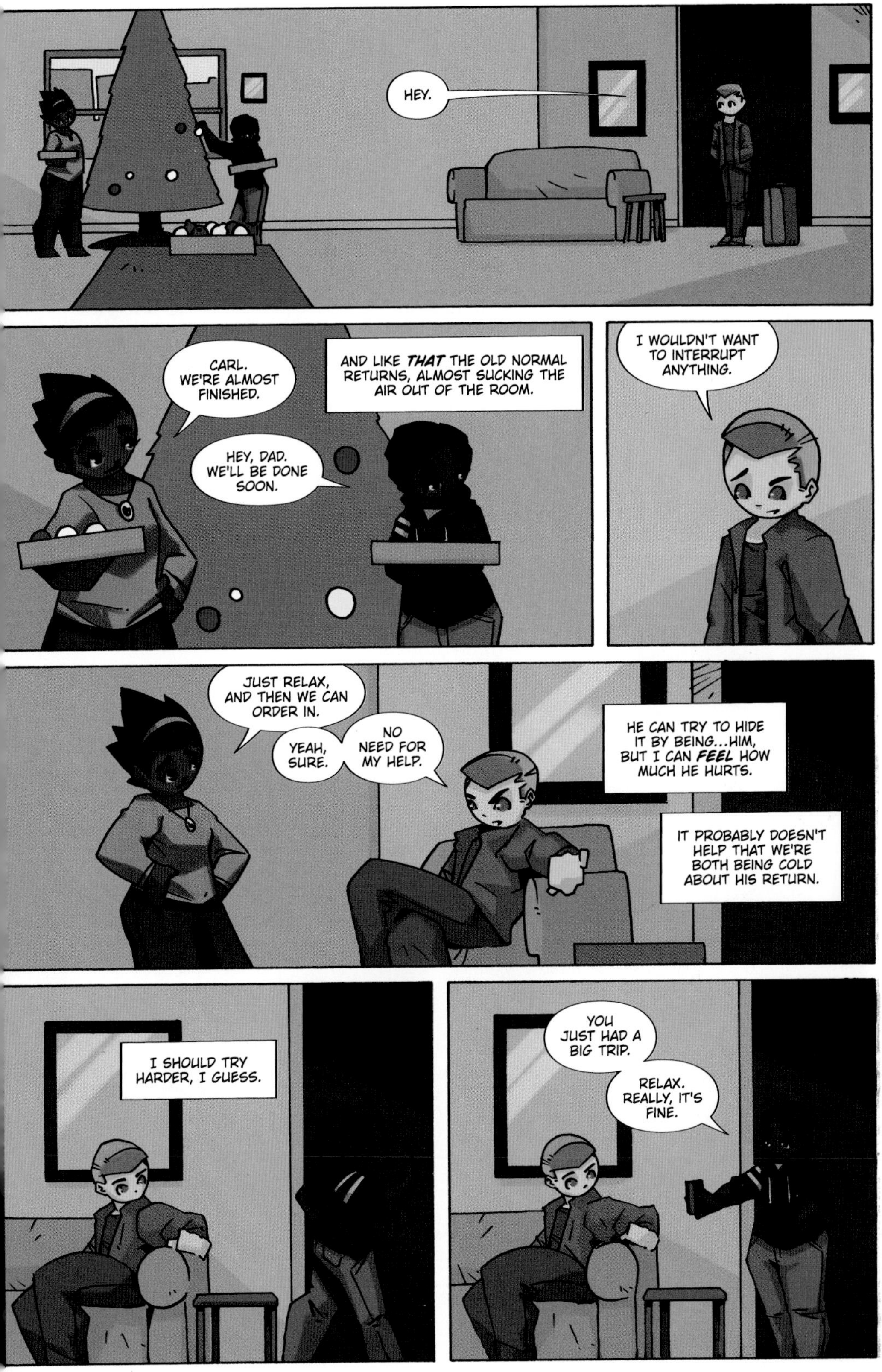
HEY.
CARL. WE'RE ALMOST FINISHED.
HEY, DAD. WE'LL BE DONE SOON.
AND LIKE *THAT* THE OLD NORMAL RETURNS, ALMOST SUCKING THE AIR OUT OF THE ROOM.
I WOULDN'T WANT TO INTERRUPT ANYTHING.
JUST RELAX, AND THEN WE CAN ORDER IN.
YEAH, SURE.
NO NEED FOR MY HELP.
HE CAN TRY TO HIDE IT BY BEING...HIM, BUT I CAN *FEEL* HOW MUCH HE HURTS.
IT PROBABLY DOESN'T HELP THAT WE'RE BOTH BEING COLD ABOUT HIS RETURN.
I SHOULD TRY HARDER, I GUESS.
YOU JUST HAD A BIG TRIP.
RELAX. REALLY, IT'S FINE.

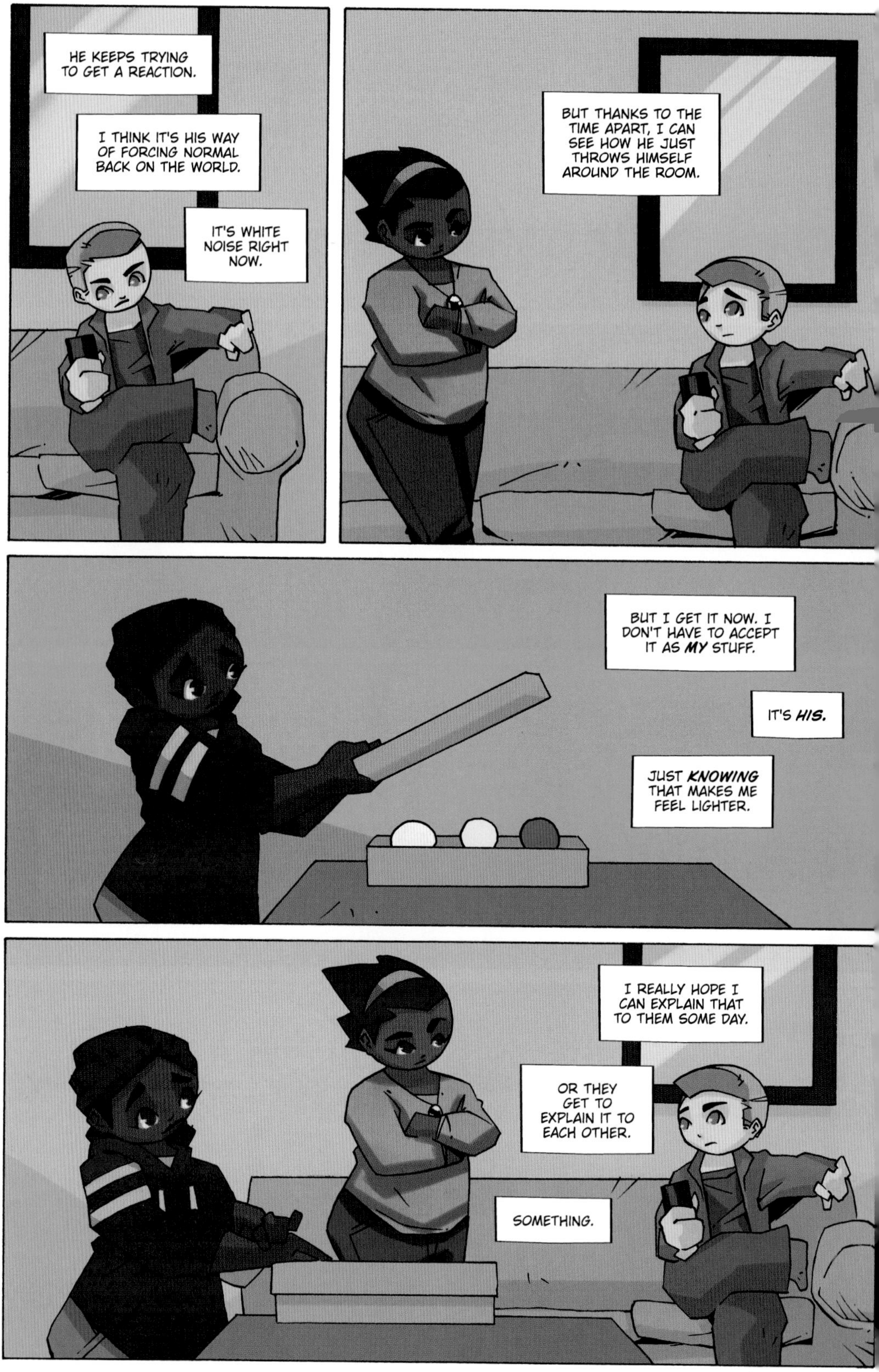
HE KEEPS TRYING TO GET A REACTION.
I THINK IT'S HIS WAY OF FORCING NORMAL BACK ON THE WORLD.
IT'S WHITE NOISE RIGHT NOW.
BUT THANKS TO THE TIME APART, I CAN SEE HOW HE JUST THROWS HIMSELF AROUND THE ROOM.
BUT I GET IT NOW. I DON'T HAVE TO ACCEPT IT AS *MY* STUFF.
IT'S *HIS.*
JUST *KNOWING* THAT MAKES ME FEEL LIGHTER.
I REALLY HOPE I CAN EXPLAIN THAT TO THEM SOME DAY.
OR THEY GET TO EXPLAIN IT TO EACH OTHER.
SOMETHING.

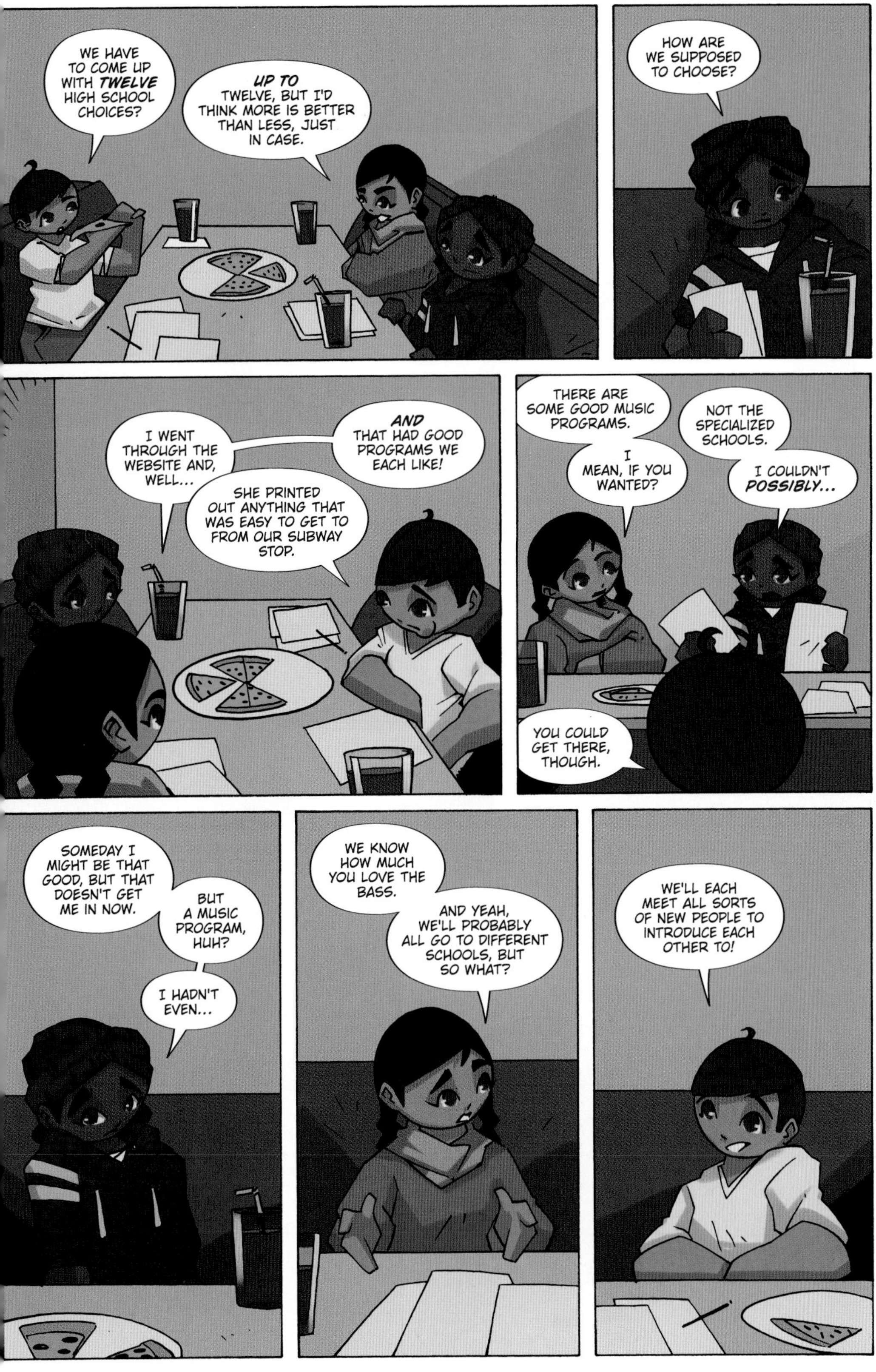
WE HAVE TO COME UP WITH *TWELVE* HIGH SCHOOL CHOICES?
UP TO TWELVE, BUT I'D THINK MORE IS BETTER THAN LESS, JUST IN CASE.
HOW ARE WE SUPPOSED TO CHOOSE?
I WENT THROUGH THE WEBSITE AND, WELL...
AND THAT HAD GOOD PROGRAMS WE EACH LIKE!
SHE PRINTED OUT ANYTHING THAT WAS EASY TO GET TO FROM OUR SUBWAY STOP.
THERE ARE SOME GOOD MUSIC PROGRAMS.
I MEAN, IF YOU WANTED?
NOT THE SPECIALIZED SCHOOLS.
I COULDN'T *POSSIBLY...*
YOU COULD GET THERE, THOUGH.
SOMEDAY I MIGHT BE THAT GOOD, BUT THAT DOESN'T GET ME IN NOW.
BUT A MUSIC PROGRAM, HUH?
I HADN'T EVEN...
WE KNOW HOW MUCH YOU LOVE THE BASS.
AND YEAH, WE'LL PROBABLY ALL GO TO DIFFERENT SCHOOLS, BUT SO WHAT?
WE'LL EACH MEET ALL SORTS OF NEW PEOPLE TO INTRODUCE EACH OTHER TO!

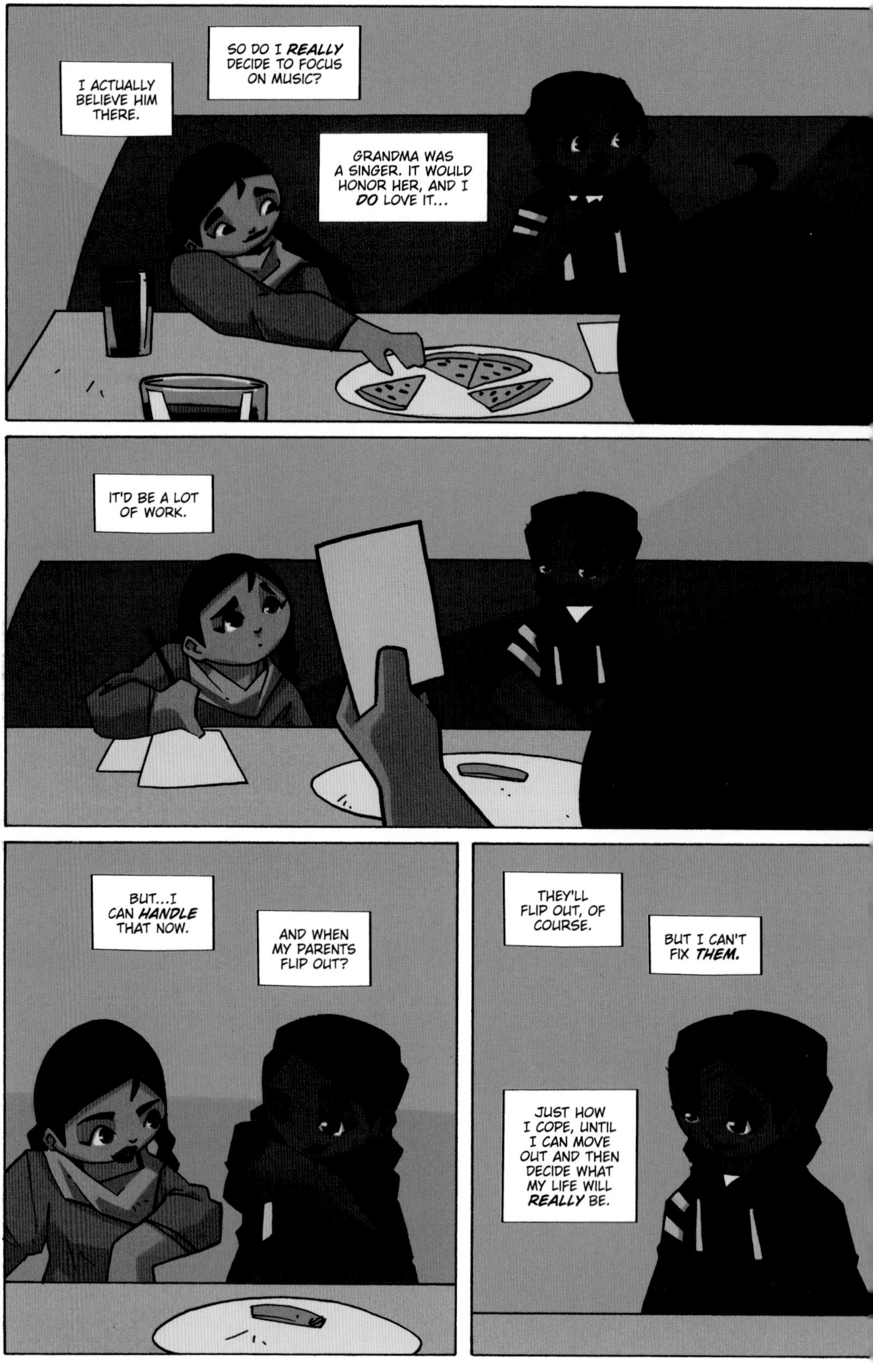
I ACTUALLY BELIEVE HIM THERE.
SO DO I *REALLY* DECIDE TO FOCUS ON MUSIC?
GRANDMA WAS A SINGER. IT WOULD HONOR HER, AND I *DO* LOVE IT...
IT'D BE A LOT OF WORK.
BUT...I CAN *HANDLE* THAT NOW.
AND WHEN MY PARENTS FLIP OUT?
THEY'LL FLIP OUT, OF COURSE.
BUT I CAN'T FIX *THEM.*
JUST HOW I COPE, UNTIL I CAN MOVE OUT AND THEN DECIDE WHAT MY LIFE WILL *REALLY* BE.

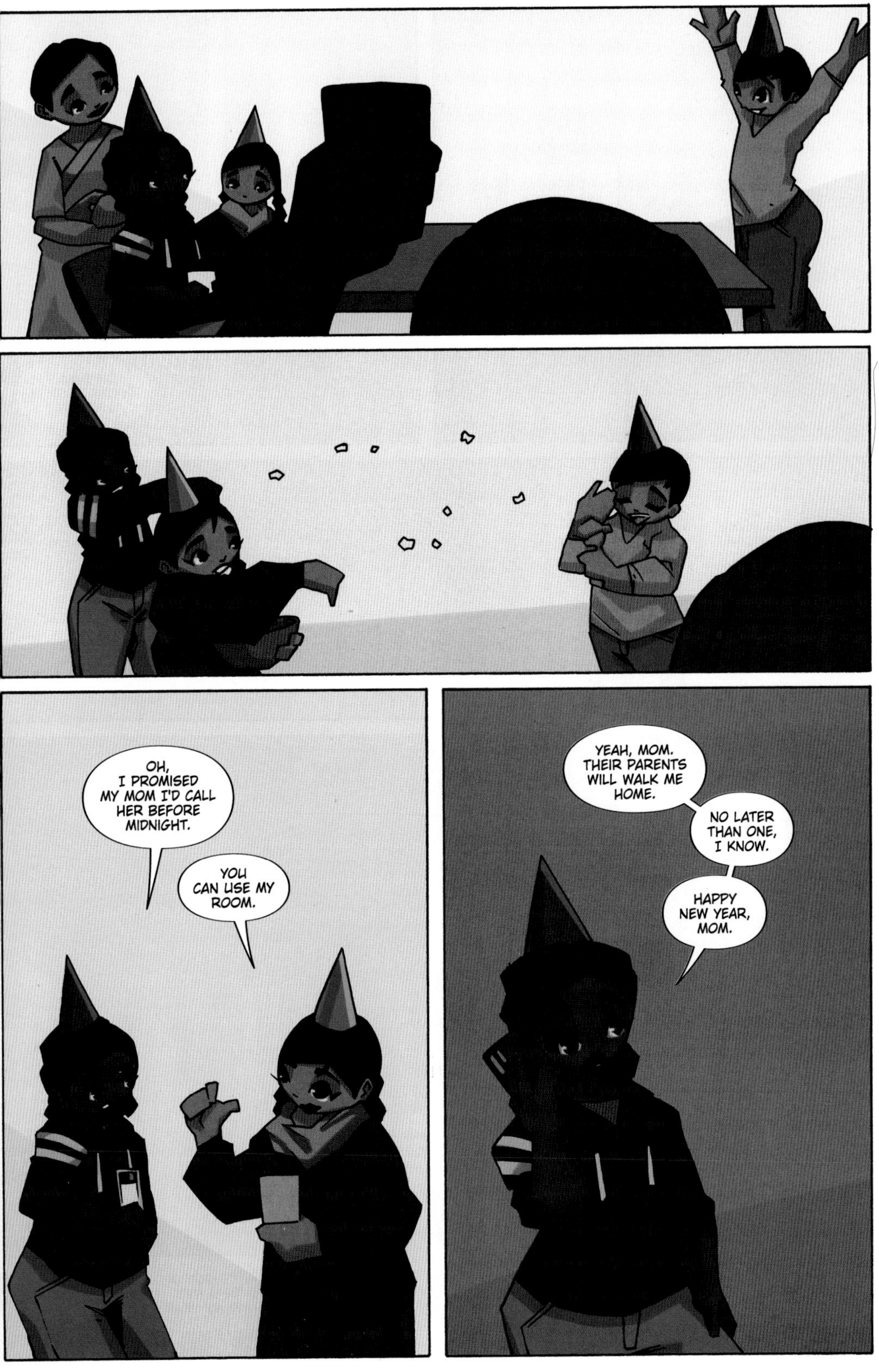
OH, I PROMISED MY MOM I'D CALL HER BEFORE MIDNIGHT.
YOU CAN USE MY ROOM.
YEAH, MOM. THEIR PARENTS WILL WALK ME HOME.
NO LATER THAN ONE, I KNOW.
HAPPY NEW YEAR, MOM.

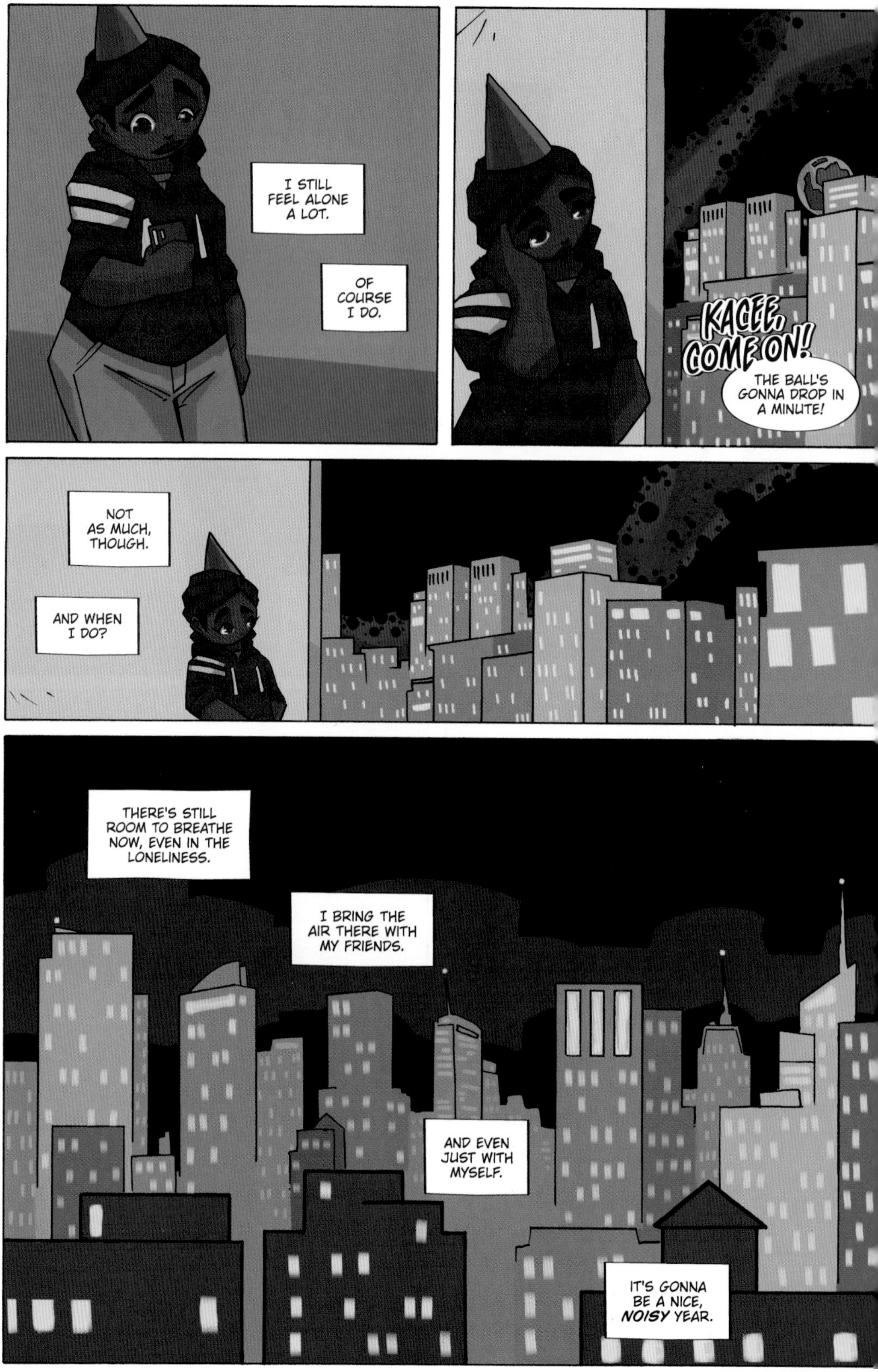
I STILL FEEL ALONE A LOT.
OF COURSE I DO.
KACEE, COME ON!
THE BALL'S GONNA DROP IN A MINUTE!
NOT AS MUCH, THOUGH.
AND WHEN I DO?
THERE'S STILL ROOM TO BREATHE NOW, EVEN IN THE LONELINESS.
I BRING THE AIR THERE WITH MY FRIENDS.
AND EVEN JUST WITH MYSELF.
IT'S GONNA BE A NICE, *NOISY* YEAR.

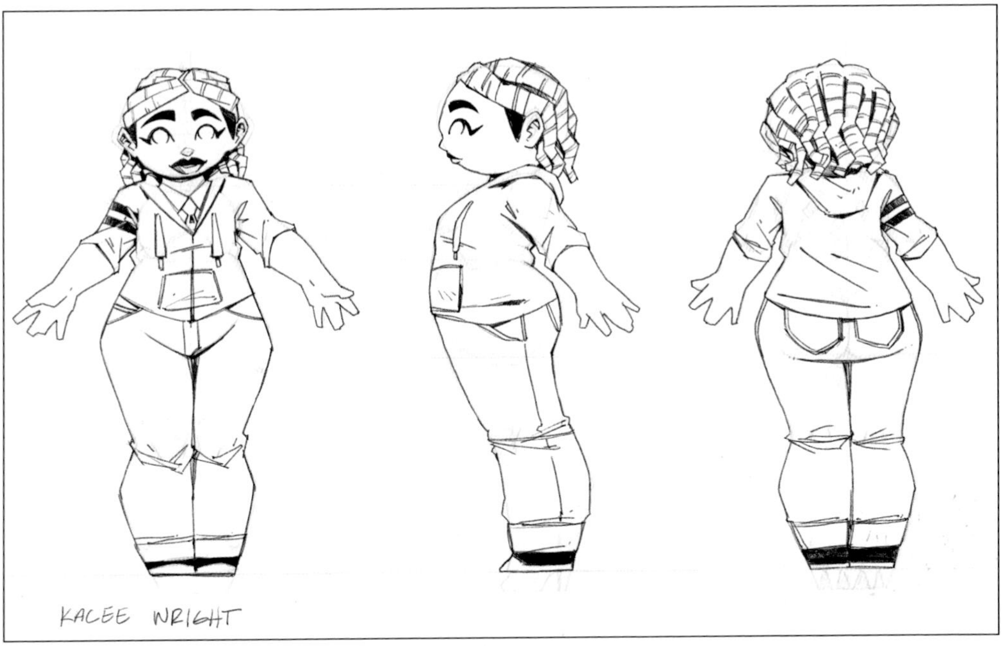
KACEE WRIGHT

Preliminary designs for Kacee

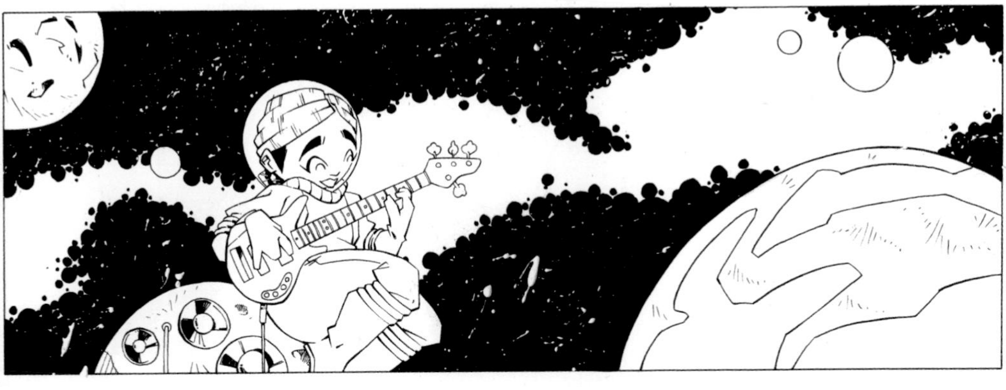

The sci-fi headspace that helped her avoid her everyday problems turned out to be more of a burden than an escape.

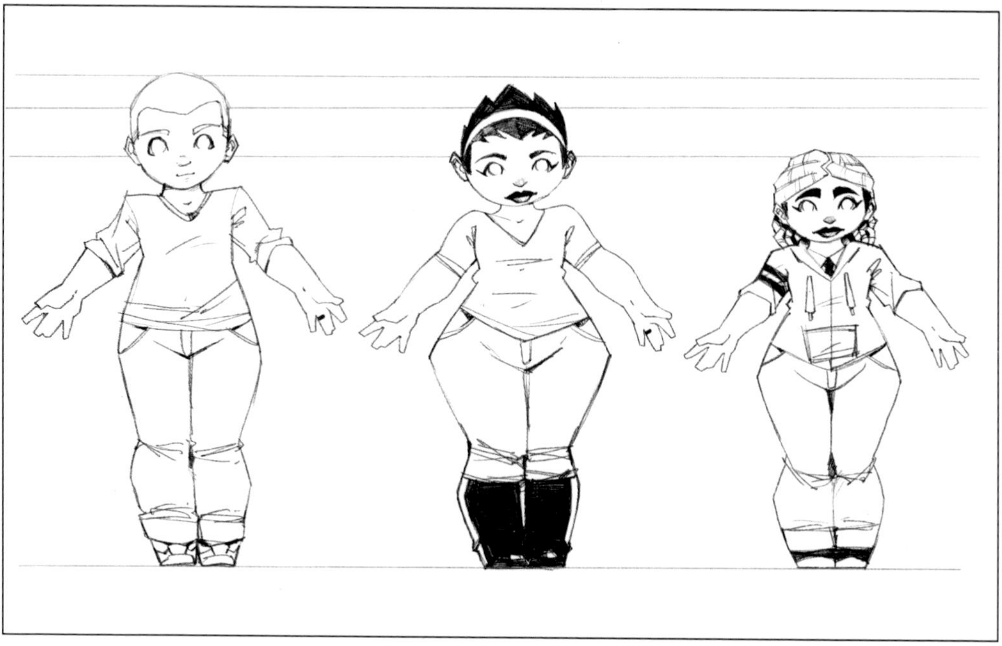

In the original designs Kacee's father was taller than her mom, but as the story came together the height comparison shifted.

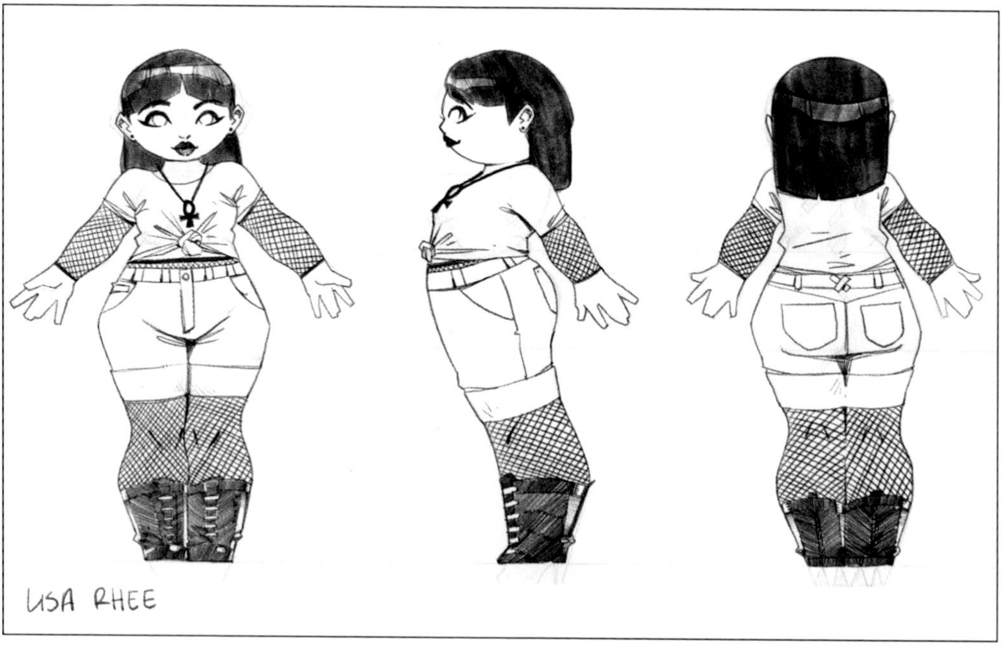
LISA RHEE

Lisa Rhee

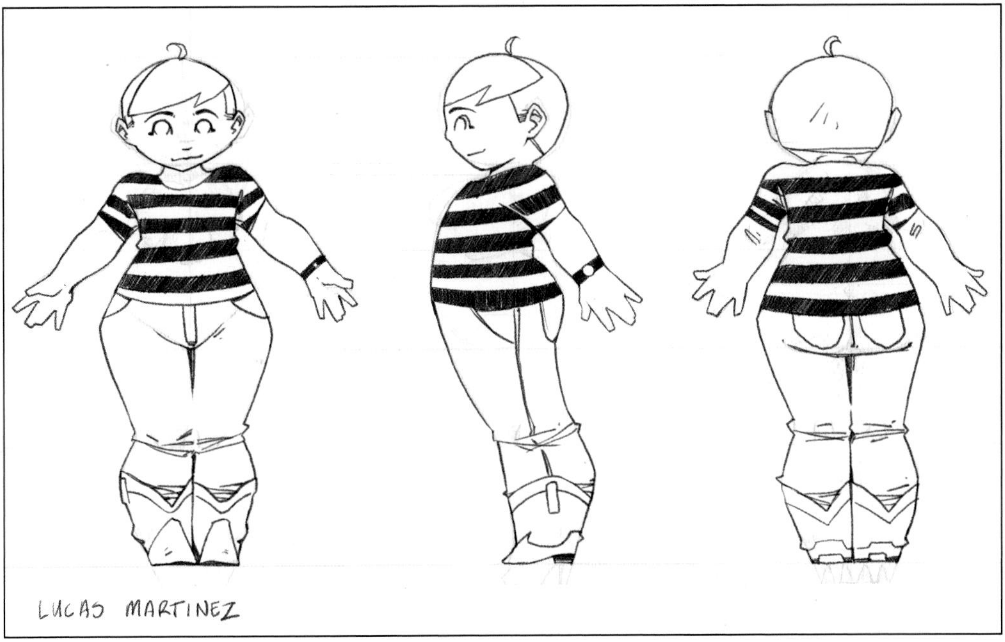
LUCAS MARTINEZ

Antagonistic twins Zoya and Lucas Martinez. Their love for Kacee is stronger than their sibling rivalries.

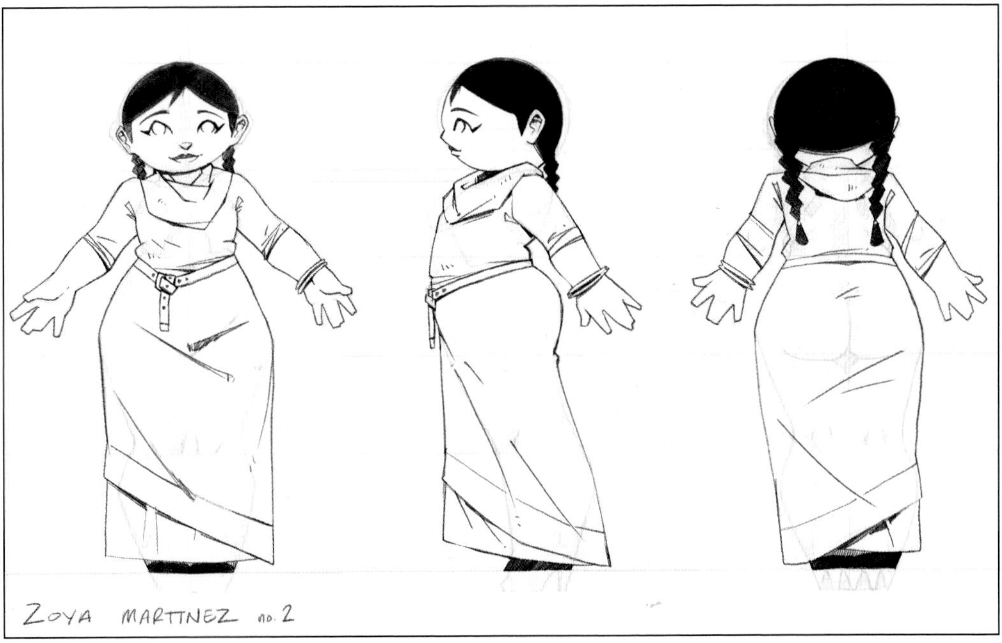
ZOYA MARTINEZ no. 2

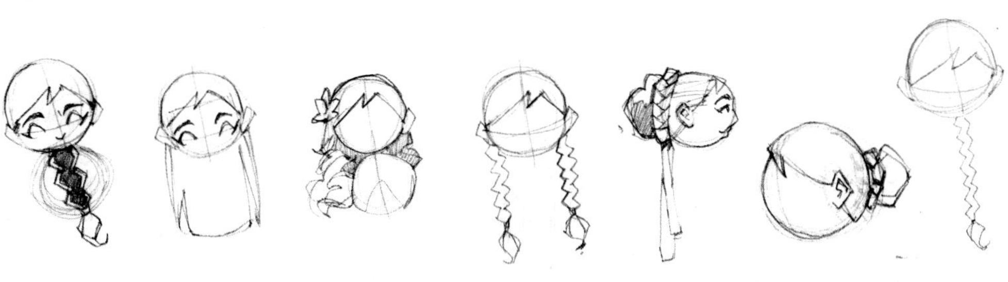

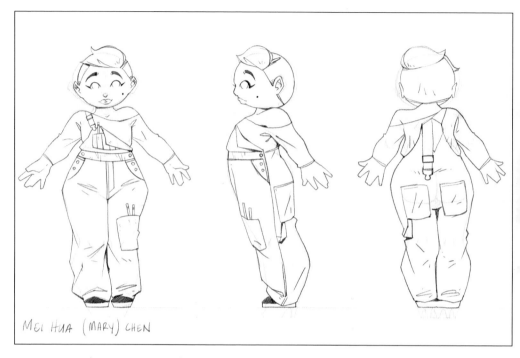

MEI HUA (MARY) CHEN

It was important to the entire creative team that a multitude of genders, cultural identities, racial backgrounds, and dress styles be represented in this comic, but that they not be the focus of the story. Diversity is the norm.

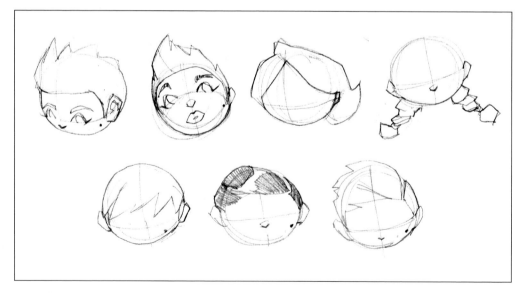

Mei Hua Chen

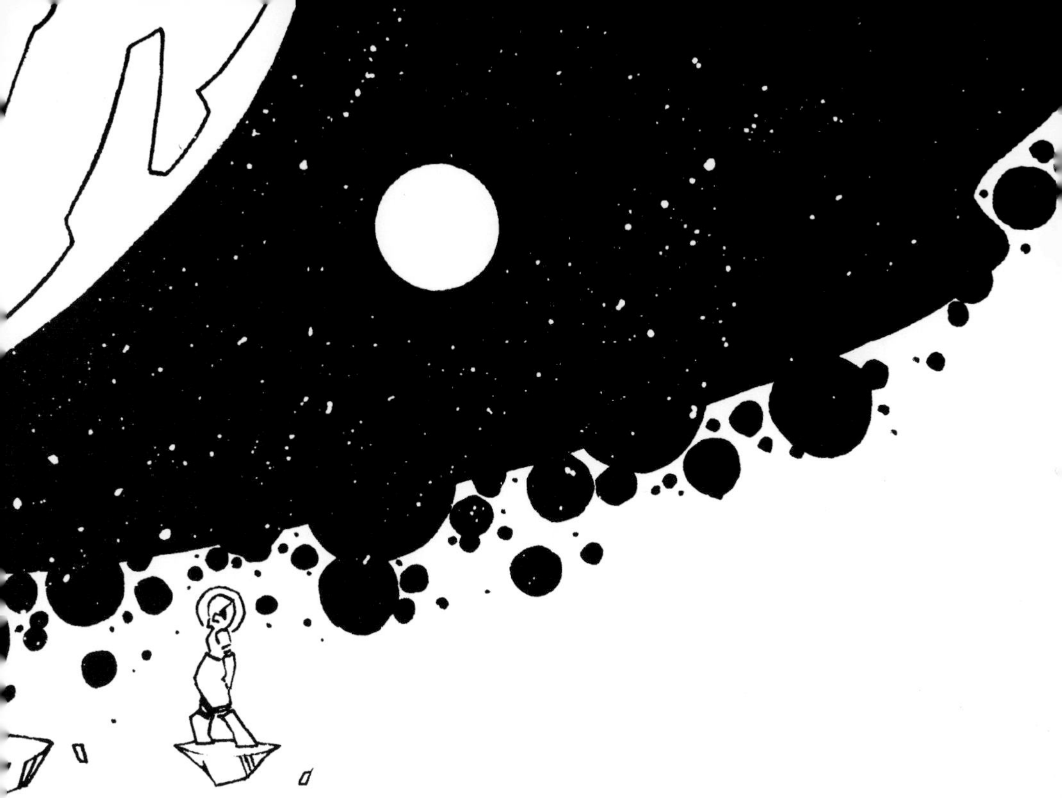

WHERE DID THE IDEA FOR *THE AIRLESS YEAR* COME FROM?

Adam P. Knave (writer): Valentine and I have meant to work together for years. One day we were sitting on my patio, listening to music, and decided that was it, we were going to find a story that spoke to us deeply and just do the thing. We started to find the core of the idea. Given both of our lives when we were younger, the emotional core of the characters revealed itself to us quickly.

Valentine Barker (artist): Ultimately, I think, we wanted to tell a relatable story. Middle school is kind of a crucible and there's a lot of growth that can happen in those few short years. Adam and I were discussing this idea and found there was a lot of overlap between our personal stories, and I think we just wanted to try to help other kids know that their personal stories were possible to grow past.

Frank Cvetkovic (letterer): While Adam and Valentine came up with the initial idea behind *The Airless Year*, I think we all related to the hardships of having to navigate through difficult relationships with family and friends, troubles at school, and all the uncertainty that comes with being thirteen. We each put a little bit of ourselves into this story, in hopes that it might help young readers who may be going through similar experiences realize that they're not alone.

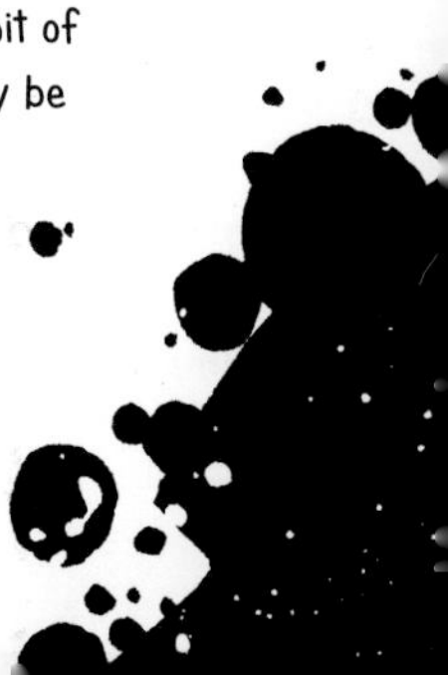

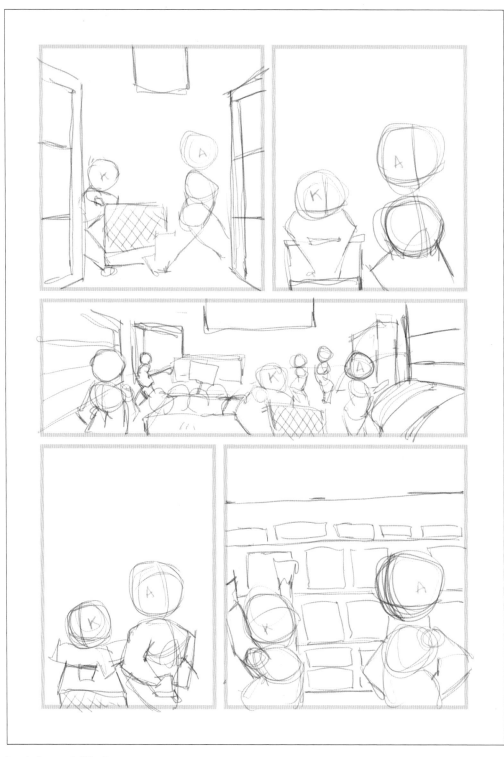

Layouts for page 7 of the story.

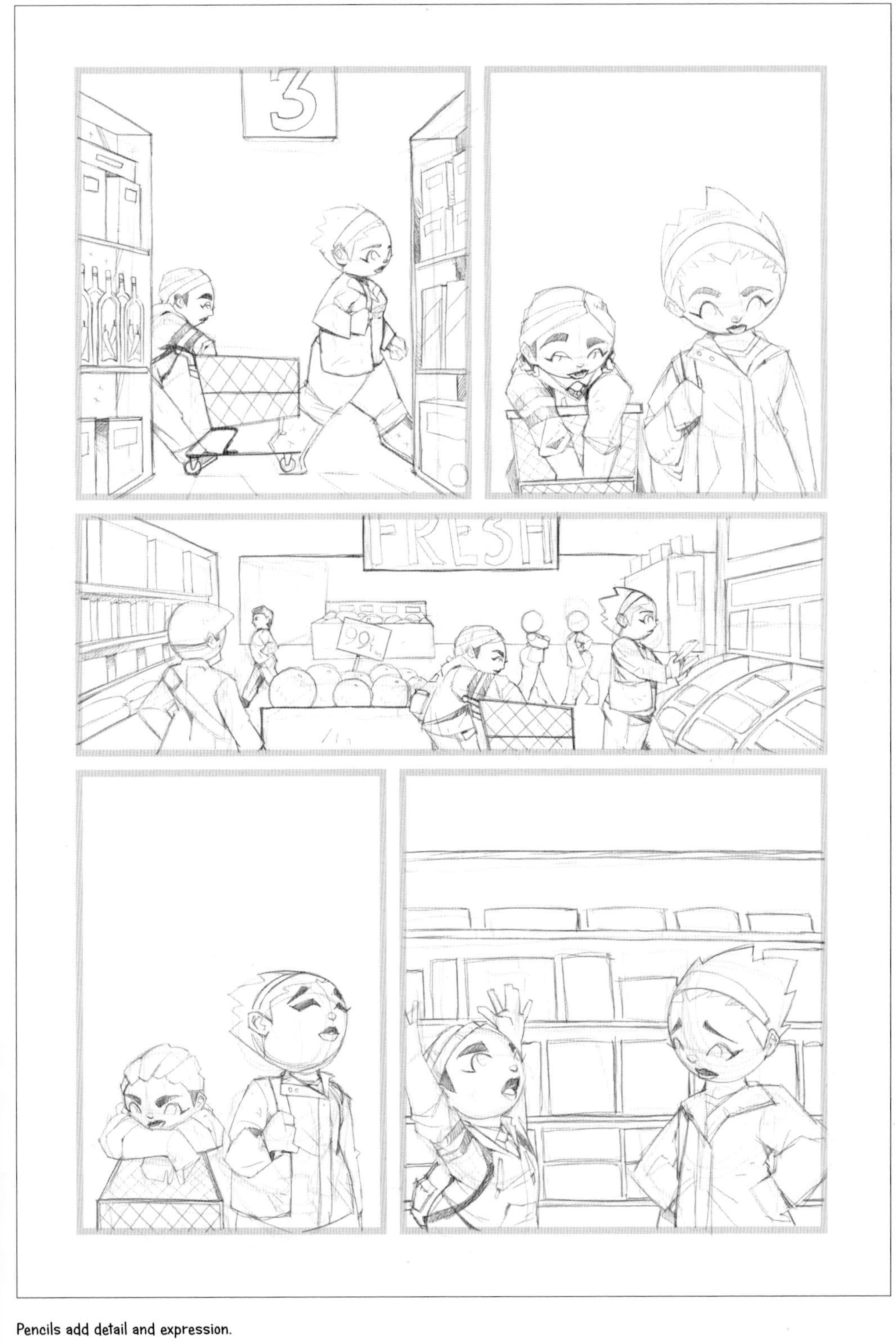
3
FRESH
99¢

Pencils add detail and expression.

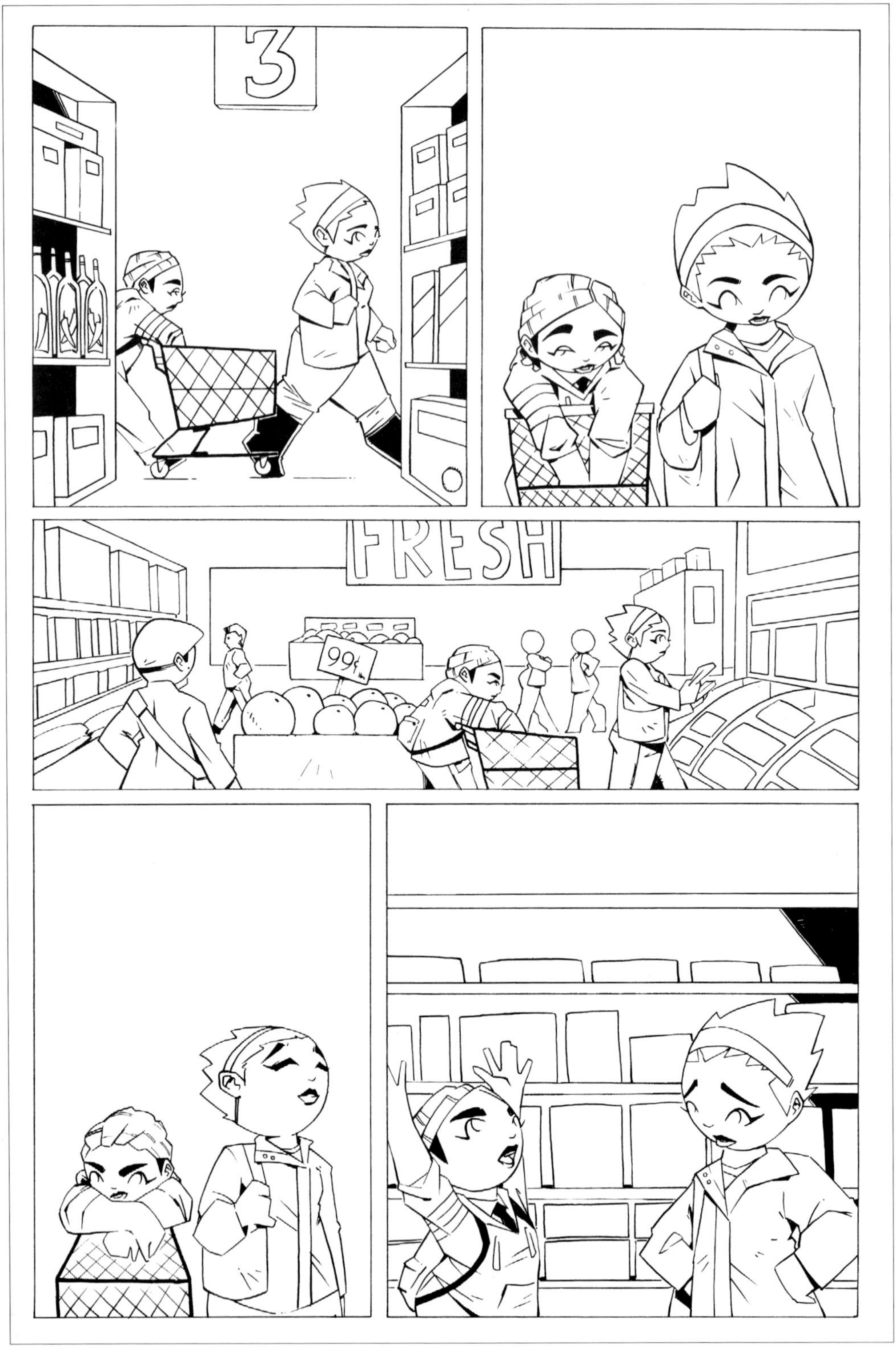
3
FRESH
99¢

Line art streamlines and finalizes the images.

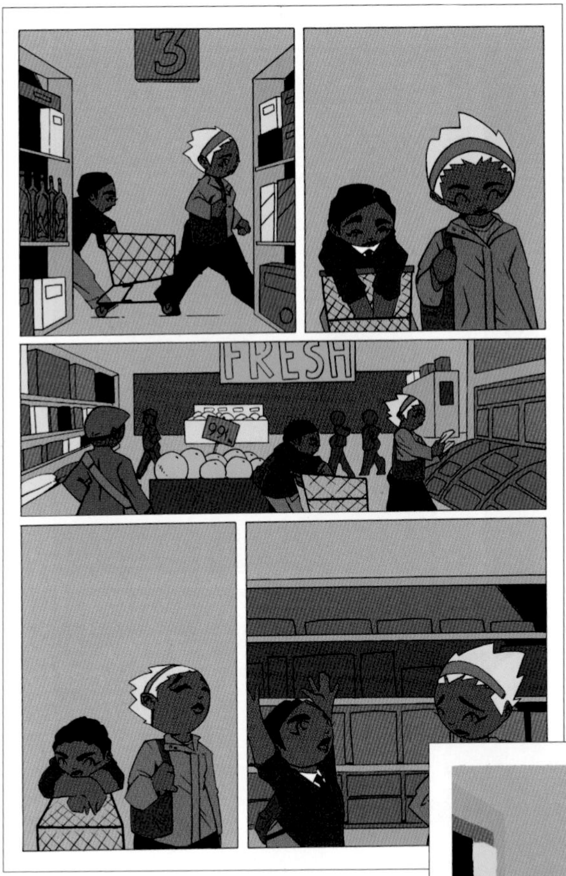
3
FRESH
99¢

Flatting helps the colorist separate out different parts of the comic and plan for palettes and contrast.

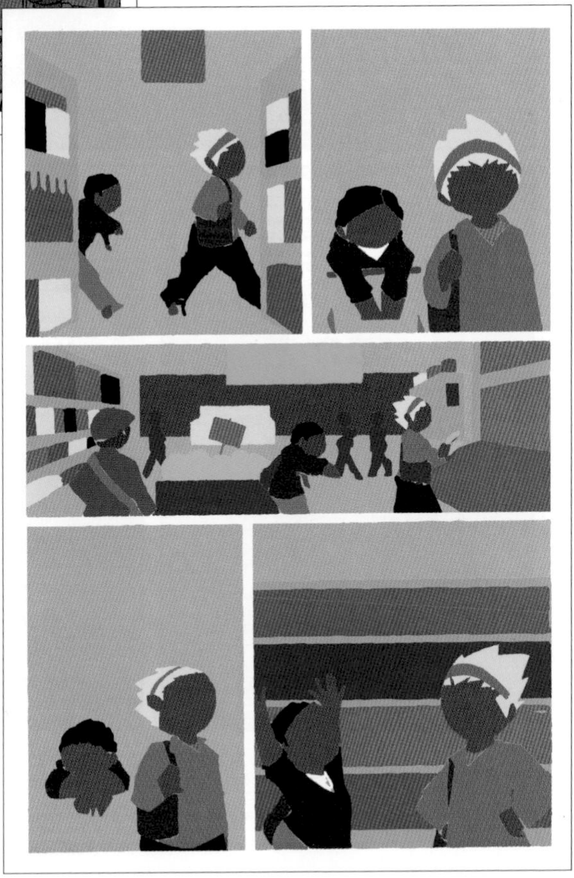

A trick that some flatters use is digitally turning off the black line art. If the images are still legible without the lines, the flatting is done.

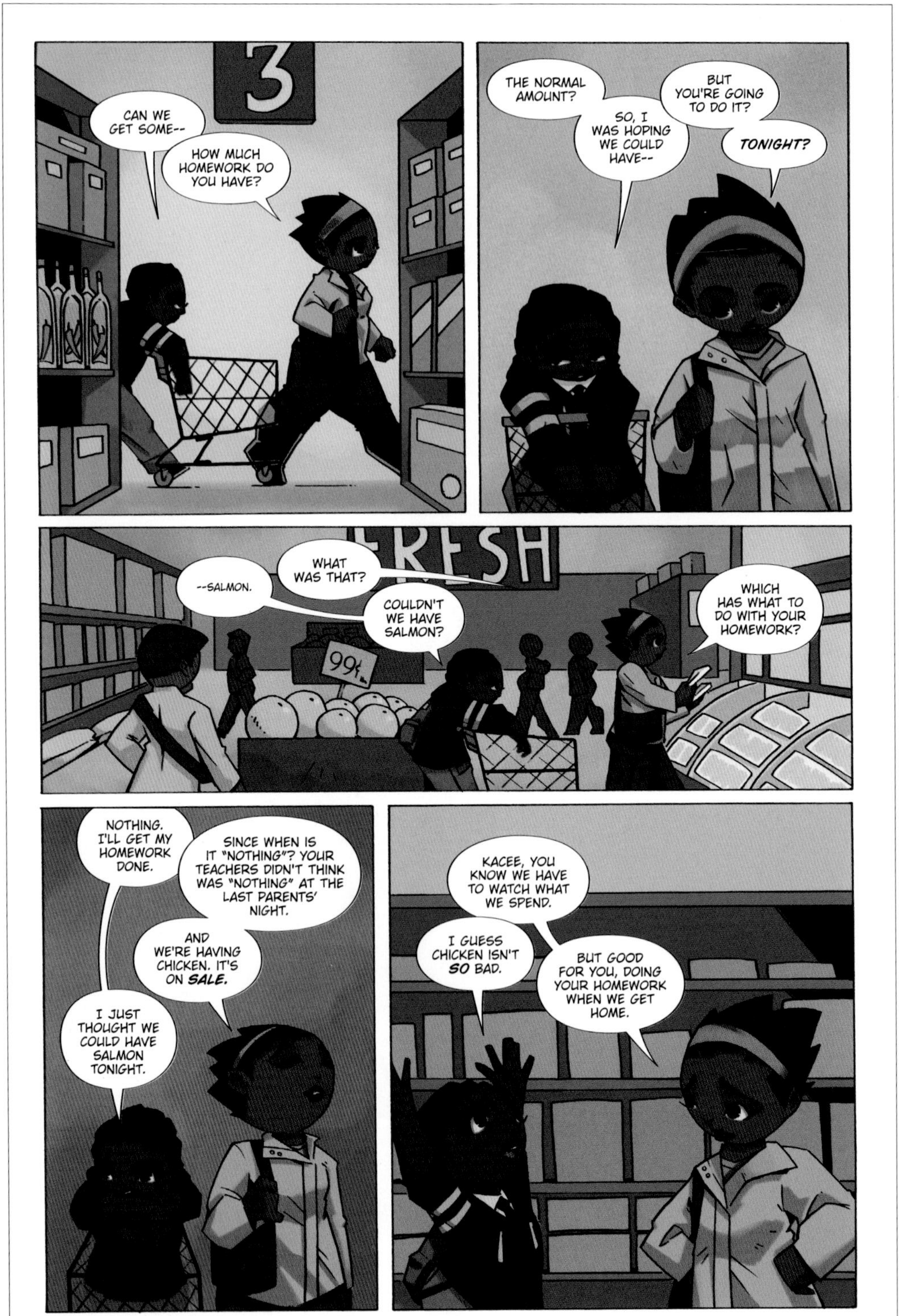
3
CAN WE GET SOME--
HOW MUCH HOMEWORK DO YOU HAVE?
THE NORMAL AMOUNT?
SO, I WAS HOPING WE COULD HAVE--
BUT YOU'RE GOING TO DO IT?
TONIGHT?
FRESH
--SALMON.
WHAT WAS THAT?
COULDN'T WE HAVE SALMON?
99¢
WHICH HAS WHAT TO DO WITH YOUR HOMEWORK?
NOTHING. I'LL GET MY HOMEWORK DONE.
SINCE WHEN IS IT "NOTHING"? YOUR TEACHERS DIDN'T THINK WAS "NOTHING" AT THE LAST PARENTS' NIGHT.
AND WE'RE HAVING CHICKEN. IT'S ON SALE.
I JUST THOUGHT WE COULD HAVE SALMON TONIGHT.
KACEE, YOU KNOW WE HAVE TO WATCH WHAT WE SPEND.
I GUESS CHICKEN ISN'T SO BAD.
BUT GOOD FOR YOU, DOING YOUR HOMEWORK WHEN WE GET HOME.

Once the final coloring is completed, letters are added on a separate layer over the art.

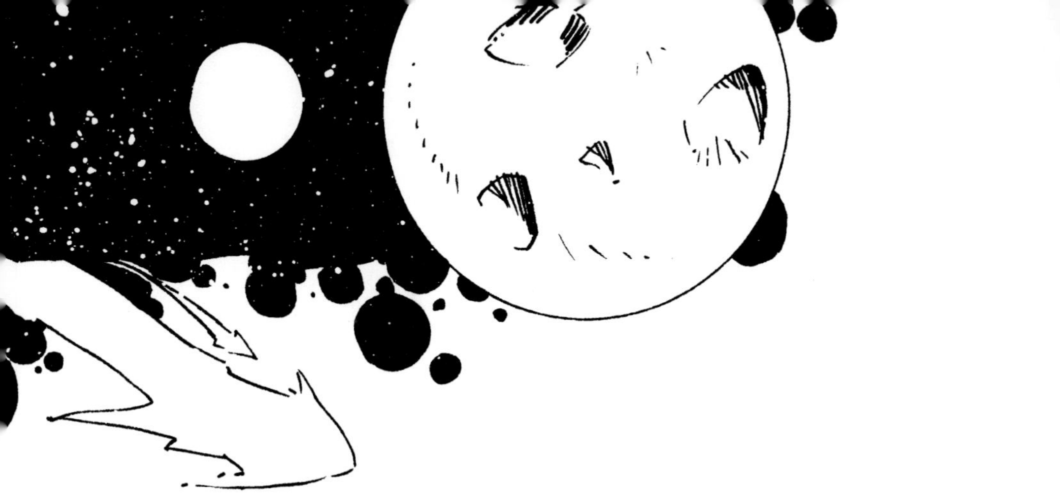

HOW DO YOU LETTER A COMIC?

Hi! I'm Frank, and I lettered *The Airless Year!* My job as the letterer is to combine the dialogue from the writer with the artist's illustrations, so that it all looks like one unified piece.

With *The Airless Year* I chose to use a font called Wild Words, which is commonly used in manga lettering, because it looks clean and easy to read even when printed at a slightly smaller size. And because Valentine uses a lot of beautiful round shapes in his character designs, I wanted to make sure I used nice, big, roundish balloons that matched his art style.

Once I had a lettering style that the entire team was happy with, I laid out the balloons, caption boxes, and sound effects in a way that easily led the reader's eyes from one character to the next, from panel to panel, and throughout the entire page.

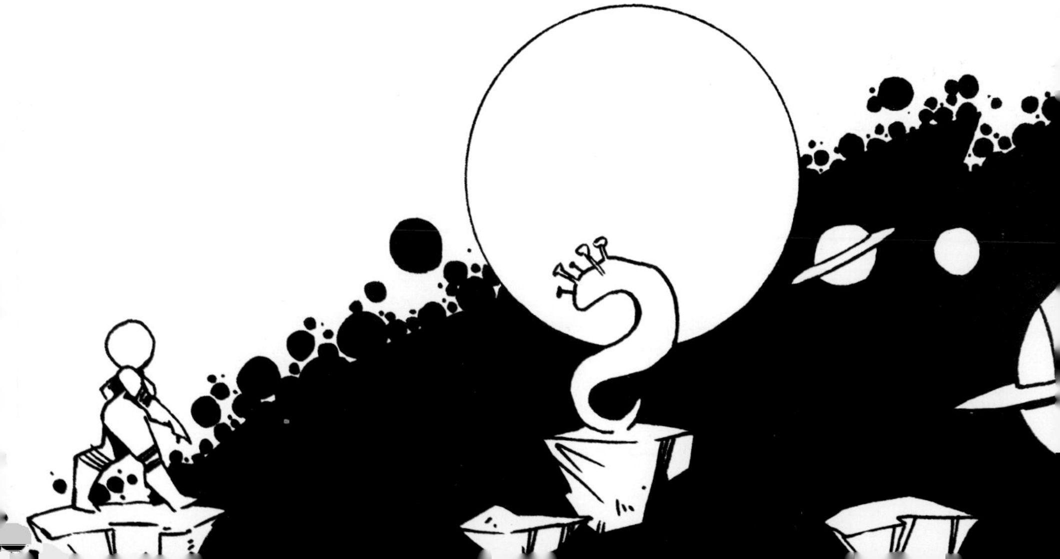

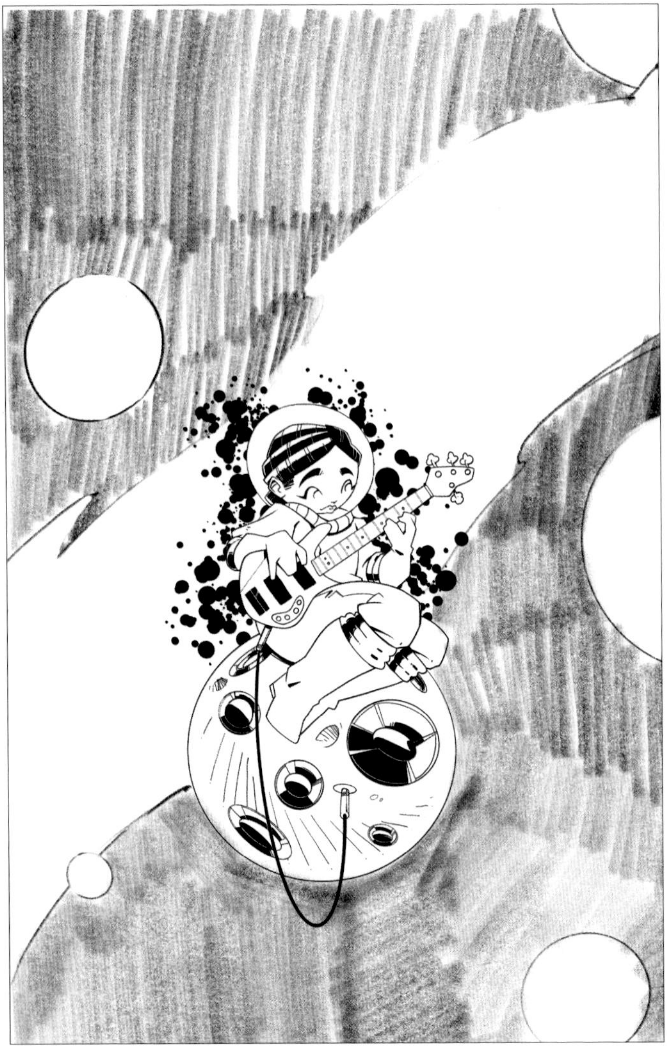

These were some preliminary cover ideas that Valentine sketched out.

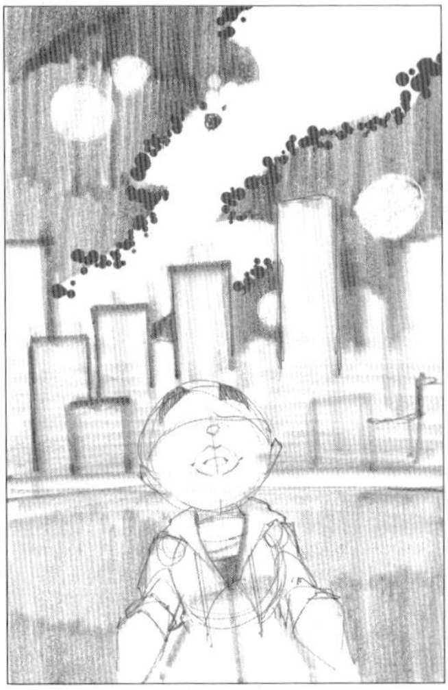

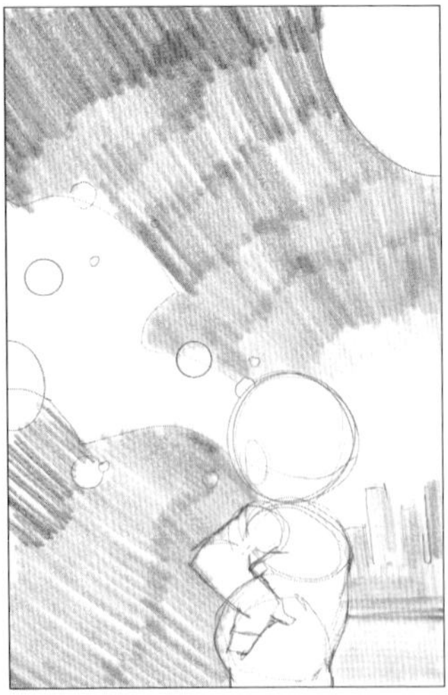

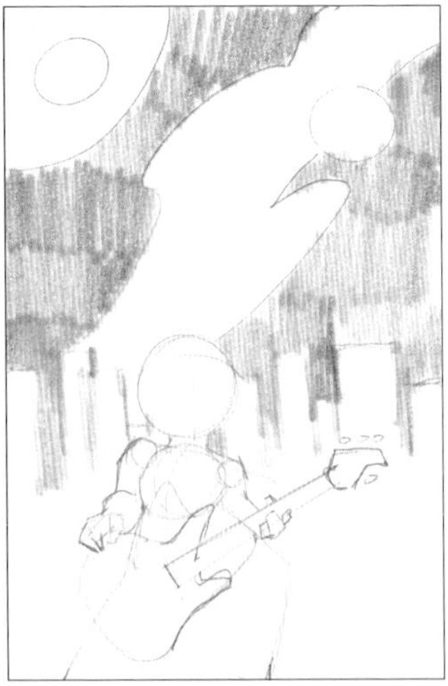

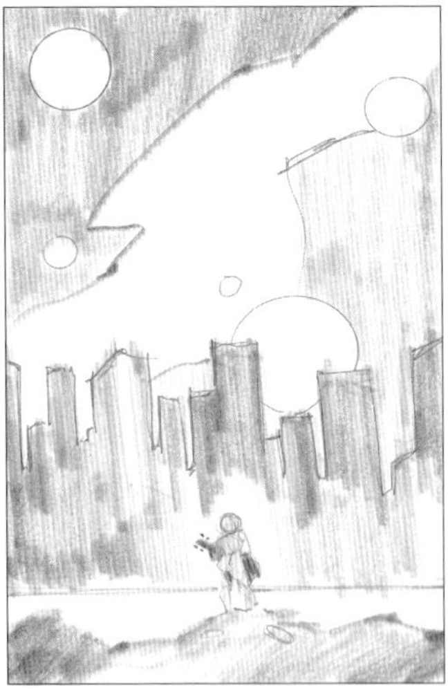

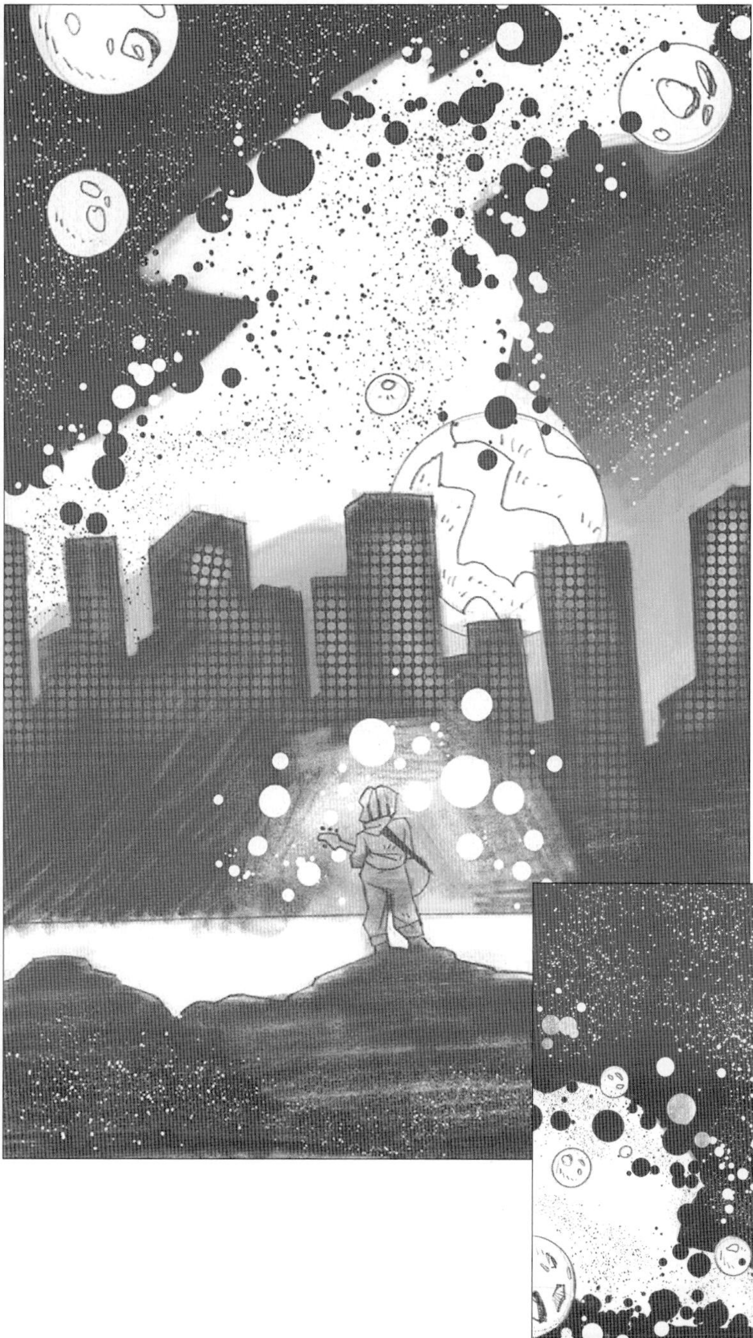

The team selected two possible candidates from the sketches, and Valentine developed them both a bit further before a final decision was made.

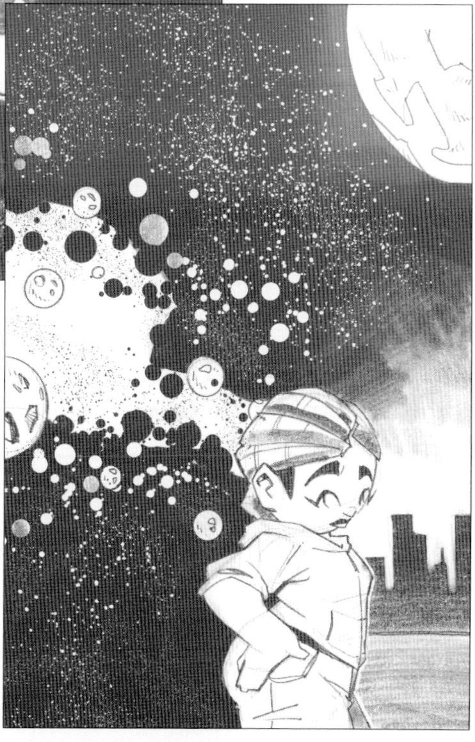

HOW DO YOU WORK TOGETHER AS A CREATIVE TEAM?

APK: We worked on *The Airless Year* in ways I've never gotten to work on a book before. It was an extra special time. We would have meetings after every step: every section of script, batch of pencils or inks, etc., and Valentine, Frank, and I would all suggest things, shape and reshape the story, and so on. We each let the others be as involved in our jobs as they wanted. That's why we say this book is by the three of us instead of "written by, art by, letters by."

VB: We worked very closely as a team throughout the whole process. We shared a lot of work in progress, which helped shape and guide the final results. And we were stronger for it. Nothing is created in a vacuum, and we were all available to help the others as needed.

FC: Comics are a collaborative medium by nature but, most of the time, they're made on a sort of assembly line. The writer writes a script, then gives the script to the artist who draws the book, who then passes the art to the colorist, and so on. With *The Airless Year*, Adam, Valentine, and I made the conscious decision that all three of us would build and shape the story together, which meant that we would go through every single page of outline, script, art, and lettering together, each of us suggesting and incorporating whatever changes helped make the best possible version of our book. It was a truly collaborative process.

Adam P. Knave (he/him) is an Eisner and Harvey Award-winning editor and writer who writes comics (*Amelia Cole* and *The Once and Future Queen,* among others) as well as prose fiction (*Culture's Skeleton, Turn To Paige Never,* and more) from a secret lair in Portland, OR. He denies that he is secretly a robot controlled by his cats. No one believes him.

Valentine Barker (he/him) is a comic book artist and oil painter based in Portland, OR. His work focuses on female empowerment, body positivity, and celebrating diversity. When he's not drawing, he can be found at home playing bass or out in the wilderness painting landscapes.

Frank Cvetkovic (he/him) is a comic book letterer who
hates when people assume that all he does is put
words in bubbles. There's a *little* more to the job than
that. For instance. sometimes he puts them in boxes.
His work can be seen in *Count Crowley: Reluctant
Midnight Monster Hunter. Cyberpunk 2077: Trauma
Team.* and *The Once And Future Queen*.